Fresh Start

KAREN MACLEOD-WILKIE

ISBN-978-1-9990957-0-3:

DEDICATION

To Mom and Dad—Carolyn and Victor MacLeod—who always encourage me to pursue my dreams. You treat life as an adventure, full of possibilities, which has given me the courage to make this fresh start in my life.

ACKNOWLEDGMENTS

My husband Paul's desire for us to walk the Camino de Santiago together started me on a journey that reached into my heart and awoke my long-buried dream of writing a novel. Thank you for sharing that incredible adventure with me. I am extremely grateful for your steady support as I crammed every possible moment between work and vacation with writing. The love you so generously pour into my life I offer back to you with delight.

My children—Julia, Suzanne and Nicholas—encouraged Mom to go for it and willingly gave feedback, guided me on the business aspects, set up my dedicated computer, and so much more. You three are awesome, I love you!

I appreciate each one of my amazingly patient friends and extended family, who read rough drafts and were wonderful cheerleaders along the way.

To my caring congregation at South Shore United Church, I say thank you. Your willingness to accommodate my unusual sabbatical allowed me to write for a week out of each month for a year. Your interest and support are true characteristics of a spirit-led people.

I am grateful for all the healing practitioners of many modalities who have shared their gifts of healing with me over the years. You are a power for good in the Universe. A special thank you to Healing Pathway Canada—a group I joined in 2000—who have continued to be a transformative influence in my life since my very first workshop.

I could never have asked for a better editor than Maeve O'Connell. You are able to take my words and make everything read better while maintaining the integrity of my original intent. You bring out the best in me with your gentle questions and encouraging words. Thank you for making editing such a pleasurable experience!

To my writing coach, Patti Larsen, I offer my appreciation for guiding me through the business side of book writing. What feels overwhelming to me, you make manageable. Thank you.

CHAPTER ONE

What the hell are you doing?

I pushed in the clutch and plastered a smile on my face, trying to convince myself all was well. But my heart hadn't quite got the message. It continued to race as the engine of my trusty Toyota Corolla ignited and the car rolled slowly down the driveway. I took a few deep breaths of crisp spring morning air. Breathing is good, I told myself. My chest thumped maybe a few beats slower, but the sense of panic still hovered, threatening to merge into a full-blown attack. Foot to the gas, I pulled out onto the road. Just begin, I muttered through clenched teeth.

New beginnings—that was what this was all about. For twenty-five years I had been a church minister. I knew week to week, month to month, what I was supposed to do. I baptized, married, visited, preached to, and buried people—not always in that order! My role was clear and, although my daily activities varied, I had figured out a rhythm that worked for me.

At least, it had worked for me; but in the past few years a rising discontent had begun to gnaw at my insides. What had always seemed to fit, no longer matched who I felt I was. Old dreams began to haunt my sleep and even disturb my waking moments. I doubted my words, my hopes, and my purpose. I resigned my ministry position and decided to try something new.

Holy shit, are you out of your mind?

That doubting voice was extremely tough to silence. It kept shouting in my head every time I thought I was ready to take another step forward. Did that voice think it was easy to resign? I didn't do it on a whim, in a moment of madness. It took two years to finally let go of that identity and to be willing to venture into unknown territory: going into business for myself. And here I was, heading out in my Corolla to look for the right property to match my dream.

You have no business background. Are you crazy?

I clasped the wheel as I drove and I repeated my mantra, "I can do this. I can do this. I will learn."

Yeah, if you want to fail!

"Be quiet voice!" I snapped, stomping my foot on the brake as I pulled up at a red light. "I trust this will unfold as I need it to."

My gaze was drawn to a poster in the window of an optical store on the corner. It read "Seeing is Believing". I took it as a message that my ramblings were not a sign that I was crazy; they were just an effort to be in command.

At first, I couldn't even imagine leaving the church. I had grown up in the church and served in ministry all my life. It was second nature to me. Then, in little ways, a word, a meeting, or an experience would chafe at me and erode that firm foundation. Things I had always believed didn't make sense anymore. Rituals that had been so meaningful felt empty to me. The words I spoke felt like hollow echoes that reverberated through space and didn't affect anyone or anything. I felt as though less and less of me was showing up each day. I needed to change things before I was lost altogether.

I had no idea what else I could do. All that was clear was that I needed to stop what I was doing.

That was three months ago. I finished out my notice just after Christmas and, since, I had struggled to find words to respond to the numerous questions from well-meaning people such as, "What will you be doing?"

"That's a good question." I would fumble around for answers, but I didn't have any.

Fortunately, my husband, Dan, was supportive through all of this. Thanks to the Universe (my go-to higher power these days), Dan had a steady job, so we wouldn't starve. How do people on their own take risks like this? They truly amaze and inspire me!

Once I no longer had to show up for paid employment every day, I cleaned house. I mean, I literally cleaned my house. I sorted and tossed piles of junk that had accumulated over the years. I got rid of furniture I didn't like and books that I was someday going to read. It was cathartic and necessary, and it felt great!

Then, I sat. I walked. I watched TV. I drank lots of wine and gorged myself on warm buttery popcorn. What was I doing? I had no direction. I felt aimless and lost. I looked in the mirror and wondered, Who am I? Where am I going? Diana Ross' song "Do You Know Where You're Going To?" kept repeating in my mind.

You haven't got a clue. Why would you give up your nice secure job to do nothing? You're a loser.

The critical, doubting voice was everywhere during that time of transition. I let it speak its concerns. After all, they were a part of me. But I did not let those fears triumph. I held on and rode out the waves of terror, doubt, and grief that crashed over me. I could figure this out. I would figure this out. I was figuring this out.

Eventually, my mind began tossing tidbits to me. I knew I wanted to help people. I remembered a dream I once had of having a healing centre. Possibilities began tumbling around in my head. I played with them, drawing out each idea, until I woke up one morning and I suddenly knew I needed to start looking at properties.

Another mortgage? Do you want to be in debt when you're 90?

"I hear you, Fear. Relax. Just because you can't figure it out doesn't mean it isn't possible. You need to breathe."

And that's how I found myself rolling down the highway, trying to keep breathing, ready to start exploring. I did my research. The prices online were astronomical on some of the listings and they didn't even look like much. But I decided not to get caught up in the money aspect. This was going to be investigation time: How did these places feel on the inside? How were they laid out? What were the locations like? How much work would they require? I could do this.

Siri's soothing voice guided me to the first stop.

"Right turn on Franklyn Street. Your destination is on the right."

Number 1445. Ugh! The description said chartreuse-coloured which I guessed was a fancy name for puke green. Who on earth would choose to paint their house that shade? Did I dare check out the inside? The curtain twitched; I'd been spotted. I opened the door and thought the inside couldn't be any worse than the outside.

Why do I always set myself up? It can't be that bad—oh yes it can! I could hardly conceal my cringing as I stepped into the foyer: black tile floor and orange walls. Was the last tenant on drugs? Even the woodwork was painted, so I couldn't tell if it was good quality or not. This was definitely not the vibe I needed for a Healing House. However, the eager agent in her well-fitted business suit seemed so anxious to give me a tour and do her spiel that I acquiesced and trailed after her, room by room.

Coffee—I deserved a premium cuppa. That thought kept me going as I was assaulted by colours that even the most garish 1970s decorator would have rejected. My mind whirled, trying to compose a compliment with some iota of truth that I could speak convincingly.

"Lovely view from the bathroom window. I'm sure it will be right for… someone else. Thank you for the tour!" I stumbled past the sales agent and skipped down the steps as fast as I could.

Seat belt fastened, key in the ignition, I screeched away in my reliable ride. My eyes couldn't take any more.

Timothy's Coffee beckoned and a parking place appeared right outside. Thank you, Universe, for small mercies! I quickly smeared Burt's Bees lip balm onto my lips and flicked my fingers through my hair. Best I could do. Make-up and I don't really have a thing going, so what you see is pretty well what you get. I clambered out the door and locked the car without looking at my keychain as I hurried toward the café. My mouth watered in anticipation of coffee and a tasty chocolate treat as I entered Timothy's Coffee Shop.

There was a line, of course. Ah well, it gave me time to consider all the options. I scanned the descriptions of all the fancy coffees and felt tempted, but, as usual, my party- pooper friend, Frugality, whispered in my ear: "You're not really going to pay that much for coffee are you?" And, as always, I relented. Farewell Caramel Latte Bene, maybe someday you and I will get to know each other! I spied something called Midnight Magic dark brew in one of the urns and thought that a half mug of that with my sensible decaf smacked of a bit of adventure.

As the line moved forward, out of the corner of my eye I saw Mildred Smith making her way from the bathrooms at the back of the café. I ducked behind a stand of Colombian Arabica and prayed that she hadn't seen me. I really wanted that coffee, but I didn't want conversation. Too late! She bustled toward me, wearing a chic suit, her kitten heels clicking assertively on the tiles. Stately and in her early sixties, Mildred was not hurting for money. She was also a champion conversationalist and prolific gossip. I did not want to add to her fuel tank, but I was trapped between a potted plant, a coffee stand, and a woman with a service dog. The only way out was straight through Mildred. I plastered a fake smile on my face (I should have been getting used to it by then).

"Alisha, how lovely to see you," she cooed.

"You too, Mildred," I gagged. I was lying through my teeth! Good thing I didn't believe in a God of retribution or I'd have been blasted on the spot!

"It's been ages. I'd love to catch up on all your news." I tried to smile and thought, don't do it. Don't ask me to sit with you.

"I was just going to get another Chai Latte. Won't you join me?"

Of course Mildred buys only the expensive, decadent drinks. Not that I was jealous. I was not envious. I make my own choices. But I had to decide how I was going to gracefully get out of that encounter. If I was going to open my own business at some point, she might end up being a customer; I couldn't afford to offend any potential clients. I sighed and thought, so much for sitting and relaxing in a comfy corner in the café.

"What a kind offer, Mildred, but I was just flying in to grab a coffee."

"Where are you rushing off to?" I could see the wheels turning in her head.

"An appointment—I have an appointment."

She didn't need to know the appointment was with myself.

"Is this appointment related to any new opportunities?" She definitely knew how to dig for information.

A shout from the barista was a welcome intervention. "Next, can I take your order?"

"That's me! Great talking with you Mildred!"

Wow, the Universe was watching over me. I dodged that bullet.

"Half and half Midnight Magic and whatever decaf you have on brew."

I looked mournfully at the baked goodies and resigned myself to forgoing any chocolate decadence. I made my way over to the cash and, as soon as my coffee was in my hand, I hurriedly waved at Mildred and scurried off out the door.

Back in my car, I wondered, now what? Where was I supposed to go? I couldn't sit there; I was easy prey if she came out the door. I turned the engine on. As I backed onto the street, I thought of the park at the end of town. It overlooked the water and wouldn't be too busy during the day. I could sit in my car and savour my coffee without interruption.

Sure enough, a few walkers were dotted along the boardwalk, but they were far enough away from the parking spaces that I could sit there unnoticed. I found a spot far down the boulevard where no other vehicles were nearby and I pulled in with relief. My introverted self seemed to need more alone time as middle age progressed. My tolerance for general conversation had been stretched to the limit in the last months of my ministry. Perhaps that was one of the reasons why working with healing touch was so appealing. It demanded less in the way of conversation; any dialogue in my healing sessions was about significant issues.

I decided to leave the car running in case a quick getaway was needed and I dug into the glove compartment to see if any of my emergency chocolate stash remained. My hand clutched a dark chocolate orange-spiced bar and I heaved a sign of contentment. Life was good.

Even with the car running, the coolness of the spring air seeped in around the door and window frames. The coffee and chocolate were a happy memory in my belly and it was time to make haste to my next realtor appointment. I took a deep breath as I gazed at the water for a final time. Here we go again!

Located on a quiet side street, this house looked more promising than the last. It was a creamy yellow two-storied residence, with well-tended bushes flanking the walkway to the front door. I strolled along, then stopped and turned in front of the house to get a sense of what the neighbourhood looked like from that vantage point. A dog, straining at its leash, pulled a white-haired woman along the sidewalk. There was a vividly coloured pirate-themed playground a block to the left. I counted five children scrambling over the slides and two adults chatting together. I wasn't sure this was what I was after or even if zoning laws would allow a business in such a residential area; something else to research. The further I delved into this dream, the more I realized I didn't know!

Facing forward again, I reached the door and rang the bell. A robust woman with a large smile on her face opened the door. I extended my hand.

"Ms. Peyton?"

"Alisha, how wonderful to see you again. Come on in."

Again? What did she mean, again? Had we met before? Shit! Who was she? I quickly trawled the memory banks as the door closed behind me.

"It's been a while." At least, I hoped it had been! I silently implored the smiling woman for a clue.

"It sure has. It was a beautiful baptism."

Inside my head I yelled, that is not enough information, lady! Do you realize how many baptisms I've done over the years? Was it ten years ago, last year?

Can't remember? Should you really be thinking of starting a new career at your age? You can't even remember people's names!

I quickly hushed the naysayer voice. I couldn't let it trigger the fear response or I'd never access that memory bank effectively.

"Such a beautiful baby." Everyone wants to hear that, don't they?

"He sure was. You wouldn't even recognize him now. Ten years old and sprouting like a weed. My brother Brad and Pam had two more boys since you were at their church. Their house is pretty rambunctious. And they love their sports."

Bingo! I hit the jackpot! She'd thrown me enough memory markers to clue me in. Thank you, Universe! "I can't even imagine, Deirdre."

"Shall we begin the tour?"

"I'd love to."

The tour proceeded without further event. Thankfully, she focused on showing the house and not dragging up old memories, and she was professional enough to not ask any uncomfortable personal questions I didn't want to answer yet. The house made good on the promise of the pretty front garden; it was lovely. The rooms were spacious and well laid out. The kitchen was immense, with stainless steel appliances and a gorgeous oak-topped island. It would be an awesome home for entertaining, but it didn't really feel like it had potential for what I was seeking. After thanking

Deirdre, I climbed back into my car. I would not feel discouraged. I'd only looked at two places. I didn't really expect to find something immediately, but that spark of hope had been there under the surface. Maybe I needed to cruise around and simply check out different areas of town, to see if a particular section tugged at me more than another.

I spent two more hours aimlessly meandering up and down the streets of Bright Haven. I spotted a few places for sale, but nothing truly resonated with me. I decided to call it a day.

My cellphone rang. Dan wanted me to pick up a few groceries on my way home. It was time to get back to the mundane and set dreaming aside.

I had spent two weeks painstakingly working through the list of homes for sale and old buildings that had seen various businesses go through their premises—and nothing! Not one of the listings called out to me to say, "I'm what you want." I had a clear picture of what I didn't want, but the elusive dream of a healing place just wouldn't present itself fully to me.

My car was due for an oil change so, once again, I drove toward Bright Haven and tried not to think about all the gas I had burned in what seemed to be a useless quest. I would not worry about money. I was done with letting money drive my decision-making processes. I turned onto Starling Drive on the outskirts of town, leading toward the industrial area and the airport. I passed what seemed to be a very overgrown Leyland Cyprus hedge and a sign caught my eye: "For Sale". At a wide break in the hedge, I caught a glimpse of a richly coloured log building, set back from the road. The wood looked like eastern white cedar. The lot was unkempt-looking, but I couldn't drag my eyes off the building. I pulled onto the shoulder of the road. Why hadn't I seen this on any lists or when I was driving around?

My pulse raced. I was enraptured by the beauty of the wood. It felt warm and inviting. I wanted to go in and see if the inside was as wondrous as the outside. Cars whizzed by as I continued to gaze at the vision before me. I hadn't driven this part of Starling Drive when I was searching around Bright Haven. But there was something about this place; it was tugging at my heart and pulling persistently.

My phone buzzed with a reminder that it was time for my oil change. Shoot! I was going to be late. I glanced at the "For Sale" sign and, sure enough, there was a phone number listed. I dug into my purse, fishing around for a notebook in which to record the number. I knew I kept a pen in the glove compartment, so I quickly dashed the number down as my senses buzzed. I did a shoulder check as I pulled back onto the road and my eyes wandered back for another glimpse of what just might be a part of my future.

The auto shop was a short drive down the road and I impatiently checked my car in and wandered out to the parking lot to make the call. My stomach tightened as I punched in the numbers. Three rings.

Please be there!

"Hello, this is Anderson's Realty."

"Hi. My name is Alisha Langley. I just drove by a place on Starling Drive with a "For Sale" sign listing your number."

"Ah yes. The old Fredrick place."

"Is it still for sale?"

"Yes." There was a tone to the man's voice that I couldn't quite pin down. What was going on, I wondered?

"Would I be able to take a look at it? I'm just down the road at an appointment. Would anyone be available in the next hour?"

There was a slight hesitation before he answered, "Let me check with one of our agents. Can I get back to you?"

I gave him my number and paced the parking lot for the next fifteen minutes. What was taking so long? My car would be ready soon and I didn't want to hang around indefinitely. Yet anticipation was building so strongly that when my phone finally rang I nearly jumped a foot off the ground.

"Alisha, Frank Proud from Anderson's Realty here. It appears I'll be the one meeting you at the Fredrick place. I can be there in twenty minutes if that's convenient?"

"I look forward to viewing the building," I replied as soberly as I could, trying not to reveal my giddy excitement.

As I pressed the end call button, I thought I heard him mumble, "Let's hope that's all you see."

CHAPTER TWO

Eagerly counting the minutes at the garage, I paid for my oil change and exchanged the usual small talk with my mechanic. With five minutes to go, I enthusiastically jumped into my car and sped down Starling Drive. My focus was entirely forward, until a roaring sound slowly impinged upon my brain. I looked in the rear-view mirror—a police car with flashing lights. Shit! How fast was I going? I glanced down at my speedometer: eighty kilometres per hour. What was the speed limit on Starling Drive? I frantically tried to remember as I pulled over. I could see the Fredrick house just ahead of me; so close, but I was busted!

The female officer ambled over to my window. I rolled it down with a sincere smile, hoping to appeal to her forgiving side. She didn't seem affected.

"Ma'am, do you realize how fast you were going?"

I gulped. "Officer, I just peeked down at my dash and saw it read eighty kilometres. What is the speed limit here?" I tried my best innocent look.

"The limit is fifty kilometres per hour. Ignorance is no excuse." (I guessed she'd used up all her tolerance that day already.) "You were thirty over the limit."

"I'm sorry. I just wasn't paying attention. You see, I'm so excited. I'm going to view that house over there and all I could think about was arriving on time to meet the realtor."

My words tumbled over each other and she wasn't the least bit interested in my gabbing on. I shut up and waited for the verdict.

"Can I see your driver's licence and registration, please?" I extracted my licence from my wallet. Then, I pulled open the dash, and my stash of pens and chocolate tumbled out. I dug under the stack of car receipts.

"I know it's here somewhere. Just hold on." Why is it that what you need is always at the bottom of the pile? I could hear her foot tapping impatiently. You'd think she'd have been through this enough times to have a little compassion for what I was feeling! Finally, I pulled out the plastic registration holder and handed it to her. She flipped it open and looked at me hostilely before handing it back. It was empty. I gazed disbelievingly at the holder and then I looked back at her blankly. I had no idea where it was. The insurance card was where it was supposed to be, but the registration was missing. I hurriedly pawed through all the papers in the dash. Out of the corner of my eye, I noticed the officer turn in annoyance and lean against the car as I searched. Her body angled toward the Fredrick place; suddenly, she straightened up and leaned into my window.

"Going to look at the Fredrick home, are you? Well, you make sure you find that registration and slow down when you leave there. Have a good day now!"

I sat there stunned as the officer made her way back to her vehicle. The flashing lights stopped and she pulled away with a wave. What the hell had just happened? Relieved and totally confused, I jammed everything back into the dash and crept back onto the road. I turned on my signal to enter the Fredrick property. No realtor yet, so no witness to my encounter, thank goodness!

As soon as I had turned off the ignition, a car pulled in behind me. The driveway was rutted and the yard was obviously neglected. Yet the house beckoned. I climbed out just as Frank Proud clambered out of his Miata. He was obviously doing well for himself! As he made his way over to me, he glanced around in a rather nervous manner.

"Ms. Langley?" he extended his hand. We shook briefly.

"Would you care to look over the grounds first?" he inquired.

I really wanted to see inside the house, but I was willing to follow his lead, so I responded, "Sure!"

He described the lot as being five full acres.

Apparently, this part of Bright Haven had been farmland years ago and this was the only farm homestead remaining. Other homes and buildings had been demolished as the airport bought up land and as businesses developed in the area. There was a generous amount of space in front and to the sides of the house. I imagined the potential the front possessed to become a parking lot—a necessity for any business. Zoning wouldn't be a problem in this area of town. My mind zipped ahead from one detail to the next. We hiked around the right side of the house and I could see a small pond, choked up with old leaves and brush. A few sheltering trees were scattered around it. I could envision a Zen garden there with seats skirting the trees, just like I'd seen on Pinterest.

At the back of the house, the land extended into a copse of trees. There was room for a labyrinth walk and maybe a few pathways through the trees. Continuing around the house, I observed a tangle of weeds covering a plot of ground and hypothesized it had once been a vegetable garden; it was a ready-made spot for a healing herb garden. Returning to the front, I felt in a daze as my mind wandered from possibility to possibility. Had Mr. Proud been speaking to me as we traversed the outdoors? I had no idea. Hopefully, during my internal interlude, I hadn't missed anything significant.

As we approached the house, he cleared his throat. "Ms. Langley, you seemed very engrossed as we navigated around the property."

My wandering mind hadn't gone unnoticed after all.

"Perhaps you'd like to take your time and roam through the house at your own pace. I have a few calls to make, so I can wait out here for you. If you have any questions, I'll gladly answer them when you've completed your viewing."

It seemed a little peculiar, but an answer to my prayer nonetheless. I didn't want anyone else's energy intruding as I went from room to room, giving my imagination full reign. I observed him shifting from foot to foot as he awaited my answer.

"That's very thoughtful of you, Mr. Proud." I tried to keep the eagerness out of my voice and sound businesslike. I'm sure he saw through my effort, as I grasped the key and my feet betrayed me with a slight skip when I attempted to walk sedately up onto the veranda.

The veranda extended all the way around the house. A few boards looked rather weatherworn but still intact. I slid the key into the lock and the door opened invitingly. I stepped over the threshold and into the charm I had seen reflected on the outside. I was in a wide entryway with a blue tiled floor. Lightly coloured stained glass windows on either side of the door let in plenty of light and added to the welcoming beauty of the entrance. I stood and just let it soak into me for a moment. I had no idea of the price of this place, but I was fast beginning to believe that this wasn't something I could pass up. This was the fit for which I'd been searching.

A property this size, you'll never be able to afford it.

Not now, voice, I chastised silently. No negativity allowed here. I'm trusting the Universe to let this unfold. It wouldn't have shown me this property if it didn't have the possibility of working out for me.

"Of course it will work out. Didn't I make that cranky police woman leave you alone?"

My hand clutched into a fist around the front door key. This voice was not the same as the one in my head—that negative one that never seemed to let up. This one sounded different; a soft, silvery, female-sounding voice. What the hell?

"Stop making a fuss dearie. Come on in and take a look around."

Okay, I was definitely hearing this. Did I want to go any farther or did I just want to turn tail and run? I truly wanted to explore the rest of the place, so a timid step took me forward into the Great Room. It extended up the full two floors of the house and abundant light poured through the windows. Off to the right, I could see a half wall with columns which supported beams overhead. The wall separated a section that was the kitchen and dining area. In the dining area there were sliding doors leading outside to a screened-in section of the veranda. I could envision a small café on that side, while on the left I imagined the reception and maybe a small store in the Great Room. Stairs rose to the second floor at the back of the room and directly across from me there was a doorway into another room. I edged toward it. The chatter in my head had quietened, so I kept going. It was a large bedroom with a huge bathroom off to the right; the perfect layout for an aesthetic area, if I wanted one.

I climbed up the stairs to a cozy landing overlooking the Great Room, but which also had a viewing area at the end which captured the sights outside. Doors off the landing led to four bedrooms, an upper bathroom, and lots of storage closets. This space was ideal for setting up a variety of healing rooms. My dreams were coming alive in my mind and heart as I finished looking around. Could this truly be happening? Was I on the verge of something wonderful? Then, it happened again.

"Okay, dearie, that poor man outside is getting rather anxious about you. It's time to show yourself, so he knows you're all right."

I spun around. The voice I was hearing inside my head felt like it was coming from outside of my being. I searched the room. No one was there. I pitched my gaze upward and flicked it side to side. Nothing. Was I going crazy?

"You're not crazy! You just can't see me yet. Your visual perception needs some development. Your listening and feeling senses are pretty good, but you haven't worked on seeing what's around you."

What?

"You ken exactly what I'm talking about. Now stop blethering about and get out there and make that man an offer. Be sure it's less than the asking price. It's time you got this next stage of your life going."

I was stunned, but I played along. "Who are

you?"

"I'm Essie. This used to be my place. Now I want it to be yours."

"You used to live here?" I felt kind of ridiculous, but I was reluctant to stop the conversation. I hoped Proud didn't decide to step through the door until I was done.

"Lived here. Died here. It's a bonnie place don't you think?"

"You seem to know what I'm thinking, so you know I feel it's wonderful. But if you're a spirit or ghost or whatever, how can I take this place on and develop it into a business?"

"This used to be a beautiful wee place and I can help you restore it. When I died, I felt my life's purpose wasn't complete. I decided not to go on to the next dimension. I've been waiting around for something to unfold and I believe you're it! You want to make this a healing place? I can guide you. I can help you with what people are thinking and feeling."

"We can't intrude that way. That's not ethical. Besides, what if clients hear or see you?"

"Very few do, lassie, except those who are gifted or those who are open to me. I'm very particular about choosing to whom I show myself."

"I can't believe I'm talking to you. I can't believe I'm even considering this. But…."

"But this house has a hold on you, doesn't it? You can see the possibilities. Skedaddle. Go talk to that fellow and see what he has to say. This is important for both of us!"

"You're the reason he didn't come in here, aren't you?"

"I wasn't going to let just anyone take over my place. Most of them just wanted to tear everything down. My husband and I built this place, on my family's land. I couldn't bear to see it ripped apart. There's so much beauty here and they couldn't see it. They just saw room for business development. All that realtor wanted was top dollar, so he'd get a nice commission fee."

"What did you do?"

"I made some interesting sounds in different parts of the house. I encouraged things to move; you ken, the usual ghostly pranks."

"That's all?"

"I did give that one man a rather firm push into the pond.

"No!" I suppressed a giggle.

"Another day, the realtor seemed to have trouble with his footing on the stairs and plopped down on his behind with a solid thump! I haven't really seen too much activity here since then. Rumours have a habit of circulating."

"And knowing this about you is meant to encourage me to want to buy your place?"

"You do have quite marvellous dreams that I could really get behind."

"I do. However, every time you have a difference of opinion with my dreams, what can I expect?"

"I'm sure we'll get along just fine, dearie!"

"If we're going to do this, you might as well call me Alisha," I sighed. I must have been crazy. Not only was I talking to a ghost, I was actually thinking of buying her house. What was I getting into?

CHAPTER THREE

I thanked the agent for his time, as he slipped his phone into his pocket. He indicated the listed price had been reduced; even so it made my stomach clench with anxiety.

"Mr. Proud, as you can see the property has captivated me. However, before making an official offer I would require someone with building knowledge to inspect the building and property with me, to ensure there are no hidden costs I might be overlooking."

Mr. Proud shivered and looked around. What was that ghost up to now? "I understand your hesitancy. Be assured the price is negotiable. Whenever you want to go through the place, why don't you just drop by my office and pick up the key."

That didn't sound like standard policy to me, but who was I to look a gift horse in the mouth. Eagerly, I made my way back to my car and waved farewell to

Mr. Proud. I needed to get home to Dan. There was so much I had to share with him. My dreams were very rapidly threatening to become a reality.

Keeping my foot light on the pedal to avoid any further encounters of the cop kind, my mind raced back and forth. I had conducted a few Internet searches on mortgages, but it was all very confusing. Would I need a home loan, an investment property loan, or should I create my business name and buy the property through the business? Were there other options of which I wasn't even aware? Would any bank even consider me for a mortgage when I wasn't working? How was I going to unload all of this on Dan? Should I tell him about the house first? Should I tell him about the spirit I'd heard or wait to see if he heard her himself? Questions bubbled up to the surface, crowding my mind with their intense demands for attention.

Before I ended up hyperventilating, I held the wheel with one hand and began tapping the meridian points on my face with my free hand. It was time to put into practice my methods for managing anxiety, especially if I was going to open a business highlighting anxiety management as one of my skill sets. Gradually, the grip on my guts eased and the excess firing in my brain settled down. Home awaited me, just over the hill.

The driveway was empty. I glanced down at my watch. It felt like hours had passed, but it was only mid-afternoon. Dan wouldn't arrive home from work for another hour, at least. Perhaps putting my energy into cooking something nice for supper would help order my thoughts and set the mood for our discussion. My mind was running menu options as I opened the front door. I kicked my shoes onto the mat and slipped into my comfy Birkenstocks. I reached behind and unhooked my bra. I slid it down my arms and I threw it over the upstairs railing. Freedom!

Into the pantry I went to collect the ingredients for an Asian stir fry. It wouldn't take a lot of concentration and the scents would be mouth-watering, greeting Dan as he arrived home. I happily chopped vegetables as my mind began to put in order how I would share my news with him. The doorbell rang and I scurried to wash my hands and get to the door promptly. Just as I swung the door open, I remembered the bra on the upstairs railing and the lack of one on my chest. Damn it! There was a chill wind outside and if it blew inward I knew my light t-shirt would leave little to the imagination. Too late.

The dreaded wind gusted in with force as I stood in the open doorframe. The UPS guy was eye-candy handsome but short, which put him directly at eye level with my chest. Although my cheeks blazed red, I refused to try to hug myself or obviously attempt to cover up. To give him credit, his gaze didn't linger any obscene length of time, but it was enough to leave me in no doubt that all had been revealed!

"Good to see you, Ma'am." He blushed. "I mean, good afternoon."

"Hi there. What can I do for you?" Did I really ask the UPS guy that?

His gaze zipped down and up again before he cleared his throat and stated, "I have something for you."

"How big is it? I mean the parcel. I don't see it." The conversation couldn't get any worse.

"It's between my legs."

I glanced down. Sure enough, the parcel was tucked between his legs, leaving his hands free to hold the pen and clipboard I assumed I needed to sign. I looked up and caught his grin which he quickly wiped off his face.

I grabbed the pen and clipboard as he bent to retrieve the parcel. The clipboard caught him on the temple and he staggered back with blood spurting from a cut I had inflicted.

"Shit! I'm sorry! Let me take a look at that." I leaned toward him just as he brought his head down and I realized my top was more low-cut than was wise for such an angle. He looked up and didn't bother to hide the grin this time.

"It's nothing. Don't worry about it." He passed me the parcel and sauntered over to his truck. I closed the door and leaned against it, hugging my breasts, cringing and laughing. Then I smiled to myself—at least my ego appreciated being ogled by a younger man. Maybe Dan would be just as appreciative!

I set the parcel aside and returned to the kitchen to resume supper preparations. A nice glass of merlot would go well with the rich flavours of the meal. I selected a bottle from my small stock and uncorked it to give it plenty of time to aerate.

I heard the thump of the front door and Dan called out, "Hey, I'm home."

"Hi honey." I jaunted out to meet him.

He glanced at my top. "Nice shirt."

"Want to play postman?" Dan gave me a slightly confused look as he hung up his coat.

"Never mind. I've got so much to tell you! Would you like a glass of wine? I've made supper. I found a house." The words just wouldn't stop spilling out of my mouth.

His mouth descended on mine, shutting me up for the moment. "Why don't we get that wine and sit on the couch? Supper can wait a few minutes, even though it smells delicious."

I restlessly nodded as Dan's arm came around me and guided me to sit. He poured our wine and came to sit beside me as I tried not to squirm too impatiently.

"Okay, what's up?" he said.

For the next half hour, Dan calmly listened as I recounted the afternoon's events. He hooted when I told him about the speeding incident. Then, he confessed he had taken the registration out of the car to process the renewal and had forgotten to tell me. One mystery solved at least! When I got to describing the property and all my ideas for it, I could see the excitement lighting up his eyes. I was so fortunate to have him on board with me. But there was still the slightly more complex issue of Essie.

Dan raised his eyebrows as I chronicled my interaction with Essie. It wasn't exactly doubt or concern that I felt emanating from him; it was more like curiosity.

"I'd like to get a look at the property myself, before you call in an inspector. Do you think we could go back out there tonight?"

"Is it the property you're hoping to see or Essie?" I asked.

Dan chuckled, "Can't get much by you, can I?"

"You load up our plates with supper and I'll call Frank Proud."

Frank answered on the second ring. He seemed keen to have me return to the Fredrick place with Dan, and suggested he meet us out there. He said he wanted to make a stop at the hardware store and he would do that while we took our time looking around. Hah! Frank got himself out of going into the house yet again—fine by me.

We set our wine aside for later and hastily ate our supper.

"Tastes awesome, Alisha," Dan mumbled around a mouthful of food.

I made noises back at him as I quickly finished up. We piled the dishes on the shelf. In five minutes, we were in the car and on the road, with my bra back on!

Anticipation churned the air in the vehicle as we drove along. Would Essie show up again, I wondered? The evening light was soft as we pulled into the driveway. The log house was bathed in the colours of twilight. It looked elegant and bewitching.

Dan exhaled in astonishment. "I don't recall ever seeing this place." As we alighted, he looked around with pleasure. "It has incredible potential."

He was as captivated as I had been.

Just then, Frank drove up. He rolled down his car window. He wasn't even going to get out of the car! Dan walked over, extending his hand.

"Good evening. I'm Alisha's husband, Dan."

"Frank Proud, nice to meet you. I mentioned to Alisha I had some errands to run, so feel free to take your time looking around."

With that, he placed the key in Dan's hand and rolled up his window. We looked at each other and grinned. We quickly proceeded around the grounds before the light was gone. I sketched out my ideas as we traversed the land. Dan was keen to take a closer look at the woods at the back of the property and to check the survey markers, but that would have to wait for daytime. As we rounded the house, he took a look at the foundations for any obvious signs of cracks or crumbling.

No signs or sounds of Essie so far. I didn't know if that was a good indicator or not. The steps creaked as we clamoured up them and onto the veranda. Dan excitedly grasped the opportunity to open the front door. As we stepped over the threshold, I reached in to the right where I recalled seeing the light switches. Dan gasped. I whirled to look at him. His face was agog with anticipation. He continued forward.

"It's just like you described."

I sucked in a breath and followed beside him.

"What did you say?" he asked.

Scanning the room to see if it was as I remembered, I turned toward Dan with a puzzled expression on my face. "What?"

"You were whispering. I didn't catch all that you said."

"Dan, I didn't say anything."

"Yes, you did. Something about isn't this a bonnie house." Dan's expression changed. "It wasn't you?"

"No." I paused for a moment. "Essie, this is my husband Dan."

"Well, I can see that dearie. Picked a braw lad, didn't you? Reminds me of my beloved Stanley. Pleased to meet you, Dan."

The bemused expression on Dan's face assured me he was hearing the whole conversation. "Nice to meet you, too, Essie. We'd like to take a look around so I can assess any repairs we might need to take into account if we buy this place."

"I can help you out with that."

Essie proceeded to lead us through the house, pointing out a few windows that would need replacing and assuring us of the overall structural integrity. The wiring had been updated so that wouldn't present any issues. Dan appeared to be having fun, so I let him pose the questions. I let my mind wander creatively and continued to add to my dreams of the afternoon. Next time, I'd have to take a notebook to start making lists of questions and sketch out ideas. I suppose if my kids had been present they'd have told me to use my phone. Somehow, writing on a phone just doesn't cut it the same as writing on a piece of paper. I'd read somewhere that the act of writing stimulates nerves on the side of the hand and creativity is enhanced in a way that doesn't happen when you type. Maybe my generation isn't so backward after all.

Eventually, I heard an engine sound outside. Frank must have returned. It was time to go. Reluctantly, I handed the key back to Frank and assured him we were interested in the property. I indicated that I would be in touch the next day, once I had an opportunity to book a licensed inspector. The prospect of a sale must have emboldened Frank, because we watched him climb the steps and make sure the door was locked as we pulled out of the driveway.

Dan immediately began making suggestions and I put my hand up to stem the flow.

"Wait until I dig in the glove compartment for something I can write on," I told him. Putting a list on paper would make it all feel more real.

"Okay, go for it," I encouraged Dan, pen poised and ready to record.

"It's a beautiful and well-kept place, from what I could see, but obviously no one has been in it for a while. I'd say all the windows should be replaced, not just the few Essie pointed out. If you replace them all at the beginning you can be sure they're the same type, to maintain a consistent appearance. It should help with air flow too. I noticed a bit of a draft in a few spots. The furnace likely needs replacing—get the inspector to check that. I think the foundation looked okay, but it should be assessed also. Other than some paint and groundwork, everything else looks to be in great condition. They must have replaced the roof not too long ago—it's made of steel."

"I love the red colour. It's so vibrant, especially with the sun reflecting off it, just as it was setting. Dan, it all feels like such a fit for my dream of a Healing House, but I don't know how I'm ever going to figure out the finances."

"Trust, honey. It all boils down to trust. I believe in you and your dreams, so don't stop believing in them yourself, just because you can't see it all clearly yet."

Dan switched off the ignition and I realized we were home. All of a sudden, I felt exhausted from the rollercoaster of emotions I'd ridden through that day. I dragged myself out of the car and inside the house, pulling my coat off and turning to the left to hang it up in the closet. As I did, my foot caught the package which had been delivered earlier. Dan grabbed my hand to prevent me from falling and then reached down to retrieve the parcel. "What's this?" he asked.

I'd forgotten all about the delivery when I got caught up in sharing with Dan my discovery of Essie and her house.

"I don't know. I don't recall ordering any books;

I'll grab the scissors and we can take a look."

As I walked over to the everything drawer in the kitchen that held our assortment of scissors, tape, tacks, and various coupons, Dan plonked down at the table.

"The return address shows some lawyer's office from out West," he declared.

"We don't know any lawyers out there, do we?" I wondered out loud, as I began to cut through the seal.

"Not that I can recall."

I pulled out a sheaf of papers. The top sheet was a cover letter. In utter shock, I looked up at Dan and dropped down onto a chair.

"What is it?" he asked worriedly. I scanned the letter again and then I wordlessly handed it to him. I clung to the arms of the chair and sucked in deep breaths as he read. He glanced up at me every now and then. I nodded, reassuring him I was okay.

It looked like the Universe was really taking a hand in helping my dream move forward. The letter, which Dan was reading, came from a law firm in Calgary, Alberta. Sarah Finestone, a woman from an earlier congregation who had no close relatives, had chosen me as her main beneficiary. I had shared my healing gifts with her in the past and told her of my dream of developing a Healing House.

In the package, there was a short thank you note which expressed her appreciation for the healing she'd received and the healing she hoped to help me offer to others by supporting my dream after her passing. Aside from generous donations to various charities and a few mementos designated for her friends, the bulk of the $300,000 estate was to be mine. The will had already been probated, so I simply needed to present myself at the bank with identification papers and the money would be transferred to me.

I heard a wild tapping noise and I realized Dan's foot was rapidly drumming out his exhilaration. I didn't know if I should shout aloud, dance, or do cartwheels to express all the pent-up energy I now felt inside. Dan decided for me by grabbing my hand and whipping me into an exuberant twirl as he danced me around the kitchen. We whooped and hollered and scooped up our wine glasses from earlier. With broad grins on our faces, we toasted Sarah, who we were sure would have appreciated Essie and her house.

Eventually, we slowed down and slipped out onto the back deck. The moon was riding high in the sky and the stars were brilliant that night. We snuggled together for warmth and chatted about the next steps I'd need to take. The lump sum, even after paying inheritance tax, would be enough for the purchase of the home and renovations, but I would need to make a solid business plan to project what kind of start-up loan I might need to get the Healing House up and running.

First things first, I needed a good night's sleep; maybe there'd be time in the morning to play postman!

CHAPTER FOUR

Events progressed rapidly over the next few weeks. The inspector was thorough. He recommended a new heating system and suggested we look into more environmentally friendly options than simply replacing the old oil furnace. He also agreed that the windows should be replaced. No other major concerns were identified. Dan took window measurements and we scoured the local building supply stores for the most energy efficient and economically feasible choices. We contacted a few energy consultants regarding the heating and obtained quotes for options in that area. With a clear sense of what the improvements would cost, we made an offer on Essie's house. Whether by Essie's intervention or just the fact that it had taken so long for the house to move, our offer was immediately accepted. The closing date was set and, before I knew it, I was sitting on the front step, keys in my hand—a proud new home owner.

A light breeze wafted by and I heard, "*You did it dearie! We're on our way now.*"

"We sure are, Essie. Things are going to get a little busy around here for a while as the contractors install the windows and the new heating system."

"Don't you like the old one?"

"I'm trying to create a Healing House, so I not only want to offer healing for people, but I also want to make sure the house itself is healing for the land and not taking from it. There's plenty of land around the house, so we can install a geothermal system."

"I've never heard of such a thing."

"It's a heating system that transfers heat to or from the ground. Underground tubing takes heat from the ground to the pump and the pump delivers the heat through the house as hot air or hot water. During hot weather, the process is reversed so that it acts as a cooling system. There's no combustion, so it's a clean system. Plus, it's less expensive than electric heating and requires very little maintenance."

"I rather like the sound of that dearie. Good for you!"

"I'm really excited about being able to lessen my footprint on the environment. Now Essie, are you going to behave yourself while all these folks are working here? Not all of them might relate well to the idea of a spirit inhabiting the place."

"I'll keep a keen eye on them, but I won't interfere. I ken how important this is for you. As long as they do a proper job, I'll keep mum."

"Even if you have concerns, Essie, please save

them and tell Dan or me. Don't talk to the workers, okay?"

"Fine, but I don't want anyone doing shoddy work on my home."

"Thanks, Essie. Now, I wonder who that is?"

I saw a swarthy man in his early thirties running up the drive. He had a full beard and long hair that flowed over his bare shoulders as he ran. His leg muscles were well-defined and he moved with a fluid grace that suggested he was an experienced runner. His face, however, was arranged in a bit of a grimace.

"Can I help you?" I inquired as I stood up on the step.

"I'm so sorry to intrude, but is there any chance I could use your washroom? I have a few kilometres to go in my run, but last night's beans are doing their business and I could really stand to use your facilities!" I could feel the urgency of his request as I listened to his slightly accented speech.

"Just a second. The house is still locked up." I opened the door and he bolted in behind me. I quickly pointed to the bathroom located at the back of the Great Room, next to the large bedroom. Just as the door slammed, I thought, Oh shit, what if there's no toilet paper. I hadn't even considered any supplies yet. Should I call out or give him some privacy? How do I get myself into these predicaments?

I decided to err on the side of necessity, so I called out, "Hey there, I just bought this place, so I have no idea if there is toilet paper or not. I can go grab some tissues out of my car if you need them."

His rich baritone voice rumbled out, "Don't worry. I always carry some in my shorts for emergencies."

I left him to his emergency and walked back onto the front porch. A few minutes later, a very relieved runner came out to thank me. He looked around the estate as we stood there and said, "This is quite the property you've got here."

"Yes, I'm pretty excited about it," I replied.

"Just imagine the gardens you could create." No sooner were the words out of his mouth then I felt a nudge from behind me. Essie. What was she up to?

"I've had a few ideas about what I'd like to develop. Are you interested in gardening?"

"I've worked with a local landscaping company for twelve years, but I'm kind of at a turning point in my life," he said.

Another nudge from Essie.

He continued, "I really want to focus on growing healing plants and creating a place that isn't just attractive, but has a healing energy to it. But I'm not ready to start my own business just yet." He smiled, "As they say in India, patience is the best prayer."

Then he shook his head. "I don't know why I'm telling you all this. I'd best get on with my run."

Before he stepped off the porch, I spoke. "Wait. I do know what you're talking about. I've experienced it, but I don't know how to create it. I want to create that on these grounds, but I need someone to work with me. I'm planning on developing a Healing

House with various types of healing modalities offered here. Would you be interested in talking with me? I can give you my number and you can call me if you want to follow up."

I could see interest and hope stirring in his eyes. He extended his hand to shake mine.

"My name is Raman. I definitely want to talk with you about this. When can we meet again?"

"I'm Alisha. What about later today after your run, maybe at a coffee shop?"

"Sure, I'm off work today. Let me finish up and grab a shower. How about we meet at Timothy's? It's my favourite."

I flinched at another nudge from Essie. I could sense Raman's curiosity, but pushed it aside as I agreed to meet him at two o'clock.

Once he had turned the corner of the hedge, I whipped around and exclaimed into the thin air where the nudges had been coming from, "Essie, what the heck is going on?"

"Well, he's perfect isn't he? He wants to do healing things like you. He's ready for a change. You're going to need a full-time gardener, plus he could start a whole line of herbal remedies for your shop. Besides, he likes the same coffee shop as you do. It's Karma."

"Aren't you getting a little ahead of the plan? I don't know anything about this guy yet. I need to get into this slowly and carefully."

"Careful, smareful. When it's right, it's right! When I first set my eyes on Stanley, I knew he was the one for me. When the heart knows, it doesn't plod along, it leaps!"

"I don't think there is such a word as smareful and this isn't about love, Essie. This is business."

"When it comes to business and love, the principles are the same, dearie. To be successful in either, you have to be all in and listen to your heart. I can just tell that Raman is going to be a wonderful asset for your Healing House. You just wait and see!"

"Okay, Essie, I'll try. Now, I want to go through the house and start picturing the colours I want for the rooms. Are you going to help me?"

"I wouldn't miss it!"

Essie and I spent a pleasurable couple of hours bickering about colours. I wanted soft, soothing, inspiring colours and she insisted I needed bright, fun tones. I agreed to fun for the kitchen and dining area, where we could use a combination of a warm brown below the wall trim and golden orchard as the shade above it. I had researched information about the energetic impact of colours. Orange shades supposedly increase oxygen supply to the brain, produce an invigorating effect, and fuel mental activity. Orange is very popular with young people; it's associated with healthy food and stimulates the appetite—perfect for a café.

A softer yellow shade would suit the reception area, reflecting the light from the many windows. Light yellow promotes pleasant, cheerful feelings; this would be a good introductory colour to make an impression on new clients. Green is a healing colour and the shade aqua is particularly helpful for emotional issues; I definitely wanted that for my healing rooms. A silvery grey would blend with that in the bathrooms. My eyes were getting blurry from concentrating on so many different colour palettes, but I felt a sense of accomplishment and contentment with our choices. In my notebook, I carefully listed each room and colour with descriptions.

Glancing at my watch, I gasped. Time had flown.

"Essie! I need to get into town to meet Raman!"

"Scram, dear. I'm just going to savour the vision of these rooms coming alive again. Just remember to keep your foot light on that accelerator!"

I dashed out the door and down the steps, then back up the steps, as I remembered to lock the door. As much as I wanted to believe the community was a safe place, I didn't think it wise to leave it open for anyone to wander in.

Carefully navigating the potholes in the driveway, I turned onto the road and headed to Timothy's to meet Raman.

What are you going to say to him? You don't even have a business proposal drafted yet.

Doubt was back, raising her voice loudly and clearly! Very quickly, I began to feel I was in over my head. I had no idea what I could offer him as a salary. I could feel tension in my clenched leg muscles and my hands gripped the steering wheel tightly.

For a moment, it felt as though a soft hand rested lightly over mine. I sensed the presence of Archangel Gabrielle gently assuring me. I felt my insecurities loosen their grip and my muscles relaxed. I wasn't alone. As usual, my guardian angels were keeping watch over me. For a while, I had been so closed off I couldn't sense them; but I had been practising my awareness over the past weeks and my sensitivity to them had increased notably. I was just going to have a conversation with Raman; there didn't have to be any commitments right away.

There was a parking spot a few blocks before Timothy's, so I nabbed it because it was often crowded the further downtown one drove. The chance to stretch my legs would be welcome and grant me a moment to clear my mind. I spotted Raman sitting at a table near the window and he waved as I moved into the entrance. I shuffled around other tables to join him.

"Can I get you anything?"

"What would you like?"

We both spoke at the same time! Grinning at each other, I insisted, "You're here at my invitation, so my treat. What would you like?"

"Whichever rainforest certified one they have brewed would be great, please! Black, no sweetener."

"Anything else?"

"Honestly, my stomach is too jumpy right now to consider adding anything sugary!"

It was comforting to know we were both feeling nervous. There was no line, so in a few moments I was back with our coffees. My insides were flip-flopping around. What should I say first?

Raman took the onus off me by speaking first.

"Why don't you tell me about your idea for this

Healing House?"

I spent the next ten minutes telling Raman about leaving my career, willing this old dream to re-emerge, finding the house, and feeling my dream confirmed. I was honest with him that I was still in the very early stages of planning and I didn't have anything concrete to offer yet. I also confessed that our meeting had seemed so fortuitous that I felt drawn to speak up when he shared his interests. As I spoke, Raman nodded his head and appeared to be caught up in my story. As my words drew to a close, Raman leaned forward.

"For the last two months, I've felt as though I was standing at a threshold, but I couldn't find the handle to open the door. Today, it feels like that door has cracked open and this is the new possibility I've been waiting for. I understand you can't make me any promises. What if you hired me through the company which presently employs me? You can contract me to consult with you for the layout of your grounds. Not a lot of the physical labour can be done until after the geothermal heating system is installed. We would get a sense of how we work together and you could figure out the financial outlay required to develop your grounds. We can brainstorm and you can see if there is space for me as your business plan unfolds."

"You mentioned an interest in healing plants?" I queried, not wanting the conversation to end.

"I completed a Clinical Herbalist Diploma a year or so ago. It was mostly online studies, with bimonthly hands-on workshops. I also completed 400 internship hours in the final year. Fortunately, with my work, I could juggle my hours. As long as I completed the jobs assigned to me, my boss didn't mind me studying."

"You almost sound too good to be true," I smiled.

"I feel the same way. I've been looking for opportunities around here and nothing seemed to be quite the right match. So…?" Raman probed.

"I like your idea of starting with a contract. It feels less pressured. I don't know how long it will take to get this business off the ground and I don't want you to be dependent on an income that I might not be able to offer."

"Sounds like a good start to me. Even if the door only seems to be open a crack, I'm confident, when the time is right, it's going to blow wide open!" Raman declared with conviction.

I extended my hand across the table and Raman clasped mine between both of his. "Let it be so."

Placing my other hand over his, I concurred, "Let it be so."

I promised to contact his business to request an appointment with him for a consult on my property. Dazed, I walked out of Timothy's and down the street to my car. When I had set out that morning, little did I anticipate yet another step forward toward my dream.

CHAPTER FIVE

The days zipped along as the contractors installed the heating system and another company took care of installing windows. Raman and I walked the grounds, conceptualizing ideas for the healing garden, the Zen garden, and the labyrinth. We also discovered a small brook when we traipsed through the woods and he had ideas about a meditation area he could develop near it. A rather run-down-looking shed was at the edge of the woods, but we left it for exploration at another time. We seemed to have established a comfortable rapport, which boded well for the potential of working together more permanently.

I was still struggling with the business aspect of things and trying to work up spreadsheets. I decided it was paramount that I take a break and give my mind an opportunity to rest by going to a hot yoga class. Sinking into the poses and the breathing was a phenomenal way to ease stress. I felt invigorated and renewed as I returned to the change room. As I emptied my locker, I overheard some of the women chatting on the other side of the room.

"Congratulations, Cheri! I heard you got your business degree!"

"Thanks, Rayna. I actually finished my yoga instructor certificate at the same time. I must be crazy!"

"Good for you, girl!"

"I just hope I can find work locally. My fiancée and I want to stay here in Bright Haven, but with our student loans we'll have to go wherever the jobs are."

My ears perked up. Business and yoga sounded like another match for my Healing House. This class was going to do more than just clear my mind! I wondered how I could nonchalantly join in their conversation.

I closed my locker and turned around. There were several women on the other side of the room hastily changing their clothes. Awkwardly, I stepped around the bench and inquired, "Excuse me, but which one of you is Cheri?"

A burgundy-haired young woman in her mid-twenties, generously covered in tattoos, replied, "That's me."

Not quite what I had imagined, but who was I to judge? "Hi Cheri! I overheard your conversation—you mentioned that you're looking for work. I'm in the process of setting up a business. I could really use someone with your skills. If you'd be interested in applying, here's my number."

Cheri's face opened up into a broad grin.

"I was about to grab a juice at the Rawsome Juice Bar. We could hang there for a bit and discuss what you're after. What do you say?"

We quietly walked through the studio hallways and, once outside, Cheri suggested, "Why don't we walk, it's not far?"

I nodded in agreement.

Cheri sauntered briskly along for a few steps; then she blurted out, "So what's the deal?"

I began to explain some of my journey thus far. As I talked, Cheri called out to various folks as we walked by.

"Good morning, Clint. You're doing a great job there," she yelled to a young man who was raking a lawn. "Clint is in recovery," she shared with me, "and needs lots of encouragement. He has really low self-esteem."

"Hey, Mrs. Schumacher. Ready for your daily hug?" Cheri bounced up the walkway to a veranda, where an elderly woman sat in a rocking chair. A grand smile swept over her face as she carefully stood up and opened her arms to receive her hug. In seconds, Cheri was back and we were on our way again.

"Mrs. Schumacher lives alone. Her family all live hours away, so she has very little company. Human touch is so important, so I try to share a hug whenever I can."

As I took up my story again, I rapidly assessed

Cheri as an extrovert with excellent people skills. She would be awesome at reception, if she wanted to be involved that way. I had reached the point in my story at which I had to confess to Cheri that I had all these ideas, but no business background to figure out how to move it all forward.

She asked, "Do you have a vision statement? Have you identified your core values? Is there a name for your business? Have you looked into permits?"

Cheri began to slow her questions as I kept shaking my head in reply to her inquiries. "So, you have the big idea, but none of the practical work is in place yet?"

"That would be a very accurate assessment," I mumbled. "I've had the vision for a long time. I now have the place, the environment, and some start-up money, but no idea how to effectively progress from there. I desperately need someone with a passion for this kind of work and a willingness to be in from the bottom up."

At the juice bar, we intuitively agreed to postpone the discussion until we placed our order and found a seat. The juice called "Enlighten Me"—a blend of strawberries, pineapple, blueberries, apple, lemon, and beets—sounded yummy and the name felt like it matched my situation right then. Cheri ordered "You and Me", which contained beets, pineapple, strawberry, red apple, and ginger. I wondered if her choice was simply a favourite or if the Universe was trying to communicate something more through its title.

We found a seat and took a few refreshing sips before picking up the conversation again.

Cheri began, "When I started looking for work, I initially wanted something already established and fairly stable. However, my heart-strings are resonating with your story. During my business degree, I did some summer interning with an agency which helps small businesses get started; I do have experience in the area you need. Being with you from the ground up sounds both terrifying and exhilarating! I would need to talk this over with my fiancée to make sure she is on board. You'll probably want to interview other people too." Cheri paused for a drink. "My energy is just vibrating thinking about this. Definitely not what I expected when I went to yoga this morning!"

I interjected, "It wasn't on my agenda either! But, I'm learning to trust these portentous meetings. The Universe or my guardian angels or fate seems to be on my case. I keep meeting the right people at the right time for this work to go forward. Why don't you talk with your fiancée and, if she's supportive, send me your resumé. I'll check your references and we'll see what unfolds."

Cheri hauled in a deep breath. "Okay, let's go for it!" I handed over my contact information and wrote hers into my trusty notebook. She grinned when I admitted that I just couldn't trust some things to technology. I finished the last of my juice and stood up to go. Cheri bounced up and gave me a big hug. I could feel the energy streaming off her body into our embrace. I could sense her excitement, but also there was a warm compassion that flowed through the core of her energy. This was another confirmation for me that Cheri was the next person for my team.

I could hardly wait to tell Dan! But, it would be hours before he'd be home from work, so I decided to go back to the property and catch Essie up on the latest development.

As I pulled onto Starling Drive, I remembered the painters had started on the house. I glanced at the dashboard clock and noted that it was past noon. Maybe they'd be taking a lunch break and I could chat with Essie without risk of being caught.

As luck would have it, I could see the workers seated on folding chairs around a makeshift table on the lawn. I meandered over and gestured to the foreman, whose name I thought was Bob, to stay seated. "I'm just going to take a quick look around while you're on break. I'm eager to see how my colour selections actually look on the walls."

"No problem. Base and first coat are on in most rooms. Just be careful where you step; there are buckets and ladders strewn around. The drop cloths on the floor can be a little tricky too."

I eagerly dashed up the front steps and into the house. Closing the door behind me, I turned and stood still, absorbing the beauty before me. To the left, the soft yellow glowed and, on the right, in the kitchen and dining area, the brown and orangey hues gave depth and warmth to the whole place. I couldn't wait to check out the healing rooms, so I darted across the reception area to the room at the back. As I pushed open the door, I heard a noise behind me and glanced back. Bob was coming through the front door, calling out to me, but it was too late. I had already advanced into the room and directly into a ladder with a worker and a tray of paint on it! The nimble worker managed to leap off the ladder before any disaster befell him. I, however, was not so lucky. The paint tray flew up into the air and flipped onto my head. Aqua paint dripped through my hair and over my clothes.

Bob's voice echoed from the Great Room as I turned toward him.

"Alisha, I forgot to mention, Ronnie is still finishing up the back room, so don't go in there." His words drifted to a halt as he confronted the situation. I could see startled amusement wash over his face before he got a grip on himself. Fortunately, the tray landed in such a way that my face wasn't affected; it had hooked on my head and dripped all down my back. The drop cloths I was standing on protected the floor. I took the tray off my head and handed it to him.

"Ronnie, grab some cloths for Alisha," Bob directed, as he gingerly took hold of the tray and placed it on the floor.

Ronnie rushed over and began wiping the paint off my hair and body.

"That's an interesting way to get a man's hands on you, dearie!"

I could hear Essie's chuckling reverberating

through my mind. I glared up at the ceiling, but then realized the men would think I was angry with them.

"It's okay. This was my fault entirely. I wasn't watching where I was going."

"I think I've got most of the excess wiped from your hair. There are a few spatters on your skin, but most of it seems to be on your shirt and pants. You might want to get out of those clothes," Ronnie urged.

"*Ooh, how exciting!*" Essie exclaimed teasingly.

I spoke firmly to Essie in my mind. "Stop that!"

To Bob, I grumbled, "My kitbag is in the backseat of my car, with my sweaty yoga outfit in it. I can switch into that, if you'll go get it for me."

"Back in a jiff, don't go anywhere," he cheerfully replied—as if I was going to go and drip more paint around the house!

Ronnie resumed with his helpful instructions.

"All the paints we're using are zero VOC qualifying paints, like you specified, so you shouldn't worry too much about getting it off. Scrub firmly with soap and water, then rub mineral or coconut oil over your skin. Leave it for a few minutes, then scrub again. Lavender or rosemary essential oils work well too, if you're into that kind of stuff."

I looked at Ronnie with new respect.

He shrugged his shoulders sheepishly. "My wife is an aromatherapist. I've picked up a few things."

All of a sudden, my interest was piqued. "Where does she work?" I inquired.

"She just quit her job with A Natural Nose

because they inflated their prices for clients but pay their staff a pittance!"

"You don't say." I began to wonder if Essie might have been at work again.

"Now, dearie, I didn't make you rush into this room."

"And how was it that I was perfectly on target for that paint tray?" I hissed internally.

"Now don't flap, I protected your face!" Essie sounded a little disgruntled.

Bob re-entered the room and handed me my kitbag. They threw a drop cloth onto the bathroom floor and closed the door behind me. There was a full bar of soap and finger-brush scrubber at the sink, so I was able to get rid of a good bit of the paint before it dried on my skin. I continued my conversation with Essie.

"Thank you for protecting my face. But couldn't I have met him another way?"

"You presented me with the perfect opportunity. I just helped it along a little. I didn't mean any harm."

"No harm, Essie. Just a big inconvenience."

"Will you talk to his wife?"

"I'll give her a call and get a feel for her." Then I remembered, "Essie, the whole reason I was rushing out here is that I wanted to tell you I think I've found a business administrator! No, I know I have. Her name is Cheri. She just finished her degree, has experience in new businesses, and she's also a yoga instructor. She just has to speak with her fiancée and make sure she's supportive."

"Isn't that something, two women getting married."

"Is that going to be a problem?"

"Nay, Alisha. I'm profoundly grateful this has finally come to be. My sister had to keep her true self in hiding all her life. She had a 'friend' who lived with her, but they could never openly share that they were lovers. It was so heartrending to know they could never openly be themselves. Congratulations on finding the right woman to get the next steps going."

"Thanks, Essie. I don't have her for sure, yet. But my heart says yes. I better get back out there, so the guys don't worry about me." I opened the bathroom door and stepped out.

"You look a sight better," declared Bob.

"Thanks. I'll be fine. Go on back to your lunch. I just have a quick question for Ronnie."

Bob nodded his head. He glanced around and, since everything else seemed in order, he made his escape. Meanwhile, Ronnie looked at me inquisitively, so I pushed ahead with my agenda.

"Ronnie, you know I'm working toward developing this as a Healing House. I'll be looking for an aromatherapist to be on staff here. I would love to interview your wife if I could have her contact number."

A splendid smile split Ronnie's face. He quickly rhymed off his wife's cell number and I told him to hold on as I went out to get my notebook. Once I had recorded her number, I thanked Ronnie for his help. He had one final suggestion before I left.

"You might want to try a hairdresser before you get home, although they might use a lot of chemicals. Otherwise, just use lots of soap and then soak your hair in the oil and soap up again a few times."

I took an extra drop cloth to cover my car seat and decided to opt for home and natural remedies for paint removal. Hot damn, Dan was going to get an eyeful and an earful once he returned home from work. I wondered what to cook up for supper? It would have to be from supplies in the pantry because there was no way I was stopping at any store, looking and smelling the way I did!

Dan's amusement over my predicament was full blown. He was also excited about the possibility of Cheri as my business manager. When I checked my emails that evening, her resumé was in my inbox. Obviously, her partner had no reservations that would hold her back.

It was still early evening, so I called Cheri's referees and heard glowing reports of a pleasant-natured, dedicated worker, with a sense of humour and who deeply cared for others. Although one referee mentioned that she could be stubborn at times, wanting to wrestle through an issue until it was resolved, I didn't see that as a terrible thing. Therefore, I called Cheri to see if she'd be available to meet the next morning. I thought it would be helpful for her to see the property. We agreed to meet there mid-morning. I knew Raman would be there at that time and she'd have an opportunity to connect with him as well; we could get a sense of how the three of us meshed together.

I went to bed exhausted and exhilarated. What a day!

CHAPTER SIX

The next morning, when I gazed into the mirror after my morning shower, I fatefully accepted the faint shade of aqua that permeated my hair. The paint itself was gone, but the dye seemed determined to hold on. I had completed a run and strength workout and felt invigorated as I prepared for my morning meeting. After a healthy breakfast of oat-bran, chia, and flax, sprinkled with dark chocolate chips, I set off.

When I pulled into the driveway, I saw Cheri was already there. She was contentedly sitting on the steps, leisurely looking around, while sipping from a large mug. She languidly stretched upward as I got out of the car.

"What an incredible place! And I've only been outside. It just makes me feel exceptional. Geez, listen to me rave. I'm so pumped yet so chill about all this. I brought coffee, by the way. Don't know if you drink it or not, but it's decaf and I have a thermos full. I have fresh farm milk in a little cooler. It's from my parents' place. I'll stop talking now!"

I smiled widely at her, "You hit it perfectly! Decaf is my favourite and I take milk. Let me grab my mug from the car." I eagerly filled my mug and we savoured the flavours together with a clink of our mugs as a toast.

"Do you want to check out the grounds with me first? We should see Raman at work somewhere. He's the landscape artist I contracted to do the grounds. I'm hoping once we get the business up and running that he can come on as full-time staff. He has training as a clinical herbalist."

"Sounds interesting. I'd love to see more of the grounds."

As we began the tour, I could see where Raman had already been hard at work. The pond was clear of dead leaves and debris; a few new bushes had been planted nearby with fragrant mulch surrounding them. I mentioned to Cheri the plan for a Zen garden in that area. At the back of the house, the lawn had been cut and it looked like parts had been re-seeded. A pile of hand-sized rocks were ready for planning the labyrinth. My gaze flitted over to the old shed. I'd have to take a look at that soon, because we'd need storage room for tools and supplies in the near future.

As we came around the far side of the house, I saw Raman diligently preparing his herb garden. The transformation here was a result of incredible hard work. Raman had extracted all the weeds; then he had enriched the soil with compost and manure. Bales of straw on the side were ready for lining the rows around the plants. I hailed him and he glanced upward, waving us over.

"Hey, Alisha. And you must be Cheri. I'd offer my hand, but it's coated in dirt." Raman looked back at me. "That's an interesting shade; something new you're trying?"

I raised my eyebrows. "You've been talking to Bob and Ronnie!"

He burst out laughing.

Cheri spoke up. "I noticed it right away. I think it's quite attractive on you."

"It's growing on me, but it wasn't an intentional choice. Yesterday, after I met you, I had a run-in with a tray of aqua paint. This is the toned-down version."

Still chuckling, Raman rubbed his lower back and suggested, "I've been at this over an hour and a half. Why don't we grab a seat for a few minutes and chat?"

We walked around the house to the seats the painters had used the day before. Cheri pulled an iPad out of her purse and started in right away. "I was so excited after you called me last night that I stayed up until two a.m. framing things up for your business. There are two ways we could look at this. Firstly, you could own the business and hire the rest of us on an hourly wage, as contracted employees or salaried positions. The second way is that you own the house and grounds, but lease it to the business, which all the employees buy into. We put a start-up amount in and we become shareholders, with shares according to how much we put in. This gives us all a more vested interest in the success of this place and gives you more to work with for starting things up. We would each still be given a set wage or salary as we work out each job description, so we'd have money to live on."

"I like this lassie! What a wonderful way to do business! That sounds just and fair to me," Essie exclaimed.

"I'm sorry, I didn't see you earlier. Hi, I'm Cheri." Cheri extended her hand to the space beside me.

Raman looked puzzled and I blurted out, "You can see her?"

Cheri looked at me, ponderingly. "Yes. Why?"

Raman interjected, "Hold on. This voice I'm hearing is for real?"

"Aye, I'm real," declared Essie.

I heaved a sigh. "I suppose I should have mentioned Essie earlier."

"You truly should have!"

"Essie Fredrick and her husband… Essie I don't remember your husband's name?"

"Stanley, dear, he was my beloved Stanley."

"Okay, so Essie and Stanley built this place. The land was in her family for five generations. Stanley died years ago, and Essie died, hmm…"

"I died back in 2008, just before my 98th birthday."

"So, this place has been vacant for ten years?" asked Cheri.

"We lost both our sons, John and Harry—John in the

Korean War and Harry died of tuberculosis. My sister didn't have any children and my husband was an orphan. Other than a few distant cousins, no one was interested in the place. They just wanted the money, which is why it has been in the hands of a realtor. But they've had to be patient. I didn't hang around for just anyone to buy this place. I've been waiting for the right person to show up."

"Essie is a ghost?" Raman quizzed.

"I prefer the term 'spirit', dear."

"And some people can see you?" he persisted.

"Yes. People like Cheri—who are visually perceptive—are able to see my energetic imprint."

"But you can't see her?" Raman swivelled his head to look at me.

"Not yet," I said testily. "I've been practicing my visual acuity, but the most I get is a quick impression of movement, not an image of Essie."

"It'll come, dearie, just be patient."

"This is so frosty; our very own spirit," gushed Cheri.

"Yes, but, be cautious. Sometimes she gets ideas and things happen. Let my hair be testimony. She wanted me to meet Ronnie and—kablooey—I had a tray of paint on my head! Anyway, you've both met Essie now. Perhaps we can get back to business."

Raman smiled in the direction of Essie's voice. "Glad to formally meet you, Essie."

He paused, then continued, "I honestly feel Cheri's suggestion that we all invest in the business is the best way to move forward. I'd been thinking of starting my own business, so I've been putting money aside the last few years. If we all feel we're in this together, I think we'll be more committed to all aspects of the business and making this work."

"I have to say, I'm drawn to that proposal as well," I concurred. "I've been rather anxious about trying to carry the load of owner and director. This seems more like a team approach, where we draw on each other's strengths, and value each other as an asset. I'd like us all to receive the same salary, because we're all important to the success of this operation. The only difference in income will be related to income from our shares.

"Stupendous!" exclaimed Cheri. "We're all on the same page then for our business set-up. My parents gifted me a small investment at my graduation. It's not a lot, but I can add something to the pot. Will this apply to new team members we bring on board?" Cheri scrolled her way down her iPad notes.

"Makes sense to me," affirmed Raman. "The more we include everyone from the start, the more this will feel like a team."

"But what if we find someone we really want to work with us, and they don't have any buy-in money?" I asked anxiously.

Cheri frowned thoughtfully. "Perhaps they could be taken on as a salaried position and, at the end of each business year, all team members will be given the chance to invest or re-invest with the company. Shares are then redistributed accordingly."

"That sounds like it could work," I enthused.

"I'll look into how we set that up," Cheri stated.

"Next, we need to determine exactly what services we want to offer, how many staff members will be needed, furniture, specialized equipment, ongoing supplies, and so on."

"Wow, your brain sure does a lot of thinking in the middle of the night!" exclaimed Raman.

"Why don't we move inside to show you the layout and share what I've visualized for the space? Raman, do you have time for this?" I inquired.

"My time's your time, Alisha," Raman smiled, "I'm keen to see the latest updates."

Cheri practically floated off her chair, she seemed so eager to get moving. "I can't believe I'm actually going to see inside this place. A year ago, I saw it on the Internet when I was dreaming about houses, but I knew there was no way we could afford it. The last few months, I've driven by over a dozen times and felt this strong connection tugging at me. I couldn't understand it! Now I do and I'm so excited!"

We briskly walked to the front door and I pulled the key out of my pocket. The painters were on another job, so we had the place to ourselves. As I opened the door, Raman and Cheri crowded in close behind me. I could feel the anticipation oozing from them. We stepped inside. Cheri sighed in appreciation. Raman drew in a deep breath and kept nodding as he looked around.

"Essie, you have a beautiful home," Cheri cooed as she looked to one side where I saw a slight ripple in the air. Wow! My sight was improving.

"Alisha did a great job selecting windows that maintain

the old-fashioned look of the place and they also provide some of this newfangled insulation and UV protection. Do you like the colours we chose for the rooms?"

"The windows appear to be good quality and certainly offer a pleasant brightness to these rooms. The colours show up well and reflect the light nicely," Raman assessed as he moved further into the Great Room.

Cheri casually strolled into the Great Room. Then, she stood at the entrance to the kitchen and dining area. "It feels so welcoming and cheerful—a happy place."

"It was a happy place for Stanley and me for sixty years. I'm so glad the essence of our bonnie home will bring joy to others," Essie sniffed.

I quickly reclaimed the conversation by explaining my ideas for the reception area and the café. Both Cheri and Raman were in agreement. Cheri suggested keeping the space flexible, with easily moveable furniture so that a small yoga or meditation class could be held in the Great Room during quieter hours. I interjected with the idea of a café journal-writing class, featuring different coffees and treats. Raman became very animated as he considered various herbal remedies he could make for sale. He did raise a concern regarding a place he could properly store supplies and make his preparations. There was a back pantry behind the kitchen that might suit for his preparations and I suggested we could take a look at the shed to the back of the property. Although decrepit-looking, it might be repairable.

Cheri diligently took notes on her iPad as we made our way to the back room. I saw the exchange of looks and smiles as they noted the colour on the walls and glanced at my hair, but no comment was made.

"I wondered about setting up this room with aesthetic services, because of the bathroom attached to it," I posed to the others.

I could sense Raman's hesitation and I noticed Cheri screw up her nose. "Spit it out," I urged, as neither of them were speaking. "Share what you're thinking. Remember, we're a team. Just because one of us has an idea doesn't mean we have to follow it."

Raman responded immediately. "I get that aesthetics can be a renewing experience for some, but I'd be concerned about the chemicals and smells that such treatments often exude and how that might affect our other clientele."

"That was exactly my thought!" Cheri declared. Pointing to her hair, she stated, "Even though I go for hair colour fun, the smells drive me crazy in those places, so I limit my exposure. I'd rather we focused on aromatherapy, mud wraps, massage, and maybe even hydrotherapy in this area since our focus is on being a healing place."

"Me too," Essie chimed in. *"But what's a mud wrap?"*

"A mud wrap uses a mix of herbs and clean clay or mud which is spread over the skin to draw out toxins. It's an exfoliator and it refreshes the skin. You feel so revitalized afterward," Cheri enthused.

"Sounds interesting. Isn't there someone you can contact about this part of the business Alisha?"

I had completely forgotten about Ronnie's wife, so I explained that the painter I'd crashed into was married to an aromatherapist. We agreed I'd get in touch with her and see what suggestions she might have for us. We finished with the upstairs rooms, which could easily be used for a variety of healing modalities. By then, Raman was itching to get back outside to his garden and Cheri was beginning to fade from her late-night brainstorming session. We felt it best if we took a few days to do some independent thinking and research, before coming back together for a second meeting. Raman sauntered out while Cheri embraced me with a warm hug. I felt another hand on my shoulder and a slight surge of energy.

Cheri smiled softly, looking slightly to my left. "Thanks for the boost, Essie. See you again soon." She scurried out to her car, leaving Essie and me on our own.

"That went well, don't you think?"

"Yes, but it's not fair that she can see you and I can't!"

"Stop fashing. She hasn't had as many years as you've had to be conditioned into thinking I'm an impossibility!"

"You're telling me I'm too old for this?"

"Are ye daft, I'm still going at ninety-eight! Alisha, what's really going on?"

I plopped down on the floor and hugged my knees to my chest.

"Things are happening so fast. At first it was just me, consulting with Dan, making all the decisions. Now these new people are in my life and, don't get me wrong, they're great, but…."

"But you feel like your dream isn't your own anymore?"

Exactly! I'm delighted with Raman's work so far. Cheri has excellent ideas and seems to have a firm grasp of the business perspective, which overwhelms me. But, it almost feels like the first day I sent my kids to school.

"I remember those feelings, dearie. The excitement, the fear, the pride, the hope, the sorrow, the knowledge that my children would no longer be just shaped by Stanley and me. Your dream has launched and it's now being shaped by others. It may turn out a wee bit differently than you first envisioned it."

I heaved a huge sigh and ran my fingers through my hair. "You've hit it on the head in one swing! I'm excited about the possibility of what we can create together, but I'm terrified I'll make a mistake and it won't just be me that sinks; they'll go down with me. My dream was so nebulous at first and now it's taking shape in ways I didn't expect. I suppose, if I consider myself a life-long learner, I'd better accept that I still have a lot to learn about life and about myself. Thanks for listening, Essie. I think I'll go take a look at that shed out back."

"Why don't you leave that for now, dearie? Go home and soak in the tub and let yourself sort through the morass of emotions that are seething around inside you. Put a few drops of frankincense in the water. It helps with emotional release."

"How do you know that, Essie?"

"I just do, lass. Skedaddle, take some time. Even though your dream seems to be moving on fast forward, hit pause for a bit. You can take the time you need."

"I will," I spoke definitively. "I need to write some of this down as well. Journal writing helps me get my thoughts in order. Sometimes, as I scrawl it all down, clarity will push through when I least expect it."

"Why don't you come back after lunch tomorrow and we can take a stroll down to the shed together?"

"Sure." I dragged myself up from the floor. "I'll be back tomorrow, Essie. Keep an eye on things." I saw a flicker of movement and felt a light, reassuring hand on my shoulder again.

"Thanks, Essie. See you!" I meant it!

A few hours later, I had very wrinkled skin, but a much-soothed spirit as I climbed out of the tub. The fragrance of frankincense had done its work and tight muscles which had been holding my mixed emotions had suppled out. I choose a comfy, thigh-length blouse in a swirl of blue and pink hues that flattered my colouring, even the new tint of my hair! Snug-fitting leggings stretched with me as I moved around. Dream catcher earrings gently caressed my shoulders. They were a personal favourite and, for me in that moment, symbolized that not every detail of a dream catches; some parts flow through. I needed to trust that what was good would hold.

I took my journal out onto the shaded back deck

where a light breeze kept the temperature manageable. Sketching out my thoughts and feelings in prose further calmed and centered my certainty that I was on the right path. I felt playful and wrote a poem which captured my Healing House journey thus far:

Breaking ties, a dream beckoned.
Searching days, my heart reckoned.
Universe guided and surprise support:
Spirit presence, unique rapport,
Gifted allies, met by chance—
Dream unfolding, joyful dance!

My stomach rumbled and I decided it was time to start planning something for supper. I looked at the clock and jolted; it was almost 5:30 p.m. What kind of comfort food could I rustle up in twenty minutes? Portobello mushrooms, red peppers, sun-dried tomatoes, and sliced olives, tossed in the bottom of the pie plate, lots of grated cheese, spices, and well-beaten eggs. Whew, I did it in fifteen! I had remembered to pre-heat the oven, so I slid the crust-less quiche in and opened a bottle of red wine to breathe. Briskly, I chopped veggies, grabbed a package of rice crackers, and pulled a container of hummus out of the fridge that I had made earlier in the week. Wow, look at me go. I even had hors d'oeuvres!

I heard the front door opening as I reached for two wine glasses. Dan was home.

"Hey honey," he called out.

"I'm in the kitchen. Supper needs time to bake,

but I have wine and crudités for us to munch while we catch up on our day," I replied.

Two strong arms encircled me and I felt Dan's warm breath swirl over my ear as he nibbled a greeting. I turned around and felt his gaze burn up and down me.

"You look good enough to eat!" he joked.

More than willing to be his appetizer, I grabbed Dan's hand and pulled him toward the couch.

After a delightful interlude that left me even more limber than my bath, I heard the timer sound for the oven. Lazily, I sashayed over to check our quiche. It looked perfect. I turned off the heat and pulled the oven door ajar. The aromas wafted out and my stomach let out a wild growl. I giggled, pressed my hand to my stomach, and turned to Dan.

"Ready for solid food yet?"

He grinned and said, "Let me go grab my sweats, then we can start with the veggies and wine."

I pulled my slightly squashed clothes back on and poured our wine as Dan came back down the stairs from our bedroom.

"How was your day?" I asked as I handed Dan his wine.

"Actually, it was a rather strange day. Lately, I've been thinking about how you're chasing your dream and making it into a reality. I've started contemplating my own dreams, latent ones that I set aside years ago. Then, today, two clients cancelled in a row and I found myself with a chunk of unexpected free time. Before I knew it, I was immersed in sketching out plans. Hold on, let me go grab my briefcase."

I watched as Dan strode toward the front door. There was a vitality emanating from him that was enthralling. Whatever he was going to show me had obviously spiked something in him that I hadn't seen in a while. When he plopped down next to me, he placed a sketchpad on my lap. I glanced at him and he nodded. I opened it and gasped! It was my café, with beautifully styled wooden tables and chairs, a unique island, and serving trolleys laid out on the page before me. The following pages had specific sketches, with exact dimensions, for each piece of furniture.

"These are incredible!" I exclaimed. "You've captured exactly what I want and I didn't even tell you."

"We've been together for twenty-five years. I've picked up a few things in that time." Dan grinned as I swatted him.

"Truly, Dan, I love the shape and feel of each piece you've sketched. So, tell me more about your dream?" I inquired.

"You know I've always loved working with wood. It has been a healthy outlet over the years—a contrast to working with people in need. But mostly, I've done practical things, like build the kids' bookshelves, make footstools for the family room, repair dressers, and things like that. I've always wanted to do more, but there was never time and there were always bills to pay, so I didn't let my mind go there. Since you've been dreaming, it's as if I can't shut my own mind off. I have my workshop and the tools I've collected over the years, so there's no set-up cost. I have other ideas for the rest of your Healing House and some creative pieces. But I've also been thinking that, as I listen to friends and seniors in the community, I hear them repeatedly say that there's no one out there to do small home repairs. That could be the bread and butter part of my business, as long as I allow myself a day or two a week for specialty type projects."

"That'd be quite a shift from psychology and counselling," I reflected. Dan had worked for the last fifteen years in the outpatient clinic at the local hospital.

"Exactly! My compassion metre has been dipping really low lately and I'm concerned I'm on the edge of burnout. I want to get out while things are good, not wait until I'm forced out because I've lost it," Dan confessed.

"I knew some days were rough, but I hadn't realized it was that serious. I've been so caught up in my life transition and you've been so supportive. Dan, I'm sorry I haven't been there for you," I uttered guiltily.

Dan clasped my hand between his. "Alisha, I wasn't even aware of how all this was pressurizing inside me. I don't expect you to understand what I didn't even know was going on. But, this afternoon, when I opened that sketchbook and started, it was like taking the lid off the pressure cooker. I don't think I can put it back on. All these ideas and wants just keep pouring out. It's not like I'm going to quit my career tomorrow, but it's time for a change."

I climbed onto Dan's lap and gave him a hug. "It seems the times they are a changing for both of us! Let's take it one step at a time. First, I'm starving. Let's eat."

Dan hugged me back. "Change—it's terrifying and exhilarating at the same time."

"Essie and I had this very conversation this afternoon," I shared.

As we ate the slightly cold quiche, I filled Dan in on my discussion with Essie, as well as my meeting with Raman and Cheri. He was impressed that Cheri could see Essie and he was glad Raman could hear her too, so he wouldn't be left out. Dan concurred with their reluctance about having aesthetics in the back room and was interested in their suggestions for other types of therapies.

Once we'd stacked the dishes in the dishwasher, we made our way out to the porch swing on the back deck. Gently swinging back and forth, we enjoyed the view of our gardens and the comfort of full bellies.

"Ready for part two of my strange day?" Dan began.

"There's more?" I replied.

"You know the 'Twoonies for Teens' draw we hold each week at work? The pot reached $50,000." Dan said.

"Did you finally win?" I laughed; this was a running joke we exchanged every week.

"Actually,"—he paused for effect—"I did."

I stopped the swing and turned to stare at him. "You're kidding me, right?"

"Nope." He grinned broadly.

"You won $50,000 and you're just telling me now?" I jumped up off the swing with such force, I almost wobbled off the veranda as my voice rose in volume and in disbelief. I shook my head, "I can't believe that wasn't the first thing out of your mouth when you came through the door. And you let me ramble on about my day all through supper." I felt stupefied.

"To be honest, the money wasn't the most important part of the day for me," Dan explained. "Delving into my dream and hearing yours unfold are more valuable than any dollar figure. The money is just icing on the cake."

"Pretty expensive icing," I mumbled.

"I wanted to share everything else first, so we can more clearly look at what we want to do with the money. For now, why don't we put it in a short-term investment to earn some interest and then we can decide how to use it, when our emotions aren't as jumbled?" Dan suggested.

"Makes sense." I replied. "You really won $50,000?" I was still in shock.

"I did." Dan stretched out his arm and drew me back onto the swing, tucked close beside him. Gently, he set the swing in motion again. "Breathe, Alisha. Just breathe. And I'll do the same. God, what a day!"

If life kept up the way it was going, I was definitely going to get in an extra supply of frankincense.

CHAPTER SEVEN

Details like laundry and clean bathrooms kept me busy at home the next morning, while my mind busily pictured Dan's designs fitting into the café. I was eager to share with Essie our latest news, so, after a quick quinoa salad for lunch, I set off for our Healing House once again.

I began to think about a name. The place was more than just a Healing House; the grounds were important too. What would capture the essence of our vision for the place and communicate it simply but powerfully? Maybe I should text the others and get their brains mulling it over too. We'd need to register our business soon and I wanted the official name, representative of our dreams, on those forms.

When I pulled in and turned the car off, I fired off a text to Raman and Cheri. Then, I tucked my phone in the dash of the car, so I could meet with Essie undisturbed. There was so much to tell her. I had barely opened the door when I felt her presence.

"There you are. I've been waiting for you dearie!"

"Hey Essie! You told me to come after lunch and I had chores to do at home. So much has happened since yesterday." I gulped in air as my words tumbled over one another.

"Aye, aye, we'll get to all that. But the painters are gone for now and I want you to see that back shed," Essie exclaimed impatiently.

"Okay, but Essie I want to tell you…."

"You can tell me after we see the shed."

"What's so important about a shed?"

"Get those legs moving, dearie. Time's running out!"

"Essie, what are you talking about?" I protested grumpily, even as my legs carried me around the house, along the path to the shed.

"Just keep going. You'll see once it all unfolds."

"Once what unfolds, Essie? What are you manipulating now?" I asked suspiciously as I arrived at the shed door.

There was no reply as I looked at what seemed to be a fairly new-looking lock on the door. I hadn't noticed it previously, but then none of us had really been up close to the shed because we were busy with all the other details. I estimated that the shed was about twelve by twenty feet as I sized it up. I reached out to turn the handle. It moved in my hand and the door opened. I gasped in surprise, which turned to a scream, when I came face-to-face with a person holding the door on the other side. My scream was echoed by theirs and both our hands fell from the door handles as we each took a startled step backwards.

"Easy, dearie. Go gently here."

"Essie, what the devil is going on?" I expressed firmly in my mind, certain she could hear me!

"You don't have to shout! There's no danger here. Just be open and listen."

"I'm sorry, ma'am. I didn't mean to scare you." The words came out in a velvety smooth voice. The person before me had wispy silvery hair falling around a finely boned young face. A fairy-like beauty emanated from him. Or was he a her? I couldn't tell.

"My name's Alisha and I own this place. Perhaps you can tell me who you are and what you're doing on my property?"

"I was going to leave, truly, but this voice kept telling me to stay put, that there was no rush, and I haven't been able to find another place yet."

"A voice?" I inquired in a careful tone.

"Yeah, almost like my grandmother's, but not quite. I felt like I had to listen."

"I understand. Believe me, I understand. What's your name?" I gently prodded.

"My name is Leigh." The name wasn't going to tell me their gender either.

"So, Leigh, what brings you to my property?"

"Why don't you come in and take a seat. This could take a while." A heavy sigh gushed out with this statement, as I was gestured into the shed. I looked around in astonishment. What had looked like a decrepit place from the outside had been made lovely on the inside. Thick, beautifully-designed quilts covered the walls, around the edges of which I could see evidence of caulking foam which filled holes and spaces between the boards. A few old boards and bricks had been used to make a bookshelf in one corner, with what appeared to be textbooks and cookbooks side-by-side on its shelves. Next to it, an old aluminum shelf held various food supplies and dishes. A small table with an embroidered cloth covering held an electric burner on a cork board and offered two wooden chairs at each end. Along the other wall, a bed with another gorgeous quilt had folding carriers under it, holding various bits of clothing. An ancient-looking wood stove stuck out in the last corner.

I was sure I needed to pick my gaping mouth up off the floor as I slowly took it all in. Leigh gestured to a chair and I gratefully sank into it. I didn't know what to say, I was so stunned.

"Maybe, I'd better start from the beginning," suggested Leigh.

"Sounds like a good place to start," I affirmed.

With a deep breath, and an intense look at me, Leigh blurted out, "I came here to be a student and to get away from my home town, where I was bullied all my life. I was continually beat up because I'm gender-neutral."

"Okay," I replied, looking carefully at Leigh. Then I confessed, "I'm not sure I know what that means."

"It means I don't identify as either male or

female. It doesn't have anything to do with my biological makeup or my sexual preference. It has to do with my identity. Not many people get this and the small town that I'm from is totally intolerant of anything they perceive as 'different'. It took a long time for me to understand who I am, and to accept myself. I tried to talk to my parents about it, but they freaked. I just couldn't stay there anymore."

"Sounds pretty intense, Leigh."

"It was. But I was nineteen, so I could take off. I let them know I was safe. I love them, but they just don't get me—at least, not yet."

"How did you end up here?" I encouraged Leigh to continue speaking.

"I hitchhiked my way to Bright Haven a year and a half ago. My final ride was a delivery guy from a business just up the road from here. I got out and started walking. When I came to this place, something seemed to draw me in. Nobody was around and it was getting late in the day. I didn't have much money, so when I spotted this shed, I thought it might be okay to crash here for the night. I've been here ever since."

"You lived here through the winter?" I gasped.

"Yeah, it got a little chilly at times, but the wood stove works and there was enough old wood out back to see me through. I filled in the holes as much as I could and went to second-hand stores to pick up some old quilts to insulate the walls a bit. I got by."

"Leigh, I can hardly imagine it!" I was overwhelmed thinking, back to the cold winter we'd had. "Where's the bathroom?" I blurted out anxiously.

"I found a small composting toilet in a cubby behind the woodstove. It's well insulated and I read up on how to care for it."

"My Stanley put that in!" Essie interjected in my mind. *"This was his little getaway place. We loved each other, but we needed our alone time too and this is where he liked to put his feet up and whittle his wood carvings with the wood stove burning."*

Taking in Essie's comments, I said, "I'm just trying to wrap my mind around how tough it must have been."

"It was okay. I found work at a grocery store for the first few months and registered in a culinary course at Smith College. Back in my hometown, I took some online courses about food preparation and I also worked at a local diner there. I've always loved food and herbs and blending flavours." I could hear the excitement building in Leigh's voice. "I used the money my grandmother left me to cover tuition. My work supervisor was willing to give me evening hours, so I wasn't here a lot. I took showers at the school gym. It all worked okay. I noticed when the sale sign was taken down and work started on the property, but every time I thought of going, it just didn't seem to happen. I graduated last month and now I'm trying to find a place that will take me on as a chef."

My ears twitched and I felt a gentle nudge at my shoulder. Essie was getting involved again. "Did you specialize in any particular area of culinary arts?" I inquired.

"That would take another year and I couldn't afford it. My passion is for organics, natural foods, flavours, and helping people discover the healing power of foods. There isn't anything out there with that focus in Bright Haven. I've just been experimenting with some of my own stuff. Would you like to try my cocoa cranberry mint crisps?"

I could hear the anxious excitement in Leigh's voice. Would I like to try something made with chocolate? How could I resist?

"I'd love to, Leigh."

Leigh went over to the pantry shelf and arranged a small plate with a slice of dark deliciousness in the centre with a small sprig of mint to finish it off. I eagerly accepted the offering and admired the presentation. I sniffed. The chocolatey aroma was pungent and enticing. I lifted the treat to my lips and the flavours burst in my mouth as I bit in.

"Chocolate, cranberries, and mint are all high in antioxidants. They have trace minerals our bodies need to keep healthy. They help lower blood pressure and improve brain health."

I held up my hand to stem the flow of words as I savoured the experience of Leigh's offering.

"Leigh, you don't have to convince me. This is incredible. I think you've found your calling, if this is anything to go by! Just give me a minute to thoroughly encounter this wonder."

Stunned by the sensations in my mouth, it took

all my effort to gain enough control of my facial muscles to speak. I continued, "Leigh, this voice you've been hearing...."

"I know it sounds weird, but every time I got discouraged or felt like I really needed to move on, this grandmother-like voice in my head kept telling me to stick it out."

"It's not weird at all Leigh. The voice you've been hearing is Essie. I've heard her too." I watched for any signs of discomfort, but Leigh seemed calm. "Essie used to live on this property. After she died, well, it seems she decided to hang around."

"I can talk for myself, dearie. Now that you and Leigh are getting along we can all talk together. I think Leigh will be perfect for your Healing House."

"Now Essie," I spoke firmly.

"Don't patronize me, Alisha. You cannae deny Leigh has another skill set you need."

Leigh interrupted, "All right, I'm hearing this voice and you are too?"

I nodded.

"What's this Healing House she's talking about?"

"I'm in the process of making this place into a business, offering healing grounds, healing sessions, and various approaches that help people on their healing journeys. Part of the building will host a café with healing foods. I think that's what Essie was referring to."

"Watching the workers around, I thought someone was fixing the place up to move in," Leigh commented.

"No. My dream has always been to offer a Healing House and this is the place that chose me, or Essie did! So far, I've found my landscaper who is an herbalist and a business administrator who also teaches yoga. It seems Essie has the idea that you may be the person we're going to need for the café!"

"There's nae maybe about it. Just look at those books on Leigh's shelf. They're all about the healing power of food. He's perfect."

"Essie, I don't mean any disrespect, but I'm not a 'he'. Remember, I'm gender-neutral," Leigh said softly.

"Sorry dearie, but then what do I call you?" Essie asked.

"You can just refer to me as 'they' or 'them'."

"Just look at how much they can teach us," Essie declared. *"Leigh is just what you need here."*

I took a deep breath. "Leigh and Essie, I'm not the only one involved in this place now. I'll need to introduce you to the others because we've agreed we're a team and we will work like one in all situations. My interest is piqued by what I've heard about you and your cocoa treat was awesome. It looks like there might be potential for you and Raman to work together with foods and the herbs he produces, but he needs to decide for himself and you need time to think about this too. Is this what you want? And not just because Essie has been pushing you in this direction. We may not be up and running for a couple more months. Is that going to work for you?"

"I still have my job at the grocery store, but I'll

have to find a place to live." Leigh weighed in.

"You're going to kick him out! Alisha, you disappoint me," Essie scolded.

"Let's not rush to any decisions here. Essie, I didn't say anything about Leigh having to leave." I looked deeply into Leigh's eyes and sighed, "You've been here this long, you might as well stay. Let's take this one step at a time. I really want you to think this through. Listen to your heart, not what Essie wants or what I want. Truly consider what's best for you."

I stood up. "Leigh, thank you for sharing your story with me; for trusting me. Do I have your permission to share this with my husband Dan and with my co-workers in the business?"

Leigh stood up as well. "Definitely. If I'm to be part of your Healing House I want people to accept me for who I am and what I've been through."

Leigh looked down at their watch. "Cripes, I'm going to be late for work."

"I can drive you, don't worry," I reassured, as Leigh grabbed their bag.

"Essie, no more pressure! Trust us and let us figure this out," I expressed sternly as we hurried to my car. Hastily, we fastened our seatbelts and I peeled out of the driveway. Once again, life had taken an unexpected turn and I hadn't even told Essie about Dan's news.

CHAPTER EIGHT

When we arrived at the grocery store, I asked Leigh if they could send me a resumé. Leigh affirmed there was free wifi at the grocery café and they could send it after work. With a wave, Leigh hurried in. Since I was already there, I decided it would be a good chance to pick up a few supplies.

I scanned my memory banks, trying to recall what I needed. Maybe that phone app for groceries our kids had suggested would relieve some stress. I grabbed a basket and headed to the health food section. I knew I needed my special oat bran cereal. I dodged around other customers as I simultaneously thought about my list and wondered if there was time to go back and chat with Essie. My mind elsewhere, I didn't notice the water that had seeped onto the floor from a faulty freezer unit. My foot made contact and suddenly I was sliding, my arms twirling. I saw the tower of bottled chili sauce, but there was nothing I could do. Impact was imminent!

The force of the encounter tossed me backward onto my buttocks and toppled the tower. Bottles rained down upon me and the floor beside me. Unfortunately, they were glass bottles. With a smash, the bottles that connected with the concrete floor splattered their contents all over my stretch pants and shirt; fortunately, very little landed directly on my skin. Not again! How could this happen twice in one week? Essie wasn't even around. I looked around in stunned dismay as the sauce oozed over my clothing and a few small patches of skin. It began to sting as it soaked into my pores.

A store clerk rushed forward, calling out, "Don't move ma'am. There's glass all around you. Do you have any broken bones?" What's with the ma'am thing? I thought. I'm not that old!

I assured him nothing was broken. My derriere was sore and my pride rather battered, but that was all. I asked for something to wipe off the chili sauce to lessen the burn.

I stayed put as instructed, chili sauce dripping. I studiously kept my gaze downward, hoping no one else would see me.

Then, I heard a calm voice, with a hint of humour in it, say, "Perhaps this would help?" A hand holding a small towel reached into my line of vision. "It has rubbing alcohol on it to help remove the chili oil that's causing the burn."

As I grasped the towel, I glanced upward. The hand belonged to a petite Asian woman in a stylish flowing dress. Colours bisected the dress diagonally with a soft yellow on the top and charcoal on the lower segment. Butterflies were scattered irregularly, offering bright flashes of colour. Sparkly sandals enwrapped meticulously manicured feet. Of course, it would be someone gorgeously put together who would be my witness!

I mopped at the mess all over me and carefully pulled off any glass that was attached to me. I heard scurrying footsteps. "Alisha, are you all right?" Leigh gasped. Leigh had their store uniform on and had been called to assist with the cleanup.

"I'm fine, Leigh. Perhaps, you could get this glass out of the way, so I can move?" I encouraged, anxious to get out of the limelight.

I noticed the woman had simply stepped to the side, as Leigh and the other clerk worked. At this point she intervened again, politely inquiring, "Would you happen to be Alisha Langley?"

Oh great. What an auspicious start to meeting someone!

"Yes, that would be me."

"I'm Tadame, Ronnie's wife. He told me about you." I bet he did, I thought to myself. Here I was, immersed in goo again. What an impression I must have been making.

"Nice to meet you, Tadame. I'd actually planned on contacting you today, but I got a bit tied up," I spoke sheepishly.

Tadame smiled gently. "We live in the apartment complex on the other side of the grocery store parking lot. Would you like to come over and clean up before you go home? It might help to soak the affected areas of your skin in milk to counteract the capsaicin that was in the sauce. I could loan you something to wear, so you don't get chili sauce on your car."

"Seriously?" I exclaimed.

A large grin stretched over Tadame's face. "We could also take a few minutes to chat, if you have time? See, my motives aren't totally altruistic."

I matched her grin as I clasped Leigh's hand and stood up. It felt good to stretch my sore and cold behind! As I wiggled to get circulation flowing, I thanked Leigh and the other clerk. Just then, I saw the store manager hurrying to the scene of the crime. Darn, I wasn't quick enough in my getaway!

Before I could speak, he blurted out, "Ma'am, I sincerely apologize for this incident. Please, let us make amends for your inconvenience." He handed me an envelope which seemed to be stuffed with gift certificates.

"Thank you," I stammered. "I apologize for the mess."

"No worries," he replied. "Clark and Leigh will have this reset in no time."

"Come on," interjected Tadame. "Let's get you out of those wet and messy clothes." She guided me away from the others and toward the exit. "They're just trying to cover their asses so you don't sue for negligence," she whispered.

"I wouldn't sue. I wasn't hurt." I muttered back.

I ignored the curious glances cast our way as we exited and crossed the parking lot. "Maybe there's a silver lining to being so accident-prone lately," I pondered. "First, I met Ronnie and, now, you. Plus, I have some start-up money for our café!"

I took time to soak my arms and feet in basins of milk which Tadame provided. Then I reveled in a shower and sniffing all the wonderful aromatherapy bottles in Tadame's bathroom. I used the aromatherapy shampoo and conditioner, so all scent of chili was eradicated. The calming fragrance of ylang ylang wafted around me as I walked out to the kitchen, where the aroma of coffee embraced me. Tadame turned, "Ronnie mentioned you prefer coffee, so I brewed some in case you still needed warming up. I'm a tea drinker myself," she confessed as she lifted a porcelain cup to her lips.

"Coffee would be wonderful, with milk, if there's any left," I grinned.

"Why don't we sit in the breakfast nook," Tadame suggested. "The window overlooks the river trail and the flowering bushes are just coming into bloom."

"So, Tadame, Ronnie shared with me that you're looking for a new job and that you might be interested in what we're planning at our Healing House?" I inquired.

Our conversation flowed rapidly back and forth as Tadame shared her work history, her love of aromatherapy, and her training in reflexology. I sketched out our unfolding vision and who was on the team so far. We agreed it would be a good idea for her to meet the others before any further decisions were made, so we could assess how well we all meshed together. I briefly mentioned Leigh as a potential chef, but thought I'd wait and allow them to share the fullness of their story at the next meeting.

I thanked Tadame for everything and took my wet clothing, which she had soaked to remove the chili stains. Feeling worn out, I decided to forgo visiting Essie and climbed in my car to head back home.

CHAPTER NINE

I arrived home to discover Sabina, our middle child, sitting in the living room easy chair with her feet up and pouring over Dan's plans. She glanced up as I traipsed through the door.

"Nice outfit!" she declared. "I love the colours."

Although usually attired in jeans or coveralls for her work, Sabina had a yen for pretty clothes and wore them well on her tall, curvy figure.

"Don't get too excited. The clothes aren't mine." I kicked off my shoes, dropped my bag, plopped down in the other chair, and proceeded to share my grocery store experience with her. Before I knew it, she was holding her stomach from laughing so hard. No family or female sympathy for me!

When she had herself under control again, Sabina held up the pile of plans in her hands. "Sounds like things are really moving forward for your business, Mom. What's all this?"

Proudly, I responded, "It's your dad's work. This is the layout and all the furniture for my café."

"Dad did all this? These designs are incredible! I know he's done stuff around home for years, but I didn't know he had this in him," Sabina exclaimed admiringly.

"We're so excited!" I bubbled and I blurted out the rest of our news. I couldn't hold it in any longer and, since I hadn't been able to tell Essie, I needed to share with someone. Sabina was beyond astonished and then leapt up to begin pacing around the room.

"Is everything okay, honey?" I asked cautiously. "I didn't ask why you've dropped by?"

"I came to do laundry. The machine in our building isn't working again."

"Anything else going on?" I teased, as she continued to pace.

"I quit my job!" she declared.

The tension emanated from her as she hitched her shoulders up and down. I listened without comment, which was the most effective approach with Sabina.

"I can swear with the worst of them on the job, ignore their stupid jokes, but I just got fed up with continually trying to prove I was as good, if not better, than most of them!"

Sabina was five feet eight inches and strongly built. I knew from watching her work with Dan that she could handle the heavy work.

"I've been with the company five years and the new kid they just hired is doing more complicated work than me. At our last job, I was told to clean up after the guys until they were ready for the trim work; then I could help. The latest supervisor was afraid I'd injure myself carrying heavy boards or using heavy equipment."

Sabina let her frustrations spill out for a few more minutes and then collapsed back into the chair with a sigh. "Guess we've both had a rather eventful day."

Sabina had studied carpentry and cabinetry, sharing her father's love of working with wood. She had returned home to do her apprenticeship so that she could be close to her friends and family. It hadn't been easy in such a male-dominated workforce, but I hadn't realized just how much she'd been struggling. She had earned her Red Seal, but that obviously didn't make a difference to her newest supervisor.

Before I could respond, the front door opened and Dan strolled in. A smile curved over his lips as his gaze fell upon us.

"This is a nice way to end my day!"

Sabina jumped up for a hug. He looked over her head inquiringly at me as she squeezed him tightly.

"I have lentil gravy and biscuits in the freezer. Why don't I heat that up while you two catch up? I think I have some craft beer in the cold room which will go quite nicely with it."

Sabina led Dan over to the chairs we had just vacated. I could hear the babble of their voices as I assembled our meal. The conversation continued as we ate, including the details of my latest clumsy episode, which caused Dan to grin and shake his head at me.

After supper, I cleaned up as Sabina showed Dan a computer design program that could help with his furniture plans. I put my laundry on and took out my notebook to go over my lists and begin experimenting with names for the business. The hours slipped by and I was suddenly startled to see it was after ten o'clock. Were they still at it? I ambled down the hall to Dan's den.

"How's it going, you two?"

They glanced at me with the disoriented look of those who'd been in another world entirely.

"Hey, Mom," Sabina said, gesturing with her hand. "Come over and take a look at what we've been doing."

When I glanced at the screen, I saw a business plan laid out. Dan pulled me onto his lap.

"Sabina and I have been talking about going into business together. She has the training and contacts which would be a significant help in getting things started. I was worried about how I'd ever be able to get the work completed for your café on my own, but with the two of us, it's completely doable. Today, I applied for three months leave from the clinic. It'll take a few weeks to process, but there shouldn't be any issue. I'll make sure I transition my clients over to other therapists, but I should be totally free very soon."

His arms hugged me with an eagerness that expressed his excitement.

"I can start comparing suppliers, so we get the

best prices without sacrificing quality. When you give the go-ahead, Mom, we'll order what we need. I can also get the workshop set up the way we'll require it for this project. By the time Dad joins me, we'll be well underway. Your café will be our top priority, but it's important to keep honing our business plan so we can start expanding our work beyond that commitment."

This was the most animated I'd seen Sabina in a long time.

"I'll pay Sabina an hourly wage, similar to what she received from her previous company, until we get the business details fully worked out," Dan assured me.

Thank goodness, I thought. She would get to maintain her independence and we wouldn't have an adult child moving back home.

"This sounds awesome, you two, but I need to go to bed. I don't think my mind can absorb another detail," I confessed.

Sabina glanced down at the time stamp on the computer. "Shit, it's past ten! I'm supposed to pick Jack up at the airport tonight. His flight gets in around eleven. I have so much to tell him!" She sprang up and started for the door, then turned around and rushed back to give us both exuberant hugs.

"I'm so excited!"

Sabina had just started dating Jack. I wondered if he was ready for all this!

By morning, I was refreshed and called Raman and Cheri in the hopes they could meet a day earlier than we'd planned. I wanted them to give me their impressions of Tadame, whom I had also called, and to bring them up-to-date on everything else. Fortunately, they were able to juggle commitments and by mid-morning, we had convened at the house. The warmth of summer was beginning to make itself felt, so we sat outside, admiring the burgeoning growth in Raman's gardens.

I quickly reviewed Tadame's qualifications and what I thought she'd have to offer our establishment. I had learned that not only was she an aromatherapist and reflexologist, but that she was also trained as a massage therapist. Cheri and Raman were both impressed, and eager to meet her. When her car pulled up, we felt ready to explore the possibility of her becoming a part of our team. Tadame gracefully climbed out and grabbed a small container which she brought over to our gathering. "I made some chili buns, in memory of our first meeting," she offered with an audacious grin.

I burst into laughter, while the others contemplated me curiously. I had to confess my latest catastrophe and soon all were chortling along. I proudly confided that I'd scored us $250 in gift cards. With a twinkle in her eye, Cheri commented, "We're going to have to invest in extra liability insurance if you keep this up!"

We took Tadame on a tour, sharing with her each of our areas of expertise. She fell in love with the place, like the rest of us. Essie was oddly silent, so I kept quiet on that front. Tadame made a few Feng Shui suggestions for the layout of our rooms. Her ideas made good sense to the flow of energy in each area and meshed with Cheri's earlier scheme to keep the spaces flexible. As we began to talk about furniture, I hauled out Dan's plans. Seeing them in context fully revealed how much they matched the setting. Raman was particularly impressed. He thought Dan should be asked to consult about the display racks and other specialty items we'd need.

We shared our business approach with Tadame, so she'd be clear about her options.

We had barely finished before she blurted out, "I am so in, if you're willing to let me join you. This is exactly what was missing where I worked before."

There was a common feeling that Tadame fit what we were looking for, so we welcomed her aboard as our next team member.

Knowing we had a lot more ground to cover, I suggested we chat over some hot drinks. I reached into the cupboard for the can of herbal tea I'd left there a few weeks previously. While we waited, Tadame hesitantly said, "Who is Essie?"

I glanced at the others, who shrugged and left it to me. I explained to her about our resident spirit and Essie finally spoke up.

"I'm so glad you're filling your team with such excellent people! I've been a tad quiet because you were very firm, Alisha, that you didn't want me pressuring any of you. I hope you appreciate how hard it's been for me to bite my tongue."

Raman, Cheri, and I grinned at the mental image of Essie biting her tongue.

"What are you all smiling about?" Tadame queried.

"Essie. You didn't hear her?" Raman quizzed.

"No, I don't hear or see spirits. I just get a feeling and a name pops into my mind, or I sense the spirit's mood. I'm not really visual or auditory in my gifts. I'm more kinesthetic, which is why I do the work I do," said Tadame.

"That's fascinating," said Cheri. "I see and hear Essie. Alisha and Raman mainly hear her. This is so cool!"

"Yer drinks are ready, Alisha. It's time to move on to Leigh," Essie prompted.

"Your spirit seems impatient," declared Tadame.

"Who's Leigh?" Raman interjected.

"Let's grab our hot drinks and I'll explain." I opened the fridge for milk and saw a plate wrapped in foil with my name on a sticker. I took it out and unwrapped a plateful of treats, obviously from Leigh. How did they get inside, I wondered?

"Essie?"

"I might have shown them where the spare key was hidden."

"Look at those goodies! What have you got for us Alisha?" Cheri drooled.

I shared the chocolate treats as I disclosed Leigh's story. Their compassion was evident as I recounted the salient points. When I finished, I sensed Raman pondering something. We waited.

"It seems to me that fate or Essie has brought us all together, and we each seem to bring something unique to this team. I feel Leigh is meant to be part of us somehow. I've actually been thinking, as work progresses and we start filling the house with furniture and supplies, it'd be good to have someone watching over the place, besides Essie. Would it be possible to renovate the shed sufficiently to make it a caretaker's cottage and then Leigh could stay there and receive accommodations in lieu of wages as a caretaker? As a chef, Leigh would come onto the team the same as the rest of us,—with a salaried position—start developing menus, supply lists, and so on. I could work with Leigh on certain healing herb combinations to complement their cooking."

We were impressed by Raman's ideas. I agreed to run the renovations by Dan and to get in touch with Leigh. We took time to go back through the individual rooms and started making lists of furniture and basic supplies needed in each one. Tadame agreed to draw up a list for her professional needs; she mentioned certain companies with whom she preferred to work. It would be Cheri's responsibility to start making a financial plan for us and she had been diligently taking notes on her iPad. It was both exhilarating and exhausting thinking about moving ahead.

Dan was a little more hesitant when he heard about Leigh's story. I valued his opinion, so I let him speak his piece, but I was also becoming more confident about trusting my own intuition. I assured him I had checked Leigh's references through Smith College, the grocery store, and the diner. All spoke highly of Leigh. They considered Leigh reliable, motivated, kind, and someone who worked well under pressure. Dan felt Leigh was young and lacked experience of the challenging work of being a chef, a career known for long hours and burnout. I emphasized that years of work didn't always equate with quality; besides, Leigh's passion for healing foods matched well with our vision. Dan still wasn't convinced.

Leigh was very animated in their reply as I proffered Raman's proposal. I stressed that everything was only in the dreaming stage; still, Leigh was eager to meet the others. Since Leigh wasn't working that evening, I volunteered Dan's services to assess the shed's potential. I didn't realize he'd also be assessing Leigh!

I needn't have worried. Leigh walked with confidence up the pathway to meet us. As I introduced the two, Leigh offered a firm handshake and a smile to Dan.

"I expect you have reservations about me, because of my age, maybe because of who I am, and because I lived on this property as a squatter. I promise I don't smoke or do drugs. I do drink the occasional beer, but I respect my body and I don't overdo it. I'm a hard worker and I really want to be a part of Alisha's dream for a healing place. There are so many people who need this. Now, if you'd like to see the shed…."

Before Leigh could move, Dan put up his hand.

"Wait. I am a little hesitant because of your age, but that's all. The decision is Alisha's, not mine. Thanks for being so up-front with us," Dan calmly articulated.

Leigh and I started to relax.

Dan was astonished at Leigh's work on the shed. Leigh shared tricks they'd used to keep the place warm through the cold months. Dan asked about some of Leigh's cooking and was amazed at the ideas for vegan recipes and savoury treats that held healing qualities, which Leigh was quick to delineate. I kept quiet as I sensed them bonding while they moved to discussing renovation possibilities for the shed. By the time we left, I felt Leigh had won Dan over and it appeared we were going to be transforming the shed.

As we walked back to the car, Essie interrupted us.

"So, Leigh will be part of the team and can stay here? I could read Dan's hesitancy. I was fashed you'd send Leigh away! I didnae dare speak up in case I made things worse."

"You've been reading my mind, have you Essie? Well, read it again, because you'll find Leigh made a great impression. I may still have a few doubts, but I know Alisha's determined this is going to work. You'll keep an eye on things while Leigh's here alone, won't you?"

"I've been doing that all along. Why would I stop now? They're like the grandchild I never had!" Essie exclaimed.

"Goodnight, Essie. I'll be back tomorrow," I

yawned as I climbed into the car. My head kept nodding on the way home. It was all I could do to stay awake. My brain needed to shut down so that all of the day's events could be processed. I kissed Dan goodnight and stumbled off to bed.

CHAPTER TEN

The next two weeks passed by rapidly. Each night, Dan would arrive home, gulp down his supper, and meet with Sabina in the workshop. They had already met with Leigh at the shed and expansion plans were underway. The first table was under construction and the excitement emanating from Dan and Sabina was palpable. The approval for Dan's leave had come through, so only one more workday and his time would be his own.

Some days, I simply showed up at Essie's place to walk through the grounds and see how the gardens were growing to feel the potential of it all unfolding. On one of those days, I happened upon Raman pacing agitatedly as he spoke on his cell phone. The usual calm lines of his face were rigid in an expression of distress. I turned to walk away, but he noticed me and gestured for me to stay.

When the call ended, he sighed and thrust his cell

into his pocket.

"Do you have a minute?" he asked.

"Sure," I replied. "What's up?"

Raman continued pacing as I stood and listened. "My parents just called from India. They just finished a lovely dinner with friends. They think the friend's daughter would be a good match for me. They called because they want to arrange another marriage for me, since I don't seem to be making any progress in that area on my own."

"Another one?" I queried.

"When I was twenty, they arranged what they considered to be a good marriage for me. I agreed because it's our tradition and it worked well for some of my friends. That was not the case for me. We came to this country to study; my wife fell in love with another exchange student and was unfaithful to me."

I murmured sounds of support as he ploughed on.

"I wanted to arrange a divorce, but I discovered he was abusive to her. I stayed with her for a year to offer her some protection and to try to save our marriage. It didn't work. She didn't feel I was exciting enough. She found another partner. That time, I ended it. It took two years and a lot of money and lawyers to finally be free. I swore to myself then that any new relationship would be one of my own choosing." Raman declared adamantly.

"You're not in a relationship right now?" I gently probed.

"No. I've dated and had a few serious relationships, but they all stalled after a few months," Raman confessed.

"It can be challenging to trust again after an experience like yours," I offered.

"I'm working on that. I have healthy friendships with people I trust. I'm trusting you right now. I just haven't found anyone I really want to give myself and my life to for the long haul. But, my parents don't want to hear that and keep pressuring me."

"Family dynamics can be tricky," I agreed.

"It's frustrating. In all other areas of my life I feel strong and capable; but when I confront my parents, I end up feeling like I'm letting them down."

"It's tough," I reflected back to him.

"Bet you didn't expect to be hearing this today," he mumbled apologetically.

"That's what friends are for." I placed a reassuring hand on his arm.

"I'd better get back to work. I was just finishing up some edging around the garden. Thanks for listening, Alisha."

I took my leave and continued my stroll, and then wandered into the house for a quick scan before I left.

"Even the strong ones need to be supported at times. That laddie carries a lot inside. You're a good friend to him, Alisha," Essie shared.

"We all have our challenges. I'm glad I was here when it was helpful. Now, I have the challenge of figuring out my supply list."

Tadame, Raman, Leigh, and I worked on our supply lists and submitted them to Cheri, who added her suggestions. She inputted those figures into the budget she'd already begun, so we had a fairly clear sense of our start-up needs. She also did a one-year projection for wages, taxes, and all the other areas I had no clue were necessary. We then knew our expenses and had to figure out what we each needed to put in to keep us afloat for the first year. Cheri knew about a local businesswomen's council, so we decided we'd attend their monthly meeting to check out any grant options or small business loans that might be available for our situation.

I had recently become reacquainted with the local pool where I swam laps. My immersion in the unfolding of our business had led me to neglect my physical fitness. My too-tight clothing finally pushed me to recommit to my self-care. An aqua aerobics class boomed out as I stroked up and down the lane. It felt renewing to be back in the water and feel it wash away not only excess pounds but the weight of worry as well. Afterwards, in the change room, I dragged my stretchy jeans up my damp thighs. Struggling to get them on without falling over, I heard a few of the women from the class chatting animatedly. One was sharing how she had discovered Spanx. My ears perked as she told the story of a family wedding where she'd worn Spanx and gotten all sorts of compliments about how fantastic she looked. She gushed on and on about the wonderfully slimming qualities of Spanx.

Intrigued, I decided to drop by the local women's store to purchase this miracle piece of clothing. My favourite dress was feeling a little tight lately and I wanted to look my best when I made my first impression at the businesswomen's council. When I picked up the package, I looked at the size chart. Although close to a large, I thought that because the material was stretchy surely the medium would make me look smaller. Once home, I threw it in the washer, so it would be free of any new clothing chemicals and ready for the big night.

Are you sure you want to go to this meeting? You've never done anything business-related in your life. Will you even know the language in which to speak to these women? Who do you think you are?

My anxious inner voice was playing prime time in my brain as I prepared for the meeting. She hadn't said much recently, but this night she reared up full force! I twitched my shoulders and took a deep breath. Everything would be fine. I would be fine.

Do you really think you'll fit in? Is that dress the best option?

I had already culled my wardrobe. There weren't a lot of options. I elected to go with my favourite fuchsia-coloured dress that was snug at the hips but flowed around my upper thighs in a swirl of material, stopping just above the knee. Chunky brass jewelry and a multi-hued pashmina scarf would keep me warm if there was a draft in the meeting room.

I picked up the Spanx and began to haul them on.

They were a little snugger than I had expected. Determinedly, I wiggled and pulled, inching them up over my thighs and hips. I kept imagining how svelte I was going to appear. I could feel the tummy fat being slimmed away as I tugged and mashed myself into them. But, the more I slimmed one area, the more the flesh pushed upward and over the top of the Spanx. When I finally had them all the way up, I shuffled around, hardly able to breathe. The end result was not pretty.

You look like you have a second set of breasts. Definitely not the look you were hoping to achieve! All this squishing can't be good for your inner organs!

For once, my inner voice and I were in agreement. I reached under my breasts to try to pull the Spanx off, but it was as if they had adhered to my body. Maybe it hadn't been such a good idea to get a size smaller than I needed. I tried various contortions, getting more breathless with each one, and the damned thing wouldn't come off.

You know what you're going to have to do? He'll have a field day with this!

"Shut up, voice. If I don't get a move on, I'm going to be late!"

I shuffled to the door as my usual stride was impossible with the vice grip of the Spanx on my body. Thank God Dan was in his office and hadn't gone out to his workshop yet. I couldn't imagine trying to maneuver my way out there! I called out and Dan appeared in the doorway of his office.

"What's up?" he inquired.

"I need your help. Could you come in here, please?" I pleaded.

Dan strode down the hall toward me and, once he could see more than my head poking out, he exclaimed, "What do you have on?"

"Just get in here and help." I sheepishly explained my predicament as he walked around me, checking out the situation.

"Very sexy," he grinned. I glared at him. We decided it might work best if I lay down on the bed. Dan began to pull but without much success. He then had the brilliant idea that if I held the headboard, it would stretch things out a bit and he might get better leverage to pull the Spanx off. I held on tightly as Dan hooked his fingers under the edge and began the tug-of-war necessary to free me. Next thing I knew, his lips were skimming their way along my ribcage.

I grunted, "I do not have time for sex right now!"

My body bowed up in response and I glared at him again. Slowly, inch by careful inch, Dan was able to peel the Spanx from my torso without tearing off a layer of skin with them. As more of my midriff bared itself to him and his fingers caressed their way downward, I felt my libido jump into action. My breath began to quicken. Carefully cupping my buttocks, Dan tugged the Spanx over them and slipped his fingers under me, teasing me into an ever more heightened arousal. Sliding his fingers around to clasp the front of the Spanx, his thumb swept over my clitoris and I gasped in response.

"Hold tight," Dan warned, as he made the final tug to bare my pelvis and hauled the Spanx down my thighs.

"Don't let go," he rasped as he quickly pulled off his jeans and threw them aside with his briefs. Swiftly, he plunged inside and my body went into overdrive. Still clasping the headboard, I swam in sensations as Dan tantalized every sensitive nerve end. The swell of my orgasm swept through me and clasped him tightly. Within moments, we collapsed together on the bed.

Suddenly, I was giggling. Dan looked at me with a quirked eyebrow.

"Maybe they should have a warning label on Spanx—may cause arousal!"

I could feel the rumble of his laughter beneath my ear. Reluctantly, I pulled away and hurriedly got myself together, Spanx free. It was time to attend my meeting. I glanced in the mirror. I might not have the smooth Spanx shape, but I had a lovely glow about me that was definitely flattering!

On the way, my nerves started to flutter again, but our happy interlude had relaxed me enough that they didn't get out of hand. Cheri, Tadame, and I had agreed to meet up outside and go in together. The car clock showed I'd get there with just seconds to spare. I sent out the intention that a parking space would open up nearby. I happily imagined pulling into it and briskly walking only a few steps to where we were connecting.

Sure enough, the thought, linked with the

emotion, allowed the Universe to conspire in my favour. I slipped out of the car as Tadame and Cheri rounded the corner and jaunted down the sidewalk. They were talking animatedly. Tadame saw me and exclaimed, "You look great! That colour is lovely on you. It really brings out the blush of your skin tones."

"Thanks," I replied sheepishly.

We still had a few minutes before we had to go inside so I risked asking, "Tell me, have either of you ever tried Spanx?"

Tadame confessed to wearing them occasionally, but Cheri said her fiancée was a firm believer in loving our bodies the way they are, so she never tried them. They both sent probing looks my way. I decided to trust them. I proceeded to share my Spanx story and my nervousness about looking my best. Tadame snorted when she heard me say I got a size smaller than my usual. Then they were both hiccupping with hilarity as I got to the good parts.

Cheri wiped her eyes and confessed, "Alisha, we're really going to have to work on your risk management skills."

Giggles erupted again and I replied, "So glad I'm able to provide entertainment."

Tadame hooked her arms through ours and proclaimed, "Come on, ladies, we've got this! We've got vision, determination, and each other. Let's make our entrance."

We strutted up the steps and through the entrance, heads held high. Inside, a poster board to our right indicated the meeting room. A greeter welcomed people as they arrived and recorded their names. We trooped over, covertly scanning the room as we went. A mix of women were mingling around the room. They were a range of ages and wearing whatever suited them. One woman wore a tailored business suit and was talking with a woman in stretch jeans and an oversized sweater. Another woman sported tights with a flowing dress. I saw silk, linen, ragged jeans, and overalls. I shouldn't have worried.

Janine, the greeter, graciously welcomed us. She shared that there was to be a guest speaker after a short business meeting, and that we'd have a chance to meet others during the social time afterwards. She indicated we could sit wherever we wanted.

"Enjoy your evening," Janine encouraged us, as she turned to the next women in line.

Cheri immediately saw someone she knew and bounced over to say hello. Tadame and I claimed seats toward the middle of the room. We watched as Cheri flitted from person to person. I saw some faces that looked familiar, but I wasn't sure of names. Tadame waved at one person she recognized, but stayed beside me, for which I was grateful. Before we knew it, the meeting was underway. It was brief, as promised. Then, the guest speaker offered a fabulous presentation on her learnings about building clientele. The three of us took notes, knowing we'd each pick up different points.

When the social time started, Cheri introduced us to some of the people she knew and we met a ream of others as well. Some were very interested in what we were starting and offered pointers from their own experiences. It was exciting to add a new layer of connections to the vision we were creating. When it was over, we agreed we'd like to join the council. The potential for additional learning and support was worth the time commitment and fee. We exchanged hugs and returned to our cars, pleased with our evening.

The next morning, we met at 8:30 a.m., before Leigh had to go to work. It was time to brainstorm names and choose one so Cheri could get our domain name registered and start working on social media development. Leigh had put on the coffee pot and the kettle for tea. Small bowls of coconut cherry chia pudding were also available for our tasting pleasure. Sensing Leigh's anxious gaze, we sampled our treats immediately. The smooth creamy consistency slid deliciously over my tongue. The tart yet sweet flavour of the cherry chunks blended beautifully with the coconut. From the expressions on the others' faces, I could tell all were impressed.

Raman spoke up first, "Leigh, this is fantastic. It's so flavourful and filled with such a nutrient burst—it's a great way to start the morning."

"And any heavy duty thinking we have to plow through," affirmed Cheri.

"Thanks for treating us, Leigh," expressed Tadame. "Could I have the recipe? I'd love to try this for myself."

"I made it last night so the flavours had time to

combine. I was nervous that the chia wouldn't absorb enough liquid to keep it creamy, but it seems to have worked." Leigh heaved a sigh.

"Looks like you have another winner for the café menu," I grinned as I addressed Leigh. "Now let's see if we can be as successful at coming up with a name."

"I went online to check out the most commonly used names for places like ours," Cheri began. Of course she had, my mind responded, smiling inside as I wondered how we'd each approach this according to our particular natures. "There were names like: 'Wholehearted Health', 'Vibrant Healthy Living', and 'Finding a Better You'. But none of them really grabbed me."

"I jotted down a few ideas that linked to my part: 'The Floating Lotus' or 'Chill Out'. But I couldn't really come up with anything that captured the whole of the place," Raman confessed.

"'Beautiful Reflections' and 'Resole Your Life' were possibilities I pondered," offered Tadame.

"Leigh, do you have any suggestions?" I inquired.

"I thought it would be kinda nice to honour Essie since this is her place. All of us offer different aspects of healing work, so I wondered if we'd all feel included if we used something like 'Essie's Healing Place'?" Leigh submitted.

We all sat in silence, letting the name sink in. Quiet sniffling echoed in my mind. Essie was obviously moved by Leigh's suggestion.

"I love it!" Tadame interjected into the lull.

"We're not just about health or fitness or good food or taking care of yourself; the whole of what we do is about healing. We could use some of the other key words we liked in the description that goes with our advertising, but our name needs to be short and easy to remember."

"Essie isn't a common name, so we shouldn't have any trouble getting this through the domain search. Wow, Leigh! Not only did you ace our morning treat, you've created a name for our business that's perfect, in my opinion," gushed Cheri.

Raman and I looked at each other and nodded in agreement. I raised my coffee mug for a toast. "To 'Essie's Healing Place'. May our journey together offer healing to all who come our way!"

Essie sniffed again.

"I can't tell you how much this means to me! I always wanted to be involved in healing endeavours. I read voraciously about it for years, but Stanley needed me, so I set those dreams aside. I never regretted my decision. We accomplished so much together, and I loved our life dearly. But now, it feels like I'm being offered a second chance. Those years of waiting for the right person to take over my home have proven worthwhile. The purpose I was sensing I had yet to fulfill is becoming clearer all the time!"

"Whatever the reason, we're glad to have you on board, Essie," exclaimed Cheri.

"So, what's next?" inquired Leigh.

"Next, I get us registered, and we need to have a lawyer draw up our business incorporation and share plan. Leigh, you and I need to meet about some of the appliances and equipment you want for the café. I've a line on some discounted items and I want to be sure they're what you need. I've finalized our budget, so our next meeting will be at the bank to open our business account, and for each of us to ante up. I also read up on grants and small business loans that we qualify for, so I need to get the paperwork for those," Cheri listed.

"You certainly have lots on your plate. What if Tadame and I start developing wording for brochures and advertising?" I proposed.

Raman agreed and then added, "As we wait for things to start growing in our gardens, I have some time. We should probably have the fire inspector in to be sure we have everything up to code. I can make that contact. Also, I can help Dan with converting the shed into a cabin. We're going to need a storage shed for my outdoor tools, so I'd like to consult with him on that as well."

"I'm off to work! I'll call you later tonight, Cheri, so we can talk equipment." Leigh sounded excited as they left.

Raman had another contract to tend to; thus, Tadame and I spent the next two hours on our own, letting our creative juices have some fun. It was also a chance to get to know each other a little more personally. I told Tadame about the challenges Dan and I were having as we learned how to parent adult children. As we grew more comfortable with each other, she confided in me that she and Ronnie had been struggling to conceive.

"We've been trying for five years, without any luck. We were both tested, but Ronnie's sperm count is in the normal range and nothing obvious showed up in my results. I don't have polyps or endometriosis. Neither of us have had STDs. At first, we were told to just keep trying, to eat healthier, exercise, drink less alcohol, and reduce stress. Then, we were offered fertility drugs, but I was reluctant to risk the potential side effects or multiple births. We've gotten rather used to it just being the two of us, but now we're discussing the possibility of applying for adoption."

I was careful not to offer advice or to jump in with a story of someone I knew who had the same issue. I chose to simply listen.

"How are you feeling about all that?" I nudged the conversation a little deeper.

"Actually, I've started to relax about it all. We spent five years putting all this pressure on ourselves and feeling like we'd failed at something others around us seemed to be doing so easily. Now I look at where we are financially compared to friends who have children. I'm grateful for the freedom we have to focus on each other, our careers, and travel. I've begun to shift my attitude somewhat, so I suggested maybe we need to give ourselves six months of not having this as an issue in our lives, and then discuss it again."

I nodded my head to encourage further sharing.

Tadame continued. "Ronnie was relieved when I made that suggestion and confessed he'd felt for a while that the whole issue of conception had been consuming us, to the detriment of us just being with each other."

"It's a lot to go through together," I affirmed.

"Yeah and some couples don't make it. I'm thankful our love for each other is still our main priority. For now, having children is a dream I need to let go of," she said with a rueful smile.

"Thanks for sharing this part of you." I placed my hand over hers.

She turned her hand over and squeezed mine. "Here's to new dreams unfolding!"

We wrapped up, feeling satisfied with what we had accomplished and much closer in our friendship. I received a text from Cheri that the name search was clear and she was just finishing with the lawyer regarding incorporation papers.

CHAPTER ELEVEN

I returned home in an exuberant frame of mind. Sabina's car was in the driveway, so I poked my head into the workshop, where she was intently focused on what I recognized to be a café table. I closed the door behind me and waited for her to notice me, not wanting to startle her and cause a possible mishap.

Her smile lit up her face. "Come and see, Mom!" she fervently invited me over.

I reached out a hand, then glanced at her before touching anything.

"Go ahead. We decided to wax the wood rather than use a varnish finish on it, so less chemicals would be involved."

My hand drifted over the surface. The wood was lovely and smooth to the touch. The edging was rounded and there was a flow that offered a wonderful sense of harmony to the design.

"What do you think?" she asked impatiently.

"Sabina, I can hardly find the words. You and your dad have captured exactly what I wanted but wouldn't have been able to describe. Just sitting at this table will be a healing experience for someone, before they even taste any of Leigh's fabulous foods. Honey, this is incredible!" I enveloped her in a huge hug. "Thank you."

Sabina is rarely demonstrative with me, so I knew my words had moved her, because she squeezed me back.

Then she said, "By the way, Jack is coming out to supper. You guys haven't had much of a chance to get to know him. I've been putting in long hours out here, so thought I'd ask him to join us tonight."

My mind jumped into hyper-drive as I assessed what was in my fridge.

"What time do you think he'll arrive?" I asked nonchalantly, trying to hide any sign of stress.

Sabina glanced at her watch. "Probably around five. Don't worry. Jack eats anything, Mom. Just keep it chill." She looked at me sternly. I could never hide much from her.

"Don't go crazy or try to get fancy, Mom. Simple is fine. Do something like mac and cheese; we all love that and it's easy. Besides it's Dad's favourite and this is his last day of work, so we can celebrate together. I can finish up out here in another hour and help with a salad or setting the table."

"Fine," I muttered. "I'll keep it simple. Next time, though, I'd appreciate a little warning."

I hurried into the house, throwing my coat on a

hook as I entered, casting a look around to see if my housekeeping was up to scratch. I don't mind a lived-in look, but I didn't want any dust bunnies that would come out to greet him like a household pet. I decided that a quick sweep of the kitchen and clean of the toilet bowls would be sufficient. Then, deciding to appease my own desires, I threw together a chocolate self-sauce pudding for our dessert.

When the table was set, and the mac and cheese and the pudding were baking in the oven, Sabina arrived to help out.

"Smells good, Mom," she declared, as she washed up.

We companionably chopped veggies for the salad and I shared the events of my day, including the name we'd selected for the business.

"You must be so pumped, Mom."

"I am. It just feels as though things are gathering momentum and we're going to be opening before I know it," I grinned.

Jack and Dan came through the door at the same time. They were busily talking about cars. One of Jack's hobbies was restoring old cars and re-selling them. He said it gave his mind a break from the mental drain of working for the government. Words of welcome were exchanged between us and we went straight to the kitchen. Out of the corner of my eye, I noticed Dan slide something into the fridge; I wondered what he was up to but then I got caught up in conversation and thought no more about it. We dove into supper and there were appreciative murmurs about the mac and cheese. Jack easily fitted into our tendency to jump from one topic to another.

After our meal, we moved into the sun room to relax and continue chatting. I claimed my preferred seat: a rocker-style easy chair. Jack and Sabina sat on the love seat, while Dan stretched out on the couch.

After a pause in the conversation, Sabina cleared her voice and stated, "Jack and I have something to share."

I gently rocked my chair and looked at Sabina in anticipation.

"Jack proposed to me last night. We're going to be married this fall."

My feet pushed against the floor as I went to surge upward, but the momentum pushed me backwards instead. Before I knew what was happening, my chair had up-ended and I somersaulted out of it. There was a stunned silence as they all looked at me on the floor.

Jack jumped up, reached out to me, and exclaimed "Are you all right?"

I waved him away and began to giggle.

Jack dryly commented to Sabina, "You said your mom might flip out, but I didn't realize you meant it literally."

I hauled myself up, desperately trying to control the giggles, but it was hopeless. So many things had been happening; I needed the release of laughter. The others joined in, shaking their heads. Jack helped me turn my chair upright; still a little shaken, I decided to settle back down on the couch next to Dan.

Taking a deep breath, I observed, "I'm obviously excited for you, but this seems a little fast, doesn't it?"

Sabina looked at Jack and raised her eyebrows. Obviously, my response was expected.

Jack took her hand in his and looked back at me. "We may have only known each other for six months, but when you know someone's right for you, I think you just know. We've both been in other serious relationships, so we can sense the difference in ours. Whenever I have to be away for work, I can't wait to get back to see Sabina. I love sharing my life with her. So, we figured, why wait?"

Sabina spoke next, looking at both of us, "We'd like to get married in the backyard at Essie's place. We drove up there last week and it feels right to us. It's a place of new beginnings and the gardens should be perfect by September. Dad, I thought maybe we could build a small arbour for us to stand under. Mom, we wondered if you'd marry us?"

Dan squeezed my hand. "We're delighted for you both!"

Then, he said to me, "You've always told the story of how you saw me, that first day at university, and you knew I was the one for you. It took me a while to catch up, but sometimes the heart just leaps in recognition of a soul mate. That's what you've always said."

I looked at Jack and Sabina—I really looked. I could sense strong energetic bonds flowing between them.

"I'm sorry if that sounded like judgement. I think the surprise of it stimulated the concerned mom voice in me to speak up before I truly sorted my thoughts," I admitted. I could feel the excitement beginning to stir and build within me. "I'm thrilled for you both and, yes, I would love to conduct the ceremony. Essie is going to be overjoyed at having the wedding at her place." My mind started leaping ahead, visioning the setting.

Dan spoke up. "It just so happens, I brought home a bottle of champagne tonight."

So, that's what he had chilling in the fridge!

"I thought it would be a nice way to celebrate my last day of work. It seems the Universe was guiding me to pick it up for more than one reason."

As we stood up, we shared hugs of congratulations. Dan popped the champagne and we toasted new beginnings.

I eased over beside Sabina. "Would you like us to host a small family gathering this weekend, so you can share the news with the rest of the family?"

"That'd be great, Mom. We're going to Jack's parent's tomorrow night. What about Sunday?"

"I think we can make that work," I grinned. "Tommy's spring courses are in full swing, but he's always keen for a break. Ginny doesn't have any performances on Sunday, so she should be free too."

"Awesome, but don't tell them, okay. I want to surprise them! We're not putting anything on social media until we've personally shared our news with those closest to us."

Then, Sabina lifted her glass. "Dad, thanks for the champagne and celebrating Jack and me, but now I want to toast you. Here's to your last day at the clinic. Hurray! Here's to your courage to pursue your dream and work with me! You both inspire me." She encompassed both of us in her smile and we all raised our glasses again.

The champagne was soon demolished and we were all tired from the day. Dan's arm came around me as Jack and Sabina headed out the door. We locked up after them as minds swirled with yet more new beginnings unfolding in our lives. In step, we made our way up to bed and gently stripped off each other's clothes. Gentle caresses soothed and aroused as we tumbled into bed. We felt the warm sweep of love flow between us and crest. Locked in each other's arms, we slid into sleep.

We awoke early, but took our time getting up. At the previous day's meeting, we had agreed to take a few hours to ourselves that Saturday morning. I decided to do a little self-care and go for a run. I had felt so much better after swimming earlier in the week that I wanted to keep my fitness moving forward. It was a gorgeous late-May morning and I set off on the trail near our home. The birds chirruped along as I ran by and the breeze was gentle enough to cool me but not be challenging. I felt totally refreshed as I walked in the front door and smelled breakfast cooking with the aroma of coffee in the air. Dan had waffles with fruit sauce and Greek yoghurt ready for me. After a few stretches, I dived in, savouring every delicious bite.

We casually shared our thoughts about Sabina and Jack's news. Dan then admitted he was too keen to get started on things to sit around any longer. I wholeheartedly agreed! After a quick shower, we were on the road out to Essie's. We had hitched up the utility trailer Dan had purchased a few years ago; it was loaded with supplies and tools for working on the shed renovations.

When we arrived, Dan glanced over at me with a grin. "Looks like we weren't the only ones eager to get rolling!"

Raman's truck and Cheri's Kia were both in the driveway. We could hear the sound of hammering as we climbed out. We traipsed around the house and could see activity down at the shed. As we drew closer, we could see Raman, Leigh, and Cheri hard at work. Raman glanced up and spotted us. A smile split his face and he gestured toward us to the others. They laid down their tools as we approached.

"So, I see we're all good at relaxing," I exclaimed.

"I finished up my other contract late yesterday, so today was totally free. When I woke up to such awesome weather, I just couldn't stay away," Raman confessed. "I called Leigh and they were already up, so we agreed to work together on the renovation steps that Dan had outlined so far."

"I don't have a shift today at the grocery store, so I was hyped when Raman called. I've been so excited to get this place fixed up and truly call it my own. I was totally on board for starting as soon as he could get here," Leigh expressed animatedly. "Then Cheri showed up…."

"I dropped my fiancée off to work so I could have the car and decided to swing by just in case anyone was around," Cheri admitted sheepishly. "When I saw Raman's truck, I knew my instincts were right. We've been working for about an hour now."

"I didn't know you knew anything about building?" I said.

"My dad was a Mr. Fix-It when I was growing up and I always tagged along as he worked. I picked up a little bit; I know one tool from another," she explained.

"This is so exciting!" exclaimed Essie. *"I can't wait for this to be a proper home. Leigh has made do, but I really want more for them."*

"We do too, Essie," affirmed Dan. "Okay, everyone, I have the renovation plans in my vehicle and a bunch of supplies we'll need to lug down here. Perhaps we can take a look at what you've started and draft a bit of a work schedule for the day so we can accomplish as much as possible."

The others showed Dan what they'd been working on. From there, we progressed back to the front of the house where we saw another vehicle pulling in. It was Tadame and Ronnie. Tadame rolled down her window.

"We were out at the beach for a walk early this morning and, driving by, we saw all the vehicles in the driveway. What's going on?" she inquired.

We told her our story and she began to laugh. I lifted a questioning eyebrow and she confessed that as she and Ronnie walked the beach they had been talking about being sorry that we hadn't planned a work party for the renovations.

"I guess we've all been guided to this, as needed," she proclaimed. "I even have old clothes on and Ronnie's work overalls are in the back. Sign us up!"

Dan hauled out the plans as I texted Sabina so she'd know what we were up to. She texted back that she was swinging by the market with Jack, but after they were done she'd grab some goodies for our lunch and join in.

By early afternoon Sunday, we had completed the add-on to the original shed. The outer walls had Tyvek on them, and all the new windows were in and well-caulked. The roof was fully integrated and ready for steel roofing to be installed. An old steel door, which Dan had picked up at some point and stored in our shed, graced the front wall. Well pleased with our efforts, we called it a day.

I had put on the slow cooker before we left home in the morning, so a black bean and vegetable stew was ready for our supper with the kids. We showered and put our feet up for a few minutes as we sipped green smoothies. Sabina was bringing dessert, so we had time to relax as we waited for everyone to arrive.

Tommy was the first through the door and, as usual, headed straight for the fridge as he called out a greeting to us. He hauled out the extra smoothie with a questioning look and, at our nods, poured it into a mug before joining us in the sunroom. After quick hugs, he stretched out on the love seat.

"How's it going?" he asked.

We filled him in on the latest developments. He knew about the team but hadn't met any of them nor been to the place. He was curious to see the design plans for the renovation, so he and Dan had their heads together when I heard the front door open again. It was Ginny, so I went out to greet her. Ginny always had a tendency to be excitable, so I knew she'd have lots to tell me about her latest show and the various real-life dramas going on between the cast members. She waved her arms expressively and her voice grew with intensity as she described the latest feud between the two main characters. Eventually, she wound down and we joined the others.

Hugs were exchanged and Dan mentioned that Tommy had just received word that he'd been accepted into a summer co-op program for his psychology course. He would mainly do grunt work for a local counselling agency—imputing data and files—but would have the opportunity to see how his courses actually applied to the real world.

"When are we going to eat?" Ginny asked impatiently. "I promised some of my friends I'd meet them later for karaoke."

"Sabina and Jack should be here any minute. It'd be great if we could just enjoy being together for a bit without pressure," I requested.

"Fine," she huffed. As she turned to ask Tommy about a mutual friend of theirs, I heard Sabina and Jack's voices. Thank goodness! Ginny was always a restless creature who found it difficult to stay in the present moment. Once we were all together, Tommy started asking Jack about the latest car he was fixing up and Ginny poured out her latest woes to Sabina. Dan and I started putting the food on the table and poured champagne for everyone before calling them over. Dan tinkled his glass to request silence and then gestured to Sabina.

"Mom and Dad hosted tonight so that Jack and I could share with you," Sabina started.

Ginny jumped in, "Oh my gosh, you're engaged! Wow, you're the first of us. This is so awesome! When are you getting hitched?" her words rolled over one another.

Tommy interjected, "Wait, what?"

"Before Ginny interrupted," Sabina stated wryly, "I was going to share with you that the other night Jack proposed to me and we're going to be married in September. We hope we can get married on the lawn at Mom's new place."

"September! That's not much time for planning! An outdoor wedding…what if it rains?" Ginny wasn't always known for focusing on the positive.

Dan jumped in, "Let's take a moment and toast the happy couple." He raised his glass and we all joined in. "Why don't we eat while the food is hot," he continued.

As Tommy filled his plate, he added his two cents. "Congratulations, guys. I'm happy for you. Anything I can do to help out, just let me know." Tommy tended to be the peacemaker and was adept at redirecting his older sisters to avoid confrontations. "Ginny, you and I will have to get out to see the new place. I can just picture something like an arbour, with all of us standing under it, and a large weeping willow in the background."

Sometimes I wondered if Tommy was precognizant, because he had described exactly the tree that was on that side of the house and what Sabina had planned to build with Dan.

"Anything else you picture?" I inquired nonchalantly.

He played along, as if humouring me, "I see a petite woman with pure white hair hovering in the background and a golden labradoodle standing beside some guy with wispy silvery hair."

Sabina jumped in for fun, "Who's the woman?"

Tommy shrugged. "Let's call her Essie."

Sabina dropped her fork. Dan and I looked at each other and Sabina gasped, "Who told you about Essie?"

Ginny, feeling left out of the conversation, joined in, "Who's Essie?"

Tommy looked puzzled. "Yeah, who's Essie? I just pulled that name out of my head."

We decided to fill both Tommy and Ginny in on Essie. Tommy was curious about her, while Ginny was rather anxious about meeting a spirit.

"What if she doesn't like me? Will she do anything to me?" Ginny asked apprehensively.

Sabina made a suggestion. "After we eat, why don't we drive over so everyone can see the place?"

The vote was unanimous. We relaxed and enjoyed our meal. Conversation jumped around from Tommy's courses, Ginny's show, and Sabina and Dan's work together. We felt pretty stuffed, so we agreed to take dessert with us. Sabina had made mini vegan cheesecakes in muffin cups; they were easy to transport and didn't require any dishes.

It was the end of May and there was still a lot of sunlight in the sky as our cars pulled in. As everyone got out, Tommy exclaimed, "This place is incredible. I love the logs used for the house. And the setting, it feels so peaceful."

Ginny huddled close to me, "Where's Essie?" she inquired in a jittery voice.

"Essie," I began, "these are the rest of our children. Ginny is our eldest. I think I told you she's in theatre. You've met Sabina and beside her is Jack, who works with the government. They just got engaged and would like to have their wedding here in September."

I heard a sniffling noise in my mind; Essie must have been affected by their idea.

"We wanted to come as a family and scout out the layout of the grounds for such a gathering. Tommy is our youngest; he's a psychology student."

"She just pulled my hair. I told you she wouldn't like me," a distressed Ginny shuddered, looking around.

"It's just the wind, Ginny," soothed Tommy. "It's ruffling all our hair. Besides, Essie is over there sitting on the steps."

"You can see her!" I exclaimed.

"Aye, he can, dearie. He has a very open third eye, just like Cheri. You've sensed that for a long time, haven't you? That's why he's so good at psychology."

"Nice to meet you, Essie. You look exactly like I imagined you. Your place is pretty cool," Tommy said to her. "This should be awesome for a wedding!"

"I don't see anyone. This is spooky." Ginny was beginning to get agitated. "Mom, I need to go."

I intervened by offering to tap with her for a moment on her triple warmer meridian and she agreed. "Take deep breaths, Ginny. As I tap on this point, let all of your fear be felt but don't hold onto it. Trust it to rise up and flow through you."

Ginny let the agitation she was feeling move through her body; I could feel the tension under my fingers—then it shifted and her muscles softened.

"Now, if you invite your mind to relax, Essie will be able to communicate with you. I don't see her either, but Dad and I both hear her. My friend Tadame just feels her presence. It's different for all of us," I explained.

I watched as Ginny's shoulders rolled back and down and her whole frame opened up. She was visibly relaxed. She glanced around and said, "I had this feeling of a gentle hand resting on my shoulder and a wave of calm washed over me. I don't hear anything, but I feel better."

"Tell her not to fash, I don't judge people. My son Harry was a dramatist and always felt things intensely, so I understand her. Tell her I like her just fine," Essie assured. She sniffled a bit again. *"I agree with you, Tommy. This would be a wonderful place for a wedding. It would mean a lot to me to have it held here."*

Tommy shared Essie's words with Ginny as I looked over to Sabina and Jack. They seemed engrossed in conversation. I stepped closer to ask if Jack was experiencing any communication from Essie.

He said, "It's the strangest thing. I don't really hear anything in my mind, but I see words in front of me, like reading a page."

"Ha! It's probably all that work with documents he does with the government; that's how his mind sees things."

"Did Essie just comment on how I work with documents?" Jack inquired.

"Yup," Sabina smirked. "This is so cool. She communicates with us all a little differently. Come on everyone. Let's look around outside. Then, we can go into the house for a tour and our dessert."

We walked around the right side of the house where the pond, trees, and Zen garden were taking shape. Tommy looked at the weeping willow beside the pond and grinned at me. Sabina led Jack over to the garden and showed him where she and Dan had talked about building an arbour. As we strolled further around the back, we could see the renovated shed in the distance.

"Can we take a closer look?" Tommy asked eagerly. As we began forward, the new door opened.

"Hey, it's the dude I described in the wedding picture," declared Tommy.

"Not a dude," I explained to Tommy as we drew nearer. "That's Leigh, who will be our chef and our live-in caretaker. Leigh is gender-neutral, so please don't refer to them in a gendered way."

"Leigh, sorry to descend on you like this, but we decided to bring the whole family out to take a look around." Dan introduced everyone to Leigh and Leigh graciously offered to let them look inside their place.

Tommy and Leigh seemed to hit it off immediately, while Ginny trailed behind looking everything over. Sabina busily pointed out to Jack the work she'd done and he admired all we had accomplished. Dan and I decided to wait outside, so it wouldn't be too crowded.

When they finally emerged, we invited Leigh to join us for dessert to celebrate the engagement. They gladly accepted and we walked over to the house to show it off. I told them that I hadn't spoken yet to the rest of the team about holding the wedding on the grounds and Leigh agreed to keep mum on the matter until I brought it up at our next team meeting. Ginny loved the colours we'd chosen for the house and suggested the café would be a perfect setting for small musical performances or poetry readings. Finally, we gathered around the table Sabina and Dan had crafted, which they had brought with them when we went to work on Leigh's home earlier that day. Sabina retrieved her dessert and we eagerly grabbed a cheesecake each. There were two flavours and she had wisely made extra of each. Leigh was very impressed and asked about her recipe. I could see another menu item unfolding.

Dusk was just beginning to fall as Dan and I said goodnight to Leigh and exchanged hugs with the family.

"It was wonderful to meet you all," Essie expressed, before we left. *"It's so heart-warming to see my place coming alive again, in so many ways!"*

"Loved meeting you too, Essie. I hope those are tears of joy running down your cheeks?" Tommy asked kindly.

"Yes, laddie, they are. Tell your sister to trust herself more and worry about others less. Jack and Sabina, congratulations! I look forward to seeing things unfold with your wedding plans."

"Thanks, Essie. We'll keep you updated as we make our arrangements," Sabina promised.

"This is the most relaxed I've felt in a long time," Ginny declared. "I might come back, just to sit in the garden or the café. It feels like this is truly a healing place, Mom."

"I'm glad you felt that, honey," I shared. "Come any time. Have fun at karaoke!"

One by one, we pulled away and drove to our respective places. I clasped Dan's hand in mine as we made our way home, content with the day.

CHAPTER TWELVE

The next day, we held our inaugural weekly team meeting. We had determined that it was necessary to keep us all connected to what each person was accomplishing and to consult on areas that required all our input. It was to that meeting that I took Sabina and Jack's request. The vote was unanimous in favour of the wedding to be held on the grounds. Essie let out a whoop that started us all chuckling.

"*This could be the start of a wonderful tradition,*" Essie exclaimed.

Cheri had a contemplative look on her face; I wondered to myself if we might have another wedding request in the not too distant future. We left wedding plans behind to discuss what we had achieved during the past weekend and what still lay before us. Tadame and I displayed our sample pamphlet and a few tweaks were suggested.

We had an honest discussion about how we all

felt about financial pressure and a reasonable opening date; we agreed to aim for September to open to the public. Cheri submitted the idea of a few open house days and tours throughout August to create awareness of Essie's Healing Place and build our clientele.

The next two weeks flew by. Our supplies began to arrive at the house. Leigh busily organized their kitchen. Cheri and I went shopping for the Great Room furniture. We found some light-weight comfortable chairs without arms that would accommodate differing sizes of people. The chair fabric was a grey-blue tweed that was pleasing to the eye. We interspersed those with walnut stained, firmer chairs with arms for people who needed such support when shifting from a sitting to standing position. We were still on the hunt for a suitable couch, coffee table, and front desk.

Leigh was eager to test out their skills and the flow of their work space, so they suggested we have a July 1st Canada Day family celebration for our team. We were all excited. Tadame and Ronnie would be there, Cheri's fiancée Melissa was keen to meet us all, our kids were all able to join us, and Raman was bringing along a running friend who was new to town.

July 1st dawned clear and bright. I stretched in bed and decided to treat myself to a few peaceful minutes to reflect on all the goodness that had come into my life. Building that well of gratitude inside filled me with energy and purpose for the day. Dan had obviously greeted the day earlier than I. Even though he didn't have to be awake as early as his previous work schedule demanded, I think he treasured the time on his own. Also, he loved his new venture so much that he was eager to get to his workshop. I slipped my feet into Birkenstocks and headed to the kitchen. I plugged in the kettle and, while waiting for it to boil, gazed out the window. Birds were warbling in the trees. Bushes and grass were a verdant green, and flowers were blooming in my flowerbeds. It was a perfect day for a party!

I savoured my breakfast and not having to rush anywhere or do anything. We weren't gathering at Essie's until late afternoon, so the early part of the day was all mine. I wrapped a surprise for the others: I had offered a friend a healing session and, in exchange, she had crafted a splendid wooden sign to put at the entrance to Essie's. The colours she used and the spiral sun she added as a symbol of healing gave it a radiant look. I loved her inclusion of the sun and the way it pointed to balance and harmony emanating throughout the cosmos.

After wrapping my surprise and throwing on my comfiest yoga tights, I made a mug of tea to take out to Dan. As I neared the workshop, I could hear him humming away—a sure sign he was enjoying himself. I stepped into the chaos of various projects underway and Dan looked up with a delighted smile on his face.

"You're just in time," he said.

I quirked a questioning eyebrow in response.

"Ta da!" He stepped to the side and gestured with his hand. I could see a completed trolley gleaming in the sunlight which trickled through the dusty window. I handed Dan the tea and moved closer to examine his work. It was three-tiered and about three and a half feet tall. There were handles at either end and cup hooks under the top tier. The middle tier had a sliding cutlery drawer designed within it. The lowest level was fashioned so that two basins could be placed on it: one to soak cutlery and the other for dirty dishes. All the edges were rounded and the corners were curved. It was magnificent!

"I thought I'd drop it over before today's gathering, as a surprise for Leigh," Dan shared. It looked like I wasn't the only one with surprises on my mind.

"It's fantastic. I love it and I'm sure Leigh will too," I assured. "Dan, I want you to know how excited it makes me feel to see you doing something that gives you such pleasure. I know you were committed to your job and cherished it, but this change seems to be giving you a whole new zest for life and I love it!"

"I've been having so much fun, this last month has flashed by," Dan admitted. "We'll see how things go over the next two, but I'm already thinking I might choose to go back to counselling just two days a week for a few more years and balance it with this business with Sabina."

"I'm sure the future will unfold as it needs to," I affirmed. I was pleased that not even a hint of financial worry had reared its head in my mind.

"Now let's get this trolley off to Leigh. I can't wait to see their face!" We carefully packed it into the back of the van, along with a few bottles of wine and some local craft beer—our contribution for the gathering. If we took the drinks over early, there'd be lots of time for them to chill before mealtime. Leigh had insisted they'd prepare all the edibles. Off we set with excitement pumping through our veins.

We arrived to hear music ebbing from the house, through open windows. Leigh was already in preparation mode. We called out as we entered and Leigh's smiling face popped up from behind the counter where they'd been pulling something out of the oven.

"You're early!" Leigh declared.

"Don't worry. We're just stopping in for a few minutes. We have liquids to chill and a surprise for you."

Placing the oven mitts on the counter, Leigh followed us outside. They waited on the step as Dan and I manoeuvered the trolley out of the van. As we carried it up the steps, Leigh's eyes popped.

"Wow!" they exclaimed. We barely had it set down when their hands were all over it, testing it out. "This is fabulous! Can I use it tonight?" Leigh begged.

"That's why we brought it out early. We thought you could give it a trial run for the party. I busted butt to try to have it finished on time," admitted Dan.

He and Leigh rolled it inside, discussing its set-up; I went to retrieve the wine and beer.

Back inside, Leigh invited us to test what they'd taken out of the oven. They'd brushed thinly sliced sweet potatoes, beets, parsnips, and carrots with oil and spices and grilled them, to make them crunchy. They were delicious. Wonderful, I thought. Healthy junk food I can eat without guilt! We confirmed the deliciousness of the veggie chips to Leigh and shared our eagerness to return later to taste the other foods they'd prepared.

When we returned home, Dan needed a shower, so I generously offered to wash his back. Well-relaxed, we puttered away at chores around our home. After a light lunch, I stretched out on the porch swing and let the hours dwindle away as I read for pleasure. If the warm sun caused me to nod off for a bit, no one was watching. Dan called out that it was time to get dressed to go; I suddenly became alert and dashed to our bedroom to throw on something fun and comfortable. Dressed in a flowing top over leggings and dangly earrings that made me smile, I threw a pashmina into my bag in case the evening turned a little cool. Dan slid my surprise in the back seat and we were off to Essie's.

My anticipation was building as we rounded the corner and onto Starling Drive. We pulled into the driveway and, before we even got out of the car, Raman drew alongside and Cheri followed behind. It seemed we were all excited to be having a party. We climbed out and met Raman's friend Lisa, who had recently moved from Vancouver to Bright Haven. We'd heard lots about Cheri's fiancée, Melissa, but this was the first opportunity for us to actually meet her. Leigh must have heard our vehicles because they came out onto the porch and introductions were shared again. Before we could get in the door, Tadame and Ronnie arrived. Shortly afterwards, our three children appeared; Tommy was their designated driver.

The setting was perfect to present my surprise. I clapped my hands, to draw everyone's attention.

"The Universe has brought us together on this journey and led us to this place. Each day I feel more joy and gratitude for the people you are and what I hope we'll accomplish together. I'm amazed at what we've already achieved! I thought tonight's celebration would be a fine opportunity to show you something I had designed to celebrate who we are. Dan'll bring it out. Leigh, Raman, Tadame, and Cheri, I invite you to unveil it."

Once Dan set the package on the deck, they eagerly joined together in tearing the wrapping off. I heard their gasps and Cheri looked up with tears in her eyes. Leigh reached out to Tadame and Raman put his hand out to draw me into their circle.

"It's perfect!" Cheri proclaimed. She tilted it up so that everyone else could see the sign. "You've captured what each of us brings to this place and how our contributions make this beautiful whole."

I heard Essie whisper quietly in my mind, *"Well done, Alisha! You've offered them all something very special here—and me."*

My friend hadn't just put the spiral sun on the sign; she had also encircled the words with a swirl of greenery. A small jar, a plate of food, a yoga figure, a bottle of oil, a hand with a heart in it, were interspersed throughout the greenery. These symbols were small in comparison to the large lettering of "Essie's Healing Place" and the large spiral sun at the end, but they were meant for us.

"So, you'd like to use it?" I asked.

A chorus of loud yeses and hearty nods from all evidenced their pleasure and agreement. Dan had brought posts and a maul; we all gave our opinion about positioning and we shared turns pounding it into place.

"Someone should take a picture with all of us around the sign," Tadame declared.

"I took a photography class last summer, so I'll make sure you all look great!" Melissa stepped forward to capture the moment for us.

As soon as our photo shoot was complete, Raman cleared his voice and spoke up. "Since we're all outside, why don't we tour the grounds together?" We drifted around the right side of the house where the Zen garden was beginning to fill in nicely. A graveled walkway led from the garden up to the screened-in veranda which offered sliding doors into the café.

Following the pathway to the back of the house,

we could see Leigh's place and the woods behind. Raman led the way. Everyone was extremely impressed with the work on what had been little more than a shack. Dan proudly shared how everyone had contributed and pointed out details of the work. From Leigh's cabin, we proceeded into the woods where Raman had a surprise waiting for us. He had completed the labyrinth.

Ginny pushed forward to question Raman, "I've never been in a labyrinth. Is it like a maze or something?"

"It's a very specific type of maze. Most mazes are constructed with multiple pathways to confuse the user, but a labyrinth is a single pathway intended to lead the walker into a meditative state. I've followed the Chartres design, with the pathway delineated by stones. The path leads a person inward and outward, back and forth toward the center. Want to help me lead the others in?" Raman invited.

"Sure!" she beamed at him. He smiled at her enthusiasm. The rest of us fell into place behind them as we walked the labyrinth with them. In the centre we could see a pedestal with a wooden bench placed beside it. As we drew near we gasped in astonishment. Raman had chosen a pedestal with a spiral sun dial. We burst out laughing and Melissa arranged us for another photo.

Leigh spoke up. "I think it's time for a toast to Essie's Healing Place, to us, and to all those who are here to celebrate with us tonight!"

Everyone was in total agreement, so we trooped

inside to the café. Leigh had made a yummy coconut, pineapple, cherry, lime, and mint smoothie which they poured into glasses chilled with ice cubes. Leigh had gracefully arranged fresh strawberries dipped in chocolate and the veggie chips on trays for our greedy fingers to grasp. Having assuaged our initial hunger pangs, we then took everyone on an indoor tour.

Raman's friend, Lisa, was intrigued by what we had set up. She asked lots of questions and wanted to know when we'd be open so she could book a session. As we went from room to room, Ginny and Sabina talked wedding plans. It wasn't long before Melissa and Cheri joined their conversation. Tommy just seemed to soak everything in. Jack, Dan, and Ronnie talked about the structural integrity of the house and then started into the latest sports news. More food and a few drinks later, the conversation flowed freely. When I glanced over, Ginny had gravitated toward Raman and Lisa, and was enjoying their company. The evening was free from mosquitos and we had set up a fire pit that we could use once darkness fell. Gradually, everyone gathered around the fire.

Tommy grabbed his guitar out of the car and encouraged Ginny to entertain us with a few tunes. Unexpectedly, Raman's rich baritone voice blended with theirs in harmony and, before long, we all joined in. Eventually, the stars came out and quiet descended as we soaked in the peaceful starscape. Then, we heard a bang and the sky exploded with colour. We realized that we were in a perfect location to be able to see the town's Canada Day fireworks. For half an hour we delighted in the array of colours and shapes on show. It was a wonderful close to our first celebration at Essie's.

I stood up to stretch and started gathering things when I noticed a dark shape coming around the side of the house. I gasped and the others looked at where I was pointing. It was difficult to see because the fire had died down and we had turned all the lights off so that we could see the stars better. Was it a skunk? A fox? A coyote? Ginny grabbed Raman's hand and we all froze in place. The shape kept moving toward us. Raman tried speaking up to see if that would scare the creature away. The forward movement didn't stop.

Then, I heard Essie say, *"Simmer down. A new member of your team is about to join you."*

I looked to see who else might have heard Essie's words. Up to that point, Essie had been respectful of having guests. No one else seemed to be reacting, other than Ginny, but Raman was calmly patting her hand. Tommy was whispering to her from the other side and she was much calmer than I would have expected. Finally, the shadow came into the light, right beside Leigh. It was a dog—a golden labradoodle. It sat down beside Leigh and lifted its paw. Leigh laughed in delight and shook.

"Hey there fella, are you lost?"

A sigh of relief echoed through our group. Leigh fumbled with the dog's collar.

"There's a tag here. Let me just shine my flashlight on it." They fumbled a small penlight out of their pocket. "It says, 'Toby, Therapy dog'. There's a phone number on the back. Shall I call it?"

It was rather late, but we thought someone might be missing him. When Leigh placed the call, a puzzled look came over their face. "It's disconnected," they said. "There isn't much more we can do tonight, so Toby can stay with me. I'll fix up a bit of food for him and tomorrow I can call the local radio stations and get word out."

Toby stayed by Leigh's side the whole time we cleaned up. We all agreed it had been a fabulous night, but we were ready for some sleep. Goodbye hugs were exchanged, as were promises to be in touch soon. Yawning, I climbed in the car and promptly fell asleep as Dan drove us home.

Sunday was a quiet day on our own; we'd promised ourselves not to do any work. After a leisurely morning, we decided to truly relax and go to a nearby beach. We threw water bottles, a few snacks, novels, and beach towels into a bag. In no time, we were stretched out in our bathing suits, soaking up the warm sun with the lulling sound of the surf soothing our minds. We read. We napped. We swam. We strolled the length of the beach, pausing frequently to enjoy the beauty of the day. I purposely avoided putting on a sundress and allowed myself to feel confident in the slightly rounded, petite body I inhabited. I smiled at other walkers, feeling more content in this new self I was becoming.

Early in the evening, we showered off the salt and sand that had accumulated on our bodies. Refreshed, we ordered a vegetarian pizza at a local pizzeria. Our appetites were hearty after our time in the fresh air, so we ate with gusto and chowed the whole thing down. Although a little voice inside wanted to feel guilty and fearful about eating so many treats in the last few days, I hushed it. I accepted this lovely food with pleasure and as nourishment.

Even though Monday was a holiday, we were back together for a staff meeting. As none of us had planned to be away, we wanted to keep things rolling. I had managed a quick run just after dawn, so I was feeling revved. We met in the café. Leigh had prepared iced mint coffee and sun tea. Toby obediently sat outside on the veranda. I had heard Leigh's announcement on the radio earlier that morning, but Leigh told us that, as yet, there had been no response. I heard the sound of relief in Leigh's voice. It appeared the two had bonded since our party.

Cheri interjected that she had done a bit of research on therapy dogs while she was relaxing on Sunday. Of course she had, I thought to myself. After sharing with us her findings, Cheri proposed, "If no one claims Toby, he might be an asset to our business."

Essie interjected, *"Toby's meant to be part of the team."*

Tadame held up a finger, "I feel Essie's in favour of that move."

Cheri grinned while looking to my left. "He has my vote."

"Whatever we feel, we have to try to track down his owner first," I asserted.

As we chatted, ideas popcorned out of all of us, back and forth around the table. Eventually, I reclaimed our agenda and drew everyone back to items we more urgently needed to discuss. We discussed using the image of the spiral sun which connected the representations of our gifts on all our print materials.

Tadame grinned and pulled a pamphlet out of her bag. "I thought that might be a possibility, so yesterday I pulled up our template and added the spiral sun to see how it would look. What do you think?" She held it up for our first impressions.

"I think it makes the pamphlet look more complete," said Cheri. "I'd felt something was missing before, but I couldn't really put my finger on it."

Raman pondered, "What if we used our own personal symbol on one corner of our individual business cards and the spiral on the other? That would show how we're each unique but connected."

"Like this?" Tadame reached into her purse and pulled out an envelope which she handed to each of us. When we opened them, we saw the original template for our cards, but this time, after the title "Essie's Healing Place", the spiral sun beamed back at us. Under our names and information, the vine twined along the bottom of the card with each person's personal symbol in the centre.

"These are awesome!" Leigh exclaimed. Their excitement spread contagiously. Cheri popped up and hugged Tadame. Raman offered an approving smile. I reached my hand out and put it on top of Tadame's.

"I think we're ready for production. What do you say, gang?" I asked. Three other hands piled on top of ours and I sensed a fourth.

"Aye, I'm with you on this!" Essie's voice was laden with emotion.

We all seemed to be feeling Essie's emotions. With slightly watery eyes and some throat-clearing, we pulled our hands back to get on with other business. Tadame agreed to take our newly revised templates to the local print shop to place our order. Then, I raised a new suggestion.

"I've been thinking…."

The others groaned.

"Seriously, I think we've covered pretty well every furniture store in Bright Haven. We haven't been able to find exactly what we're looking for here. I don't want to shop online, so I propose a trip to Hope Falls. They have stores we don't have and stores with greater variety. Who's in?"

Raman declined, "I have a job I'm trying to finish up with a very particular client. I agreed to two more bookings after this one. Then, I'll be done. I'm ready to focus full-time here. I trust your judgement on those purchases, so the rest of you go ahead. Don't worry, I don't feel left out. Shopping isn't really my thing."

Leigh piped up, "I'd love to go! We've ordered all the specialty equipment for the café, but I wouldn't mind wandering through some of the stores in Hope Falls, just to see what they have. I've only been there twice before and that was to visit relatives, so I didn't get to see the city or to shop. Just let me know when and I'll switch shifts with a friend if I need to."

"There's this divine little café that Melissa and I discovered on our last trip to Hope Falls. It'd be fun to show it to you all and maybe you can even check out their menu for ideas, Leigh. I'm definitely in!" Cheri proclaimed.

"Ronnie's working extra hours with the good weather, so he essentially comes home, eats, and falls into bed," said Tadame. "I'm sure he'll hardly notice I'm gone. Plus, it'd be helpful if we could finalize our furniture, so the Great Room can be arranged."

Tadame paused and then continued. "Alisha, you weren't the only one thinking." She smiled and turned to Cheri. "Melissa's photos from the party were excellent quality. Do you think she might consider doing a photo shoot for us, once we're set up?"

"I agree with Tadame. I saw the photos on Facebook and they rock! We could get her to do a layout of the gardens, the café, maybe a steaming cup of coffee, and one of my treats," Leigh enthused.

"We could capture someone walking the labyrinth

or relaxing on one of the bench's in the Zen garden. Perhaps you could do a demo of what's offered in the healing rooms and take some of the mystery out of it for people who know nothing about what you do," Raman suggested.

"I like it," declared Cheri. "Melissa will be pumped her photos went over so well and that you want more. I keep telling her she's really good, but she thinks her main talent is in graphic design, so that's been her focus. In fact, she has an interview later today for a full-time position," she confided. Then, lifting her hand with fingers crossed, she invoked, "Universe do your thing! We're ready to be out of the contract-to-contract lifestyle."

"Sounds like we need to get moving on finishing our set-up. Would everyone be able to leave by Thursday morning? I'll book a hotel, so we don't feel rushed and we can have some fun. We can keep receipts as part of business expenses, can't we?" I asked Cheri, who nodded in reply. She was busily taking notes of all we were covering.

Raman spoke up again. "There's a supply store in Hope Falls, with good quality glass jars for storing herbal creams and mixes. If I make a list of what I need, could you pick them up? We'd save on shipping costs that way." I agreed that was a good idea and he continued.

"I was thinking…."

"You too?" Leigh interjected saucily. I arched an eyebrow at them and gestured to Raman to go on.

"I know Cheri's been working on our website and

we've all contributed to that. What if we started a blog to go with our website? We could post something new each week—a kind of a teaser to keep people coming to our site. Maybe we could start with a little history of Essie and Stanley and their place. I could do a few write-ups on some of the herbs I have in the garden here and how they help with healing. Once we have photos, we can add them in. Some of you could write about the healing benefits of some of the different practices you'll be offering."

Cheri high-fived Raman. "Sweet idea! We can get the message out and maybe cop some invites to speak about our place and what we do."

"The archives of the local library should have some photos of Stanley and I when we were married. Also, there's a photo display of our property back in the 1960s. There was a gardening competition in the community back then and we won. It might be fun to contrast the property then with now." Essie suggested.

Tadame inquired, "I feel Essie's approval, but I suspect from the way you've all paused she's making some suggestions?" We passed on what Essie had shared, and we decided to add Essie and Stanley's history to the place. Cheri offered to do the library research and get the blog set up for us. Then, we'd take turns doing a write-up for it.

We moved on to discuss professional insurance companies that Cheri had checked out and which ones would cover each of our areas of expertise. She went over things like getting the health inspector in for the kitchen and the steps of applying for a liquor license. Leigh provided all the necessary certificates they had obtained for handling food and operating the café. We also made sure we were all up to date on our professional memberships, so Cheri could set up our billing system for people with health insurance. Raman indicated the fire inspector would be back for a final inspection once we were all set up.

During our review, it became clear none of us had up-to-date first aid or CPR certificates. Cheri checked her iPad, and a two-day course was being offered in two weeks' time. We decided we'd all register, so we'd always have someone on site with the necessary training.

We planned for the four-hour trip to Hope Falls and we agreed to take my vehicle because it was the most spacious. I arranged pickup times for Thursday bright and early! Raman offered to keep an eye on the place and check on Toby while we were away.

CHAPTER THIRTEEN

On Thursday morning, I was up and eager to be on the road. I had packed the night before, so a quick shower and breakfast were all I needed. Dan sensed my excitement. He gave me a prolonged kiss and encouraged me to have fun. As if I needed encouragement! Sunglasses on and tunes blasting, I patted the dash of my trusty car as I pulled onto the street.

"Road trip!" I whooped.

Cheri was the first pickup. I didn't even make it to the buzzer of her apartment when I saw her clumping down the stairs with a gorgeous fabric travel bag over one shoulder and a small cooler in her other hand. She flung open the door and did a spin.

"We're tripping!" she sang out, and she grabbed me in a hug.

"So, you like road trips?" I asked tongue-in-cheek.

Cheri grinned and threw her stuff in the trunk. She pulled funky sunglasses out of her purse and called dibs on the front seat, since she was the first in the car. As we pulled away and the music kicked back in, I saw her expression and laughed. Obviously, my musical preferences were a tad different to hers.

Tadame was next. We drove up to find her outside her apartment building, giving Ronnie a hug. He hopped into his truck and waved as he set off for work. Tadame looked gorgeous in mint green leggings with a coral and green off-the-shoulder top. She looked pretty revved as well. After placing her bag in the trunk, Tadame climbed in the back. I pulled away and she eagerly leaned forward. I turned the music down slightly, so we could hear her.

"I went through all the furniture places in Hope Falls and some of the other spots we wanted to hit. I made a map so we could visit them all in the most efficient way, without a lot of back-tracking."

"Chill, Tadame!" exclaimed Cheri. "Did you allow time in there for a visit to the café?"

"Of course. And, I also checked out the Hope Falls theatre company. They have a musical playing right now, if anyone's interested?" I could sense Tadame's longing as she posed her question.

"Better wait for Leigh's input. We're almost there." I swung the car into Essie's and Leigh was waiting on the front steps. They had a kitbag, two thermoses, and a small cooler. They jumped into the back seat with Tadame before anyone could get out of the car.

"Ready to roll?" Leigh asked impatiently. We all burst out laughing.

"Have a wonderful trip!" Essie cooed.

Cheri waved to where I presumed Essie was standing.

Leigh and I chorused, "We will!"

Tadame nodded, feeling Essie's good wishes.

As soon as they were buckled up, we were on our way. Tadame asked about the musical again and Leigh responded immediately, "I love musicals, but will we be able to get tickets at such short notice?"

Tadame cleared her throat and sheepishly admitted, "I put them on hold, hoping you'd all want to go. I know we didn't budget for this…."

"This part of the trip is my treat," I declared.

"Wait, that's not what I meant," Tadame spluttered.

"It's what I want to do," I insisted. "I filled in for a friend and did a wedding a few weeks ago. The cheque came in the mail yesterday. I was wondering what I'd do with it. Now I know. You can treat me at the café. How's that?"

"That's majorly generous." Leigh affirmed. "I say, thank you."

"Ditto for me," Cheri avowed. "Tadame, book those tickets for us! Now, can we please change the music?"

We comfortably argued back and forth about what constituted great tunes. In the end, we agreed to half an hour of each person's favourites. Leigh offered us fresh coffee and tea from their thermoses.

Tadame had chocolate truffles she'd picked up as treats. We took a few bathroom breaks but made do with our own snacks. Cheri contributed Havarti cheese and crackers with fresh apple slices. I had chunks of pineapple and a can of mixed nuts. Conversations flowed easily as the miles slid by. As time passed, however, Cheri seemed to withdraw into herself; a very unusual state for her.

Tadame picked up on it first. "Everything okay, Cheri?"

"Oh, it's probably nothing. I'm sure I'm just overreacting." She attempted to brush her mood aside.

"You're not usually one to overreact." I observed.

"It's relationship stuff. I don't want to dump it on you guys. This is supposed to be a fun trip."

Leigh stretched a hand out to her shoulder. "We're here if you need a sounding board. Sometimes sharing things can free up the fun again."

Cheri reached up to squeeze Leigh's hand. "Thanks. I just don't want to influence your opinion of Melissa."

"Hey, no judgements allowed in my car," I proclaimed. "Only listening ears allowed on this ride." I tried to ease the situation with a little humour.

A small smile tugged at Cheri's lips. "Okay. Here goes." She pulled in a deep breath. "When Melissa and I first met, she was in a polyamorous relationship with three other people. We really hit it off, but I wanted a monogamous relationship. She was willing to give that a try because the sparks between us were pretty rad. After two months of dating, she completely ended her other relationships and we became exclusive. After a year we had moved in together and just before graduation in April, she proposed to me." Cheri paused.

"And you said yes...." Tadame encouraged her on.

"You bet! I love her so much," Cheri stated emphatically.

"Sounds like there's a 'but' in there," Leigh probed.

"But, this past week she's been going out at night without me. Granted there are times I've been working on things for our business, but she doesn't say where she's going. She didn't get that job we'd hoped for and we were both pretty bummed about it. I thought we'd talked it all out, but she comes home exhausted and falls into bed asleep before I barely do more than kiss her good night. I'm afraid I'm not satisfying her anymore," Cheri said miserably.

"Have you asked her about it?" I inquired gently.

"I brought it up once and she brushed me off, saying she was just here and there, nowhere special."

"Has trust been an issue for you before?" Leigh contributed.

"I've trusted Melissa, but I don't know if I trust that I'm enough when she's had this other type of relationship." Cheri looked out the window and back to us. "Wow, this is about me, not her, isn't it?"

"Great insight," Tadame encouraged.

"Guess I need to do some more thinking on this.

But with your help I have a bit more clarity, so I can let it go for now. Thanks for listening."

We arrived in Hope Falls early in the afternoon. Our first stop was the café Cheri had recommended. It was a tiny place tucked in between two larger businesses. A few tables under umbrellas stood on the sidewalk. The day was warm and sunny, with very little breeze; we decided to sit outside. Cheri told us we had to go in to place our order, so we traipsed inside first. The interior was painted a soft creamy white and decorated with pastel paintings by local artists. At the counter, the signs indicated all products were organic and fairly-traded. Produce was mostly locally sourced. A chilled avocado soup with ginger and basil accompanied by a cheese biscuit was the special of the day, which caught my attention. The others each decided to try something different. Tadame ordered a quinoa and kale salad. Cheri chose a pita stuffed with a barley, walnut, and fig salad with a tarragon-orange dressing. Leigh hummed and hawed before finally selecting a salad with mixed local greens and herbs, topped with Cajun shrimp and veggies. We asked for extra forks and spoons, so we could try each other's selections. The flavour combinations were exquisite, so Leigh posted notes on their phone so they could experiment with similar ideas back home.

As we enjoyed our meal outside, Leigh spoke up. "I noticed a display shelf inside with the same pottery bowls and plates we're eating from. What if we did something similar? I've been working with Cheri to try to pin down the dishes we want to stock the café, but nothing seems to fit. We were just looking at basic kitchenware, but what if we mixed in some local pottery as well? We could see if a local artisan might like to be connected to us, or we could purchase from a variety of people?"

Tadame finished her mouthful of salad and said, "At my monthly book club, there's a woman who's a potter. I have a couple of her bowls and mugs. They're sturdy and stand up well, while still being lovely. She also paints healing symbols on her dishes. She doesn't have her own store, so she sells by consignment. I could see if she'd do a deal for us if we'd sell her stuff through our business."

"Wow, this trip is turning out to be productive already and we're just getting started," Cheri quipped. We all urged Tadame to speak with her friend. We took the fact that she used healing symbols on her work as a potent indicator that she was meant for us.

We left the café and began our shopping tour. Raman's supply store was first on the list. It didn't take long to obtain the items he'd listed for us to pick up. The next three stores were a bust. Our spirits lagged a little as we entered the large IKEA store. At first, we browsed the kitchen supply areas and Leigh discovered more and more items on their list. I went back to grab a cart and, before I knew it, we were excitedly loading it up. Small display shelves for our pamphlets and cards, cloth hampers that would be perfect for our laundry, and items we hadn't even considered we needed caught our attention. We had fun bickering about colours and which things were essential. Then, we saw the furniture area. A wooden slat sofa with a full-length cushion drew me over. I snuggled in and the comfort surprised me. I urged the others to take turns trying it out. We sat on various other types too, but I kept finding myself back at my first choice. A vote was taken. It was unanimous. We agreed to order two for delivery—one for the downstairs reception and one for the upstairs look-off area. We chose cushions in a contrasting colour to the chairs we already had back home.

Thinking of clients who might require back support, we sought out the pillow aisle, where we chose a rainbow of colours and shapes. With the cart heaped high, I eagerly pushed it around the corner to head to the check out. As I did, one of the wheels stuck, and I had to give it a firm shove to unlock it. As I shoved, the weight of the contents pulled the cart out of my hands. I looked with horror as it glided away from me down the aisle and crashed ahead into someone else's cart. We rushed to the crash scene and discovered that a man who had been crouched down looking at an item on the shelf had been knocked off his feet. Fortunately, the cart careened to the side without falling on top of him as he lay, stunned, on the floor.

I'd thought my clumsy capers were over—and I couldn't even blame this on Essie! Tadame shrieked. Cheri clasped a hand over her grin. Leigh rushed over to help, while I stood in disbelieving shock.

Leigh held out a hand and blurted out, "Are you okay?"

The man looked up and exclaimed, "Leigh?!"

He stood up and I rushed over to apologize. Before I could say anything, the man repeated, "Leigh McCreary? It's really you."

Leigh nodded and grinned. "Mr. Conter, good to see you. Sorry about the accident." He gestured us over. "I'm here with my friends. We're starting a business together, so we've been picking up supplies. Alisha, Cheri, Tadame, this is my former high school English teacher, Mr. Conter. He was super supportive when I first came out."

We exchanged handshakes, pleasantries, and, in my case, an apology. "Is your business here in Hope Falls?" Conter inquired.

"No. We're setting up in Bright Haven. We decided to do a road trip to Hope Falls to suss out the stores here." Leigh gestured to our cart. "As you can see, we've struck it lucky! Alisha had a dream for a healing place and we've all come together to help make that happen."

"Good for you, Leigh," Conter said warmly. Then, he addressed all of us. "I was going to grab a coffee on the top floor after I finish here. Would you care to join me? I'm keen to hear about your business venture."

I offered to check our stuff out and load it in the trunk, while they went to the coffee shop, on the condition they ordered me a medium decaf with a flavour shot. When I rejoined them a short while later, they were earnestly sharing what our healing place would offer to the public. Mr. Conter nodded and appeared to be listening attentively. I joined the table, gratefully sipping my coffee.

"Alisha, Mr. Conter, I mean Jace—because he's not my teacher anymore and he told me to call him that—Jace has been telling us that he just completed two years of massage therapy."

"Ten years teaching high school was enough for me. I was taking too much of it home with me. When my wife left me, I decided I needed a different outlet. I've always been drawn to healing modalities, so I decided to move away and try something new; hence, massage therapy. I just finished packing up my apartment here in Hope Falls, so I can move to Bright Haven to be close to my extended family. I'll be looking for work there."

I didn't need Essie in my head to tell me this was another match for us! Leigh seemed to be enjoying catching up with their former teacher, so we stayed a while longer. Then, I suggested Jace get in touch with us once he settled in Bright Haven, if he was interested. A wide smile spread across his face as he took our contact information.

"Leigh, it's really great to see you so happy. I'm a little bowled over," Jace winked at me, "but also excited about what the future may hold. I'll definitely be in touch. Enjoy the rest of your time in Hope Falls!"

We meandered our way through a few more stores on the way to our hotel. Other than a few more basic purchases, we felt we were done. While we were emptying out the trunk, Tadame noticed a small shop across the street. It was called Milky Way Mystic and looked intriguing. We still had an hour before our supper reservation at a pub close to the theatre, so we gave in to the pull and dashed across the street. Bells chimed as we entered. Glowing salt lamps were scattered throughout the store. Crystals in gorgeous pottery bowls gleamed. The scent of honey wafted through the air from an arrangement of beeswax candles. A cosy chair and side table placed next to a book shelf invited visitors to sit and peruse the latest array of authors. We were hooked.

The attendant behind the counter smiled at us and encouraged us to look around. Time drifted as we became lost in the wonder and whimsy of the shop. Suddenly, a woman breezed into the store from the back room. She was tall and curvaceous, with rich mahogany skin. Multi-hued scarves hung from her shoulders and flowed with her movement. Clear crystal earrings and a necklace reflected the captivating colours, and seemed to glow with an inner fire. She stopped abruptly in front of me.

"I am Mirabelle, the Mystic in the Milky Way Mystic."

I could feel the others falling into place around me.

"Hi, Mirabelle. You have an awesome store," I offered.

"Hrmmph," she replied. She proceeded to walk in a circle around our group. We weren't sure what to expect when she spoke again. "You are one. Your gifts spiral in and around each other. You have much to offer. Let me see your hands." I could sense the others' curiosity, mixed with a little apprehension. What had we gotten into?

"Your hand, please," Mirabelle snapped.

Taking a deep breath, I offered my hand. Mirabelle gently cradled my hand in one of hers. Her long slender fingers traced my palm in the hush that had fallen over us.

Looking at me directly, she proclaimed, "You are the heart. You nurture the whole. There is generosity here, but remember the lesson of the heart; there must be balance. The heart not only gives, it receives. Practice this receiving."

With a firm nod, Mirabelle turned to Leigh. "You next."

Leigh cautiously lifted their hand. Again, Mirabelle took her time. When she was finished tracing, she enclosed Leigh's hand between both of hers.

"You are becoming whole. Stay on the journey, it is right for you. You bring delight through the senses. You're the youngest, but you're the wisdom. You carry knowledge from times past. Listen deep within. Trust your voice and ideas."

Her gaze bore into us all. "Listen to this one."

Feeling enthralled, we nodded our agreement.

Tadame quickly offered up her hand, without being asked. We waited with baited breath for the next pronouncement Mirabelle would offer.

"You are the connector. You draw things together, to the whole. You know through your feelings. You feel through your hands. Your hands will bring relief to many. But do not carry more than is necessary. Let go. You must practice letting go."

Tadame dipped her head, obviously feeling Mirabelle's message strike home.

Mirabelle turned to Cheri, who bemusedly held up her hand. A warm smile floated across Mirabelle's face.

"Such light—there is such light in you. You bring the joy that makes the whole shine. Ideas radiate from you. Energy and laughter infuse your being and grace those around you. Trust this beauty that is in you. It never has to be proven. Share because you want to share, not because you want to earn approval or attention. You understand?"

"I do," Cheri affirmed.

"You are the last, but not the last. There is another. He is earthy, strong-rooted. He brings strength to the whole. He nurtures yet needs nurturing too. He soothes with his gift. You can depend on him. Be careful you don't take him for granted."

Nodding, we indicated that we were listening.

Mirabelle continued. "Yet, he is not the last either." She scrunched up her face, concentrating. "There is one, she's hard to capture. Ahh, you have a spirit guide. What a delight! Enjoy what she offers. Others will join you, but you are the core. It's exciting what you have brought together."

Mirabelle looked at each of us, her eyes communicating kindness and promise.

"Yes, exciting. Blessed be."

Swirling around, she exited before we could respond. We stood together feeling rather stunned.

"You folks must be pretty special. Most customers have to book and pay for readings," said the attendant at the desk. "It's rare for her to come out like that. Now, is there anything I can help you find? I'm supposed to close up in ten minutes."

We gasped at the time. We decided we would each choose something that would remind us of our experience with Mirabelle. I found a green heart necklace with a silver spiral encasing it; the word 'give' was inscribed on one side, and 'receive' was etched on the opposite side. Leigh decided upon an amethyst they could carry in their pocket as a touchstone to remind them of the wisdom they carried. Then, they saw a shelf of mortar and pestles. Leigh really wanted one in marble and they suggested we purchase a granite one for Raman. We all agreed to chip in and take it back as a gift for him. Cheri fell in love with crystal prism earrings that dangled from a brass spiral. Tadame joined us with a bracelet made of obsidian and malachite, threaded onto interwoven wires.

Pleased with our choices, we rushed back to the hotel to freshen up for the evening. We chattered about the incredible experience with Mirabelle and I bemoaned the fact that I'd never remember all she'd said.

Cheri piped up. "Don't worry. I was so intrigued with the store's layout that I was using my phone to record for ideas we could look at back home. I just kept it rolling when Mirabelle appeared."

"You wonderful woman," I exclaimed as I rushed over to give her a hug.

"Don't worry. I won't post it or anything. This is private and just for us. We'll share it with Raman and, personally, I'd like Melissa to hear it too, if that's okay?" Cheri queried.

"I'd like Ronnie to listen to my message. What about you Alisha?" Tadame turned to me.

"I'm good with those closest to us having the chance to observe the Mirabelle experience, but once we write down our messages, I think we should delete it. We didn't ask permission to record her and it doesn't feel right somehow. What do you think, Leigh?" I called through the connecting door to the second hotel room.

"For me, it felt like a special spiritual message to each of us. I'd like to be respectful of how we share the experience. I vote we play it for those we've mentioned and then delete it. Are we ready to go? I don't want to rush supper or be late to the show!"

We were all set, so we piled back into the car. Supper was typical pub fare and we each had one drink to celebrate our day. We enjoyed relaxing over food and reviewing the day. I grabbed the bill as part of our business expenses. At the theatre, we were wowed by the show. The quality of music and dance had me tapping my toes the whole evening. I could tell from the body language of those around me that everyone was fully engaged and loving it.

It was a weary crew that finally crawled into bed back at the hotel. We agreed to no alarms. We'd wake up when we woke up.

CHAPTER FOURTEEN

I eased out of bed just after 8:00 a.m. I had laid out my running clothes before going to sleep, so I quietly pulled them on and snuck out the door. I jogged along the street to the park that I knew was nearby. It offered walking and running trails which wove along the riverside and, at one point, led to a look-off at the falls that gave Hope Falls its name. I settled into a comfortable pace and allowed the peace of the morning to fill me up. I arrived at the look-off and began to laugh. Cheri was there snapping pictures, while Tadame was showing Leigh some Tai Chi moves. I was trying to be so quiet leaving, that I hadn't realized the others were already gone!

They glanced over at the sound of my laughter and waved. I jogged over with a quick good morning and a promise to see them back at the hotel. Breakfast was included, so we sampled the buffet. We unanimously agreed that the hotel coffee was not to our liking.

By mid-morning, we were loaded up, back on the road, and tunes were pouring out the window. The trip had been über-successful and it felt like we had taken another solid step forward with the business. We were promised a furniture delivery on the first of the following week, so the Great Room was really coming together. Rolling down the highway, my eye was drawn to a sign advertising 'Gramma's Treasure Chest'. I called out to the others, over the music.

"Have any of you noticed that sign before?"

"I don't recall it from the last time Melissa and I came through here," Cheri responded.

Tadame turned down the music, "I seem to recall reading an article about it just last month. I think it's a new place. It sounded interesting in the write-up."

"Anyone ready for a break?" I asked. "Want to check it out?"

"Sure," Cheri chimed her assent. "I need a bathroom break anyway. Two cups of coffee, orange juice, and water with breakfast may have been pushing it!"

I had only had a glass of water and one decaf coffee, and I needed to go. Oh to have a young bladder, unstrained by childbirth! Tadame was enticed by the idea of the store. Cheri shook Leigh awake, although how they could nap with the volume of the music was beyond me. There were multiple signs for the store. Each one displayed a treasure chest, but they were all different. A hand lifting up a piece of treasure out of the chest displayed a different item each time.

The building at which we found ourselves was an elegant yet aged farmhouse. The front door led us into a welcoming area where we were greeted by a petite, white-haired, woman in an attractive sundress. She greeted us charmingly.

"Welcome to Gramma's Treasure Chest. Please feel free to wander from room to room. Each one is brimming with treasures in keeping with each setting. Even the bathrooms at the back of the hall have unique finds in each one. Enjoy!" She turned to greet another group of shoppers and we made a bee-line for the bathrooms.

Feeling much relieved, I began to wander through the room designated as holding office treasures. Antique letter openers and paper weights lined a shelf on one side of the room. As I stepped further into the room to see more of the contents, I heard a gasp behind me. Cheri slid around me and darted to the far side of the room. Her hands smoothed over a leather-topped, mahogany and walnut, oval-shaped desk.

"Alisha, look at this. It's magnificent," she whispered reverently.

I drifted over to take a look. I had to admit it was beautiful. She looked at me with longing eyes. Even in the Hope Falls stores, we hadn't been able to find a desk for Cheri that we thought would fit the Great Room. I walked around it. The wood tones and the shape were ideal for our setting. There were lots of drawers for whatever odds and sods she'd need for her work. The desktop was large enough for a computer monitor with plenty of extra space around it. It looked like someone had modernized the desk because under the center cutaway, rather than a central drawer, a pullout keyboard shelf had been installed.

"Well?" she pleaded.

"I love it," I assured her. "Let's get the others in to see their reactions."

I set off in search of Tadame and Leigh, who I found chortling over pantaloons and old-fashioned bathing suits. I didn't tell them what we'd found; I simply said that I wanted to show them something. They traipsed merrily along behind me. Cheri was standing outside the room, fidgeting from foot to foot.

We had barely entered the room when I heard Leigh exclaim, "Wow, look at that desk."

Tadame was just as enamoured with it. We tried to assure a balanced perspective in making a decision, by considering how we'd get it home and noting that we didn't yet know the price. Cheri searched around the desk for a price tag, while I went in search of the woman who had welcomed us at the door. She'd been replaced by a young woman who cheerily said, "Gramma's out on the veranda, just a sec." She opened the front door and hollered for Gramma, who quickly appeared.

"Now, Christine, what have I told you about proper deportment around our customers?" Gramma reprimanded gently.

Christine didn't seem too worried about Gramma's ideas about manners. She just shrugged and said, "These people want to talk with you about a desk."

Gramma turned to us inquiringly. We mentioned our interest in the desk in the office display room, but that we couldn't find a price tag. Gramma followed us down the hall and into the room.

"I recall that desk. It's a shame, really. A beautiful antique, but someone tried to modernize it. It's still quite lovely from this side, but I'm afraid its value has been greatly diminished if you're a collector. Normally, it would be in the price range of eight hundred to a thousand dollars."

"As it has been altered, what would you be willing to accept for it?" I probed.

Gramma walked around the desk, shaking her head sadly. "It's the only piece in the store that isn't in mint antique condition. I'd be glad to let it go. I shouldn't have picked it up from that estate sale last week, but for some reason I couldn't seem to resist it."

Cheri, Tadame, Leigh, and I interlocked gazes. We knew exactly why she couldn't resist it. This desk was meant to be ours!

"Would you be willing to pay two hundred and fifty for it, taxes included?"

I explained our transport issue and Gramma assured us, "My husband, Reginald, goes back and forth regularly to Bright Haven. He picks up items from estate sales or other things I've purchased online from that area. He'll be there next Monday, if my memory serves me. I'd be glad to have him deliver it to your place. Let's go to the computer so we can work out the details of your sale."

Cheri beamed as Gramma walked by and she did a happy little dance when she thought no one was looking.

Back in the car, we all sang along to Tadame's choice of "Best Day of My Life", while Cheri took photos of us all. We were eager to share with everyone back home the events of the past two days. Approaching Bright Haven, we decided to drop Leigh off first and texted to see if Raman might be free to meet us. He responded that he'd be there, albeit a bit sweaty and dusty after his contract job.

We drove into Essie's place and saw Dan's vehicle and trailer in the parking area. He must have finished another table! Great, we'd be able to share our news all at once. I could hear Essie buzzing in my mind with excitement.

"It's so good to have you all back!"

I popped out of the car and saw the front door open. Dan stepped forward to greet me with a huge hug. Toby bounded out the door, making straight for Leigh, who crouched down to receive Toby's head butt.

"Welcome back." Dan spoke over my shoulder to include the others in his greeting. "You all look like you're bursting with news. I just made a supersize batch of orange, mango, kefir, and almond butter smoothies. I figured you might need something cool and refreshing at this point."

"You're an angel!" I declared. Raman's truck pulled into the drive. Cheri danced over to give him a hug as he stepped out. He laughed at her barely contained excitement and waved at the rest of us as he strolled over to join us.

"We're just heading in for smoothies to sustain us as we catch you up on our doings." I shared. We trooped in together, turning into the café. All of the tables were surrounded by chairs. I looked at Dan. He beamed with pride.

"Sabina and I really pushed this week to give this area a more finished look. We have one set of table and chairs left to complete and the other trolley, but by prioritizing the chairs, this area can now be used for a photo shoot." Dan explained.

"It's both terrifying and exhilarating to see everything falling into place," Tadame confessed. We responded with a chorus of "I hear you" and groans of assent.

A knock on the door made us turn our heads. Ronnie poked his head in. "I wondered if I'd find you here. I got off early tonight, so I thought I'd check in on my way home." He strolled in and placed his hand on Tadame's shoulder, offering an affectionate squeeze. She placed her hand upon his.

"What's the latest?" he queried.

Dan offered Ronnie a drink. Once he was seated, we took turns telling our road trip story. Our voices sometimes chorused over each other, adding details we wanted to remember. Cheri and Leigh both had photos on their phones to illustrate various parts of the trip. When it came to sharing the video clip of Mirabelle, there was complete silence. Finally, Cheri dug in her purse and presented Raman with his gift. "This is from all of us. We hope you'll remember, you are strength to us all." Raman opened the box. There was a long pause. He cleared his throat, "Thank you," he said, with a tone full of emotion.

I could hear Essie sniffling in the background.

"Essie feels sad and joyous at the same time," Tadame observed, shifting our focus.

"She included me as part of your team."

"Mirabelle's message about her seems to have touched Essie quite deeply," I shared with Tadame.

Leigh and Cheri both looked toward the next table over, where I assumed they could see Essie seated near us. Concentrating and opening my mind allowed me to see a soft glimmer in that direction. My sight was improving.

"You are part of the team Essie. You've been watching over me and guiding us all. You're an important part of who we are," Leigh affirmed.

Cheri nodded in agreement and offered a warm, gentle, smile.

"I know I've been helpful in bringing you all together, but now that things are really getting off the ground, I wonder if my purpose has been fulfilled. What more can I do?"

Raman interjected. "Essie, for a long time I struggled with equating my worth with what I did or offered to the world. I felt my value was related to how many projects I could accomplish with satisfactory customers and how much money I could bring in. Yet, the more I chased the dream, the emptier I felt inside. It took a while and some outside help before I realized my worth is in who I am, not what I do. Your worth to us is in who you are, Essie, not in what you can do for us."

Cheri offered, "Maybe we haven't told you enough that we appreciate you."

"Thank you. I think I've been a little down because you've been away on your trip. Dan and Raman were working elsewhere, and I'm tied to this place. I've been lonely. I know that sounds crazy, since I spent years alone here. But I've gotten used to you all."

"I feel a wave of loneliness from Essie," Tadame described.

"It's only been a few months, but we've all created a bond that's pretty special. Now, would you all like to see what we picked up to help us remember we're each unique and worthy in our own way?" I suggested.

"What did you get?" Essie asked with interest.

We each pulled out our treasures and what they represented to us. Essie was delighted and the others were impressed by how well each symbol matched us individually.

Before anyone left, Cheri spoke up again, "I didn't share this earlier because I wanted us all to be together." She looked over to Raman, who smiled his appreciation. "Melissa is really stoked about doing our photos. She can borrow some lighting equipment from a friend of hers who does professional photography; she just needs to know when we want to do the shoot."

"Our furniture is supposed to be delivered on Monday," I reminded everyone.

"I dropped off our print supplies and the print shop told me things would be ready for pickup on Wednesday," Tadame noted.

"The weather forecast is good for the end of the week, so our outdoor shots wouldn't be a problem," Raman added.

"What if we asked Ginny if some of her acting friends would like to help us out?" Dan suggested. "They're used to being photographed."

"I could cook up a variety of dishes and treats for the shoot. Then, we could eat together once we're done," Leigh proposed.

"I bet some of my running friends would be delighted to come too, especially if food's involved," Raman contributed.

I concurred. "Maybe we could give each of them a gift certificate for a mini-session as a thank you and as a way to encourage them to come back."

By mutual agreement, we unloaded the car of supplies and dumped them in the Great Room to deal with on another day. We decided we'd each pop in over the weekend to sort out our particular purchases as needed, but otherwise we'd make our connections for the photo shoot and be together again on Monday morning for our staff meeting. Trip tiredness was beginning to set in, so we said farewell to Leigh. Tadame switched her things to Ronnie's truck and I promised Dan I'd meet him back home after dropping Cheri off.

Cheri cat-stretched in her seat and heaved a huge sigh. "This trip has been savage. I'm eager to see Melissa. She'll be so bummed she wasn't there for Mirabelle and the show! I can't believe how much we packed into such a short trip."

Cheri climbed out and grabbed her bags.

"Sleep well!" she chirruped.

With a cheery wave she bounced into her building. I returned her wave and sent an intention for healing energy to surround her relationship. I drove for home, more than ready to kick back and let the events of the last two days process in my mind and heart. Dan was in the kitchen when I arrived. He had tossed together a mixed green salad and grilled cheese sandwiches were cooking in the pan. Simple and comforting food—just what I needed. I kicked off my shoes and let the silent peace of our home slide over me. I refilled my water bottle and sipped refreshing well water. Road trips were fun and stimulating, but I always treasured the return home.

CHAPTER FIFTEEN

Monday dawned rainy and cloudy. I pulled on a rain jacket as I yawned my way out the door, heading off for our staff meeting. The weekend had been busier than I expected. Tadame had called and we ended up spending the weekend visiting local artisans, including her book club friend. Enough were interested in our enterprise to agree to selling some of their wares through us on consignment. We had a whole collection of samples to show the others. Excitement over our finds and expectations about the day's deliveries had kept me tossing and turning throughout the night. I sipped my coffee, which I had made half decaf and half regular; I needed the extra zip from the caffeine.

Raman was already at the house when I arrived. He was standing on the veranda, looking out over the grounds with a pleased look on his face. I figured the softly falling rain would replenish his various plants.

He sauntered over as I arrived. He hadn't bothered with a jacket and the mist of rain glistened on his skin. He truly was a very attractive man.

"*Isn't he! I just love watching him when he's hard at work—all those delicious muscles!*" Essie declared.

I glanced at Raman, but he didn't appear to have heard; Essie must have been able to share with us selectively, if she so chose. When he saw the boxes on the back seat of my car, Raman offered to help me carry them in. Between us, we managed them all. I gestured to the café, where I wanted to array our samples on the café tables. Once we set them down, Raman bent over and looked in my face as I turned around.

"Hold on." He gently clasped my chin with his fingers, turning my face side to side. "You've got shadows under your eyes. You're not looking your usual energetic self. What's up?"

I blushed. "Do I look that bad? Sheesh! One poor night of sleep at my age and I look pathetic."

"*Alisha, that's not like you!*" Essie exclaimed.

Raman let my chin go and guided me to a chair. I plopped into it as he sat at an angle to me.

"Come on, Alisha. You know you're beautiful."

I jerked my head up in astonishment. "What?"

Raman paused before continuing. "You're a beautiful woman. You have a spirit and energy that shines through in a very attractive way. We've been friends for months now and I've not seen you like this before. I've seen you tired with all we've been trying to accomplish, but this seems to go deeper. I trusted you when I told you my parents are pressuring me to remarry. I told you about my first marriage and how my wife was unfaithful. You listened when I needed support. Do you trust me?"

"Alisha, you know you can trust him. Remember Mirabelle's message?"

I looked at his kind and caring eyes, which noticed more than I'd realized. I placed my elbow on the table and leaned my head into my hand.

"It seems I underestimated your intuition. I do trust you, Raman. Sometimes, I need to work on letting myself receive support, not just give it." I heaved a heavy sigh. "It was a rough night. Not only was I excited about today, but we had a call at midnight from the police station. Tommy was arrested."

Raman didn't comment. He simply placed a comforting hand on my arm.

I continued, "He went to a party with some friends. He was their designated driver. But, the cops got a tip about the party and there was a big drug bust. Tommy was rounded up with all the rest. Apparently, the guy hosting the party had a private lab in an old trailer at the back of his property. It took hours to get Tommy cleared. He passed all the drug tests and obviously wasn't in possession of anything. Some of the other kids testified that Tommy had no knowledge of the drug enterprise. Fortunately, the cops let him go after taking his statement and telling him not to leave Bright Haven." I felt lighter, having shared what happened.

"Being a parent can certainly stretch us to our limits," Essie commiserated.

"Life throws us some pretty wild curve balls, doesn't it?" Raman patted my arm. "It can be scary, considering what could have happened. But it didn't. Tommy's lucky you're there for him. Don't let 'could haves' drain your energy."

"I'm so grateful for Tommy. He's such a wonderful person. I know young adults need to push boundaries, but I'm eternally thankful he didn't choose to do so in a way that would've been destructive to his future. Thanks for listening. I feel better having told someone about it."

"Secrets have a way of sucking us dry. I try really hard not to keep them anymore, but I will keep yours until you feel ready to share with the others," Raman assured me.

"I'll tell them all at the staff meeting. You've reminded me of the importance of being honest about what's going on in our lives. So often we can sense it from each other, like you did just now. If we're not upfront about it, our work and friendship together can suffer," I concluded.

I heard the front door open. Leigh and Cheri's voices tumbled over and around each other. Tadame followed behind them with a box in her arms.

Cheri rushed over and crouched before me. "Is Tommy all right? I read about it on Facebook in a post by an old friend of mine who was at the party. She mentioned the names of others who were there."

I looked at everyone and smiled. "Grab a seat," I

suggested. "I have a story to tell!"

Everyone found a chair and I caught them up on the details of what had happened. Their compassion and understanding reaffirmed for me the rightness of this team we'd formed.

"Okay. I feel better now that you all know what's going on, but it's time to focus on the happier side of things. Leigh, could you make a fresh pot of coffee because you make it the best, while the rest of us unload these boxes? Then, we can shift to the newest happenings for our business," I requested.

"Well done, Alisha. They all needed to be part of this with you."

Raman went to retrieve something from outside, while the ladies did the unpacking. Cheri and Leigh were curious as they joined in to help, and soon pottery, paintings, and handcrafted journals began to appear on the tables. I could hear Essie's exclamations of delight as we unpacked more items. Tadame could feel her excitement.

We reconvened with coffee mugs in hand and Tadame shared with the others our scouting spree over the weekend. Leigh was enthralled with one set of pottery in particular. It was a red–brown clay with a simple flower design and white glaze wash. Each plate was irregularly shaped and had a touch of whimsy, with the addition of an animal gazing out of the plate. One had a lion, another a fox, and yet another sported a gazelle. Then, they picked up a set of mugs that had fairies etched in them.

"What if we purchased four sets of varying kinds

of pottery?" Leigh spoke up. "Any of them would mix and match with the basic white settings we had ordered as our base dinnerware. They'd brighten up the tables and add some fun for our clients. It would show off a variety of artists, rather than just one. We could place display shelves with the pottery for sale in that corner of the café."

"Excellent!" I exclaimed. The others nodded, so I encouraged Leigh. "Why don't you choose the sets you like the best and we'll pick them up tomorrow? Dan was working on display shelves when I left this morning, so hopefully we'll have some ready for the photo shoot."

Cheri lifted up two paintings. "I love this blue-green etheric being that seems to emanate healing power. This one with the rich browns and greens of the forest and a pathway beckoning me right into the painting would be perfect behind my desk."

Tadame and I grinned at each other.

"I chose the forest scene and Alisha chose the other. We put in a few extra options, in case our instincts were off, but those were our first choices for your space," Tadame confessed.

"We'll purchase these two and Tadame has selected one for each healing room. Maybe we can select others to go on the back wall and the upstairs hallway, where the sun wouldn't hit them directly; those can be for sale. We also liked the look of these journals and thought they'd complement our café programs and any recommendations we make to people to journal as part of their healing journey."

Affirmations came from all around and we were ready to move to the next item on our agenda, when we heard a knock at the door.

Cheri leapt up and scurried out to see who it might be. We could hear her voice excitedly responding to whoever was on the other side; we wandered out to join her. We could see a delivery truck in the driveway with 'Gramma's Treasure Chest' emblazoned on the side. A burly gray-haired man was holding a clipboard for Cheri to sign.

"Hello there!" he chuckled as he took us all in. "I'm Reginald. I have your desk. Glad you're excited to receive it!"

Raman offered to give him a hand unloading it and we moved out of the way to give them room. As they approached the front door the two men looked at the desk and the opening. There was no way it was going to fit, even if they turned it on its side. They set it down.

Cheri poked her head out. "The patio doors are wider. I think we can get it through there," she offered helpfully.

We all rushed to assist in any way we could. There was no way that desk was going to be left outside. Tadame grabbed a blanket to protect the desk from the patio door casing. With a lot of fiddling, we successfully maneuvered it into place.

Thanking Reginald for his help, we all then stood back and admired the desk.

"It sure is a beaut!" Raman declared, running his hand over the wood. "You can finally get our business computer up and running."

"I can't wait!" Cheri avowed. "Working on my laptop is convenient when I'm out and about, but I'll really feel like we're taking off once I have everything centred here."

"Can I watch you? I was just getting into computers before I died. Facebook was fairly new. I'm sure a lot has changed since then and there hasn't been anyone in the house, so I'd love to learn from you, Cheri." Essie sounded excited.

"Sure, you can watch me, Essie. I'm surprised you're interested. My grandmother hates computers and gets agitated every time she has to use one."

"Och, I suppose not everyone takes to technology, but I love to learn, whatever the field."

"I hope I take after you when I'm ninety-eight. I'll be studying whatever's new then!" Cheri declared.

"With all your energy, I think you will, dearie."

"I have another surprise," Tadame divulged. She led us back to the café to the box she had brought in but not opened. She lifted the cover and we saw our pamphlets. "I dropped by the print shop on my way here. Our order was ready early, so I picked it up." We crowded around her and pulled out all our print resources. The work was excellent and we were well pleased.

"I sense Essie's pleasure," Tadame smiled.

Leigh encouraged us to take a seat and to taste some of the chocolate mousse they had made with grapefruit oil and fresh berries.

"These are anti-inflammatory, and the grapefruit oil is a stress-buster. I didn't realize just how much we'd be needing this today!" they confided.

We took a few minutes to let the healing power of food nurture us. Then, Raman offered to unpack the computer components for Cheri's desk as she put it all together. Tadame and I decided to start hanging the paintings in the healing rooms, with a bit of guidance from Essie who had definite opinions about their placement. Then, she helped Leigh sort through the pottery and make their selections, exclaiming over some of the unique designs.

CHAPTER SIXTEEN

Mid-afternoon, we heard another truck pull up outside. It was the delivery from IKEA. The rain had eased up a bit, so the transfer inside went without a hitch. We tore off the plastic coverings and placed one couch in amongst the reception area furniture. The other we carefully hoisted up the stairs. Pillows were added and Cheri's paintings were hung. We filled the small display shelves with our cards and pamphlets. One fit perfectly on the far side of Cheri's desk. The others we would place on the larger display shelves at the entryway, in the upstairs hall, and in the café. The Internet and phone line had been installed in the first week of July, so Cheri was able to hook everything up at her desk. Tadame had inventoried everything we had chosen to purchase, including which items we had selected for selling via consignment and what we'd decided to return. Those items were repacked and ready for us to deliver on

Tuesday.

"Hey gang, I need you all out here," Cheri cheerily called out to us.

We gradually drifted in from the various parts of the house we'd been working in.

"Over the next few days, I'll be installing our work programs and spreadsheets. I'll transfer all the data from my laptop and keep back-ups in the cloud. I will also set up our billing program and our website. It's important that I'm not the only one who knows how to use our system. So, we need to set a training day when I can work with you all to go through the basics," Cheri proposed.

A few moans were exchanged, but we all agreed it was necessary. Next week was our first aid course, so we decided that the following Monday, after our staff meeting, would be dedicated to computer training.

My cell dinged and I read out to the others that Ginny and four acting friends had agreed to come out on Friday mid-morning until mid-afternoon. Raman indicated his friend Lisa could also come. He was still awaiting responses from the rest of his running buddies. Leigh asked if they could invite one of their former classmates to assist in preparing and serving food on Friday. It would be a good chance to give someone a trial run as an assistant, which we would need once the business got established. We agreed to the wisdom of Leigh's suggestion. Feeling we had accomplished a lot, we planned for the rest of the week and decided to call it a day.

"It's truly coming together, Alisha. This dream of yours

from a few months ago is no longer just an idea. It's flying forward with this wonderful team you've pulled together." Essie's voice flowed over us as we prepared to leave.

"I feel that Essie is experiencing a profound sense of pleasure," Tadame indicated.

"I think seeing everything arrive today and observing the transformation of her home makes Alisha's dream seem more real to Essie. We're not just playing at this—it's for real!" declared Cheri.

"This may have begun as my dream, but it has evolved as each of you came into my life. This is not just my vision; it belongs to us all—you included, Essie. You had a feeling this house had something special to offer. You led each of us here and you've offered your input all along," I affirmed.

"Not that you always listened," Essie huffed.

"We listened, Essie," chuckled Raman. "We just might not always have agreed with your ways! It's exciting seeing it all take form. Just wait until we start taking bookings and we have to pay taxes. Then, we'll feel the reality of it all!" He waved as he went out the door.

The next few days flew by. Dan and Sabina finished the display shelves for the main room and café. Tadame and I picked up the pottery Leigh had selected, along with the various other items we had agreed to sell on consignment. Cheri spent long hours setting up all the computer programming, putting finishing touches on the website, and preparing our first blog posting. Raman juggled his last two job assignments and put in overtime to be sure our grounds looked to be flourishing for the photo shoot. Leigh helped set up displays and baked up a storm so we'd have a variety of foods to depict the café's creative cuisine.

On Friday, Leigh was up at 4:00 a.m. with their friend to assist in making all the fresh treats, so the café was redolent with delightful aromas as we arrived.

Melissa arrived early to set up indoor lighting. We began with the café. She captured Leigh working behind the counter. She arranged plates and bowls of food, and mugs of coffee, snapping steadily with her camera. She focused in on the pottery displays. When our volunteers arrived, she positioned them in casual groupings—some with food, others with coffee mugs and a journal. It was fascinating to watch her work: a quick adjustment here, an encouraging word, a quip to bring a smile, and—voilà—a fantastic photo. It felt like Melissa's finger was constantly depressing the shutter button, moving from one angle to another to capture something her artist's eye had spotted.

"This is so exciting. Melissa is doing an amazing job. She seems to know exactly how to handle each person and each setting," Essie whispered eagerly in my ear. *"I like that the mixture of actors and runners are different ages, sizes, and shapes, and come from different cultures. It shows that what you're offering here is for everyone."*

We shifted to the main room and then used one of the therapy rooms with different people set up as clients and each therapist doing their thing. While that was happening, the rest were able to dive into Leigh's treats. I could tell by the exclamations of pleasure that all appreciated Leigh's talents. When I came out from my photo session, Ginny gestured me over to her table.

"Mom, my friends and I think Leigh's food is fabulous. We were wondering if we could book a cast party here a week from Sunday—that's our dark night, no shows. I know you don't have everything finished, but it'd be the perfect spot. One of our cast members is leaving Bright Haven to accept a part in Toronto. We'd really like to throw him a party before he goes. What do you think?"

"I'd have to check with the rest of my team, but it sounds like a possibility," I responded. "Can I let you know tonight? How many people are we talking about?"

Ginny looked at her friends for confirmation. "Probably fifty or so."

Ginny's friends nodded in agreement and bubbled over with how much they loved the setting and the food.

Melissa nabbed a quick snack break and then selected a few models for the outdoor shots. Raman went with her to point out areas of interest, including the labyrinth. Ginny headed out with him and I noticed she and Raman talked animatedly to one another. While they headed out, Raman's friend Lisa beckoned me over.

"Alisha, my friends and I were just talking about a

race we have coming up. We were thinking, what if you set up at the race with one or two tables and offered mini-sessions to runners afterward? It would be a great way to get your name out there," Lisa eagerly shared.

I sat down with the table of runners. This sounded like an idea with great potential. One of them pulled out his cell phone and called up a calendar of races over the next month. He highlighted the most popular ones and then bounced the information to my email. I thanked them all for volunteering their time and they declared the food, gift certificates, and the brief energy work they'd received were well worth it!

Shortly thereafter, Melissa returned. Ginny and her crew had to leave. As she waved goodbye, she called out to Raman, "See you later."

I turned an inquiring look toward him.

He shrugged. "Ginny invited me to join her and her friends at a karaoke bar after their show tonight. I thought it might be fun."

He directed his attention to his running friends and expressed his thanks as they departed. Leigh's friend headed off as well.

The final photos were our individual and team photos. Melissa had us pose in various places and positions, so we'd have lots to choose from for our website. She skimmed through a few of the day's photos, so we'd have a feel for what she'd captured. We were delighted. Leigh had made up a tray of food to send with her as a thank-you. She eagerly stashed it in her car after dismantling and storing the lighting and other equipment she'd brought. Cheri gave her an enthusiastic kiss and hug before she departed. Melissa offered an eager response. Since I had notified everyone I needed a brief team meeting, Tadame offered to drive Cheri home later.

As we went to sit down, Cheri whispered, "I still don't know what she's up to some nights, but I'm practising trust. Things feel good between us."

I quickly filled everyone in on Ginny's request and the runners' suggestions.

Raman responded first. "These both sound like solid opportunities to begin building our clientele. But, the party is going to impact Leigh more than the rest of us."

Leigh was busily scratching notes and ideas in a journal I'd noticed them use before. Leigh said, "I could do this, but I'd need the rest of you on deck to act as hosts and servers. We could set up various food stations in the main room, in the café, and on the veranda. It can be buffet style. We'd have to keep the stations replenished and circulate with trays now and then. We can have seating inside and out, depending on the weather. I'd suggest we offer fresh fruit and or vegetable drinks. If we serve alcohol, that should be sold separately at the counter so we can control consumption."

Cheri jumped in. "That's good. Our application for a liquor licence was approved. It arrived in this week's mail. If we set the event up this way we won't need extra staff."

"Wow, Leigh. I'm impressed!" Tadame exclaimed. "This would be a great way to highlight our café and we could write it up in our blog. Perhaps Ginny could do a short write-up for the newspaper afterwards? I'd be down with serving, Leigh, but how do we figure out what to charge?"

"Once Leigh develops a menu, I can work out the food costs, the cost of napkins and accessories, a portion for our overhead, our labour time, and add a percentage for profit. It's really important that we keep this consistent, even when we're dealing with friends and family," Cheri said firmly.

"I agree," Tadame asserted. "We're not a charity. We're a business. A lot of our early clientele are going to be family and friends. They'll be trying to support us, so we need to show the value of what we're offering from the beginning."

Raman looked around at each of us. "It seems we're all in for this. Once we know the date, I'll arrange to finish early that day, so I can be available to help as needed."

"Leigh, could you draft a sample menu for Ginny and her friends, and work with Cheri on the cost estimate so they'll know what they're committing to?" I suggested.

Leigh nodded as they continued writing in their notebook.

"We should be able to have this decided by our Monday team meeting," I surmised.

Raman interjected, "I know we usually meet at nine, but could we make it ten on Monday? That would give me time to get a few hours in at work; then, I'll be ready to sit a bit. I need to get as much done on Monday as possible because of our course on Tuesday and Wednesday. I can't wait to complete this final job!"

Tadame rested her chin in her hand. "Raman, I admire how you're juggling all this. I'll be glad for you when you're done, too. Now, what about this race suggestion? It sounds like a fun idea to me for some free advertising."

Cheri added, "Races include a cross-section of ages, so we'd reach a good mix of people. I'd like to do it."

"I can look into it a bit more and contact some of the race directors. We can discuss it at our Monday meeting," I offered.

"Agreed!" everyone chorused. We were all starting to come down from the adrenaline rush of the day. We gave Leigh a hand cleaning up and each of us selected a few treats to take home. With a cheery farewell, we took our leave of one another.

CHAPTER SEVENTEEN

Over the weekend, I enjoyed a long slow run and time in my sorely neglected flower beds at home. Our rhubarb harvest was abundant, so I transformed a portion of it into jam. I texted Leigh to see if they had any interest in the rest of the crop and they were thrilled at the prospect of bottling sauces to use later in the café. All in all, I spent a lovely weekend calming myself before the next rash of busyness hit.

On Monday, I awoke early and decided to make gluten-free rhubarb tarts to take to our team meeting. I experimented with coconut flour and lots of butter for the crust and added some of my jam as the filling. I popped one in my mouth and the flavours blended exquisitely together. Excited, I arranged them in a pretty tin and set off for Essie's place.

When I arrived, a quick glance into the café revealed Leigh at the coffee maker, preparing a fresh pot. I called out a greeting and Leigh turned with a smile. The door opened behind me and Tadame slipped in with Cheri. Through the open door, I could see Raman's truck pulling into the driveway. As I hugged the others in greeting, he climbed out with a small container in his hand and sauntered over to join us.

As we went into the café, I held up my offering.

"I've brought gluten free rhubarb tarts. Leigh, I don't want you to always feel you have to prepare a treat for our meetings. I know you enjoy trying things out on us, but I'd like you to feel you can take a break sometimes too!"

Raman grinned and held up his tin. "I had the same thought! I have a small strawberry patch in a sheltered area and some of the early berries have ripened. I have strawberries dipped in dark chocolate to share."

Tadame laughed, "I texted Leigh yesterday to say I'd bring something. I have strawberry mint squares with a rhubarb cream sauce to pour over them."

Cheri chimed in. "Glad I checked in with Tadame or we'd be spending our whole meeting eating! Are we foodies or what?"

"How lucky you are to be able to taste the tartness and sweetness of those treats! One of my fondest memories was making Stanley's favourite strawberry rhubarb crisp," Essie recalled.

As they set the coffee pot in the middle of our table, Leigh put a hand on my shoulder. "I appreciate you doing this. While I enjoy making treats for you all, and it has never felt like an expectation you put on me, it's also fun to experience other's cooking. It often stimulates new ideas for my work," they reassured. "Getting the proposal ready for the cast party has taken a lot of time, so I wouldn't have had time to prepare any treats for today."

"That had crossed my mind when I texted," Tadame confessed.

"Maybe we could take turns bringing in a treat," Cheri suggested. "I enjoy experimenting now and then. It certainly won't be up to Leigh's standards, but I think it's fun to share."

"Sharing food isn't really meant to be a competitive experience, in my opinion," reflected Raman. "It's an expression of affection and creates a bond between people."

"Let's get this bond established. I skipped breakfast and I'm famished!" Cheri declared.

We dove in with a mutual agreement that we would give our full attention to the food and our taste buds before starting into business. As we savoured the morning's offerings, our moans of pleasure echoed around the café. We sipped our coffee, crunched the tarts, slid the tangy delight of Tadame's squares into our mouths, and licked melted dark chocolate from Raman's berries off our fingers. It was an unforgettable feast. Leigh insisted on having our recipes to add to their collection.

Well satisfied, we settled into Leigh and Cheri's presentation and cost analysis for Ginny's cast party. They had received approval from Ginny and her friends. Leigh had mapped out the food stations for us and a detailed checklist of duties for everyone. Cheri suggested they email it to her, so she could enter it into our database for future reference. The only area requiring discussion was with regard to liquor. Leigh recommended we choose two local wineries and two craft beer stores to offer a few selections. It was agreed we didn't want to get into a full bar service because that didn't jive with our healing focus. We tossed around the names of local places with which we were familiar and that had established reputations. From these, Leigh chose wine and beer that would complement the food they had planned. Raman volunteered that he had taken a bar tending course to supplement his income while studying, so he could supervise that station.

After making a few minor changes, Cheri sent the revised fee structure, which included the liquor costs, to Ginny for her friends. Next, Cheri indicated she'd need to obtain a cash float to be able to make change as people paid us. Since we hadn't planned on starting quite so soon, the debit and credit machines she'd ordered for the business hadn't yet arrived. An additional text was sent to Ginny, letting her know we'd need cash payment for everything.

I directed our attention to the next agenda item: offering mini-sessions at local road races. I had heard back from four of six race directors, and all were eager to have us participate at their races. Leigh inquired about offering protein bites to help race recovery which would introduce people to our café as well. Raman wondered about having some of his herbal creams and Tadame's healing oil samples for people to try post-race. I agreed to clarify those possibilities with the race directors to ensure we didn't conflict with local businesses that might be involved. The first race was in ten days, so we had time to figure out the details.

Raman reported that he'd be finished his final job that evening. Cheers erupted all around. He went on to share an idea he'd been mulling over. "What if we sent invites to local yoga studios or churches to experience a walk through our labyrinth?"

"We could offer a short introduction in the café, where they could return for a light snack and discussion after their experience." Leigh proposed.

"Would the walk be free? Guests would still be paying for what they purchase in the café," said Cheri.

"My original vision was that people who wanted to experience the beauty of the gardens and the power of the labyrinth could do so freely," I shared.

"I agree. If we ran programs such as 'growing healing herbs' and I used the gardens to educate people in that discipline or if we ran, say, a four-week program on 'seeking healing direction in the labyrinth', then I feel we should charge a program fee," Raman suggested.

I could see the gears shifting in Tadame's mind as she listened to our conversation.

"Sounds like the labyrinth walk will be similar to our mini-sessions at the races. It will introduce people to our setting and what we have to offer; I agree they should be free. I wonder if we could have a jug of sun tea and a plate of chocolate cranberry wafers—again for free—as part of our invitation. Anyone wanting anything more can then purchase from the café. We could include tours of the building and have our pamphlets available as handouts. Of course, all our consignment items would also be for sale."

I looked at Raman. "What about developing your ideas into programs that we could offer early in the fall, for which people could pre-register?"

"I've actually been thinking about this. I feel four weeks is a manageable time for people to initially commit to trying something new; then, we can offer longer, more advanced courses if interest builds. September will be harvest time, so I wondered about doing a series on harvesting and storing healing herbs. I also thought of a series on cooking with healing herbs," Raman offered.

"Back in my mother's day, people knew the healing power of local plants. With the advent of the pharmaceutical industry, people turned to quick drug fixes and lost the wisdom of natural sources for healing," Essie declared.

"I'd love to team up to do the cooking one," Leigh volunteered.

"I was counting on that!" Raman grinned. "Tadame, I was wondering about a series on essential oils to support wellbeing and, Alisha, you have experience of leading groups for spiritual development, so perhaps you can work with the labyrinth or journal writing. Cheri, with your yoga background, I wondered if you might be able to do a yoga series specifically for runners, because we'll already be interacting with that population."

"Somebody's brain has sure been in high gear," Cheri exclaimed.

"When I was out working those last few jobs, my mind kept jumping ahead to all these ideas. It's like this swirl of excitement inside that I can't hold back any longer. It's coming unleashed!" Raman confessed.

"I say, let it roll. I love all those ideas. Perhaps we could plan two program nights a week, because we'd need other nights free for people who can only book sessions with us in the evening. Also, we don't want to stretch ourselves too thin by trying to do everything at once," Tadame cautioned.

Cheri jumped in. "We haven't really talked about how we'll handle scheduling or sharing the cleaning."

"I have some ideas if everyone wants to talk about that now?" Leigh inquired, looking around at the rest of us.

Nods encouraged them to continue.

"I was thinking we should have at least one day of complete shutdown, like Sunday. We should each have another full day off every week. If we work some evenings it would be important to take another block of time off, maybe in the early morning or afternoon. We need to model good self-care if we're going to truly be a healing place."

"Listen to them! Leigh is making a very important point."

"I wholeheartedly agree," Tadame asserted. "I've

worked in places that expect you to be at the client's beck and call—coming in early, or late, or whenever is needed—and you never really get time off. Don't get me wrong, I care about the people who come to us, but if we create a schedule and stick to it, they'll find a way to make it work. I've watched friends tumble into burnout and try to drag themselves to work, with nothing left to offer the client. I don't want to see that happen with us!"

"Along that vein of thought, I strongly feel we should hire someone to clean for us on our closedown day. We can maintain a daily touch-up in bathrooms and sanitize our rooms, but at least once a week we'll need a deep clean of floors, bathrooms, and the café area. We'll have more than enough on our plates, so a professional cleaner would be best, in my opinion," Cheri shared.

"I bet you've even checked some out," Tadame conjectured.

Cheri grinned wryly. "You'd win that bet. I checked out a variety of local cleaning businesses and I have two that were within a similar price range with good ratings in the better business bureau listing." On her laptop, she pulled up the information on each business, so we could all peruse them together. The prices seemed reasonable to us, so we authorized Cheri to contact and book one to start with us in September. We would begin with a two-month trial to be sure they were suitable and consider a longer-term contract after that period.

Leigh and I preferred to have two days off in a

row, so we opted for Monday as our day off. We agreed the café would be open Tuesday to Saturday and only on the evenings we booked programs. Raman suggested we hire Leigh's friend part-time or others as needed, depending on the response to the café. This was critical since Leigh would need early morning prep time and opportunity to do the shopping.

Cheri liked to go out dancing on Friday evenings so she said Saturday would be a good second day for her. Since we all would be trained on the computer, we'd take turns covering the desk on Saturdays. Tadame claimed she'd enjoy a day off during the week so she could go to her own appointments and do things at home; Thursday was her choice. Raman chose Wednesday. With everyone's preferences in mind, I suggested that perhaps Tuesday mornings from 8:00 a.m. to 9:00 a.m. could be our staff meeting. That seemed favourable to the whole crew.

Cheri busily took notes and promised to put this into a schedule format for us, so we could all get a sense of the flow of who would be working and if there were any gaps we'd need to cover.

As Cheri was tapping away on her laptop, the doorbell rang and I heard Essie gasp, *"Oh no!"*

As Raman went to answer the door, Tadame asked, "What's happening? I sense Essie's distressed."

I shrugged my shoulders. "Essie?"

"Prepare yourselves. You've got company, and I didnae send them!" she huffed.

A man and woman in their mid-thirties followed Raman into the café. He wore a business suit. She was dressed in a teal blue silk pantsuit, four-inch stiletto heels, and a floppy hat atop a perfectly coiffured hairstyle. Words gushed from her mouth as she pirouetted around, taking in the café and Great Room. The man ignored her as he focused on his iPhone. Raman's eyebrows arched as high as they could go.

"Just look at this place! I told you it was worth more than we got for it. The grounds are larger than I remembered and could easily have fit four apartment complexes—maybe more. Bradley, are you listening to me?"

Bradley grunted in reply, without looking up. The woman finally noticed us as we stood up from our seats. She took a few mincing steps toward me.

"I recognize you from the website. I read the blog posting about Essie and Stanley and I just had to come over. My grandmother, Petunia, was Essie's favourite cousin and this place should have been ours, right Bradley?"

I heard Essie's loud snort echo in my ears.

Eventually, Bradley tore his gaze from his phone. "Cassie, you know it was left to all the cousins equally."

"We should have bought it out from the others! This could have been a wonderful income property for us," Cassie declared.

"If you hadn't taken that trip to Rome, the jaunt to Australia, and that cruise down the Nile, maybe it would have been possible," Bradley pointed out, his eyes drawn again to the phone vibrating in his hand. "Excuse me, I have to take this," he said as he stepped into the Great Room.

None of us quite knew what to say, but we needn't have worried because she barrelled onward.

"Those other cousins, they had no real connection with Ellie," she proclaimed dramatically.

"You mean Essie," I interjected.

"That's what I said," Cassie retorted. "My cousins were only interested in the money and they wanted it quickly."

"Wasn't this property for sale for ten years?" inquired Cheri innocently.

Raman coughed into his sleeve, trying to cover his snort of laughter.

Cassie glared at the interruption. "That's my point. They wanted the money immediately and the realtor had trouble selling the place, so we were paid much less than it's worth."

"Would you like a cup of coffee or tea?" Leigh offered in an attempt to be hospitable, or perhaps as a ploy to stop the words erupting from her mouth.

"Thank you, young man. One cream and one sugar, and make sure it's hot," she snapped condescendingly. I opened my mouth to correct her gender mistake, but Leigh shook their head. I remained silent.

After a small sip, Cassie spoke again. "At least you make good coffee. Now, I would like a tour to see what you've done with this place. I would have torn it down, but I can see it did have some potential."

No one else seemed eager to do the job, so I stepped forward to guide her through the house. It was a quick tour because Cassie wasn't really interested in what we were offering; she simply wanted a look around. We passed Bradley animatedly striding up and down the Great Room as he dealt with a client. On our way back through, he thrust his phone into his pocket and joined us. "Okay Cass, you've had your look and your say. It's time to go."

"But if I spoke to my lawyer and had him come out here…."

"Cass, let it go. We all had our chance and didn't take it. Just because you saw these people doing something wonderful here, doesn't mean you can barge in on them and try to get more. From what I can see, they've put a lot of money and effort into restoring this place. It may be worth a lot more now, but when they bought it, we got what it was worth then."

"But…."

"Oh stop your caterwauling. I never liked your grandmother and you seem an awful lot like her. You got what you deserved—now git! These are good people, doing something good for the community and I want them in my house!"

It seemed Cassie heard Essie's proclamation because her head started to swivel from side to side as she looked for the source of the voice. She turned very pale. She clutched Bradley's arm, but he seemed unaffected; he was obviously not tuned in.

"Did you hear that?"

"Hear what?" Bradley asked impatiently. "Cassie, I have to get back to the office for a client meeting. Let's go."

Cassie looked at the rest of us. I drew in a breath for confidence and stepped forward.

"As you can see, we have very different ideas about what is best for this place. It's always a pleasure to share with others our dream of Essie's Healing Place. Our tour is complete. Let me show you the way out."

"Go! Do the travelling you love so much, Cassie, but leave my place alone. Be satisfied with what you have and appreciate that brother of yours who's so good to you."

Bradley extended his hand to Raman and to me.

"Thank you for letting us in, and for giving Cassie a tour. I hope we didn't inconvenience you too much. Good luck with your business. If Essie were here, I think she'd approve."

Bradley took the arm of the now-quiet Cassie and guided her toward their car.

The door closed firmly behind them and the room erupted in squeals of laughter.

"Look at you go, Alisha!" Cheri hip-bumped me.

I inquired for all of us. "Essie, care to explain?"

"I'm sorry you had to experience that! I wasn't paying attention, so they were at the door before I had an opportunity to prepare you. They're part of my delightful extended family—the distant cousins I mentioned before. I didn't think any of them would actually show up. I thought I had scared them all off and that they were glad to be rid of the place. I

should have warned you about them, especially Petunia's daughter; they're money grabbers. Although, I must say I was pleasantly surprised by young Bradley."

Cheri continued in conversation with Essie. Raman set off to finish up his final job. I knew Tadame could feel Essie's earnest concern, so I filled her in on what Essie had revealed as we tidied up our mugs. The doorbell pealed again. We looked in apprehension at each other. Had Cassie come back on her own?

CHAPTER EIGHTEEN

Leigh answered the door this time. We heard excited conversation and, as we looked to the entryway, we could see them talking with Jace Conter. Together, they walked into the café.

"Wow, this place is incredible! I checked out your website and first blog posting. The photos are fabulous, but I couldn't wait to come see it for myself." Jace crossed the room to shake our hands.

"I'm glad our posting is getting traffic. Good to see you again, Jace," said Cheri.

"Have you found an apartment and settled in?" Tadame inquired as she shook his hand.

"Yes, I was fortunate. Someone had to break their lease. I called and the manager wanted a new tenant right away, so it all fell into place. It's a lovely, spacious apartment located behind a grocery store, which is convenient," Jace replied.

Tadame grinned. "It sure is! And it overlooks a

local trail system so if you like hiking, biking, or running, we have immediate access. Welcome to the neighbourhood!"

"You live there?" Jace queried.

"My husband Ronnie and I do, yes. So, if you need a hand any time, just drop by. We're in Number Six."

"Welcome to Bright Haven." I extended my hand to Jace's warm friendly grip. "How's the work search going?"

"Do you have a few minutes to sit and chat?" Jace looked around at us.

Leigh suggested we might be ready for a fresh pot of coffee. Tadame put a plate on the table so Jace could try some of the leftover treats and Cheri wiped off the table. As they made preparations, Jace meandered around the café with me. He ran his hand over the tables and chairs, admiring the workmanship. He chuckled over the whimsical pottery designs on display and flipped through one of the hand-crafted journals. When Leigh called out that the coffee was ready, we gathered around the table.

Jace took a mouthful and then began. "Before I met you in Hope Falls, I'd done some initial searching and I continued that when I arrived in Bright Haven. I did receive an offer from a good clinic, but after meeting all of you and listening to your vision for this healing place, all I could think about was that I wanted to be part of what you're building. I know you're not up and running yet, but I could probably get seasonal work through the summer, bartending or waiting tables. I did that every summer when I was teaching."

Jace paused to take a breath and I intervened.

"Jace, there are some things we'll need to share up front. We set our business up as a team, so no one person makes the decisions; we work things out together. We each have different areas of expertise, but we value each other's questions and opinions in all aspects of the business. We're set up as a corporation and we've all put in varying amounts of money to get things rolling. We each have shares based on that contribution. The number of shares we own doesn't affect how much say we have; the shares only influence additional income we receive at the end of the year. We're all salaried in this set-up, although any part-time staff we hire will be paid a fair hourly wage."

"I fully support a team model and the way you've set up your business. I do have some savings invested from when my wife and I sold our house after our divorce. If you accepted me onto the team, I can contribute to the corporation. Other than Leigh, I know the rest of you don't really know me. I can give you some references and offer free massages, so you can get a feel for my work," he grinned.

"You haven't met Raman, who's another key team member, or Essie," stated Cheri.

"We're on our first aid and CPR course tomorrow and Wednesday," I reflected.

"The one hosted at the Delta?" Jace inquired.

"Yes," I replied.

Jace laughed. "I guess I'll see you all there. I enrolled to update my skills."

"That's great," Tadame contributed. "We'll all have the chance to get to know each other and sense how we would work together in a fairly low-key setting."

"Jace, you've got me thinking. We've had lots of opportunity to try out Leigh's specialties and see the results of Raman's handiwork outdoors, but we haven't actually experienced all of each other's talents. Our focus and energy have been on getting our business setting prepared and organized. What if we took Friday as a self-care and sharing day?"

"I could lead everyone through a basic yoga session," Cheri volunteered. "And I'd love to receive a massage or any other healing session."

"Some things we could do as a group, like an introduction to some of the essential oils I use," Tadame suggested.

Cheri texted Raman to let him know what we were planning and he responded, "Count me in!"

We spent the next twenty minutes planning the day. Then, Jace raised the question of Essie. "You mentioned Essie. I know you've named the business Essie's Healing Place and I read the history of Essie and Stanley. Is that the Essie to whom you're referring?"

"That would be me, dearie!" Essie chimed in.

Jace didn't respond.

"That's strange. I spoke directly to him. There must be

some blockage there," Essie asserted.

From the direction of Cheri's gaze and the slight ripple I could see in the air, Essie was standing close to Jace. Jace was looking inquiringly at us because of the long pause we had allowed in the conversation.

"What's your opinion of ghosts or spirit voices, Jace?" Cheri inquired.

Jace looked uncomfortable. "Is that pertinent to my work here?" he asked cautiously.

"It might be," I confessed. "You see, the rest of us see, hear, or feel, Essie, who is a spirit still inhabiting this place."

"You all believe in that stuff?" Jace probed.

"I didn't understand at first," Leigh assured Jace. "I just kept hearing this grandmotherly voice in my mind, helping me out. It wasn't until I met Alisha, who told me it was Essie, that I began to realize she was for real, and as others heard her too, I started to truly believe."

"Essie doesn't reveal herself to everyone, but all of us as the team of this healing place need to be aware of her. As Leigh mentioned, she communicates with us all, in slightly different ways. It's okay if you don't believe in spirits, but you'll need to be comfortable with the rest of us experiencing that type of interaction." I explained.

"It's not that I don't believe in spirits. When I was a child, I heard voices all the time. I was too young to understand what I was experiencing, but it scared my parents and they passed that fear on to me. I eventually learned to shut off that hearing sense and block out any communication other than in this dimension. Until today, I've never spoken to anyone about this kind of thing," Jace shared courageously.

"I knew something was awry!" Essie exclaimed. *"If he had extrasensory perception at a young age with only fearful people to guide him, no wonder he shut that down. He was probably terrified he'd be labelled as crazy!"*

"Jace, some of the healing work I do is with people who've been through traumatic experiences. If you're interested, on Friday we could work with a tapping protocol to ease some of that childhood fear?" I offered.

"I'll think about it," said Jace. "I'm comfortable with all of you hearing Essie. I may need time before deciding if I want to open up to that experience myself."

"It's entirely up to you," I assured him.

"On another note, this food is amazing! Thanks for sharing. Would it be possible to get a tour of the house and grounds?" Jace inquired.

"I can do that," offered Tadame. "Let's take a look inside first."

"I'm going to tidy up here; then, I'll join you for the outside tour, so I can show Jace my place." Leigh jumped into action.

"I need to get onto the computer to deal with some of the things from our meeting earlier this morning," Cheri stated as she gathered up her laptop. "It's hard to believe that was only a couple of hours ago!"

"Was that even today?" I groaned. "I have work

from that meeting as well. I'll just pour another cup of coffee, help myself to one more strawberry, and work from that table over there." I settled down in the back corner of the café and set to work on catching up on email correspondence. I barely heard the others walk through to the veranda and outside.

Jace left after his tour, commenting on the tranquility invoked by the grounds and his curiosity about the various healing herbs in Raman's garden. We promised to watch out for him at the course the next day. I was left with an impression of sensitivity and strength emanating from Jace. His place on the team wasn't as clear to me as it had been with the others, but I trusted that all was unfolding as it needed to.

We all arrived early at the Delta the next morning which gave us the opportunity to introduce Jace and Raman. They discovered a common interest in Wayne Dyer's work when Raman spotted the book *Excuses Be Gone* protruding from Jace's backpack. As they explored which of his books they'd each read and started delving into their favourite teachings, the rest of us led the way into the conference room where our class was to be held. We found a section of seats together and settled in. We took a moment to flip through the booklets we'd been handed at the registration table while Jace and Raman continued to chat. Leigh was avidly listening and at one point asked a question. Cheri stirred the pot, opining that she sometimes found Dyer to be condescending.

Tadame and I grinned at each other as a lively discussion ensued.

The room slowly filled with other participants and the leadership team entered. The day flew by. Even though I'd taken the course before, there was a lot I'd forgotten because I didn't use the information on a regular basis.

Jace, Leigh, and I decided to take a walk during our lunch break. We kept the conversation light, talking about favourite movies. Jace asked Leigh about the best place in Bright Haven to pick up fresh herbs for cooking. He had learned how to cook for himself in the last few years and preferred using fresh over dried herbs whenever possible. Leigh became very animated as they discussed one of their passions. I let their conversation flow over me as I soaked in the sunshine and fresh air. I admired the way Jace drew out Leigh's strengths and demonstrated a willingness to learn from Leigh's expertise, even though Leigh was younger and had been Jace's student. There was a kindness to Jace that I appreciated.

The next day, Tadame, Raman and I walked together. The others had decided to try a sushi bar nearby. As we walked, I invited their impressions of Jace.

"I like him. He's confident, but not overbearing. He's interested in each of our areas of work and seems genuine in seeking to understand what we offer. He seems to flow well with our team," Tadame offered.

Raman took time to form his response, so we walked in silence for a few minutes. "I feel comfortable with him. He seems to exude a feeling of trustworthiness; yet, I have this sense there is a part of him that he holds back. It's difficult to put my finger on it exactly."

We hadn't had a chance to share with Raman Jace's response to Essie, so it was interesting that he picked up on a block in Jace.

We shared what Jace had told us and Raman suggested, "We've all had different issues we've been dealing with on our individual healing journeys. Some of us have been fortunate to have had the people and support we've needed show up when we were ready for them. I wonder if we might be the people for Jace, if he chooses to deal with that part of his journey?"

Tadame contributed, "It's helpful to be reminded of that, Raman. I know when I quit my job, I'd gotten to the point where I just couldn't do anything else; I had to move forward in a new way. Then, you all came along and we seemed to click, but it has taken time to build trust and feel safe with each other. Jace needs his own healing time and we need to give him the opportunity to know us better. I feel he was hugely courageous to share as much as he did with us on Monday."

"I was a little shocked he was willing to be that vulnerable with us, but I appreciated the trust he put in us to hear what he had to say. I feel his honesty was a solid first step in building a relationship with us. Perhaps Jace is a good reminder that we don't have to be perfect with each other," I expressed wryly.

"What? You're not perfect—the former minister, mother, and healer?" Raman teased.

I lightly punched him on the shoulder. "I pulled off that mask when I left the ministry and there is no way I'm putting it back on. What you get is the real me, like it or lump it!"

Tadame put her arm around me and gave me a quick squeeze. "Oh we like it, most of the time," she quipped with a smile. "Seriously, that's why I'm on this team. There's room for me to be myself—to share my story, to voice my opinion without fear of losing my job."

"I suspect we all have pieces we haven't shared yet with one another, but from the beginning, Alisha, you've set a tone of open, honest communication amongst us. I'd like Jace to be a part of our team. I feel he's meant to be with us," Raman added.

"Shall I check in with the other two when I get a chance? If there's any strong disagreement, I'll call a team meeting but, if not, shall we welcome Jace on Friday morning before we do our sessions together?" I asked.

"That sounds good to me," shared Tadame. "Then Jace can relax into the sessions and not feel he's being evaluated."

Raman and I nodded in agreement with Tadame's insight. The conversation shifted to more general topics as we made our way back to the Delta.

As I was driving home after the course, relieved to have it completed, my cell phone buzzed with a message. I found a spot to pull over in case Dan had messaged me to pick something up, but it was from Sabina, asking me to call. I dialled her number and she picked up on the first ring.

"Hey, Mom."

"What's up, honey?" I asked.

"Are you free Saturday?"

"I think it's clear. Why?" I tried to draw out more information.

"My friend Trish is going to be home this weekend and we thought we'd go shopping for my dress. Do you want to come along?"

Does she really want you to go or is she just asking because she thinks she should?

My old friend Doubt leapt into expression. Sabina and I didn't always have an easy relationship; I had been careful not to ask too much about the wedding, so she wouldn't feel I was pressuring her with my ideas. But to go dress shopping with her....

"Mom?"

"Yes, yes! I'd love to join you. What time and where?" my excitement leaked out.

"There's a wedding boutique here in town that I'd like to try first. Then, there's the Wedding Barn twenty minutes east of Bright Haven. Can you meet us at my apartment around ten a.m. and can we use your car? Tommy's borrowing mine to run errands," Sabina proposed.

"Sure, I'll see you at ten." I hung up, excited and

apprehensive. I decided to be proactive on Saturday and allow myself time to tap and set the intention that it would be a fabulous day together!

Back on the road, I headed home for an enjoyable supper with Dan, catching him up on all the latest developments at work and with Sabina. We decided to take a short hike after eating and then snuggled in for a light romantic comedy that had us still chuckling as we made our way to bed.

CHAPTER NINETEEN

On Friday morning, we gathered at 8:00am at Essie's place. We spread our yoga mats out in the Great Room, ready for a class with Cheri. Cheri was the last to arrive, stretching into a huge yawn as she came through the door.

"I was out dancing last night. I'm still waking up." She looked around. "We're all here?"

We offered nods and murmurs of assent in reply.

"Alisha, you have something you want to share before we start our class."

I stepped over in front of Jace, who looked up at me with a curious expression.

"Jace, by unanimous decision, our team would like to invite you to become a part of Essie's Healing Place."

Jace's face lit with pleasure.

"We wanted to express this before we got into our day, so you can relax and enjoy the day without feeling like you're being judged or assessed by us for a position here."

"We appreciate your honesty and we think you're a good fit for us. But, you don't have to give us your answer right away," Raman began.

Jace jumped in. "Are you kidding? I want in! I was drawn to the vibe you guys emanated when I first bumped into you in Hope Falls." He grinned wickedly at me. "Seeing the environment you've created here, and the respect you have for each other, solidifies for me that this is where I need to be."

"Awesome!" cheered Leigh, who immediately raced over to hug their former teacher and new teammate. We all took a moment to extend a handshake or hug of welcome to Jace.

"I'm definitely going to enjoy this day!" he exclaimed.

"Let's get this show on the road, then," Cheri proclaimed. "First, you all may see me as the energizer bunny, so this side of me may feel different. The whole reason I have steady energy is because I practice yoga daily. It's a wonderful practice for all stages and situations in life as it builds flexibility and strength in the body, but also helps you relax. It improves focus and is the best stress buster I've ever experienced."

"I joined a yoga class when I was in Hope Falls. One of my instructors recommended it as a way of managing the physical demands placed on our bodies as massage therapists," Jace shared.

"I have to confess, I've only tried it sporadically,

so please go easy on this beginner," I pleaded.

The others had varying amounts of exposure to yoga but we were all keen to give ourselves over to Cheri's guidance.

"Let's begin on our mats, lying on our backs, slowly breathing in and out. Let your body soften and sink into your mat. Feel the support of the ground below you. Deeply breathing, pull in that refreshing breath to the very core of your being, and release all the pent-up energy you've been holding as you breathe out." Cheri's voice flowed in and around us as she led us from one movement to another, walking around our mats and gently repositioning us as needed, or demonstrating how to make a movement easier or more challenging for us.

We finished lying quietly on our mats in the Savasana pose, feeling supple, refreshed, and energized for the rest of the day together. We each got up in our own time and quietly exited to the café where Leigh had set out jugs of mint cucumber water. We quenched our thirst and looked at the schedule Cheri had posted for our day. Leigh was scheduled to receive a reflexology session from Tadame, Cheri was to receive a massage from Jace, and Raman was with me. We allowed time to change out of our sweaty yoga clothing and moved to our assigned healing rooms.

Surprisingly, I was feeling a little nervous. Although we'd all been sharing in a variety of ways with each other and we talked lots about our healing approaches, this was the first time I had offered this aspect of myself to a team member. Raman entered the room and I could sense the stiffness in his body.

I decided to speak up, "Welcome to my den of iniquity."

Raman looked startled and Essie piped in, *"Really Alisha!"*

I apologized. "I'm sorry. I was trying to be funny in an effort to relax us because I'm feeling nervous."

Raman released his breath with a laugh. "Yeah, me too."

"Why don't you have a seat and we'll just chat for a minute."

Raman sat on the massage table and I sat in the chair. "I've been doing this for years as part of my ministry and I believe in what I do, but whenever I offer it for the first time to a new person, I worry that it won't be what they're expecting. I don't usually tell them this. I just push myself to trust the work and to let it flow. But doing this with each other today, there just seems to be more weight to it somehow," I confessed.

"Why don't we agree to let go of the weight and simply trust each other?" Raman suggested. "I don't have any particular expectations for this session because I've never had one like it. I've experienced massage, but not what you do. Just start with your usual spiel and if I have questions I'll ask. Okay?"

"Agreed," I affirmed with relief. "Essie, this session is private. Perhaps you could leave us alone." I spoke to the corner of the room where I could see a slight waver of energy.

"I just wanted to see what you do, Alisha. It's new to me too," Essie stated crossly.

Raman extended his hand in the direction I was looking. "It's okay with me if you watch, Essie."

"Fine," I affirmed. "However, everything we do, say, or experience here is fully confidential. Raman is the only one with permission to share whatever happens here. Essie, neither you nor I will mention any of this to the others. I don't even share anything out of my sessions with Dan. If we're around others, I won't ask Raman about how he's doing in relation to any aspect of the healing time we share. I might say, 'how's it going?', but Raman is the one who decides how he wishes to respond."

"Didn't I keep my sister's secret all her life? I'd never reveal someone's private information. Dinnae fash, I'll keep quiet and simply observe."

"Thanks, Essie. I guess I just wanted to reassure Raman that this is a safe place for whatever healing he wants to explore today. Having said all that, Raman, you understand the complexity of the energy field and how our emotions, experiences, relationships, environment, thinking patterns, and so on impinge upon our field and affect its harmony and balance?"

Raman nodded.

"Sometimes there are things, like physical injuries, of which we're aware, or habits that've been troublesome to us. Other times, there may be incidents or belief systems we've buried within our cells that are influencing our well-being. When I offer to balance your energy field, any of these things may rise up, if your body or spirit self feels ready to do that healing work. We'll set an intention to focus on whatever you choose for this healing session but, occasionally, other things come to our awareness. You're always the one in charge and can choose to address an issue or not. If anything feels too much, you can ask me to stop at any time. This is your healing and I'm simply a facilitator. You're in charge. Any questions?"

"Do you just work in my energy field?" Raman asked.

"Some modalities do, but I learned a hands-on approach that recognizes the power of healthy human touch. If you're not comfortable with touch, that's okay. I can work off the body. It's your choice," I explained.

"I'm comfortable with touch," Raman responded.

"Again, you're in charge. If my touch is too light or too heavy, or uncomfortable in any way, please let me know. I usually begin doing an initial scan with my hands moving through your field, then place my hands at your feet, moving up the legs and the core of the body, up the arms and heart to the head."

Raman nodded his understanding.

"Is there a particular healing for which you'd like to set an intention at this time?" I inquired.

"My shoulders have been tight and sore because I've been trying to get all my final contracts completed," Raman shared.

"Anything else?" I invited.

"No. That seems good for now," he stated.

I set aside his shoes as he got comfortable on the table. I checked the height of the pillows and removed one because it put his neck at an awkward alignment and I added one under his knees to ease his lower back. I dimmed the lights and put quiet nature music on to dull any outside noises. Clasping our right hands together, I explained that this was a way to connect our energy fields as I intentionally connected us to Universal energy to facilitate Raman's healing request and this session we would share.

The further we moved into the session, the more relaxed I became and I settled into the familiar rhythm of offering a healing session. I could feel Raman relaxing as my hands moved from his feet to ankles to knees. The gentle warmth and flow of energy seeped through me and to wherever his body most needed it. When I reached the right hip, a strong resistance pushed at my hand. I gently spoke.

"Raman, I'd like you to focus on your right hip where my hand is. Simply notice anything that may be here."

"There's pain. It's really tight. I've been having trouble in my runs recently," he stated.

"Let the healing energy soak into muscles, nerves, ligaments, tendons, whatever needs assistance. Keep open to any information your hip may be trying to share with you," I encouraged.

All of a sudden, his left leg stretched out, full of tension.

"Something happening here for you Raman?" I inquired.

Raman seemed to drag in his breath. "Fear. Dark, dense, tight."

"Raman, you're doing well. Keep paying attention. Is this fear yours or is it someone else's?" I felt drawn to pose the question.

After a pause, he replied, "The outer layer is mine. I have some fear about our venture. Will we succeed?" After another moment, he continued. "The inner core is my father's fear. I see him sitting in the kitchen, his head in his hands, his body shaking as my mother sits across from him. His business failed. We were bankrupted. He went to work for other people after that. He never tried to go it on his own again."

"What do you want to do with that fear, Raman?" I invited.

"I want to forgive it. I want to release it. Just because he failed doesn't mean I will."

"Let those messages soak into your hip, into your body or spirit self, with this healing, loving energy." I continued to hold his hip as his leg gradually relaxed, and I could feel his muscles softening into my hand. "As I move on, let that release continue."

When I reached his shoulders, I added some energizing ultrasound where I could feel congestion. As I gently reached my hands under his shoulders, I encouraged Raman to fully relax them into my hands. Letting my fingers be drawn to particular spots, I directed the healing energy to flow and support

Raman's sore muscles.

Before I could move on, Raman spoke up. "I feel this heavy weight, pushing on my shoulders."

"I wonder what that weight might be?" I asked.

"The word that comes to me is expectations," Raman replied. "I don't want to let anyone down. I don't want to be like my father. I don't want to disappoint others. I feel like I have to make up for his mistakes."

I encouraged him to keep going.

"It's interesting, my family never said any of this to me, but I kept saying it to myself. Looking back, I can see I judged my dad pretty harshly. Ever since, I've been trying to make sure I didn't do anything that would bring that judgement on me. I even got married the way they wanted. Resisting their expectations in that area now has created a lot of tension in me. I guess it's time to ease up a bit," Raman confessed.

"With that awareness, let some of that weight of expectation drain into my hands. Release its weight on you and its influence in your life for your healing." I could feel a pulsing push into my hands, waves and waves of it. I held my position until the pulsing eased.

I moved my hands through the final positions and then invited Raman to do a scan of his body and spirit to see if there was anything else he felt needed further attention. I waited. He shook his head.

"I feel lighter. My hip feels looser. I think that's good."

I explained that I'd finish with a few sweeps through the energy field to further clear some of the emotions he had released. I completed the session by clasping my hands just below one knee, and then the other, pulling firmly down the calf muscles and off the foot to ground him again; then, I clasped his hands to speak words of release to free our energy fields from one another. When he sat up, I passed him a glass of water that I had placed on the side table earlier.

"Any questions you'd like to ask?" I offered.

"Is it always that intense?" he quizzed.

"No. It depends on the readiness of a person to do their healing work and their level of awareness. Some people feel warmth or tingles. They may say they feel more relaxed or at peace, or more energetic, but others can delve into some wonderfully healing insights and release. I'm just the conduit—the encourager. It's up to the individual what they choose to receive."

"Thank you. I feel like I received a lot. It was much more powerful than I expected." Raman wiggled his shoulders. "I can't believe how much looser and lighter they feel."

"Am I allowed to say anything now?" Essie interjected.

"Go for it, Essie. What did you think?" Raman encouraged her to share.

"It was incredible. Alisha, I could see the energy streaming from your hands as you moved them from place to place. At your hip and then at your shoulders, Raman, when you began

to release, I saw thick dark strands pull out of each place, then break up, returning to pure energy. As that happened, the colours of your field became brighter and lighter."

"Cool! Can you see energy that way, Alisha?" Raman asked curiously.

"My visual perception isn't fully developed yet, as you know. In the same way I can only see a flicker of energy when I try to visualize Essie, when I'm using this technique I sometimes see colour or vibrational waves; but, it isn't consistent."

"Is there anything Raman should do after this session to continue to support his healing?" Essie inquired.

"Good point, Essie!" Raman exclaimed.

"There're a couple of things. Maybe talk to Cheri about a few helpful yoga moves to encourage hip and shoulder flexibility from the physical angle. I also have a body and mind workbook that offers a few pages of reflection on each part of the body. It suggests issues that may show up in connection with particular body areas. The questions can help you read more deeply into the linkage between physical and emotional issues. You've identified a few things, so you may want to continue to affirm the release of those old emotions and beliefs and set some new more freeing affirmations for your life," I suggested.

"You mean like telling myself that I'm free of fear?" Raman asked.

"What if you tried 'I'm confident in the choices I'm making'," I offered.

"I like that! It feels different when you say it that way. I feel the confidence, not the fear," Essie proclaimed.

Raman expressed each statement out loud and agreed with Essie. “It does feel different. I guess I have some things to work on. Thanks again, Alisha.”

Raman headed out to the café for the next exchange and I switched the pillow case and sheet so that the room was ready for someone else to use.

CHAPTER TWENTY

This time, I was booked to receive a massage from Jace. Tadame was going to Cheri to consult on yoga moves for lower back pain and Leigh was consulting with Raman on herbs for skincare for their sensitive skin. I followed Jace to the room he'd prepared for giving massages. He had already changed the bedding, so after checking with me which areas I wanted him to work on, he left to give me time to disrobe and climb on the table. When he knocked and inquired if I was ready, I told him to enter, while shifting nervously on the table to try to get my breasts into a comfortable position. As he entered, I suddenly realized that of the hundreds of massages I had received, this was the first I would receive from a male therapist.

Jace calmly walked over to the iPad to select music. I recognized the thrum of a heart chakra clearing piece that was a favourite of mine. I wondered if he had somehow discovered that or if he was in tune with what I needed.

Before I could ask, Jace commented, "I tend to choose music for each client as it presents itself to me. I don't always know why a certain selection comes to me, but I trust my instincts and put it on. If for any reason you don't like the music I've chosen, let me know and we can select something else."

"Thanks, but don't change it. You hit the bull's eye, Jace. Heart clearing is my biggest challenge," I admitted.

Jace checked that I was comfortable and asked if I wanted an essential oil to be used during the massage. I invited him to recommend one and he chose hyssop. Jace's hands were strong and soothing as the massage proceeded. He had an instinctual sense of the places he needed to probe more deeply or gently stretch. Once I had turned on my back, he spent a lot of time on my arms as expressions of my heart chakra.

Then, he paused and spoke again. "Alisha, there's one area most people don't have massaged—the abdominal region. It's an area of our body that cries out for loving energy and I'm sensing that especially with you. Would you be comfortable if we draped a towel over your breasts and I pulled the sheet down to cover the pelvic area, so I can access this area of your body?"

I blushed furiously. Jace's instincts were, once again, pure gold. My abdomen was the least favourite part of my body. I hated its stretchy, droopy skin. I hadn't let it see the sun since I was a young teen. It embarrassed me that I couldn't discipline myself to get it in better shape. Was I ready to let it be seen and felt by someone else? Jace placed his hands on my shoulders and began to brush out from the neck and across the shoulder blades.

"Alisha, just focus on my hands for a moment. I can feel the tension my question has caused in you. Usually, I'd wait until I'd had a few sessions with someone before offering this, so they could feel comfortable with me. Let yourself feel my hands as instruments of loving energy, never judgement. Can you trust me with this?"

I drew in a deep cleansing breath and I felt my shoulders begin to soften. I shared with him my thoughts and the struggle they created in me.

"That's why this is so important," Jace affirmed. "If you focus on breathing in the scent of the hyssop, it helps with centering and supports the cardiovascular and nervous systems. Allow the hyssop and my hands to calm and communicate love." I gave him the go-ahead; I took the large towel he handed me and draped it over my breasts under the sheet. Then, he drew the sheet down. I was sure my face was scarlet, but Jace's soothing voice invited me to draw my attention to his hands. Loving, soothing strokes circled my abdomen. Gently pulling together and easing apart, Jace's hands left no spot untouched. As the massage continued, I felt tears leak from under my eyelids. This sorely rejected part of me was finally receiving some of the attention it deserved. My breathing became deeper and my body calmed. Jace pulled the sheet over me again and finished with some gentle pressure and a massage of my scalp.

"Take whatever time you need, Alisha. I'll be just outside."

I felt like a limp noodle, yet I felt a burgeoning wholeness that had eluded me for a long time. I allowed myself a few more cleansing breaths and then got up and dressed. I opened the door and beckoned Jace in. I clasped one of his hands between both of mine and looked directly into his eyes.

"Thank you. You bring something extraordinary to the work you offer. I feel very fortunate to have received from you today and to have you on our team."

Jace seemed a little embarrassed. "I try to listen to my instincts."

"Your intuition seems very well developed. Keep trusting it! Now let's clean up this room and rejoin the group."

We companionably changed the bedding and returned to the café. Slowly, the others drifted in to join us. This time, I was on deck to offer an introduction to the labyrinth followed by a labyrinth walk.

"Labyrinths have been around for thousands of years but have been recently rediscovered for their spiritual potential. Their imagery of a circle enclosing a spiral pathway can represent our journey toward wholeness. There are no confusing choices along the way, only the choice to walk the path and to trust our core self. Walking the labyrinth invites us on an inward journey, by accessing our right brain's intuition and creativity. The weaving back and forth along the meandering pathway encourages new perspectives and inner growth. As we travel the inward path to our deepest selves, we seek the wisdom offered at the core of who we are; then we traverse the outward path to take this wisdom back into our daily lives.

When I was trying to discern if I should leave my ministry position last fall, I walked a friend's labyrinth. I asked for inner guidance for my situation. As I walked the path inward all that I was feeling became clearer to me with each step. I noticed the clouds above me suddenly split apart and the sun shone through. It felt like a message for me to open up to new possibilities. Lines from songs sang through my mind, and each line offered a message I needed to hear. Once I reached the center, I felt filled with peace. I looked around and thought of all my life had offered me so far and I was thankful. Following the path outward, I was filled with energy and hope for all that was yet before me in life. I skipped along feeling ready for the next steps I'd take to resign my position."

"I looked up some information online about labyrinths, and from what you've just described, it sounds like a really personal journey. How do we do it with other people around?" Cheri posed inquisitively.

"Great question. I suppose it's a lot like your yoga classes where people learn to dwell in their own body experience. During this experience we'll maintain silence and we'll stagger our entrances, about three minutes apart. As you come close to another or if someone passes you on their way out, do what feels comfortable to you; perhaps nod to them or smile, or keep your eyes directed to the path if that's best for you."

"I've walked both alone and with others on the path. Each time I was amazed at how much I received during the experience," Jace divulged.

"Today, once we arrive at the labyrinth, we'll take a few moments in meditative silence to set our own intention of what we seek to receive during our walk—strength, insight into a relationship, guidance on a particular life issue, it's up to you. One by one, we'll enter, three minutes apart; just watch for my nod. As you walk, keep open to sights, sounds, smells, images, thoughts, memories, song titles, movies, or stories, that pop into your awareness offering you insights that may be helpful on your journey. Just let it all unfold, as there's no right or wrong way to walk the labyrinth. You may find yourself slowly stepping along with long pauses or skipping freely. When you reach the center, you might choose to sit on the bench or on the ground. You might feel drawn to stand and face each quadrant of the labyrinth or experience them as the four directions of aboriginal teachings. When the time feels right, return to the path and follow it back out. As you exit, you might like to turn and face the labyrinth in gratitude for what it has offered you."

"Although I built it, I'm new to all this," Raman revealed. "I'm having trouble keeping it all in my head."

"I thought that might be the case for some, so I've put it in point form on a little card for each of you. If it helps, we can use them with other folks who come to the labyrinth," I expressed.

"Terrific idea, Alisha," Cheri concurred.

"Once you're finished, we'll reconvene in the café," I directed.

The day was warm with a light breeze, so mosquitoes and other bugs weren't a problem. We staggered our entrances and maintained a respectful silence. Some meandered their way through and others walked briskly. A few sat on the bench by the sundial in the centre, taking time to ponder their thoughts. Others walked to face each quadrant, then commenced their outward journey. As they returned to the café, I had left a special journal for each person on the tables. By their name was a short note which invited them to take time to jot down notes or sketch pictures to recall what the labyrinth or the morning's experiences had offered them. Regular and coloured pencils, charcoal pens, and crayons were scattered about for use. Once everyone was finished, we closed the morning with some sharing time.

"I can't believe how much clarity I received on the issue I brought to the labyrinth. I thought it would be a nice calming walk, but the weaving in and out actually works in some mystical way. I received much more than I expected," Cheri bubbled.

"I've been to a labyrinth before, but always on my own. Walking with other people also seeking insight from the same experience was very moving," Tadame contributed.

"Jace used to take his grade twelve English classes to a labyrinth in our local community. I only had that one experience. It was actually one of the experiences that affirmed for me that I needed to be myself. It was interesting to have the chance to do it again and I found it just as powerful this time. I'm glad it'll be part of what we offer here," Leigh shared.

"The setting is beautiful and I could almost hear the stones whisper their support to us." Jace confessed.

"That's interesting, Jace. When I built the labyrinth, I hadn't ever walked one, but I had heard about them and I read up about them. I wanted ours to be special so, as I placed each stone, I asked them to be a guide to whoever walked among them. It may sound a little hokey but...."

Cheri interrupted Raman. "It's not hokey. Wait, what kind of word is that?" she shrugged. "This is what we do. This is who we are. This is why we're a team and how we're creating this as a healing place."

Leigh cut in. "I speak from experience. You've got to be who you are, Raman—no apologies!"

"He can hear the rocks whisper but not me. That's a tad interesting," claimed Essie.

We shared Essie's words with Jace and Tadame.

Then, I suggested we move on to Leigh's leadership, which would take us into lunch. Leigh was going to teach us about four healing herbs we could use in everyday cooking to support our health and well-being: cilantro, ginger, turmeric, and fennel. Raman's stomach gave a loud grumble, so we laughingly agreed it was time to shift leaders.

Leigh was an animated presenter and had us sniff and taste the herbs they showed us. We had fun tempting our senses and then they presented a delicious cold soup and herbed bread, using the herbs they had highlighted. We hungrily dove in and easily chattered with one another over the meal. We all helped with the cleanup and paired up for another session. This time, Tadame was with me, Leigh was going to Jace, and Raman was consulting with Cheri on yoga moves for his tight hips and shoulders. We had one more switch later that afternoon and we finished up with Raman inviting us outside for a surprise that he had planned for us.

In the garden, Raman had laid out an array of ceramic pots of varying colours and designs. He encouraged us to each choose one that felt right. I chose a sleek black pot with rich blue swirls etched into it. The others made their choices as well. Raman pointed out that our response to colours, shapes, and plants can be very individual, as reflected by the planters we chose. He had collected a variety of annuals that he helped us arrange in our planters to take home as a piece of our healing place. It was fascinating to watch as we each chose different plants, whether we were drawn to colours, shapes, or aromas. Raman encouraged us all to get our hands dirty and to discover the pleasure of designing a mini-garden in our planters.

As we went inside to clean up, Leigh said, "This has been an incredible day."

"If our clients get half as much out of what we offer as we did today, we're gonna rock this town!" Cheri asserted emphatically.

"I feel we all received a lot today and it's obvious that we all have things to keep working on," Raman admitted. "I wonder if we should commit to our own healing journeys by exchanging sessions with each other on a regular basis?"

"I'm down for that," Cheri proclaimed.

"I wonder if we could offer a sample day like this to the public once a week during August. It could be like an open house and we'd offer mini-sessions—not the full deal like we gave each other. They could pay $30 for the day and try two twenty-minute sessions. We could have information displays and encourage them to walk the grounds. The café could be open and we'd charge our usual prices there."

Tadame was thinking ahead.

"That sounds like a possibility. Let's flesh it out at our Monday meeting," I suggested.

Jace looked at us all. "This has been an awesome welcome to the team. Thanks everyone for bringing me on board."

"Glad to have you with us," Raman slapped him on the shoulder in affirmation.

"Time to call it a day, everyone," I yawned as the healing work started to catch up with me. "Sleep well tonight. I sure will."

I yawned again and giggled. I offered hugs on my way out and Raman exited with me to give me a hand putting the planter into my back seat, so it wouldn't fall over. I drove home sleepily and stumbled through the front door and over to the couch. I was snoring before my head hit the cushion. I woke up in time to eat a light supper with Dan and share with him about some of the day. By nine, I was in bed with the lights out.

CHAPTER TWENTY-ONE

Thanks to my early bedtime, I awoke bright and early, eager to go for a run. I threw on my shorts and tee while Dan's quiet breathing assured me he was still asleep. After a half a banana and a few of my running jellies for energy, I was on the road. A light mist drifted across the fields and there was very little traffic. The early morning songbirds were busily singing their hearts out. I felt light and free as I surged up and down the hilly terrain of our country road. At five and a half kilometres, I turned around to see the full brilliance of the sun rising. Its light bathed me as I ran toward home. I walked the last kilometre to stretch out the muscles I had challenged and to give my cardiovascular system time to rebalance itself, rather than jolting it with a complete cessation of movement.

The house was still quiet, so I took out the thick sliced bacon Dan enjoyed as a treat on the weekend and put it to bake on parchment paper in the oven. I mixed up an egg batter with a bit of almond flour and spices in it, leaving it to set so I could make crepes a little later. I hit the shower and cleared away my running sweat, giving my hair a good wash so I could style it for the shopping expedition. Back in our room, I could tell by Dan's leg movements that he was becoming more wakeful. I dropped my towel and slid in next to him to offer him a warm wake-up snuggle.

The crepes turned out to be delicious, especially as I topped them with fresh raspberries and coconut cream. Dan appreciated all my morning offerings! As we ate, I talked about the team's plan to set up at local races. He thought it was a great idea. Both Dan and I ran, but only on our own for fitness. Neither of us had participated in any races. I raised the possibility of maybe trying a race or two ourselves.

Dan paused with a piece of bacon on the way to his mouth.

"I've never brought it up because I didn't think I was good enough. But, talking with Raman about his running, he assured me races include all types of athletes—beginners to long-timers—and every pace. It might be fun and it's another way to connect with that community," I proffered.

Dan set down his bacon. "I've always wanted to try a race, but I've never had the time. I didn't think you were interested."

"I'm interested, but also terrified," I admitted.

"Maybe this is a chance to face down that fear

and to try something new," Dan encouraged.

"Next weekend, a local sign shop is putting on a five kilometre run to raise money for muscular dystrophy. That might be manageable. What do you think?" I asked with a feeling of anticipation.

Dan checked his phone calendar. "We don't have anything planned. Sure, let's try it!" He grinned and picked up his bacon with pleasure.

I heaved a sigh as I stood up. "Time to get on the road to Sabina's. You're on cleanup duty," I smiled as I leaned in for a kiss.

Sabina was standing outside with her friend Trish when I arrived. She scrambled into the back seat.

"Hey Mom, I just heard from Ginny. She's down with the flu and can't come. She's so bummed. I promised we'd connect via Instagram so she's not left out."

"Poor Ginny. I know she was looking forward to this," I exclaimed.

"I can only imagine her disappointment! Good to see you, Alisha. Isn't this exciting?" Trish greeted me as she climbed into the car. She and Sabina had been best friends since they were twelve and we were very comfortable with one another.

"How are your studies going?" I asked as she buckled up. Trish had completed nursing, but had decided to go on to medicine. She was doing her residency in another city.

"Tough, but I love it. I'm really glad I could get this weekend off, so I could be part of this awesome day!" Trish had a bubbly personality that tended to make everyone around her relax.

Sabina intervened. "Okay, Mom, here's the deal. You can help pick out dresses for me to try on, but don't be offended if I don't like them. When I try a dress on, I'll give you both my opinion first. If I want your feedback, I'll ask for it. I want to choose what feels and looks right to me and not feel pressured to go with someone else's preference. The same goes for you, Trish. I need you both for support, not to oppose me, so that I don't feel overwhelmed."

Trish laughed, "This is about you, not us. Don't worry!"

"I can do that, honey. I can't guarantee my face won't sometimes reveal my thoughts, but I'll do my best to be a neutral zone unless called upon. Now, ready for some fun?" I implored.

"Yes, please!" Sabina called out. "Let's put on some tunes." I clicked on the radio as we pulled back onto the street. Sinatra blasted through the speakers, singing "My Way". We burst out laughing and loudly sang along.

The wedding boutique Sabina wanted to try first was on a main street of Bright Haven. As we approached the door, Trish grabbed Sabina's hand.

"Here we go!" she exclaimed as we entered.

A well-dressed middle-aged woman greeted us with a warm smile. I glanced around at the array of dresses displayed on racks all around the front room. What a diversity of styles! At the back of the room, a door led into another space that I could see had a seating area and fitting rooms.

Sabina extended her hand to the woman. "Hi, I'm Sabina, the bride-to-be. This is my mom, Alisha, and my best friend, Trish."

"Pleased to meet you, Sabina. I'm Mavis. Welcome to my boutique. Do you want to browse a bit first or do you have a sense of what you want?" Mavis inquired in a friendly soothing manner. She obviously had lots of experience working with touchy brides.

"I think I'd like to look around at what you have before I narrow things down too much. Pure white doesn't suit me, so I'll avoid anything that shade. I feel better in creamy white; its softer against my skin. I don't think I want anything too princess-like or big puffy skirts—they're not really my style. However, I'm willing to try one, just for fun," said Sabina.

"Alabaster is a creamy white tone that would be gorgeous with your skin and your auburn hair. The dresses are organized according to colour. That wall will have the shade you're looking for." Mavis pointed to the left wall. "Keeping in mind what you've mentioned, would you like me to select a few possibilities as you look around?" Mavis offered.

"Sure, but please don't be offended if I don't like them," Sabina warned.

"It's your dress, dear. No offense will be taken. It makes my day more interesting if I can help in the search," Mavis replied.

"Let's all have fun! What if we each choose three dresses for you and Mavis can take them back to the dressing room? That way you won't know who chose what, so there'll be no pressure to please any of us," Trish offered excitedly.

"Good idea," Sabina chimed. "That's twelve dresses—not too many—and we'll keep it fun. Okay, let's dive in!" she eagerly headed to the racks.

We spent the next hour combing through the racks, looking at every style imaginable: sleeveless, long-sleeved, cap-sleeved, beaded, lacy, fitted, frilly, poufy, wide skirts, fitted and flared, floor-length, and ones so short I wasn't sure they'd cover the crotch area! There were dresses I thought were absolutely beautiful and others I couldn't imagine being in anything other than a horror show. Finally, we each selected our preferred three and they all hung in the fitting room, waiting for Sabina to give them a try.

Trish and I flopped into two comfortable seats.

"That was exhausting!" Trish proclaimed.

"I know. I'm bug-eyed from trying to imagine so many different dresses on Sabina," I vented.

"Would you ladies like a cup of coffee?" Mavis offered.

Trish and I groaned in unison, "Yes, please!"

Mavis pointed to a little nook on the far side of the room. "The machine has a variety of coffee, tea, and hot chocolate selections. There's fresh milk and cream in the little fridge and there's a plate of homemade cookies. Help yourselves and I'll assist Sabina with her first dress."

We tried to walk sedately across the room, but all we wanted to do was race to the coffee machine!

Mavis exited the change room to find a bra that

would better match the dresses Sabina would be trying on. We were well into our coffee when Sabina called out, "Are you ready?"

"All set," we responded.

The change room door opened and she stepped out. She had opted to try a princess style dress first. It was sparkly, with beads, and the fitted top formed a V into a wide flowing skirt. It was lovely and she could pull it off with her height, but I could see as she walked in it that she felt awkward.

She moved fully into the room and walked around us to the mirrored area. Tilting her head, she said, "It's pretty and I do look like a princess, but it doesn't feel quite right for me. I'm glad I tried it on, so I know for sure. What do you think?" She turned to us.

"Trust your instincts. If it doesn't feel right, it isn't right for you," I offered.

"Well said, Alisha. I agree. With your height, Sabina, you're probably going to look good in a lot of what you try on. It's about waiting for that one that just grabs you and says, 'I'm the one for you'," Trish advised.

Sabina exhaled a pent-up breath of air. "Thanks guys, that's helpful. So, our first no—now, we can avoid any more of this style. Oh wait, take a photo and send it to Ginny. Tell her it's a thumbs down."

She strode back to the change room and proceeded with the next option. It was a Grecian style gown that draped over her figure. It was interesting, but it didn't really flatter her. Number three was a jaunty modern mid-thigh length dress. It was sassy and fun, but it just wasn't a match. The next was a modified princess style, but still too fussy for Sabina's preference. Then, she tried one in a satiny fabric that skimmed over her curves and gently trailed out behind her. The only drawback was a square neckline which she felt made her shoulders look too broad. The more dresses she tried, the clearer she became about what she wanted for each aspect of the dress. Now all we needed to do was to find all her preferences in one dress! We received smiley emojis from Ginny as we shared the dress photo journey. She even sent a photo of herself looking miserable, holding a bucket on her lap.

Mavis was extremely helpful and kept notes. She even sketched out the basic shape and styling Sabina had identified as she nixed certain dresses and pointed out what she liked in others. Mavis admitted she didn't have anything in her store that quite fit what Sabina had pieced together. She recommended trying Wedding Barn, but if we still had no luck, her boutique used a seamstress who not only handled alterations but could design a dress as well.

We thanked her profusely for the tremendous support she'd offered us and told her that the cookies had been delicious. We made our exit to the car.

We were all ravenous from the strenuous work of shopping, so we stopped at a local café for sustenance.

"How're you feeling about the search?" Trish

asked Sabina.

Sabina chewed her salad thoughtfully before replying, "Better than I thought I would," she admitted. "It has been fun and I have a really clear idea of what I want now. Each of us picking three dresses was helpful, because it encouraged me to try a slightly wider variety and discover design aspects I might have missed on my own. Let's use this sketch Mavis did up for us and I think we should try the same approach at Wedding Barn."

Trish and I nodded our agreement. The day was going well. I was grateful I'd remembered to do some early morning tapping after my run. I felt centered and focused on Sabina, and not on my worries about my mothering skills.

The afternoon was warm, so we opened the car windows to let the fresh air blow through as we drove into the countryside toward Wedding Barn. There were a few cars in the parking lot, but thankfully it didn't seem overly busy. The interior was much like a barn and the dresses were in rows of racks down the centre. Shoe and purse displays extended around the outer walls. At the back of the barn, there were dressing rooms and mirrors with a few seats close by. A couple of women were perusing the racks and a small group were in the fitting area. We could overhear some bickering going on as a mother and daughter argued over the merits of a dress the mother wanted her daughter to try on. Sabina rolled her eyes and we walked to the farthest rack away from that area to begin our search.

A harried looking attendant hurried over to us. "Can I help you?"

Sabina took charge. "I'm looking for a dress in this style, in alabaster." She held up the sketch. The woman quickly glanced at it; then, she looked behind her as the angry voices escalated.

"Our dresses are arranged according to style, not colour. This rack is mainly princess style. Aisle three has more the design you're looking for. If you'd like to take a look, I'll check in with you in a little bit. Dressing room four is free, so you can place your dress choices in there." The woman spoke rapidly and we could feel her tension; this was quite different from our earlier experience.

As the woman scurried to the back, Sabina grinned. "Aren't you glad that's not us? Let's have our fun and see what we can find."

She led the way to aisle three. It was a long aisle and we bravely started culling through the shades and styles it offered us. I found two with most of the design elements Sabina had identified, but not all in the one dress. I swiped dress after dress and then I gasped. Trish was close by and she glanced over. A huge smile broke across her face and she gave me a thumbs-up. She swiftly swept it off the rack and between two of the dresses she had already chosen. Nonchalantly, she walked them back and placed them in the dressing room. We made our final selections and eagerly took our seats. Sabina was still seeking her third choice, so we tried to contain our excitement.

Fortunately, the bickering customers had left. The earlier tension was relieved and we were alone in the dressing room area save for two friends who seemed to be enjoying themselves as they tried on dresses together.

The attendant who had spoken to us earlier came over.

“Can I be of assistance?”

Sabina, who had just joined us with her three dresses, said, “Sure, I could use some help with fastenings. That way, they can both see the dress on me at the same time.”

The attendant followed her into the spacious fitting room and we impatiently waited for the modelling to begin.

The first two were set aside. One clumped awkwardly over her bum and the other bunched under her arms. We expectantly watched for the door to open for another viewing, but nothing happened. We waited. We listened.

Trish called out, “Sabina, is everything okay?”

“Yes,” she answered, sounding rather teary. “I’ve found it. This is it, so you can’t say anything negative, okay. This is my dress.”

The door opened. She looked radiant. The alabaster fitted top was textured with a dragonfly design. Subtly placed beads offered a glint of sparkle. The sweetheart neckline gracefully lengthened the appearance of her neck. The skirt flared gently out from her hips and there was a small bustle behind. Wide straps reached over her shoulders and continued down the back. A band connected them behind her neck where there was a small series of pearl buttons. The strap material extended down the back and was shaped into an oval cutaway which revealed the strength and beauty of her back. The buttons continued again just below the waist, down her hips to the bustle. The dress seemed to flow from her and with her as she moved over to the mirrors to check all the angles.

"So?" Sabina inquired as she turned to us again.

By this time Trish and I were holding hands and the tears were flowing freely down our cheeks.

"It's perfect!" we exclaimed together.

"Which one of you found it?" she asked as she continued to admire herself in the mirror.

"We found it together," I affirmed.

The attendant stepped around Sabina. "It could take a little tuck right below the breast-line and we'll need to check the hem with whatever shoes you decide to wear. Otherwise, you're nearly a perfect fit for this dress, which is pretty unusual."

We grinned at each other through the tears. "Not when the Universe has your back. Right, Mom?" Sabina declared. "How much is it? I don't see a tag anywhere."

The shop assistant stepped up to Sabina and checked the back of the neck of the dress.

"There's a small red tag here, which means it's a return. I remember now. A young woman bought it, thinking she'd use one for her ceremony and one for the dance. Then she decided that was too extravagant, so she returned this one. All returns are forty percent off the book price, which I'll check for you."

The attendant went to check the computer at the front of the store. We looked at each other in delight.

I spoke up. "Sabina, your dad and I would like to buy your dress for you. I know you like being independent, but we're very happy for you and would like to celebrate with you by giving you your dress as a gift."

Sabina walked over and hugged me. "When you put it that way and since it's on sale, how can I refuse?"

Trish joined in the hug and tears began leaking out again.

The attendant returned. "This dress is by a new designer we're trying out. Its original price was one thousand dollars. With the return discount, it's six hundred before taxes."

"We'll take it!" Sabina twirled in her dress, full of delight.

The shop assistant added, "In that case, if you buy any accessories from us,—say, underwear, shoes, a hat or veil—we offer an additional ten percent discount."

As it was only mid-afternoon, we decided to take our time and see what they had in stock.

The shoes were pretty straightforward. Sabina wanted comfortable flats and they had plenty to choose from. Finding a headpiece was more challenging. Hats didn't really suit the dress and

Sabina didn't want a veil. It was Trish who found a slightly sparkly floral tiara, with creamy ribbons that trailed down the back. We decided to go all out; we purchased underwear that would slide comfortably under the dress and Sabina found tiny crystal-cut dragonflies that would nestle in her ears. We were done! We left the dress for the few alterations that had to be made and joyously traipsed out to the car.

Before we climbed in, Sabina gave me a big hug.

"Thanks, Mom. This has been an awesome day."

I hugged her back, quietly thanking the Universe for this special memory we'd created together.

"You're welcome," I whispered in her ear.

As we drove back, Sabina reflected, "I think I'll invite Ginny over for brunch this week once she's feeling better. I'll share with her what we found today and maybe book a time to shop for her bridesmaid dress. I want Trish, Ginny, and Tommy as my attendants. Ginny looks really good in royal blue, so I thought we could find a style she likes in a mid-length dress. Tommy can wear black dress pants with a white shirt; I know he has those. Maybe he can wear the red vest he had made when he did that musical a year ago. I'll check with him. Trish, what colour would you prefer for your dress?"

"Actually, I picked up a dress for a Christmas dance that I didn't end up going to last year. It's mid-length and an orangey red colour—like fall leaves. I could wear that," Trish offered.

"You posted that dress on Instagram, right? It looked fantastic on you. With the wedding in

September, vibrant colours will work perfectly. I can't believe how this is all coming together. Synchronicity, keep doing your stuff!" Sabina shouted out the window.

Having left Trish and Sabina back at the apartment building, laden with the spoils of our trip, I drove slowly home.

I had texted Dan I was on my way, so the barbeque was sizzling with supper as I pulled in. A glass of wine was waiting for me on the counter. I picked it up and went out to the back deck to join Dan. He attentively listened to the day's adventures, gently rubbing my feet, which I had lifted into his lap.

CHAPTER TWENTY-TWO

Leigh hired their friend to help with the prep work on Sunday morning, so the rest of us had it off. We needed to be on deck for 4:00 p.m. to help arrange furniture, set out dishes, and go over our responsibilities again. Dan and I decided to go for a bike ride and picnic beside a small brook. We were very thankful that the weather was co-operating, both for our bike ride and for the party. I had texted Ginny and she was feeling better. She felt she'd be okay to attend later but would avoid any alcohol. I was relieved for her that she wouldn't miss out.

After my shower, I sat and journaled with a healing book. It was a beneficial time to follow up on some of the emotions that had come up during my sessions on Friday. A memory popped into my mind as I wrote. I recalled my grandmother always commenting about my weight, describing me as a husky girl, or stating that I had put on a few pounds since I'd last seen her. I remembered feeling a wave of shame in response to her words. From an early age, my war with my belly was established. I took some time to tap on those early memories, the emotions associated with them, and the beliefs I had developed about myself. I placed my hands on my abdomen and gently rubbed them in a circle, saying, "I am learning to appreciate you. We are healing together." There was more to do, but that was enough for the time being.

I switched out of my lounging clothes to black capris and a white top. I brought along a light black sweater in case the evening cooled off. Dan had decided to join in the fun, so he wore black casual pants with a short-sleeved white shirt. We admired each other and expressed our intention and hope that the event would go well.

We arrived at Essie's to find Leigh well organized. The local liquor had arrived and was chilling in the fridge. There was extra in the back pantry. It was my job to check all the beer and wine glasses to ensure they were spot-free. Leigh asked Dan to post the liquor licence, our health inspection certificate, his chef's certificate, and other pertinent forms.

The others busily arranged seating outside, using lawn chairs and small outdoor tables we'd brought from home. Toby gambolled around them, enjoying the activity. Sabina and Dan had completed small tables and chairs for the veranda and Leigh had pushed one table against the wall to form one of the food stations. In the café, the back corner was established as another food station and in the Great Room a table was moved into place on the other side of the couch and chair arrangement. People were welcome to go to the upstairs balcony to enjoy the view and mingle, but we decided against putting a food station up there to avoid having to carry heavy trays up the stairs. The upstairs healing rooms would be kept closed to avoid any unexpected contretemps in those areas.

Raman had arranged bouquets of wildflowers in small vases, which he distributed around the place, offering delightful whiffs of perfume and bright cheery colours. Baskets of napkins and cutlery were set out, and a variety of our small plates. Tadame and Cheri took a minute to pull me aside to ask about the dress shopping. I quickly shared how much fun it had been and that we had found "the dress". I pulled up a picture on my phone.

"It's fabulous on her!" Cheri exclaimed.

Tadame nodded in agreement.

Leigh poked their head over my shoulder. "Sabina looks totally happy."

I confessed that I'd been nervous at first, but I explained how we had decided to each pick three and how well that strategy had worked.

Cheri cleared her throat. "This gives me courage to go looking for my dress, even though we haven't set a date yet. Some of our friends have gone with Melissa, but they're really opinionated. Would you guys like to come with me and my mom some day?"

"Sounds like things are a little more settled for

you?" I assessed.

Cheri beamed, "Last night was our two-year anniversary and Melissa shared with me what she's been up to. The owners of the place she'd borrowed equipment from for our photo shoot were impressed when they saw her work. They asked her to do a special nighttime assignment with them for a gala photography showcase at the end of this month. If they were satisfied with her work, they indicated they'd hire her fulltime. She wanted to wait until it was definite, so she could present it to me as a surprise anniversary gift."

"Wow! That's wonderful, Cheri," Leigh exclaimed.

"Dress shopping sounds like an awesome way to celebrate. I'd be honoured to go," Tadame assured her.

"I'd love to be there," I said sincerely.

"Does the invite include me?" Leigh inquired hesitantly.

"You betcha," Cheri exclaimed exuberantly, offering Leigh a quick squeeze. "I can't wait. Can we pick a shopping day soon? Maybe later this week?"

We agreed Thursday was a clear day. Cheri just needed to check with her mom and we'd be set.

Ten minutes before the party, the cold items were set out on the serving tables: dips and veggies, cheese balls and vegan cashew cheese balls, fruit kebabs, and other delightful tidbits. Raman was behind the bar, with instructions on how to blend the veggie and fruit juices. Cheri and I were greeters stationed at the door. By 6:00 p.m., they were streaming in. Some were keen on a tour, so Tadame took on that duty. Others beelined for the food. As the place filled up, Leigh turned the ovens on for the hot items. A hotpot of vegetarian chili had been plugged in on the veranda. Outside, near a table loaded with sauerkraut and toppings, Jace stood over a barbeque lightly grilling mini sausages and small foil-covered spuds. I could hear the whir of the blender as Raman combined a juice order. We were underway!

Ginny and a small group of her friends chatted companionably with Raman. Others flowed from area to area quite comfortably. A few were talking quietly up on the balcony, taking in the view through the windows. As I looked out the veranda window, I noticed one young man sitting in the Zen garden alone, except for Toby who was cozied up to him. I wondered if I should go and make sure Toby wasn't being a nuisance, when I noticed he seemed to be talking to the dog. I saw Toby's paw reach up and almost pat the man's hand. I decided to leave them for the time being. When I checked with Ginny about taking Toby back to Leigh's place, she said to leave him because her friends loved having him around.

A young woman asked about one of our paintings; a group of colourfully dressed young people gushed over our pottery and one of them just had to have two of our fairy mugs. Everyone waxed poetic about the food, which was evidenced by the dwindling amounts I noticed at the stations. Leigh kept a careful eye on things and directed us regarding what to refill. By 8:00 p.m., we slowly shifted the stations over to dessert items. We had a few requests for coffee and tea, which Tadame handled adeptly. She had kept her skill with our specialty machines a secret!

At some point, the young man I'd noticed earlier with Toby appeared near me.

"Are you Alisha?" he inquired.

"Yes." I stopped what I was doing and offered him my attention.

"I'm Charles. Ginny told me about you and your healing place here. It feels awesome, by the way. The grounds are beautiful and sitting in the garden was really soothing. I wanted to ask you about the dog. Ginny said his name is Toby."

I nodded, waiting for him to continue.

"It's the strangest thing. My dad died of a heart attack recently and I've been having a difficult time. We had a big argument the last time I spoke with him and I never got a chance to apologize or to tell him I loved him. I was sitting out in the garden, reliving that argument in my mind. Toby came and sat in front of me, shaking his head and he butted my knee. It was like he was telling me to stop what I was doing. I ended up telling Toby what had happened. He put his paw on my hand, as if to say, it's all right. He nudged me again as if telling me to continue speaking. So, I looked into the air and said, 'I'm sorry and I love you.' Then, Toby put both paws on my lap and licked my cheek. I felt a wave of forgiveness and love. It feels really strange telling you this, but I thought you should know that that dog is special," Charles finished.

"Thank you, Charles, for being so brave about sharing something so deeply personal. Toby arrived here a few weeks back and we learned that he'd been a therapy dog. This is the first time I've seen him in action. I'm very glad he was able to help you. Would it be all right with you if I shared your story with the rest of our team, so they understand what Toby is able to do?" I requested.

"You can share it with anyone you like. People need to know how to let go of the shit they're carrying around. If sharing my story can help someone else find Toby or this healing place, go for it!" he said eagerly.

"If you ever want to do more healing work on your relationship with your father, feel free to book an appointment with us. For tonight, I hope you're able to enjoy the rest of the party," I encouraged.

"I will. I'm really thankful I came tonight!" declared Charles. "All of a sudden, I'm starving! I think I'll try some of that delicious-looking food." Charles strode over to a nearby food station and filled a plate until it nearly flowed over.

By 9:00 p.m., Jace had shut down the barbeque and fired up the campfire pit that Raman had created. Slowly, people drifted out around the fire and a few went to their cars to bring out guitars. Voices blending in song entertained us as we wandered through the house looking for dirty dishes and making sure the bathroom had sufficient supplies. Leigh looked exhausted, so we suggested they have a seat and relax while the rest of us cleaned up. Things were pretty much in order when Ginny rushed in through the veranda. "Mom, can we make s'mores? Some of my friends have never had them."

I groaned.

Before I could speak, Leigh piped up, "Don't worry. In the fridge there's some specialty dark chocolate I picked up for one of the desserts. I also made graham wafers for another dessert. They're in that tin over there." They gestured to the far counter. "Marshmallows are on the bottom shelf of the back pantry." We scurried to put it all together on a tray with some napkins.

"What'll we use to roast the marshmallows?" Ginny asked.

This time, Raman came to the rescue as he walked in the door behind her. As soon as he had heard her request, he'd slipped out the back door and gone down to the woods where he found some suitable green branches. We took a few minutes to carve them into shape. Then, Ginny gushed with thanks and Raman took the loaded tray to the outside table.

Leigh spoke up again. "With all that sugar, they'll be thirsty again. Blend together some fresh ginger, mint leaves, and cherries with a bit of water. Pour it into a large jug of cold water and give it a good stir. That should refresh them."

Dan took over the blender, while Cheri filled two

jugs of water. Tadame arranged a few trays of glasses and we met Ginny at the door.

"Cool," she said. "I was just coming in to say we're thirsty."

By eleven o'clock, our guests had left.

"I wouldn't want to do that too often," I sighed as I flopped into a chair next to Leigh. "It went well, but it's a lot of work. And we only served; you did all the prep, Leigh."

"It was actually fun to try some new recipes and see what they liked most. I had help from my friend, Jeremy, so the prep wasn't too intense. Cheri, I'll have an invoice for his hours for our meeting tomorrow, along with other expense receipts," Leigh said. "I thought fifty felt like an easily manageable number for our space."

"Can we debrief in the morning?" Tadame pleaded. "Ronnie gets up early these days, so I don't want to be too late getting to bed."

Our agreement was unanimous. In minutes, we were in our cars and on our way home.

"You're quiet," I observed to Dan.

"I was just reflecting on the event. You've sure picked a winner in Leigh. Their instincts on food, organization in the kitchen, and talent in preparation are what I'd expect in a much more mature person."

"In some ways their youth is an asset. Leigh's eager to learn; they may be more open than someone who has been in the business a while and set in their ways," I contemplated.

"There may be truth in that," Dan agreed. "It was

moving to watch all of you working as a team. There's an evident affection between you and you show each other respect as you support each other while working. You have something quite special there, Alisha."

"I see it too. I'm very grateful that these people and Toby have come into my life."

I revealed to Dan what Charles had shared about Toby's healing gifts.

"Essie behaved very well tonight and kept quiet, other than the occasional whisper in my ear that it was fun to see such a lively gathering in her home again. Five months ago, I barely saw the form of my dream; now, I have a Healing House and a truly unique team. It's pretty incredible," I admitted.

"We've been through a lot of change recently," Dan pointed out. "I'm thankful we've had each other as a constant through it all. We help keep each other steady."

"My rock, can I lean on you as I try to make it up the stairs?" I snuggled close as we went through the door and up to our room.

Monday dawned rainy and muggy. I hauled out an old Jane Fonda workout DVD rather than brave the outdoors. It was a light and fun workout, and I grinned as I watched the eighties-style outfits they wore. It kept me moving but didn't stress my body too much after the demands of the day before. I took time for a brief soak in the tub with some essential oils of northern spruce and wintergreen to invigorate my spirit. I did my tapping as I drove to our staff meeting. I couldn't do much in-depth work, but I could certainly continue reframing my inner dialogue with my abdomen and set positive affirmations for the day.

Once I arrived, I smelled coffee brewing as I walked in. Leigh and Jace were pulling a few leftovers out of the fridge and plating them for us. Raman came through the veranda door and took his work boots off before entering. That reminded me that we'd need mats at the doors and baskets of slippers that we could sanitize for our customers to keep the floors clean in the healing areas. We'd have to establish that no outdoor footwear was to be worn inside the house. I made a note to myself to remember to bring it up during the meeting.

"I was just checking to see how churned up the lawn was after last night's event. People mostly used the pathways, but I scattered extra seed over some of the grassy area. With the rain today and tomorrow, it's a good time to boost it a bit," Raman shared as he grabbed a coffee on the way to the table.

I finished doctoring mine and grabbed a seat as well. I heard Tadame and Cheri enter and hang up their raincoats. Leigh had plugged in the kettle and light steam was beginning to rise from its spout. Soon, we were gathered and ready for the debrief.

"What a wonderful event! You all worked so well together and I could tell how much fun they were all having. Leigh, they loved your food. I overheard their admiration of the house and grounds. Even Toby did his part. Well done!" Essie was hugely complimentary.

"Thanks, Essie." I said. I reported her words to Tadame and responded to the others' inquiring looks at Essie's mention of Toby. I described for them what had happened, assuring them I had Charles' permission.

"That's so rad!" Cheri proclaimed.

"Toby's presence has always been comforting to me," Raman admitted. "But, I didn't realize his gift was more than that."

"Toby has been a strong guide for me," Leigh confided. "As soon as I start doubting my abilities, Toby gets in front of me and shakes his head. When I'm not sure what to do, he gets behind me and pushes me in the butt. He's a pretty awesome friend and counsellor."

"Toby also needs the love you so generously give to him," Essie confirmed for Leigh. *"Toby needs to receive, just like the rest of you. That's why I led him to you. You're a good match."*

"It might be interesting to make a blog posting about Toby and some of what's been shared, without naming the individuals involved," Tadame proposed.

The rest of us agreed with her; then, we moved on to our agenda. Leigh shared the notes they'd taken throughout the event. The local craft beer had been very popular; they recommended we stock more of it for similar events. There had been lots of requests for gluten-free and dairy-free items, which Leigh had provided in abundance. There had been a few vegans in the crowd; had we known in advance, we could have provided a dedicated barbeque and offered some veggie dogs. The mini sausages had been a hit—there were no leftovers. The samosas had been completely devoured, as had the mini egg rolls. Leigh continued with the list as we munched on a few leftovers. We congratulated Leigh and each other on a job well done.

Cheri indicated that once the food costs and hourly wages were deducted from the event fee and bar sales, we had cleared $800. Because the event was separate from our day-to-day duties, we'd decided to pay ourselves slightly above minimum wage for the eight hours we'd each put in.

We discussed setting up special events in that way and how often we'd want to book that type of event. We agreed with the pay structure, but we also decided to limit such events to a maximum of one a month. We didn't want to direct our energies away from our main healing focus or tire ourselves out trying to do too much extra.

The agenda moved on to running events. I'd heard back from the race director of a relay race taking place Sunday of the coming weekend. The race finished at a park and the race organizers were going to provide hamburgers with beer or pop for the runners. They were fine with us offering samples of our energy bites and juices. Mini massages and healing sessions had received a definite yes. Raman was running in the race and Cheri already had other commitments that day, so Leigh, Jace, Tadame, and I agreed to attend. The next race opportunity was the third weekend in August. We agreed to wait and see what kind of response we received at the first race, to decide if just a few or all of us might attend.

Next, we hashed out our tour days for August. We needed to firm those up so that Cheri could get advertising out. We decided to invite family and friends in the first week.

"My parents and Melissa's have been eager to come and see the place. I also have a pile of relatives who are home for the summer, so I can invite them too," Cheri proposed.

"I'd suggest we go with a Tuesday for these tours, so we have Monday to prepare. Then, if folks want to make bookings with us, we can follow up immediately," Tadame piped up.

"That works well for me," Leigh advised. "That gives me a prep day for the food and I won't have to get up super early in the morning to have it all ready."

"Good point," Jace affirmed. "Do we want to put a cap on numbers with a pre-registration process or just let it happen and hope we can manage? Do people need to arrive by a certain time or can they just drop in any time through the day?" Jace challenged us to think of details.

"Either way, we'd probably need someone on the door at all times. Maybe Cheri and I could share that responsibility. We'll all be trained on the computer today, so I'll be able to handle bookings or sales," Raman suggested. "I could offer outdoor tours and talks on the labyrinth and herbs at say ten-thirty and one p.m., while Cheri covers inside. Then, Cheri could offer a short yoga experience at eleven-thirty and two p.m. while I cover the desk. That means we'll also have an extra person nearby if Leigh gets swamped in the café or if people start wanting to buy a lot of things from our displays."

"Tadame, Jace, and I will offer mini-sessions in the healing rooms. Cheri or Raman, you can collect the entry fee when people arrive and then direct people to our rooms to sign up. They'll sign up for a time slot and then they can take in an outdoor tour or a yoga class or enjoy some time in the café," I thought aloud.

"As we send invites out to family and friends, we could request an RSVP. We know some will reply and not show, and some won't reply and will show, but it should give us a bit of a guide," Cheri proposed. She hauled out a mock invite she'd prepared and we suggested a few modifications. She promised to send it to us all, to forward to our family and friends.

We discussed other groups we'd like to invite, and whether we should target a specific date for each one or just send a list of all the dates and be open to whoever showed each time.

"Summer is a busy time for many people. I'd rather we kept it flexible to reach more people," commented Tadame. "Why don't we do a media burst and list the three remaining days and the date of our grand opening all at once?"

"I agree," said Raman "I'd like to put it up on some of the running websites. Alisha, maybe you could post it on some church websites. Cheri, maybe we could advertise through local colleges. There's lots of potential."

We took time to brainstorm as many places as possible with which we had connections. We agreed to approach local newspapers for write-ups and, from there, we'd trust the Universe to send us the people who needed to be there each day.

I raised the issue of indoor shoes and we were all on the same page with that.

"Just look at the state of the floors after everyone tromped through, yesterday." Jace gestured to the dirty floors.

Tadame knew a good quality supplier for bamboo slippers, so she offered to work with Cheri to order them.

We set Tuesday as the day to clean the house from top to bottom. Raman wanted some time to start prepping some healing creams for our displays. Leigh was interested in helping him, so the two decided to dedicate Wednesday to that effort. Jace was interested in trying tapping with me; he'd come round to the idea of addressing some of his resistance to hearing voices. We agreed to meet Wednesday morning. On Friday, we planned to load my car with the supplies we'd need for the race on Sunday. With our week sketched out, it was time to delve into the computer training Cheri had planned for us.

"I know most of you are familiar with how to work a computer," Cheri said as she handed us small booklets. "However, every program and system has their own variabilities. So, I've put together some directional sheets to help you get familiar with our system." We murmured our thanks as we leafed through them.

Step-by-step, she took us through how to make bookings, how to access our website to insert information or correct items, and how to create postings for our blog. At that point, she shut the system down and had us each take turns working through those steps.

It was time for a break. We ate lunch together, cleaning up the chili and the last of the leftovers from the night before. Next, Cheri led us through the spreadsheets and billing system. These were more complex; Cheri very patiently guided us through practicing until we had a firm grasp of the steps. The handouts were particularly helpful for this part of the work.

Lastly, Cheri suggested we purchase individual iPads as dedicated work devices. We'd have them in our work areas and could quickly research information for a client online if needed, take necessary notes, or remotely access our booking schedule to check for appointments. Leigh could have their entire recipe file on the iPad and check grocery and supply sales each week. Cheri would be able to bounce emails to us without our having to wait to access the main computer.

"Having a dedicated device for work will help us stay focused on our healing place," she suggested. "If we use personal iPads or laptops, other parts of our lives—like photos, games, or home budgeting—could capture our attention and draw us away from our work together at Essie's."

"Valid point," Jace agreed. "It's helpful to keep things separate. I've watched friends lose hours of work time, getting side-tracked on their laptops. Not to say we'd do that. But it also means we can leave our work here when we go home."

Cheri had already checked out the local electronics store and there was a sale on. She confirmed there was still money in the office equipment fund. "So, what do you think?" she paused to give us time to respond.

"I'd be willing to go with you to take a look at the sales," Raman offered.

We all contributed to the discussion and agreed to authorize Cheri and Raman to make the purchases on our behalf. It was nearing late afternoon, so we wrapped things up and went our separate ways.

CHAPTER TWENTY-THREE

At Tuesday's cleanup, we cranked some tunes and had some fun. We noted we'd need to pick up another painting and order more fairy mugs to replace what we'd sold to Ginny's friends. Cheri checked our voice messages and two people had called: one asking for a massage and the other for a reflexology session. We had discussed beginning to take bookings as we entered August, even though our grand opening wasn't scheduled until September. We hoped we'd get a good response from our open house days and the contacts we made at races. Tadame and Jace spoke with Cheri about their availability so she could return the calls. We were on our way!

On Wednesday, I arrived early to meditate and set the intention of a helpful and safe healing space for Jace in the room we'd be using. Essie was curious and asked questions when I was finished. I shared with her that I found it enriched a healing encounter if I was especially clear about my role as a healing coach or encourager.

"Over the years, I've found it important to practice getting myself and my ego out of the way, so I can focus completely on the person coming to me. I create an energetic intention around the room for it to be a safe space, like a security container, so the person doesn't fear being overwhelmed by whatever may unfold."

"That's interesting, Alisha. I wonder if it's a little like when I'd light a candle, put flowers on the table in the kitchen, and say a prayer for a good evening together, before Stanley arrived in for supper. It was my way of creating a place of beauty and light," Essie pondered.

"It's exactly like that, Essie. What we give to a space and the words we pour into it help create a spirit or energy that will affect those who enter it," I affirmed.

I heard voices outside, so I went out to see who had arrived. It was Raman in the café with Leigh. They were pulling out some of the jars we'd picked up in Hope Falls. Raman had larger jars arrayed in a box. They contained various base oils and emollients. As he took each one out, he explained its properties to Leigh, who was listening avidly. I grabbed a coffee and gave them a brief wave, leaving them to it.

My phone buzzed with a text from Jace to say that he was running a little late. Cheri breezed through the door with her phone to her ear. We both arrived at her desk as she completed her call.

"My Mom's free on Thursday for dress shopping." She spun around with a little dance before plopping into her chair. "You hear that Leigh?" she called out.

"You bet! What time are we going?" they called back.

"The boutique doesn't open until ten a.m.," Cheri stated. "Can we meet there right at ten to get an early start?"

"I'll pick you up at nine-forty, Leigh." I confirmed. "Have you let Tadame know?"

"Texting her right now," Cheri said as her fingers flew over her phone keys. "Done! In other exciting news, Raman and I picked up the iPads and they're awesome. We bought the last ones. I'm going to set them up for us this morning."

The front door opened again, this time revealing Jace, who rushed in, full of apologies.

"I'm sorry I'm late. I had a flat tire. Fortunately, I had a spare, but now I'll have to find someone to repair it or replace it. Can anyone recommend a good place?"

Raman called out one suggestion and we offered our favourite places, which Jace noted in his phone. I offered to get him a coffee to give him a few moments to settle down; he asked for a decaf—his nerves were jangled enough! Eventually, we made our way to the room I had prepared.

We sat, sipping our coffees, and I shared the principles of tapping with Jace. I asserted that as we went back to painful experiences, we would not go into them so deeply as to re-traumatize him. The purpose of tapping along meridian points was to help release the energetic imprint of the trauma in his body, so that he could remember without the impact of the earlier emotions. I emphasized that he was to keep focused on my gaze to remain grounded in the present moment and not get swept away in the past.

"If you start looking away or closing your eyes, I will gently call you back to look at me," I instructed.

He felt comfortable with what I was saying and I could see his shoulders relaxing.

"Where would you like to start, Jace?' I gave the power of choice to him.

"When I was around four, I remember first being aware of voices around me," Jace claimed.

I felt the movie technique might be beneficial in helping him get a perspective on what developed over time in response to his ability. I asked him to shift his perspective as if he was filming himself as a child. I urged him to describe for me all the details of the setting, the action, the thoughts and feelings of the scene; we would also tap the whole time. I assured him that we would proceed slowly. Any time the intensity of his feelings increased as he watched the movie, we could stop and clear things from that moment. Then, we would return to the beginning and start again, to see if new elements arose in the scene. We would continue in this manner until the emotional response was triggered again.

The process fascinated Jace and he was eager to give it a try. After many years as an English teacher, he had a wonderful capacity with words; he was able to vividly set the scene of his movie. We spent over an hour gradually moving through that early experience in his life and all it triggered within him. He described the comfort he felt when he first heard voices. There hadn't been any fear, initially. That became a learned response later, which then painted over his first experience. We addressed early responses from his elders, who explained it all away as a product of his creative imagination. We dealt with some strong emotions—he had felt dismissed and diminished, and he interpreted their words to mean that they were calling him a liar.

"There are a lot of layers that weave into one experience," Jace said quietly at the end of the session. "I feel like we've just peeled off the surface, but it feels good," he reassured me.

I smiled acceptingly. "You may notice more memories surfacing as we've freed some of those layers. Just use the tapping, like we did today, if any of them have an emotional charge. Journal writing can help and we can continue with more sessions if you'd like," I counselled.

"Can we do another session on Friday; we'll be here to load the car for Sunday?" Jace was eager to continue the healing process. I agreed and we did some deep breathing to ground and release one another from the morning's experience.

Cheri was busy at the front desk working on our iPads, so we went to check on Raman and Leigh. I picked up a jar and I noticed a remarkably attractive label affixed to the top, informing me that the contents were an eczema cream. I looked inquiringly at Raman, who had noticed my choice.

"Eczema plagues a lot of people, so I thought it'd be a good standard to keep in supply for our shelves," Raman explained.

"I happen to be one of those people," I indicated a spot between my second and third fingers which was scaly and an angry red colour.

"I noticed," Raman commented. "If you'd like to take a jar to try, it's safe to use anywhere on the body."

"Thanks. Sometimes, in the heat of summer, I get patches of eczema after shaving," I admitted.

"This should help. Start with the spot between your fingers to be sure you react okay to all the elements in the cream. Then, move on to more sensitive areas," he recommended.

"Who did the lovely labels?" I asked.

"I picked up a book on calligraphy from the library a few years ago and had lots of fun experimenting with it. It complements my work quite well, so I'm glad I discovered it," Raman shared.

"Could you teach me how to do it?" Leigh begged earnestly. "I could do up some of my recipes to share with others."

"I have an extra stylus you can borrow," Raman offered generously.

Jace walked over and picked up a jar. "Got any blends that keep bugs away? Hiking on the trail near my apartment has been hazardous with the black flies and mosquitoes."

"I don't have any mixed up here, but out in my truck I have an extra jar for emergencies. Let me get it for you." Raman started toward the door.

"Great. I'm happy to buy it from you," Jace enthused.

"This one's on me," Raman grinned. "I'd like all of you to try the different creams I make, so you'll be comfortable responding to questions customers may ask. After the first jar, you're more than welcome to pay up!"

We had agreed that Raman's herbal creams and any cooking blends that Leigh created would be sold on consignment. We both expressed our thanks to Raman, and Jace followed him outside to the car.

I wandered back to Cheri, who grinned at me as she lifted up a jar she'd scored earlier. She beckoned me over to see if I had time for her to help me get familiar with my new iPad. I pulled over a chair and we set to work.

It was surprisingly easy. She helped me to create song playlists for different aspects of my work. We had remote speakers in each room so that we could play music to suit a diverse range of clients. Then, she showed me an article she and Tadame had written for local newsletters and newspapers. It looked great to me, but I suggested she run it past the others and leverage Jace's English skills to ensure it was grammatically correct.

The phone rang and Cheri answered it, while I continued to explore my iPad's capabilities. When she hung up, she had a bemused expression on her face.

"That was one of the women from the women in business meeting we attended at the end of May. She saw a Facebook post by one of Ginny's friends mentioning our place and she remembered us. She's a radio announcer and would like to do an interview with us next week. Then, she mentioned a friend in television who wants to do a spot on us for the local evening newscast. Holy shit!" Cheri jumped up and began hopping around, shaking her hands, as if trying to release her nerves.

I sat stunned; my heart, which was now in my mouth, beat furiously.

"Breathe, Alisha. Breathe," Cheri encouraged with a light punch to my shoulder as she kept dancing about. Raman and Leigh came to the archway connecting the café to the entryway.

"What's with the shaking boogie?" Raman inquired.

"Alisha, are you all right?" Leigh inquired, concerned.

I gulped in air, finally remembering to breathe as Cheri had suggested. I waved at her to tell them the news. The two of them slapped high fives with Cheri and Raman walked over to squeeze my shoulder.

"Don't worry, Alisha. We've got this."

"I can't even concentrate to think of what we'd say. Where would we start? There's so much here. We can't possibly cover it in a short interview," I worried.

"We could meet on Friday to talk about the most salient points. I think you should be the key interviewee because this was your dream, but one or two of us could join in to give a broader picture of the whole," Raman submitted.

"I agree with Raman. Besides, you're used to public speaking, Alisha. Maybe a couple of us could do radio and the others appear on TV. Let's just see how it unfolds," Cheri advised. We agreed the team would meet late morning on Friday because I had an early session with Jace.

I hurried home to tell Dan our news. Both he and Sabina were in the workshop, so I waited until their equipment was safely turned off and I had their full attention.

When I shared the latest, Sabina responded, "That's seriously awesome, Mom. Your healing place is taking off. I can tell."

Dan brushed wood chips off his overalls and sauntered over to give me a hug.

"Congratulations," he said cheerily.

"Have you guys thought of advertising your work?" I queried.

"I'm more comfortable with things spreading by word-of-mouth for now, especially since we're solidly booked to the end of the summer. One of Sabina's friend's parents has booked us to build a cedar closet into their home. Another friend booked her to build a hope chest. Two colleagues from work called me this week; we're booked to build a kitchen island and adapt a pantry cupboard for one, and the other wants a veranda built to surround two sides of their house. I don't want to start advertising and then have to turn people away because we don't have the time," he shared.

"Wow! I didn't realize things would take off so quickly," I declared.

"We didn't know either. Our time was just beginning to free up as we finished up the work for Essie's Place and—boom!—the calls started coming in," Sabina confided. "We both agreed we wanted time to do some of our own personal projects, as well. Would you like to take a look at what I finished yesterday?"

"I'd love to," I affirmed as I followed her to a back corner of the workshop. She reached out and pulled something down from a shelf, but I couldn't see clearly because it was in the shadow of her body.

"It isn't what you're used to seeing me do, but here it is." She thrust the item into my hands. I glanced down in surprise. It was a foot-high whimsical wooden figure made from polished wood scraps and curls of wood. It revealed a creative fanciful side I'd never associated with Sabina. It just goes to show our children can continue to surprise us.

"It's captivating, honey," I murmured as I carefully swept my hand over its surface. "It's really fun. It invites my imagination to think of a creature hidden in the woods."

"That's what I was trying for," Sabina concurred. "I'd like to do a sideline of these, using up scraps of wood, so nothing is wasted. I enjoy it. It stretches my mind in a different way," she admitted fervently.

Dan put his arm around her. "It's amazing watching what you can do, sweetie."

"Thanks for letting me see this. I'll let you guys get back to work and I'll take supper prep for tonight. Would you like to see if Jack wants to come over?" I volunteered.

"I'll text him. Would six-thirty be okay?"

"Sure. That'll give me time to putter in the garden too," I said, pleased that I'd get a chance to tackle some recent weed growth after the rain.

"Okay Dad, back to work!" Sabina instructed.

"Slave-driver," he grumbled good-naturedly. It was heart-warming to see how well the two of them got along. I sashayed out of the workshop and inside to put on my gardening clothes.

The gardening soothed me as I connected with the earth, kneeling beside my flowerbeds and digging my fingers deep in the soil to pull out weeds. It freed my mind to plan supper; my imagination played with different ideas and I mentally experimented with new flavours. I wanted to try a new blend of spices with some chicken I had defrosted. A half hour passed and I stood up into a strong stretch to release my back muscles and hips. I had discovered that thirty minutes in the garden was the sweet spot for me to not overdo it and end up with an inflammatory response in my joints. Regular short stints allowed me to enjoy gardening and all its benefits without hurting myself.

I scrubbed my hands well and began chopping the chicken to stir-fry it with ground fennel and cloves as seasoning. In a separate bowl, I chopped veggies that I could add later. The rice, which I had set to soak earlier, was ready to boil. I put on my favourite eighties music station and strutted around the kitchen as I completed supper preparations. I decided to make a lime gelatin using ice cubes to quicken the process and, once it was partially set, I'd fold in whipped cream, raspberries, and coconut. It was a night for inviting our taste buds to new experiences.

Sabina popped in to grab a shower. Dan jumped in when she was done and supper was just ready when I heard Jack's voice at the front door. We had a pleasant evening together and the new flavours were a hit. We tried out a fun game that Jack had picked up when he had been away on his last business trip. It led to lots of hilarity and the night closed with us all feeling refreshed by each other's company. It felt good to tend to the new bonds that were forming between us.

On Thursday, I decided I'd go for a short run before going dress shopping with Cheri. My legs were stiff and my feet made a floppy sound on the road. It was frustrating not to be able to find my usual rhythm. Some days, running was a comforting and flowing experience; other days, it felt like a battle with my body. I allowed the tiredness and stiffness to drain from my hips down my legs and into the earth with each pounding beat of my feet. I gently shook my arms out and tried to find a song I could use as a mantra to keep me going. An old camp song started repeating in my mind: "Give Me Oil In My Lamp." I imagined the oil being energy and lubrication for my joints as I let the refrain guide me along. Gradually, my breathing and movements became less jerky and the final ten minutes were almost enjoyable.

Some days, I wondered if I was crazy to keep running but, in many ways, it felt like a life lesson I had the chance to keep practicing. As I practiced running through the challenging days, when I wanted to just say 'forget it', I was reinforcing my resilience for other things in life that would challenge me even more. Learning to carry on in running had helped me many days when my life didn't make sense, when I felt like I had lost my rhythm in parenting, at work, with friends. Holding on and trusting that eventually things would smooth out again was a truth running taught me, over and over again.

I walked for a half kilometre or so, becoming conscious of the world around me again. My internal struggle had temporarily blinded me to the brilliance of the blue sky, the beauty of blossoming bushes, and a bouncy brown rabbit that loped down the bank and into the trees. Drawing in the beauty and offering a grateful heart for what the day was offering to me, I slipped into the house to shower and eat.

We met in the parking lot of the wedding boutique with Cheri, who was vibrating with excitement and nerves. "Do you think I'll find my dress here? What if I like more than one? What if you all like something different on me?" The worried wonderings whisked out of her mouth.

The woman who had stepped out of the car with Cheri enveloped her in a generous hug. "Honey, this time is for you. It's not about what we like. Let's just take this one dress at a time and enjoy ourselves."

She stepped back and turned to the rest of us extending her hand. "Hi there, I'm Cheri's mom, Tina. It's a pleasure to meet you. I've heard so much about you that I've been eager to have the chance to get to know you. I'm so excited you could all come and share this time together with Cheri."

We all took turns shaking Tina's hand and exchanging a few words. The shopping went splendidly and Mavis proved her expertise once again by finding the exact shade and style that blended beautifully with Cheri's colouring. The gang all had fun sharing their ideas.

"What if you added long gloves in a soft pink?" Leigh suggested. Mavis quickly found a set to try and they added perfectly to the ensemble. Tadame wondered about a tiara or headband rather than a veil or hat. There wasn't anything quite in the style we were looking for, but a basic one gave us the sense of how it would suit the dress.

"We'll just have to have another day of shopping," Cheri grinned.

"Sounds like fun to me," Leigh affirmed. "If we're finished, would you all like to go to the Busy Bee Café? One of the guest lecturers from school owns and runs it. They use locally sourced honey in a variety of their treats. I haven't had a chance to try it out yet and I'd love someone to come along and offer opinions," Leigh posed invitingly.

"It's fabulous," exclaimed Cheri's mom. "I'd enjoy the opportunity to get to know you all a little better."

"She means she'll bore you to death with stories of me when I was little," Cheri groaned.

Tadame poked Cheri in the ribs. "Knowing you, I doubt the stories are boring!"

It was a unanimous vote, so we thanked Mavis for her talent and time. The café turned out to be a delightful place decorated with a collection of honey pots and prints of bees in honeycombs buzzing over various flowers, and even a print of Winnie the Pooh with his paw in a hive. We listened to Tina's stories about Cheri and shared some of our own about ourselves as we took pleasure in the meals we ordered. Leigh took notes on their phone about more recipe ideas and suggested we might like to stock some of the local honey in our café. Grateful for the time we'd shared together, Cheri hugged us all before we left. Tina commented on how much she was looking forward to the open house day for families.

CHAPTER TWENTY-FOUR

On Friday, I blearily opened my eyes. Dan had left for the workshop early. I had read late into the evening, pouring over a new healing book, so I was having difficulty getting moving. My body ached for yoga, so I forced myself out of bed and googled a YouTube session with a leader whose voice I found soothing. As I gently shifted from position to position, I found my aches began to subside. I tended to store my anxieties and tiredness in my joints and muscles. Sometimes, I found it helpful to run them out, but other times I needed the contrast of calm, centering movement, as Cheri had shown us. Besides, with our first race coming up the next day, I decided my body would benefit from a gentle routine rather than a more challenging one.

I downed a glass of warm water as I quickly fried some zucchini and spinach in butter with a sprinkle of fennel. I slid them out onto a plate and used the same pan to whip up two scrambled eggs. The fennel was Leigh's suggestion and it added a delicious flavour to my breakfast while supporting my digestive system. After eating, I walked over to the coffee maker and noticed there was leftover coffee still in the carafe. I decided I'd use it for iced coffee after I grabbed a shower. Trying another of Leigh's suggested herbs, I tossed in cardamom with the ice, cream and coffee, and a splash of vanilla oil. Cardamom is supposed to aid in digestion and improve cardiovascular function. I figured my circulation needed help and vanilla oil is calming so I thought the two would set me up for the day.

Jace was due to meet me at 9:30 a.m., so I set off for Essie's place. Again, I took time to meditate the space and set my intention for our healing session together. I had texted Tadame about an essential oil to promote a feeling of safety and security and she recommended geranium. She told me it was notably helpful for connecting a person to their inner life and emotional sensitivities. Geranium also eases emotional tension and promotes a sense of well-being, so it could be helpful for both Jace and I. I borrowed one of her infusers and, when Jace arrived, I told him about its properties. I encouraged him to assess the scent for himself. He sampled the aroma and agreed to give it a try.

We began with a moment of quiet for Jace to collect his thoughts and to reflect on how he'd been feeling since the Wednesday session. He shared that he had taken some time to journal and to tap, using the movie technique. This experience caused him to recall his time at Sunday School at an exceedingly conservative church. There, he had been taught to fear the devil and to watch for the devil whispering in his ear and tempting him. As a child hearing voices, he was terrified he was going to be taken over by evil. He also remembered his paternal grandmother, who used to talk to people who weren't there. His family had moved her to a locked ward at a local nursing home. Thus, Jace was afraid he'd suffer the same fate. She had since passed away, so he had no way to check if it was solely dementia with which she suffered or if she had had the same ability as him.

"When I was tapping and journaling, I couldn't seem to reduce my fears," Jace admitted. "My whole body seemed to vibrate with a panicked response as I'd begin to describe some of those scenes. I felt powerless and I couldn't seem to shift that feeling. Is there anything we can do to break that response?"

"We can try a couple different things," I assured him. "There are a few techniques that work well with a panic response. Let's try one that focuses on the feeling of panic and I'll tap at specific points as you follow with me. We will do some eye circles and some spoken words. I'll tap on your hand as you continue to share what you feel. Whenever I speak it will be in the first person so you can easily repeat after me and fill in the blanks when needed. It may feel intense at first, but this sensation usually shifts after a minute or so. If it doesn't or it feels too overwhelming, we can try another approach."

Jace agreed to give it a try. As we progressed through the technique, Jace initially told me the feeling was intense but, after a few moments, I could see his body begin to soften. I asked him to assess his level of panic on a scale from one to ten. He shared that it was beginning to shift downward in intensity and we continued until he felt it was in a manageable zone, which he rated around three.

"Now that the panic response is integrating, perhaps we can go back to your Sunday School experience. I invite you to give it a symbol. Rather than telling me all the specifics of that time, let your imagination offer a symbol, object, or word which represents that experience for you. Just let your imagination present something to you. Don't try to force it or think it into being," I guided.

"I see a small bucket, like the ones you take to the beach as a child. It's full of dirt."

"Great. Now keep noticing this bucket of dirt and all it represents for you," I continued.

"I'm angry at this dirt," Jace declared.

"Keep tapping through the points with me," I encouraged Jace. "This anger I'm feeling at the bucket of dirt. I wonder how intense it is?"

"It's a six," Jace offered.

"This bucket of dirt which makes me angry, that I feel at a six, I notice is affecting my body…?" I encouraged.

"It's making my stomach clench and my mouth dry. My heart feels tense, too," Jace described as we kept tapping.

I repeated what Jace said and added, "I wonder if there's anything else I notice about this bucket of dirt?"

"It's blue and there's a shovel beside it," said Jace.

"This blue bucket with dirt in it and a shovel beside it makes me angry on a scale of one to ten at about…? I paused for Jace to fill in his assessment of what he was feeling.

"It's about a five now," Jace confirmed. "It feels like the shovel wants to delve in and dig out some of that dirt."

"Noticing the shovel as it empties the dirt out, I wonder what happens next?" I pondered.

"The shovel is taking the dirt and dumping it in the ocean where it's washed away."

"The blue bucket of dirt is slowly being emptied as the shovel pours it into the ocean," I repeated.

"Actually, the bucket just overturned and the whole lot has emptied into the ocean. As it turns over it seems to be full of clear water," Jace explained.

"As I consider this blue bucket full of clear water, I notice my body is feeling…?" I awaited Jace's response.

"I feel calm. The anger and dirt are washed away. My stomach is relaxed."

I probed a little, "I wonder if anything else is happening in this image?"

"I see a little boy, splashing in the water and laughing. There's only joy."

"Let's go back to your experience in Sunday

School, if that feels safe," I proposed.

"I can picture myself back then, but it's as if the weight of those beliefs and the emotional responses to them, have washed away. The fear I held—the feeling of powerlessness and my anger at having to shut away something that had been comforting to me—all that seems clear. I can remember the incident and the words spoken to me, but they carry no emotional charge," Jace described with a tone of amazement in his voice.

"If you could craft an affirmation for yourself, to represent that healing shift, what would you tap into your imagination?" I inquired. "Take a little time to ponder this. Breathe deeply as you do and let yourself play with words that make it feel really yummy and good," I suggested.

Jace had his journal with him, so he took a few minutes to write and rewrite what he wanted to claim as an affirmation for his life. When he was ready, we tapped through all the points using his affirmation to replace and transform his earlier experiences.

"I am a confident, powerful, pure, spiritual being, able to access information in a variety of ways for good," Jace affirmed.

"Well done!" Essie exclaimed. *"I just love watching you and listening to you as this healing stuff unfolds. It's so creative. I never imagined it could be so interesting."*

"It is interesting, Alisha. If you had tried to describe this to me, I'd never have believed that it'd be effective. Even as we started doing the imaging, I had to keep pushing my doubting mind aside and just follow as you were leading me," Jace confirmed.

"Jace, that wasn't me talking to you just now. That was Essie," I gently pointed out.

"How delightful! You can hear me now." Essie sounded excited.

Jace appeared a little uncomfortable. "It seems I can," he admitted. He paused. "But I don't hear any other voices."

"Your mind may do this gradually, so that you aren't overwhelmed as you reclaim this skill," I speculated.

"I'm the only spirit attached to this place, but there may be other spiritual beings and other dimensions that Jace may be able to connect with eventually. Och, this is so exciting!" Essie proclaimed.

Jace shifted in his seat. "I feel a little unnerved again, Alisha."

"Keep tapping whenever fear rises," I recommended. "Affirm and develop trust in yourself that your spirit or mind will guide you at a rate and in a way that is right for you. If you choose only to hear Essie and block off any other spiritual beings, that will be your reality. When you feel ready, other beings will present themselves when you open up to them."

Jace took a deep breath. "This is a lot to process. Two weeks ago, I didn't have a job, I barely knew you, and I had all this buried deep inside me. Now, I've trusted you and myself with some intense stuff and it feels like everything I knew is shifting. Don't get me wrong, it feels freeing and good, but it's a lot," Jace blurted out.

"It wasn't too long ago that I felt the same," I admitted. "Just ask Essie. I plonked down right over there and poured my heart out to her, sharing my fears and wondering if I could cope with all that was happening. To be honest, I still feel that way every day or so." I chuckled lightly and Jace smiled with me.

"It can be helpful to set up the tapping with an intention like 'even though all these changes in my beliefs and experiences cause me fear, I choose to trust myself.' Then, add in the affirmation you've created. Tap until the fear recedes and the confidence increases. Does that sound manageable for now?" I inquired.

"Could we do a couple of rounds together to finish up for today?" Jace requested.

When we were finished, Jace thanked me and I expressed my appreciation of his trust in me and my admiration for his courage to seek this healing for his life. We both thought the geranium oil had been a helpful infusion. I mentioned how powerful I'd also found frankincense and Jace resolved to purchase both oils from Tadame's supplies. Noting the time, we tidied the room and went out to the café for our staff meeting.

In preparation for our upcoming interviews, we spent an hour sharing what we felt were important components of our journey as a new business. Although I'd been the one with the initial vision of a Healing House, we had all experienced individual dreams of offering healing practices to others. We agreed that we would discuss being led to each other for this venture, but we wouldn't mention Essie specifically because that could take things on a tangent away from our healing focus.

"You're very important to us, Essie, and we know you guided us to find each other. However, I'm concerned some of the public would be afraid of a spirit and others might come out of curiosity to experience you but with no interest in what we're offering in healing," Raman expressed.

"It's okay dearie. I understand completely. I've watched enough people come and go here over the last ten years to know some would simply sensationalize this aspect of your Healing House and entirely miss the power of the healing modalities you'll be offering. I don't need to be recognized by the public. Being important to you is what is significant to me," Essie assured us.

"Essie, you are a stand-up lady!" Cheri proclaimed.

We shared with Tadame what Essie had spoken to us and she smiled in agreement with Cheri. We continued to talk about what we felt was unique about our specific areas of work. We wanted to feel confident in being able to present such information to an interviewer and to do so succinctly. I asked if anyone was uncomfortable or absolutely did not want to be recorded by the media, but everyone felt okay with either radio or TV. Thus, we figured the media professionals would be able to assess which of our voices would transmit best over radio and who would communicate most effectively on TV.

Cheri had received communication from the radio producer and they were due to interview us on Wednesday afternoon, after our family and friends open house day on Tuesday. That would give us the morning to tidy up and finish preparing for them. She had contacted the television crew to suggest it might be helpful to do one interview after the other and they had agreed.

"Tell them about the responses you've had to the open house, sweetie!" Essie interjected excitedly.

"Essie seems animated," Tadame commented.

"She's jumping a bit ahead on the agenda, but she wanted me to share the number of replies we've had for our family and friends' day. So far, out of the eighty or so invites we sent out, I've had thirty confirmations and ten people have said they'll come later in the summer," Cheri disclosed.

"That's fantastic!" Tadame declared.

"I've mapped out a schedule for the day, similar to what we discussed after our day together." Cheri handed it around to us. We took time to peruse it and agreed it reflected what we had considered and planned together the week before.

"It feels like everything is moving fast, but this is exactly what we've been working toward all summer," I gushed excitedly.

"I'm going to use the same menu as last Friday as I have my lists and know the time I'll need for preparation," Leigh disclosed.

"Sunday, after we do our mini-sessions and offer

our stuff at the run, I can bring Leigh and our supplies back to unload them," Jace suggested. "We'll put Tadame's oils in her room and reset the tables in the other rooms. Pamphlets will go to Cheri's desk and Leigh can store any leftover energy bites in the fridge. Otherwise, the space is pretty well set up, so there isn't much more we'll need to prepare."

"I'll pop over on Monday for an hour to do a quick inspection of the grounds, but I agree with Jace. Let's take it easy on Monday, unless you need us, Leigh?" asked Raman.

"I'll need to do a grocery run before I start into prep time on Monday morning," Leigh admitted.

Tadame spoke up. "If you send me the list and specifics of what you want, I'm right next to the grocery store. I could pick up supplies and bring them out, if that works for you?"

"That would save a huge chunk of time. I can get started with what I have and then finish up once you arrive. Then, I'll have some time off too," Leigh concurred.

"With our August open house days, our time off isn't going to be the same as we planned for the fall," Cheri pointed out. "Since the rest of us will get more downtime on Monday, maybe Leigh could take another day off."

We appreciated Cheri's organizational awareness and agreed to make sure we all took time off around the busy schedule we'd planned for August. We covered a few other agenda items and, then, set to packing up what we'd need for the Sunday run. Jace and I each took a massage table, sanitizer, and wipes. Tadame sorted through her oils and selected what would be most suited to a runner's needs. She also agreed to take the pamphlets and our cards to display on a small folding table she'd bring from her apartment. Leigh would have the energy bites and juices ready on Sunday when I picked them up.

Raman offered to carry the massage table out and put it in my trunk for me. "You seem a little tense, Alisha," he mentioned as he walked beside me. "Anything going on?"

I sometimes forgot how astute Raman was.

"I'm really nervous about a race Dan and I signed up for tomorrow," I confessed. I hadn't told the others that Dan and I were doing our first race, but I should have known someone would pick up on my tension.

"You took to heart what I shared with you?" Raman commented.

"Look where it's gotten me," I said grumpily. "I'm a nervous wreck! What am I supposed to eat for supper? What's the best way to warm up? Will I be able to do it? What if I go out too fast and can't finish?" My agitated questions rattled out of my mouth before I could stop them.

"Do you want some help with those questions or are you enjoying holding onto the nerves?" Raman queried.

I spun and nearly tackled him before I got myself under control.

Raman stepped back with a grin. "Alisha, you

have dozens of coping techniques for anxiety that you know how to use. You know I'd gladly offer advice from my experiences, yet you've chosen not to ask me until now. I'm just wondering, what's going on?"

I looked at him in astonishment. I took a couple of deep breaths and replied, "You're absolutely right. Taking a moment to breathe and think about it, I suspect I'm afraid to be excited in case I end up disappointed by the experience. If I just give in to the nerves, I'll have an excuse if that happens. Once again, it seems I've forgotten to be open to receiving help."

"It's easy for it all to end up tangled together, Alisha. Don't be too hard on yourself. Just be aware. Do you want some advice?" Raman inquired.

I agreed I did. We finished packing the table into my car and then sat on the veranda to chat together. He gave me some helpful advice and I felt calmer as I set out for home.

That evening, Dan and I followed Raman's suggestion and had a light supper of pasta with a few cookied veggies and chicken. We laid out our running gear for the morning to ensure all items were clean and in place. We relaxed together and caught up on the last few days, keeping our water intake steady up to an hour before bedtime. An episode of our favourite comedy show sent us to bed smiling.

The excitement and water consumption had us both making treks to the washroom during the night! By 6:00 a.m., we gave up and got up to eat our race breakfast: oatmeal for me and scrambled eggs with bacon for Dan. We teased each other as we pulled on our gear. Dan made a recovery smoothie to put into thermoses for after the race. He threw in avocado, kefir, coconut milk, frozen cherries, blueberries, bananas, chia, and dark cocoa. It was a favourite of ours and having something familiar was calming. With a change of clothes added to our kitbag, we set out for the race site.

Nerves danced in my belly and my thoughts darted in a dozen directions. I tried some deep breathing as we approached the parking area, where I could see various runners emerging from their vehicles. Holy shit, we were really going to do this!

"It's just for fun! It's just another running day!" I kept repeating that in my mind. I looked over at Dan, whose knuckles were white as his hands gripped the steering wheel. I wasn't the only one a bit tense. Somehow, that helped me to relax. I placed my left hand over his.

"Come on, let's go register."

As we stood in the registration line-up, people chatted cheerily with one another. We chit-chatted with a runner who was visiting the area and had wanted to take in a local race. The easy comradery of runners talking about their favorite races and their latest gear helped to take the edge off my nervousness. Then, a familiar figure sauntered over.

"How're you doing?" Raman grinned at Dan and me.

"Nervous, but good," Dan responded. "I'm

excited. I've been wanting to do a race for a long time, but it just never worked out."

"Are you going to run together?" Raman inquired.

"No way!" I exclaimed. "Dan's super fast. I don't want to hold him back. I thought you were in tomorrow's race?" I quizzed.

Raman flashed a cheeky smile. "I thought someone might need a little support. Running five kilometres today won't affect my race tomorrow. If you'd like, I can pace you," he offered.

"I won't be able to keep up," I exclaimed.

"That's not how pacing works. I'll follow your lead and we'll run at your usual pace. I'll offer encouragement and keep you going," Raman assured me.

I considered Raman's offer. If I felt we were going too fast, all I had to do was say so. Having someone next to me would probably take my mind off all the other runners around me.

"I think I'd like that," I stated appreciatively.

Dan spoke up. "Thanks, Raman! I was feeling guilty leaving Alisha alone when I know how nervous she is, but she insisted. She knows how much I want to see what I can accomplish in this race. Now maybe both of us can relax a bit!"

Raman went to register while Dan and I expressed how fortunate we felt that our circle of friends had expanded because of the Healing House. Raman returned to guide us in a few dynamic warm-ups to get the blood flowing through our muscles.

When the call came to line up at the start, we felt as prepared as we could be. Raman suggested we go toward the back third of the pack, so I wouldn't get caught in the flow of faster runners. He suggested Dan go to the front third, so he wouldn't get bogged down trying to pass slower runners.

The horn sounded and we were off! The pack surged forward and we followed along. It took a few minutes for people to space out. Raman encouraged me to settle into my own rhythm and not to mimic the beat of runners in front of me as I watched their feet in motion. He started chatting about an article he had read about microgreens. As my attention was drawn to his conversation with me, I found myself distracted from the other runners. Before I knew it, I had relaxed into the run at a pace that was comfortable for me. Near the two kilometre marker, we saw Dan passing us on the way back. He looked strong.

"Way to go!" we called out and he gave us a thumbs-up in reply.

When we turned around at the half-way point, Raman checked in on how I was feeling. He suggested that if all was well, we could pick up the pace slightly at three kilometres. I was game to try. My breathing became a little more challenged, but I wasn't uncomfortable. At four kilometres, we pushed a little more. Raman asked me to check my heartrate and breathing, and if my legs felt okay. All was good, so we pushed to the finish and I was exhilarated as we crossed over the line. I had done it—my first race! I high-fived and then hugged Raman. Dan had cheered us in and rushed over to join us.

"How was it?" he asked excitedly.

"Fantastic!" I exclaimed. "How about you?"

"It was so much fun. I loved all the cheers and words of encouragement from everyone. It kept me going. I started a little too fast, but I relaxed back when I realized what I'd done. I gave it at the end and came in with the best time I've ever had for running this distance," Dan gushed with enthusiasm.

Raman chuckled, "You're hooked! Come on, let's join the crowd to cheer the rest of the runners in."

We gathered around the finish and joined the hubbub of noise generated there. I bumped against Raman. "Thanks for making this an awesome first race experience," I expressed.

"My pleasure," he smiled. "When I first started, I was with a training group, so I didn't have to do it alone. A friend ran with me. It helped with the nerves. Glad I can return that favour today."

Most people seemed to hang around after the race, certainly until the prize draws were completed. Others stood around the water table and chatted before drifting off. I hoped it would be similar the next day when we'd be offering our sessions. Dan won a water bottle in the prize draw. Delighted with our morning's experience, we said our goodbyes to Raman and decided to go to the local market for a treat. I saw a booth offering microgreens, so I purchased a small package for our evening salad. I took the brochure to read later, because I'd only absorbed a little of Raman's conversation during the race. Dan decided on a spicy sausage with the works and I went for a raw cacao cookie. Both were delicious!

The day was very warm and we decided to drive to a nearby beach. Sweaty from our run, we thought a swim might refresh our tired muscles. We kept our swim gear in the trunk of the car during summertime, so we were prepared. We enjoyed a delightful afternoon at the beach, letting the sand massage the soles of our feet. There was a soft breeze, so we jumped in the waves. The thrust and pull of the water pummeled us, offering a full body treatment. It was a banner day!

Thankfully, Sunday dawned slightly cooler. Dan was off to meet a friend about a carpentry project. I set out to pick up Leigh and meet the others for our first race. When we arrived, Tadame was already there with her table set up and a few people were speaking with her. One had our pamphlet in her hand. Leigh slipped behind the table and set out a few of their samples. Instantly, they started fielding questions too. I set up my massage table in a shaded area to their left. Jace wasn't due to arrive for another half hour. I saw Raman speaking with some running friends and sent him a friendly wave. Then I noticed Ginny in the group surrounding him.

She saw my wave and wandered over, a coffee mug in her hand. "Hey mom," she said breezily.

"You're up early." I stated; Ginny was not known

to be an early riser.

"I know!" she exclaimed. "Hence, the supersize coffee. I thought I'd check out your set-up and watch Raman race. I've never attended a race before. I was curious. I offered to drive the van for his team."

"You and Raman seem rather chummy. Anything I should know?" I raised an eyebrow.

She grinned at me. "Right now, we're just friends. We share some common interests and enjoy being in each other's company. Don't worry. If anything develops we'll let you know." Before I could say anything in reply, she sauntered off.

Tadame and Leigh had overheard our conversation but there was no time to comment. A woman hesitantly approached me.

"I hear you'll be offering healing sessions after the race," she started.

I nodded and smiled. Before I could say anything, she blurted out, "I have a really stiff neck and I wonder if there's any way you can help before I run."

I glanced at my watch. It was fifteen minutes before the race start.

"I can do a bit of energy ultra-sounding," I offered.

Tadame joined me. "I can hold a shoulder reflex point on your hand to support what Alisha's doing."

"Have you had energy work before?"

The woman shook her head as I pulled over a chair for her. I needed her at a better height for me to work on her neck and shoulders.

"Are you okay with me working in your energy

field and are you okay with touch?" I inquired.

"I'll accept anything at this point," she declared. "I'm so uncomfortable I'm afraid it'll interfere with my race."

She held out her hand to Tadame while I quickly ran my hands through her field around her neck and shoulders to assess the areas of tension. I offered a condensed introduction to energy practices as I proceeded to ultrasound between her spine and shoulder blade where a dense knot was pulsing. I set the intention that all I was offering would be helpful for this person. Next, I placed my hands wherever they felt drawn to, so they could soak in the healing support she needed. I released her to the Universe's care as I heard the announcer calling people to the start line.

She stood and rolled her shoulders and gently swivelled her neck.

"That feels so much better! Thank you! I'll be back after the race," she yelled as she dashed off to the start.

I heaved a huge sigh of relief. Tadame and Leigh smiled widely.

"I didn't expect to jump into things quite so quickly," I confessed.

"I know. I barely got my oils on the table and people were starting to ask me questions. Hopefully that's a good omen," Tadame anticipated.

"There's the horn. They've started. We've got more than an hour and a half before the first runners will be back, right Alisha? A little time to breathe!"

Leigh joked.

"It's a twenty-five kilometre relay, circling out and back to us here. I'm told most teams will follow their mates along the route. The earliest teams usually take about an hour and forty minutes. We've got time to chill," I agreed.

They expressed gentle curiosity over my earlier conversation with Ginny about Raman. I candidly replied, "I imagine time will tell", and we left it at that.

I told them about my race experience from the day before. I was warmly congratulated on my achievement and they were impressed by Raman's support. I brought up the microgreens that Raman had mentioned while we were running and which I'd sampled from the market. Leigh had already been speaking to Raman about them. They brought up the various benefits of microgreens. Tadame shared that she loved them on salads. The case for building a greenhouse in the early fall was tempting. Our conversation jumped to all sorts of topics as we relaxed in the shade, waiting for the runners. Jace arrived before the racers returned and joined the discussion.

Eventually, we heard excited voices cheering on the first finisher. Soon, runners were swarming in. The woman I'd offered energy support to earlier had talked us up along the route. Apparently, her neck felt great the whole run and she had her best run in months. People gathered round for brief sessions with Jace, Tadame, and I. Many tried Leigh's energy balls and juice blends. The food was a hit. Others were curious about Tadame's oils. Raman briefly dropped over with a few friends. One benefited from a massage and the other was eager to try Tadame's reflexology. We answered questions and worked steadily over the next two hours as the final relay teams came in.

We were immensely thankful for the response we'd received. As we packed up, we agreed that setting up a rotation of three to four of us for such events would be best. Although it had been busy, which was good for building clientele, we didn't want to drain ourselves before we officially opened.

Tiredness set in as I climbed into my car. It had been a full week and weekend. I wished I had a jacuzzi to soak in when I returned home. I pulled into traffic and linked into a podcast to keep me awake as I drove home.

CHAPTER TWENTY-FIVE

Tuesday brought a little light rain early in the morning, but it cleared off as our crew arrived at Essie's. It promised to be fine for the outdoor tours. Leigh was busy in the café and Cheri was at the front desk. Tadame, Jace, and Raman arrived within minutes of each other. The open house was scheduled for 10:00 a.m. so we had an opportunity to touch base with each other and do a quick sweep of the place.

Cheri brought out two baskets with bamboo slippers. "I checked the mail yesterday and these had arrived," she shared cheerfully. "We won't have to worry about people tracking in the dirt today. I have a couple of signs I quickly printed off. We can post them at each doorway, but we'll need to encourage people to use them because they may not be accustomed to taking off their shoes in public places."

Tadame helped her with the signs and we were ready for action. Essie agreed to be a quiet observer throughout the day.

The door opened at 9:45 a.m. to our first attendees. There were always a few keeners who arrived early! They were members of Cheri's family who she introduced to us all. Some of Leigh's school friends were next and they beelined for the café. Only one person was reluctant to take off their shoes. They weren't wearing socks and nervous about a planter's wart on the ball of their left foot. We agreed to let them keep their shoes on and we realized we'd need to make sure we provided socks for such clients—we could sanitize the socks with bleach afterwards.

The day unfolded beautifully. From 10:00 a.m. until 12:30 p.m., I offered mini-sessions. Then, I took a half hour to mingle with people in the café and outside. Jace stepped behind the counter to give Leigh a break, so they could go out and sit with some friends on the veranda. Tadame's final session must have run over because she didn't appear until well after us.

"*Someone was asking her about a specific oil,*" Essie updated me.

I silently thanked her. Raman was on the desk, busily processing sales. Cheri was finishing up a yoga session in the Great Room.

The afternoon continued smoothly and we said farewell to our final guest as we encouraged them out the door at 4:30 p.m. We plonked ourselves down in the café, where I hauled over an extra chair to put my feet up. Cheri grabbed her iPad and a jug from the back of the fridge.

"Raman, can you bring some glasses," she called out as she waltzed to the seat beside me. "I made a new sun tea yesterday. It's nicely chilled and will refresh us as we review the day. I'd like to go over our first impressions while they're still fresh in our minds."

"It was stupendous!" Essie exclaimed. *"Every one of those people was here to support you and had an interest in what you're doing. It was so exciting watching it all unfold."*

Raman placed the glasses on the table and took a seat. "We had a larger response than I expected, but that could be because they're close family and friends wanting to show their support."

"We had sixty-five people, although only forty had pre-registered." Cheri referred to her iPad.

"I ran short on certain food items," confessed Leigh. "I had calculated for fifty to give myself a cushion, but I'll allow for more next time. Also, this crowd seemed to have a predilection for sweets. There were no cookies left by three p.m."

Jace said, "I was able to fit in about four people per hour, so I saw less than a quarter of the those who came."

"I averaged about the same. But, everyone seemed content just to have a quick experience and ask a few questions." Tadame mentioned.

"Cheri and I had around twelve to fifteen participants at our group sessions, which was manageable. Lots of people simply enjoyed wandering the grounds on their own. Some groups sat around on the veranda and in the Zen garden, chatting quietly. Others poked through our display shelves. We sold a lot of stuff," Raman shared.

"We have at least fifteen bookings for the next two weeks," Cheri highlighted. "All in all, I'd say today was a huge success. A few things to tweak, but well done everyone!"

"I agree. Well done friends!" I raised my glass in a toast. We clinked our sun tea glasses together. "I need to get laundry started for the bedding and towels. Leigh, tell us what to do in here and we'll get the initial cleanup started. Tomorrow morning, we can finish up before the interview crews arrive."

"All the outdoor areas need to be checked for any dishes and garbage," Leigh began.

"I want to check the gardens, the trails, and the labyrinth, so I'll do that." Raman stood up.

"The veranda and this area need to be cleared. Be sure to check the trolleys for dirty dishes. Once they run through the washer, we'll want to reload the trolleys with clean mugs and cutlery." Leigh instructed.

"I can handle that," Jace offered.

"I'm going to go through my supplies to be sure I have what I need for the menu I planned to display on TV and to feed the interview crews," Leigh stated.

"While you take care of laundry, I'll sanitize the rooms, Alisha." Tadame volunteered.

Cheri popped up. "That leaves me to restock our

display shelves and my desk."

We worked efficiently together. Within the hour, most things were tidied, cleaned and restocked. I put the towel load into the dryer and Leigh promised to check on it later. I waved my farewells as I dashed out the door, eager to get home to share with Dan how well our day had unfolded.

By Wednesday, my nerves were back in action. So many firsts all in a row! I dithered back and forth over my clothing choices. Finally, I called Tadame and asked her advice. "Avoid wearing Spanx," she suggested with a grin in her voice. "It's too hot and you'd sweat like crazy."

"I'm going to sweat like crazy from nerves!" I exclaimed. "I'll be a pit-stained mess."

"I have a mix of oils in a natural deodorant base that I use for times like this. Relax and tell me your options." Tadame firmly brought me in line.

I heaved a sigh and separated the clothes in my closet, as I tried to describe the most likely options for the day. We narrowed them down to two and Tadame suggested I wear one and bring the other in case I needed a change for the second interview. That felt wise to me, so I chose a sundress in vibrant swirls of colour to begin and I packed a flowing top over light capris as my second choice.

Dan gave me a hug for good luck, being careful not to wrinkle my clothes. He scrunched up his nose at the lipstick I rarely wore as he braved a kiss.

"You look great and you'll do fabulous," he

assured me. "You're an accomplished public speaker and this is something you're truly passionate about, so trust yourself." He looked me directly in the eye as he spoke. My heart swelled. I loved this man fiercely! He sometimes drove me crazy, but he always supported me.

"Thanks." I squeezed his arm. "Good luck with the veranda job."

Dan swung the door open for me and there was no going back. On to the interview!

When I arrived at Essie's, the others were restlessly prowling around, reflecting their nervousness.

"I came in early and damp-mopped the main floors early this morning," Cheri reported. "I had to keep busy!"

"I couldn't sleep, so I came in to give Leigh a hand, for the same reason!" Jace confessed with a sheepish smile.

"I brought an extra shirt because I was nervous I'd soak through the first one before I made it to the second interview," Raman admitted.

"Me too!" I exclaimed.

We broke into laughter.

"You'll all do just fine," Essie assured us. *"I have great faith in you."*

"Thanks, Essie," I replied. "Just make sure you don't decide to be part of the interview," I reminded her.

"As if I'd interfere," she sniffed.

We loosened up as we finished our preparations.

Cheri noted three more requests for appointments on the answering machine. Gradually, the time approached for our interviews. We heard vehicles pulling up outside and someone knocked at the door.

I looked around at my friends and whispered, "Ready everyone? They're here!"

I opened the door in welcome. A fortyish, full-figured woman, dressed in a crisp lemon linen top and stretchy dark grey capris led the troop. She smiled at me as she extended her hand.

"Hi. I'm Donna Banks, one of the announcers for CKSH radio. We met briefly at the women in business meeting. It's Alisha, right?"

"Yes. Welcome to Essie's Healing Place. Please come in." I stepped back from the door and gestured with my hand.

Donna introduced her crew. "This is Mike Dollar, my co-host, and Ricky Barnes, our sound man."

Mike was dressed in light cotton pants and a dress shirt. He looked tired. Ricky was in jeans and a t-shirt that proclaimed "Sounds Terrific", with images of sound equipment scattered around the words. I introduced our team and greetings were exchanged all around. Donna took charge.

"Here's how I'd like to proceed. I've checked out your website and blog. I'd like to have each of you do a tour with Mike and me, in the area where you work. We'll ask questions and get a sense of what might be juicy for an interview. Meanwhile, Ricky will find the best place to set up to record. Then, he'll test each of your voices to determine which will carry best via this medium. Alisha, I'd like to start with you because this is your dream child."

Leigh put on a fresh pot of coffee and Cheri offered to take Ricky around so he could choose his spot. I rather bemusedly led Donna and Mike into the Great Room as they peppered me with questions.

"It stated on your website that you used to be an ordained minister. What gave you the courage to walk away from a calling that had been important to you for twenty-five years?" Donna inquired.

"I don't know that I'd call it courage, exactly," I confessed. "I simply reached a point where I couldn't do it anymore. Some might call it burnout. But it didn't feel like that to me. It was more like this framework that had guided my life no longer fitted and I had to step away to discover the new person I was becoming."

"So, you had a crisis and needed new employment?" Mike interrupted.

"No." I was firm. I didn't want words that weren't mine being put into my mouth. "I had a transformative experience that led me to listen to an earlier dream in my life. I realized it was time to begin the journey to the creation of this Healing Place."

"I understand that this building was on the market for a long time. How did you end up choosing it?" Donna's interviewing technique guided me to offer my own words. She continued to ask how I had found my team and how we had set up the business. We reached the healing room set up for my sessions. I described the type of energy work I offered. Donna was keen to experience it; her knee ached constantly and she wondered if I could work on it. Mike leaned against the wall and I could sense his resistance. Ignoring him for the time being, I spent five minutes demonstrating for Donna techniques that could be helpful.

When we were finished, she stood up and took a few steps forward. "The achiness has eased significantly. I really appreciate you offering a first-hand experience of your work," Donna enthused.

I turned to Mike, determined not to be swayed by his resistance.

"Would you like to give this a try?"

"I doubt it'll do any good," he stated. "But, go ahead."

When I asked what he'd like to receive, he indicated his shoulders were always tight. I explained what I'd be offering as he sat in a chair in front of me. As soon as my hands rested on his shoulders I could feel the tension he held there. It felt like a huge weight pressed down upon him.

Essie spoke into my mind. *"The poor man is carrying a heavy load, Alisha. His wife has been sick and they have a high needs child; they're both exhausted. He never feels good enough and working with Donna exacerbates that feeling. She always seems to know the right questions to ask. He feels like he fumbles his questions."*

As I kept inviting healing energy to flow through my hands into Mike, I responded silently, "Essie, you're not supposed to be digging in his mind like that. We talked about confidentiality."

"I'm not going to tell anyone else. I just wanted to help him by letting you know, so you'd stop judging him," Essie scolded me.

"I don't have to know all of his issues to allow healing to happen. I can get my ego out of the way and I realize I was being judgemental. That's why I offered to work on him too," I scolded back.

"I just wanted to help," Essie sighed. *"Maybe that's my ego getting involved."*

"It's okay, Essie. It's a constant learning process. Now I'd better give my full focus back to Mike."

I allowed another few minutes and brought the experience to a close. Mike wiggled his shoulders and turned his head from side to side.

"It does feel looser, but I took some Advil earlier; it could be from that. Funny though, I feel lighter, somehow." Then a question seemed to pop out of him. "Do you ever work with kids?"

I was very suspicious, but Essie loudly assured me the question was all his. I explained more about our services and what they could offer to all ages as we returned to the Great Room.

They moved on to questioning Raman and toured outside, while I did a sound check with Ricky. I noticed Toby amble over and brush up against Mike. Mike's hand reached down, brushing along Toby's back. Even from a distance I could see his body relax as they walked along. When I saw Raman come in, he went to the back pantry and came out with a small jar.

"I offered a free sample to Mike for his wife," Raman disclosed. "She has severe psoriasis."

It took an hour and a half for the full tour and a quick coffee break. Leigh's treats were highly commended. Donna again took charge.

"Okay gang, Ricky tells me Alisha's, Jace's, and Tadame's voices resonate exceptionally well over the sound waves, so we'd like you three to be our interviewees. Mike and I will use some of the background information you've all shared to set up your journey together and the business you've developed. Then, we'll take turns asking you some salient questions to bring out the more interesting aspects of your story. We'll take a photo of the whole gang before we go and post that on our website with a link to yours. Ready?"

She was definitely the organizer in the bunch, but both she and Mike bounced off each other well as they recorded. They managed to keep us at ease and it went off without a hitch. We thanked them for their time as they loaded up their cars. I glanced down at my watch—there was only a half hour to go before the TV crew was due to arrive. I scurried back inside and Tadame called me over to a table she'd set up for us.

She had made a big salad for us because she knew Leigh was preoccupied with food for display and feeding the crews. We enjoyed the crisp greens, snow peas, red peppers, and small chunks of steak, tumbled in a lime oil and maple vinaigrette. It was delicious and bolstered our energy for the afternoon.

I tidied up as everyone took time to brush their teeth. We didn't want any rogue greens showing up in our smiles.

There was a knock on the door and we were underway again. This time, we gave a brief tour for the whole crew as the camera crew wanted to assess the grounds and interior for the best shots. They decided they wanted to do multiple clips which they'd later piece together. I was filmed in front of Essie's place, by our sign. Ken, the interviewer, asked me about the history of our place. Then, they did a clip in my healing room. They captured Raman sitting in the Zen garden, walking the labyrinth, kneeling in the herb garden, and behind the counter holding up one of his herbal creams. They also captured Toby outside and took notes about his history as a therapy dog. They captured Leigh in action chopping herbs, working the juicer, pulling a tray out of the oven, pushing a trolley loaded with goodies, and passing over a cup of coffee in one of our fairy mugs. Cheri led us in a small yoga class and then sat behind her desk with the phone to her ear. Ken asked questions as they filmed. It was fascinating to observe the difference in working with a visual medium versus strictly sound.

We finished up in the Great Room, with the whole team seated on the couches and chairs in a semi-circle arrangement. Ken sat at the top end of the semi-circle. He explained that he would welcome us and introduce us. He would continue with questions, but the final show wouldn't be so straightforward. He would weave all the various clips together into a whole, taking the best shots and responses from each of us. Their make-up person, who'd been working with us all afternoon, rushed in to do a final touch-up. A half hour later, we were done.

We offered the crew the opportunity to sample Leigh's treats and they gladly accepted. One person came over, coffee cup in hand, limping slightly. I recognized him as a cameraman. He introduced himself as John and sheepishly admitted he had tripped over one of the rocks forming the labyrinth when they were filming. He inquired if he could have some ice. I offered to do a little healing energy work if he wanted and Raman, who had overheard our conversation, mentioned he had some cream to ease swelling.

John gratefully sat down. We rubbed some of Raman's cream on the affected ankle and then I did my stuff. Leigh brought over a bowl of anti-inflammatory grapefruit-oil-infused chocolate mousse with berries. He delightedly tucked in. Conversation flowed around us as we continued and as everyone enjoyed the food. When it came time for them to pack up and go, the swelling in John's ankle had subsided noticeably.

Ken joined us. He cleared his throat and said, "You may not have realized, but our other camera person filmed you guys in action. He was reviewing one of his earlier clips when he saw John limping over to you. He began recording and captured the whole thing. I couldn't have planned it better myself. You three just demonstrated what this place is all about." He was almost bouncing with excitement. "We won't use it, if you don't give permission. But man, it was incredible. You simply flowed together in response to John's need. Your compassion and energy were almost visible to the naked eye. Let's take a look at the clip and you can decide."

We felt a little self-conscious as we gathered around to see the playback. John had immediately offered his permission, but we waited to see how it looked to us. We looked at each other after it was completed and nodded. Ken was correct, it was awesome. It powerfully communicated the whole of what we were about as a Healing House.

Finally, they left and the house was ours again. Cheri started waltzing around with her arms out, leading Essie in a celebrative dance. Leigh went over to join them. Smiling, I watched them.

I could hear Essie say, "*Fabulous! It was spectacular! You are such an awesome team!*"

Suddenly, the front door re-opened and John poked his head back in. "Before we leave, I wanted to say thanks again for helping me out!"

With curiosity spreading over his face, he looked over at Cheri and Leigh, who had quickly dropped their hands and come to a halt, but not before John noticed each had a hand holding empty air.

I stepped over to the doorway.

"You're very welcome, John."

The expression on my face begged him not to ask

questions. He smiled mischievously and waved farewell with a broad wink in the direction of where Essie would have been standing. The door closed behind him and I spun around.

"I wasn't paying attention. We were having fun celebrating!" Essie exclaimed defensively. *"I've been very well behaved all afternoon!"*

"I think he saw you," Raman commented.

"Leigh and Cheri aren't the only ones with vision, you know. There may be others who come who will see me. That isn't under my control." Essie sounded a little cross.

Raman tapped his iPad and grabbed my hand.

"Let's all celebrate!"

Music poured forth from the iPad as he twirled me into the Great Room with the others. Tadame and Jace joined in. We all danced with joy at another successful day.

As we swirled around Raman spoke to me. "I'd like to be upfront with you Alisha and I hope this doesn't cause any discomfort in our friendship, but Ginny and I have gone out a few times."

I made some encouraging sounds for him to continue.

"We hit it off at the campfire when we sang together. She invited me to karaoke and we've met a few other times. We're quite different from each other, but we seem to get along well. I wanted to speak to you before our friendship develops any further, so you wouldn't think we were going behind your back."

I reassuringly squeezed his hand as he twirled me

in the dance.

"Raman, you're both adults. What you choose to pursue together is your business. I appreciate you letting me know, but I care about both of you, so I'll support you both whatever unfolds."

The music came to an end. We all cheekily bowed to each other. It took only a brief time to clean the café. Jace and I had a few bookings the next day, but the others were free to go to the beach or relax as they chose. On the weekend, there was a local exhibition which Raman had looked into attending. He, Tadame, and Leigh were going to set up a table for the afternoon. We closed for the day and I looked forward to a quiet evening.

I arrived home and Sabina's car was still in the driveway. I found her in the kitchen, enjoying a blueberry beer and typing away on her laptop. She looked up.

"Oh good, you're home. Jack and I completed the online marriage course. It was actually pretty good. We had a few interesting discussions about things we hadn't really addressed before. We picked up our licence this morning and I wanted to take some time to talk about the ceremony. September's coming soon."

Throughout my ministry, I had worked with couples in marriage preparation before I performed a wedding ceremony. It was part of my commitment to them to support them in fully exploring the promises they'd be making to each other. Dan and I had gone through such a preparation and greatly benefited from it. I wanted that for Sabina and Jack, but I felt they might feel more comfortable with an electronic course rather than talking to me as Sabina's mom.

"I'm glad you got something out of it. Even though your dad and I had known each other a few years before we got married, in our marriage preparation we were surprised at some of the things we took for granted," I shared. "It's good you picked up the licence early. You can email me the information we'll need to fill in. When do you two have a night free that we could talk about the ceremony?"

"We're free Sunday. We plan to go to the beach for the day, but maybe we could come back here for supper and a planning session?" she suggested.

"I'll mark it on our calendar." I sat down beside her and she launched into a description of her shopping expedition with Ginny. It had gone well and she was pleased with the dress they'd found for Ginny. It seemed all clothing and accessories were under control, but then it struck me that I didn't have anything. I culled my closet when I left ministry, not wanting anything that felt like that identity.

"I know you're trying to keep it light and not too formal. But I'm conducting the service and I'm still the mother of the bride. What am I going to wear?" I moaned.

"Mom, you're starting to sound like Ginny!" Sabina warned. "One drama queen in the family is enough. Take a drink of your beer and a deep breath."

I followed her instructions with a wry smile, hearing my own advice being directed back at me.

"Why don't you treat yourself to a new dress? You'll want something nice for your official opening day for Essie's Place too; maybe it could double for that," Sabina suggested.

"That's a constructive suggestion," I said.

"Ginny took me to a new boutique she found when we were looking for her dress. Would you like to check it out together, as long as you don't go drama queen on me?" she qualified.

"I can agree to that," I asserted. "Would it be okay for Tadame and Cheri to come if they're free?" I asked, thinking an extra opinion or two might be helpful and that they might want to select something for the grand opening too.

"Great idea." Sabina clinked her beer bottle to mine. We compared calendars and Saturday looked free. I texted the others. Tadame texted back that she was working at the exhibition at 2:00 p.m., but she could join us earlier. Cheri was all in as long as she didn't have to get out of bed before 9:00 a.m.

Dan arrived home from his veranda job and we pulled leftovers out of the fridge for supper. Sabina joined us to give the beer time to wear off before she had to drive home.

The Saturday shopping trip was a blast. Cheri and Sabina bounced off each other easily. Cheri found a dress at Ginny's recommended boutique but the styles felt a little young for me. Tadame had a favourite place at which she had luck finding good deals, so we tried it and both of us emerged triumphant.

Sunday supper and wedding planning was full of laughter. Jack was quick to express his opinion, but also a careful listener to Sabina's preferences. Together we crafted an initial outline and I agreed to send them a ceremony workbook from which they could cut and paste the parts they liked best.

They filled us in on what they'd discussed with Leigh for the reception. The menu sounded delicious. Leigh was going to hire a few friends to help serve, since we wouldn't be working this special event. They had decided to hire a DJ so we could dance in the Great Room. They shared that they were going away for a short honeymoon, but Sabina didn't want to be away from work for very long since the business was just getting underway. They decided to save toward a trip to Thailand in a year's time. Everything seemed to be falling into place. It was good to get the details discussed without having to ask.

The rest of August rushed steadily by. Our open houses continued to be popular, although none as busy as the family and friends' day. We set up at races and a few other exhibitions, again with excellent responses. The radio and television interviews aired and we were thoroughly impressed by their quality. We also appreciated how closely they stuck to our words. We sent a note of thanks to each station. I ran two introductory sessions to the labyrinth for local church groups and both were interested in a more in-depth program.

Our appointment slots started filling up and we began to hone our program ideas for the fall. Our advertising was out for our Grand Opening and fall programs. Raman would lead one on Tuesday evenings and Saturday mornings, focusing on harvesting healing herbs. I also wanted to capture the warmth and light for labyrinth walks, so I chose Thursday evenings and Saturday afternoons. Repeating the programs in more than one time slot would ensure we reached a wider audience and meant less preparation time for those of us offering leadership. Once the wedding was over, we'd be going all out!

CHAPTER TWENTY-SIX

The Labour Day weekend approached and the forecast was for clear skies and seasonal temperatures. Sabina and Jack had sent a lovely email, with a photo, to all the extended family announcing their engagement. They asked for everyone to share their joy, but explained they would only be inviting a small representation to their wedding because space was limited. For family travelling from out-of-town they had rented two large cottages.

We expected ninety people. A few friends and cousins had babies, so we set up a temporary change table in the healing room at the back of the Great Room. Sabina and Jack had decided against a formal sit-down reception and chosen food stations like we'd done for Ginny's party. They wanted to be free to mingle and sit with people as they chose. Raman had positioned solar lights along the outdoor pathways, the gardens, and labyrinth so these areas would be well lit as evening darkness fell. A few toasts and speeches would be offered at the beginning of the dance, but otherwise they simply wanted a relaxed and fun time.

The rehearsal was scheduled for Friday at 5:00 p.m., followed by a party at Jack's family home. We went out to Essie's Place early in the afternoon and Dan set up the arbour. Sabina had consulted with Raman and he had recommended putting potted plants at each side of the arbour, so the beauty of the wood wouldn't be hidden by decorations. In the planters there was ivy which symbolized fidelity, marriage, friendship, and affection; ferns represented sincerity; white and blue hyacinth signified the constancy of love; and stephanotis denoted happiness in marriage. After the ceremony, the married couple could take the planters home and continue to enjoy their beauty.

At the apex of the arbour they had attached a small bouquet of the mixed flowers and a few red roses with trailing greenery. Sabina would be carrying a similar bouquet. We had found sparkly gauzy dragonflies at the dollar store to match those in Sabina's dress. We bought out all the store's supplies and wired a few of them at strategic spots around the arbour. We took the rest inside to hook onto the tulle we draped around the café and the Great Room walls. Essie enjoyed offering her opinion about the best placement of our decorations. She was thoroughly enjoying the only wedding her home had ever seen and Sabina graciously allowed her to join in. We put a few hearts up on the walls, but for the most part Sabina wanted it to be simple. Sabina had made coasters as wedding favours for the guests from trunks of small trees we'd cut on our property a year earlier. They were well dried out and she cut them in small circles a half inch thick. After sanding them, she had burned in either "Love is Patient" or "Love is Kind". We placed them in two baskets from which people could choose their preference.

Leigh had the stations ready. The outdoor chairs would arrive early Saturday morning. Tommy and one of Jack's brothers had offered to arrange them for the ceremony under Raman's supervision. We'd met Jack's parents and a few siblings at a family barbeque hosted by Jack and Sabina early in August. We appreciated the opportunity to get to know each other a little before the wedding. Funnily enough, Dan and Jack's dad, Frank, discovered they had been leaders together at a scout camp thirty years previous. They had a grand time, exchanging memories of that experience. Jack's mom, Linda, was a high school teacher and avid reader. I had invited Linda to Sabina's surprise bridal shower. She had eagerly accepted and revealed a humorous personality as we celebrated with Sabina. I was delighted that the rehearsal party would give us time to connect again.

With the decorating completed, I took a seat alone to go over the ceremony. I heard a knock and I looked up to see Ginny opening the door to Jack's best man, Johnny. He was loaded down with a case of wine. He called out a greeting as he followed Ginny to the café. Johnny was a wine kit aficionado and had offered to supply the wine for the wedding. We were very thankful for his generosity.

Grandparents and other members of the wedding party began to trickle in. My brother's family arrived. Their eldest, Harmony, was an accomplished harpist and Sabina had asked if she'd play for the ceremony. She set up her harp for the rehearsal, so we could figure out the sound settings. As she played, we practiced the processional.

There were a few hiccups. Toby seemed determined to get in on the action and wouldn't move from his spot between Trish and Ginny. The small table we were going to use for signing the paperwork collapsed because someone hadn't locked all the legs in place. Jack had a sneezing episode which required tissues, which no one possessed. Thus, a brief pause in the action was necessary so Dan could run inside and obtain a box to maintain the cleanliness of Jack's shirt sleeve. We were reminded why a rehearsal is necessary!

I assured them they didn't need to remember the details of the ceremony; that was my job. I would guide and conduct to ensure all went smoothly. I reminded the couple and witnesses not to imbibe in alcohol prior to the ceremony as they would be signing legal documents. With my responsibilities completed, I was eager to enjoy the rehearsal party.

Jack's family had gone with a seafood theme because Jack loved shellfish. We had steamed mussels, chowder, bacon-wrapped scallops, lobster rolls, and so much food I couldn't decide what I wanted. In the end, I tried a small bite of everything. Tommy had a surprise for the couple. Over the last few weeks, he had put together a photo journey of Jack and Sabina's lives. He had approached their friends and family, pulled stuff off their social media profiles, and dug through old albums to create a documentary for them. After the meal, we sat down with our drinks and watched it all unfold. There was great hilarity and many pauses as people took time to share stories behind the photos. It was a charming gift and superbly put together. We all agreed it should be set up at the wedding, so guests could learn a little more about the couple.

By 10:30 p.m., my energy was beginning to lag. Before anyone left, Jack and Sabina wanted a few minutes to thank us all for our support. They passed around gifts to us. They had planted small succulents in old wedding mugs which they'd had fun finding at second-hand stores. They had also found a local honey producer and created labels which read "Meant to Bee" and included their names and wedding date. We admired our gifts and then offered our goodbyes. We wanted to be sure we got our beauty sleep before this important occasion. Sabina, Ginny, and Tommy were all coming home with us, so we'd be together for the night.

As I climbed into bed and snuggled up to Dan, the tears began to flow.

"What's this?" he whispered, gently wiping the

tears away with the pad of his thumb.

"Everything's happening so fast. I haven't taken time to stop and feel. The first of our flock is leaving the nest. Our baby's getting married." My breath hitched as I tried to explain.

"But, you like Jack," Dan reminded me.

"I adore him, but that's not the point!" I exclaimed, trying to keep quiet. "Sabina will never be fully ours again. She'll be forming her own family. Our lives will never be the same."

"Sabina was never fully ours, Alisha. We've had the wonderful privilege of being her parents, but she has always been her own self. We'll never stop being a part of her, but she's ready to become even more. I feel like our lives have become richer with Jack. It's not the same, for sure; but our family has expanded," Dan said softly.

"I feel that too. But I need room to let the sadness be honoured as well." I heaved a sigh. "This marks a new stage of life, you know."

"Are you afraid we're getting old?" Dan queried. "Because I have just the thing to remind you there's lots of life to us yet!"

I knew just the thing he was talking about because it was pressing firmly against my hip. "Dan, the kids are all here!" my prudish side spoke up.

"So what? I'm sure they know their parents have sex by now." I could hear the grin in his voice as his hands began to slide under my nightshirt. Trying to keep the lovemaking noises to a minimum, we firmly established we both had lots of life left in us.

I awoke first and let Dan's calm and rhythmic breathing soothe me. I took a few minutes to offer words of gratitude to the Universe for the family we had raised and for the expansion of our family with Jack. I let memories of Sabina from birth to the present flit through my mind with gratitude. I recalled the first time she introduced us to Jack and the glow that emanated from her as she looked at him. I wanted for her the kind of love Dan and I had developed together. I set the intention that today would be one of many that led them to an abundantly satisfying life with each other. I quietly exited the room and went down the hall to the bathroom.

As I passed Sabina's room, I heard her softly call out to me. I peeked through the doorway and she beckoned me to climb into bed with her.

"How are you doing, honey?" I inquired as I slipped in beside her.

"I'm so excited," she confessed. "I was afraid I'd get cold feet or start having doubts, but all I feel is ecstatic. I've waited for someone like Jack for years. Now that we've found each other, I don't want to hold back in any way."

"You do seem very well suited to each other," I affirmed.

"I know I'm headstrong and hold myself back sometimes—I'm a lot like you, in case you haven't noticed." She jabbed me in the side with her elbow. "Jack doesn't seem to be bothered by my confidence or forthrightness. When he has a difference of opinion, he speaks up; if it doesn't matter to him, he just lets me roll. I feel safe with him and he appreciates me."

"I'm delighted for you, Sabina. I truly like Jack and I admire how you are together. If I get a little teary later, don't worry. It's not that I don't want this for you. I'll just be releasing the pent-up emotions that come with any change life brings," I confided.

Ginny appeared in the doorway.

"Room for one more?" she asked hopefully.

Sabina nodded with a smile and I scooted over to make room. Tommy showed up next and sprawled across the bottom of the bed. We joyfully spent time with some "remember when" stories, until Dan appeared. He was wearing a chef's hat and apron on which was written "Father of the Bride".

Sabina started to giggle.

"Miss Bride-To-Be, the father of the bride is here in his chef's capacity to grant you the breakfast of champions for your wedding day. Please place your order," he declared officiously. He even drew a pen and notebook out of his apron pocket. The pen had a dragonfly wired to the end of it. Then, he pulled out his phone and took photos.

Once the laughter got to a manageable level, Sabina ordered mango and raspberries for her first course, with bacon and eggs to follow. I was in charge of making coffee, while Ginny got to work setting the table. She even went out and cut a few wildflowers to put in a small cup for Sabina's place setting. Tommy offered to give Sabina a shoulder rub as the meal was prepared. The mood stayed light-hearted throughout the meal.

Ginny presented Sabina with a small gift after we ate. It was a small kit with Sabina's favourite orange essential oil. It also held a new razor, a manicure set, pumice stone and an exfoliating bath mitt. Sabina had chosen not to spend money on a manicure; long nails would be quickly destroyed as she worked. She preferred to do her own nails and spend the time together at home rather than rush around to a lot of appointments. I could tell she was touched by Ginny's gift—by both the thought and the quality of it. As she leaned over to give Ginny a quick hug, I was thankful for that special moment between sisters.

I offered to give the tub a wipe and fill it so the bride could begin her preparations. Ginny gave Dan a hand cleaning up the kitchen as Tommy headed to Essie's place to set up chairs. He would pick up Sabina's maid of honour, Trish, on his way back. I called to check on Leigh, who assured me all was in order. One of Leigh's friends was trained in cake-making and we had hired her to do a two-tiered pound cake with a fondant icing. Blue and white hyacinths and red roses would be tucked around the cake with decorative piping connecting it all. Leigh had made two dense carrot cakes with cream cheese icing at the bride and groom's request. The final dessert was a chocolate fountain with lots of fresh fruit and tiny bites of Rice Krispies squares to dip. Preparations for the main course were well underway. I was told to relax and to stop worrying.

I grabbed a shower in the downstairs bathroom, while Sabina finished her self-care. Then, she and I sat on the back deck in warm fuzzy housecoats as we painted our toenails. Ginny had already had her nails done for her show, so she kept us company and refreshed our coffee as needed. We took photos as we went along to help us remember all the special moments of the day. We heard car doors slam and knew Trish and Tommy had arrived. I left the girls to their chatter and Tommy went to take his turn in the shower.

The ceremony was to be at 3:30 p.m., followed by a photo shoot. Sabina and Jack had hired Melissa to do their photos. Cheri was thrilled. We put a light spread of salads and wraps on the table for lunch. We didn't want anyone to feel faint from hunger, so we all made sure we ate something. The girls went to help Sabina with her hair and make-up. They plaited a small braid to form a crown and used hot rollers on the rest of her hair which fell naturally about her shoulders in large curls. The braid would also help hold the tiara. I went to get myself ready and to review my notes for the ceremony. Dan joined me and I straightened his tie as we admired each other in our finery. He drew me in for a long kiss.

"Hey beautiful. It's almost time for our daughter to get married."

Who had the moist eyes now?

Melissa was due at 1:30 p.m. We planned a few official getting-ready photos and a few family photos at our place. Melissa was on time and had brought Cheri as her assistant. I could hear the laughter of the girls as she positioned them this way and that. I was called in to help Sabina into her dress. She kept her back to the others as we arranged it and then she turned to them. Melissa caught their admiration and Sabina's joyous beauty. I'm sure my motherly pride shone through as well. She took photos of Sabina with her maid of honour, her siblings, her parents, and the whole bridal party. Finally, Melissa asked the whole group to gather around a radiant burning bush in our yard for one last snap.

There was room for all of us in the van, so we piled in. We planned to arrive twenty minutes before the ceremony to provide time for bathroom breaks and any final touch ups. It would also allow me time to do a final check of the paperwork and check in with the groom's party. Jack had been given strict instructions to stay in the garden area, so he wouldn't see the bride before the ceremony. The traffic cooperated and we were a few minutes early.

Cars were lined down the road, but a space had been left for us near the front door. I chuckled as I saw Jack's car which his brothers and friends had plastered with hearts, flowers, streamers, and "Just Married" signs. I hopped out to check that the coast was clear and I saw Jack scooting out the veranda doors.

He grinned widely at me. "Last bathroom break, I hope!" he laughed. He appeared to be as excited as Sabina.

I walked over and gave him a quick hug. "I'll be out to check on you guys in a few minutes. Now scoot and no peeking through the windows." I closed the sliding door behind him. As I turned, I noticed my team standing around the café, wearing broad smiles.

"You look dazzling!" Cheri proclaimed.

I smoothed my hand down my dress. I had chosen a rich purple sheath in stretchy material that was overlaid with a flirty gauze material. It curved just above the knees in the front, and scooped down and belled out in the back.

"Thanks. Just wait until you see the bride!" I declared.

"I'm so excited I could burst! Essie gushed. *"I can't wait to see Sabina in all her finery."*

I hurried out to usher the bridal party inside.

"Just look at all of you."

I could hear the tears in Essie's voice. Trish knew about Essie and I could see from her face she was able to hear the conversation.

"This is an incredible honour for me, Sabina," Essie shared. *"My sons didn't have the chance to marry and I didn't think I'd ever be a part of something so wonderful as today. May your love for Jack and your life together be as beautiful as you are right now."*

I could see a ripple next to Sabina and she placed her hand up to her cheek, as if Essie was cupping it.

"Thanks, Essie. That means a lot to me," Sabina affirmed.

Tommy filled Ginny in on all that was

transpiring.

Then, Sabina suggested, "We'll have to keep the conversation internal from now on, Essie. There're some guests who might get spooked by you."

"I already offered Jack my best wishes, when I caught him alone. He has such a handsome smile. I'll watch from a distance and not cause any trouble, don't worry," Essie assured us.

The bridal party organized themselves and I went outside to check on things. Raman assured me the table was well braced and tissue boxes were dispersed under the front seats. Toby was quietly seated on the side lawn. I set my paperwork on the table and we did a sound check. Raman squeezed my shoulder in encouragement and slipped away to his other duties. I touched base with Jack's parents, who were admiring Raman's flower beds and the potted arrangements. I greeted grandparents and my siblings. Harmony was seated at the right front, playing the harp as people gathered. The stunning melodies she elicited from the strings added wonderfully to the day. The guests were busily filing into the seats, as directed by the ushers, two of Jack's brothers. It was almost time to begin.

I lined up the groomsmen and promised I'd return momentarily. The bridal party was ready when I went into the Great Room and I gave Sabina a final hug. Dan lined them up and they waited as I left to guide the groomsmen to the front and to make a few announcements. I invited the guests to rise and my niece swept into a lovely interpretation of Pachelbel's

Canon. Ginny emerged first, followed by Tommy and, then, Trish. I watched Jack's face as he spotted Sabina move into position and proceed down the aisle on her dad's arm. Jack's face beamed with love. I could hear Essie's delighted sigh in my mind. Sabina only had eyes for Jack. Her hands reached out to him as she arrived at the front. Belatedly, she remembered to give Dan a hug, as he stepped to his seat; chuckles rippled across the crowd.

Tommy and Jack's aunt each did a reading. Ginny sang "I Choose You" as a surprise gift for the couple and her vibrant voice echoed around with the powerful words. My reflection on marriage was only five minutes long and pulled together key words from the readings, the song, and what I knew of Jack and Sabina. They had chosen to write their own vows; with a strong voice, Sabina spoke directly to Jack the love and commitment of her heart. He responded with the words he had crafted, his voice cracking partway through. There wasn't a dry eye in the place. The boxes of tissues were passed along for all to share.

The exchange of rings followed by the marriage kiss elicited cheers from some in the audience. I placed my hand over their joined hands and made the declaration of marriage. After words of blessing for the couple, we moved over to the table to sign the paperwork. Melissa took the initial pictures, then phones and cameras were pulled out and everyone got involved. Finally, I presented the couple and harp music burst forth in a triumphant arrangement my niece had composed herself. The couple recessed down the aisle and then returned to the front for a few group photos with all the assembled guests. Melissa had a list of groupings the bride and groom had requested. She very competently directed people into position, so no time was wasted. The bride and groom wanted some fun photos of the two of them in and around the gardens. They poked heads around trees, stood amidst a group of ferns, and Jack scooped Sabina up into his arms in the middle of the arbour.

Food began to appear at the stations. I made an announcement regarding the food set-up and seating arrangements, and everyone was encouraged to enjoy the meal. For the next two hours, people mixed and mingled and devoured the food. My team filled and refilled trays, unobtrusively keeping everything moving along smoothly. The wedding cake was rolled out on a trolley into the Great Room, so photos could be taken. When the word spread that there was a chocolate fountain and carrot cake, I heard murmurs of excitement. I'd been circulating with relatives and meeting new folks; now, I felt I had earned the pleasure of dessert. I eased my way over to the chocolate fountain and waited impatiently in line to fill up a dish of the delectable treat.

Jace leaned in as he passed by. "Reward time, is it?"

I grinned at him in reply. My friends knew my weaknesses!

Tadame passed by and commented, "The red

wine has a wonderfully robust flavor. Be sure you grab a glass."

Desserts were all in the café and veranda area, so the Great Room could be transformed into a dance hall. Once the sound system was prepared, people crowded in to fill the upper balcony, the café, and the Great Room so they could hear the toasts. Trish offered a toast to the bride, sharing a few fun stories from their early years together. Jack's best man gave a toast to the groom; groans echoed around the room in response to his lame jokes. The friend who had first introduced Jack and Sabina offered a toast to the couple. Jack's parents offered words of welcome to Sabina, and Dan and I did the same for Jack. Finally, the bride and groom expressed thanks to us all, and invited us to enjoy the dance. They started us off with a waltz they had practiced. They danced beautifully together.

"Aren't they fun to watch!' Essie whispered in my mind.

Soon, everyone was up and moving.

Once things were tidied up, except for the chocolate fountain which lasted until midnight, we invited the team to join us in the dance. Raman gravitated toward Ginny and the rest cheerfully boogied along, occasionally slipping out to clear away dishes and to check on bathrooms. One of Leigh's friends was on duty at the bar, so the rest were free to relax for a while. The bride and groom left at 1:00 a.m. and we finally closed everything down at 2:00 a.m. It had been an incredible and fabulous night. I profusely thanked my team for their work. Cheri encouraged me out to the van.

"Alisha, go home. Everything's put away. The cleaners will be in on Tuesday."

Tommy was our designated driver, so I closed my eyes and replayed my favourite moments from the day. As soon as we were home, I dragged off my dress and tumbled into bed.

On Sunday, I woke to the smell of coffee being waved beneath my nose.

"Wakey, wakey, sleepyhead," Dan coaxed.

I dragged myself into a sitting position and gratefully accepted the coffee.

"What time is it?" I ask groggily.

"Nine-thirty. Relax!" He put his hand on my leg in response to my gasp and before I could spring up. We were hosting a gift-opening barbeque for the bride and groom with immediate family members and a few out-of-town guests.

"I've cleaned the bathrooms. A quick run-through with the vacuum and the house will be fine. I'm peeling potatoes now to make the hot potato salad. We'll get the kids moving around ten. Jace called and they have the gifts loaded up to drop off later this morning."

I took a large gulp of coffee and let my body recline back against the headboard. I was so thankful I had a husband who was a full partner in the kitchen. As the coffee began to do its thing, my mind slowly kicked into gear.

"I'll get the coleslaw started and the veggie tray. I'll ask Ginny to set up the gift-opening area with a few decorations and a notebook to record everything. Tommy makes a tasty guacamole and he can do the hummus too."

Ice-cream sundaes were for dessert. I'd made homemade toppings earlier in the week: caramel, strawberry, and chocolate. Nuts and sprinkles would top them off. There was time to relax for a few moments as Dan returned to the potatoes.

I threw on sweats and a comfy top and joined Dan in the kitchen. When I heard the kids starting to move around, I prepared an omelet to share with some waffles I had defrosted. I assigned tasks as we ate our breakfast together and I drew on the energy of a second cup of coffee. Jace arrived and we all helped unload gifts. Sabina and Jack landed with stories from their hotel. Apparently, Jack's brothers had planned a few surprises for them. When they opened their suitcases, everything was full of confetti. Their bed had been short sheeted with rubber snakes at the bottom. When Sabina went to the bathroom, there were happy faces stamped on the toilet paper. The tub was full of balloons and the mirror had congratulations smeared across it in lipstick lettering. The boys had had some fun! We laughed in appreciation as Sabina and Jack took turns narrating their adventure.

The gift-opening was relaxed and enjoyable. They received some lovely gifts and a few unusual ones. They raised their eyebrows at a hot pink tulip teapot from one of Jack's great-aunts, but kindly stated, "Isn't that unique!" There must have been a recent sale on knife sets because they received six. Linda and I took turns recording the gifts for them, so they could keep track for writing thank you notes later.

I was grateful for some time to visit with my brother and his family. My parents left early because they had a long drive home. Others began to drift off by early evening. Jack and Sabina also left because they'd be driving a few hours to an undisclosed location, to avoid any more trickster pranks. We agreed to keep the gifts at our place because they'd just moved the last of Jack's things into Sabina's apartment the week before. He'd essentially been living with her, but it took until the end of August to finish out his lease.

By eight o'clock, it was quiet. Dan and I had the place to ourselves again. The dishwasher hummed as it worked. We grabbed warm sweatshirts and went to sit on the deck swing to watch the stars coming out. Dan lifted his arm and I snuggled in beside him as he slowly pushed the swing back and forth.

"Six months ago, who would have thought we'd have all these new beginnings?" I expressed in wonderment. "My work, your work, new friends, new family," I listed. "Sometimes I feel like I'm caught in a dream."

"I'd say it is a dream—our dreams coming true," Dan professed. "With that in mind, Alisha, I've been meaning to talk with you about my going back to the clinic. My leave time has flown by and I've been ignoring the fact that I start back there next week." He fell silent.

"How do you feel about it," I prompted.

"I don't want to go back to that type of work again fulltime," he blurted passionately. "I know it isn't wise for both of us to be starting new businesses at the same time. I know carpentry tends to be slower in the winter months, so Sabina probably could handle the work on her own. I just don't know if I can go back to doing carpentry as my sideline."

I could sense anxiety as his arm pressed against me. I sat up and looked him in the eye.

"Honey, I apologize that I've been so caught up in my stuff that I didn't pick up on this sooner."

"Don't apologize. I've been keeping it buried. Earlier in the summer, I briefly mentioned going back just a day or two a week. But, I don't know if I'd have been ready to talk about it before now," Dan admitted.

"What's your gut response telling you now as we talk about this?" I asked.

We sat quietly, looking at the stars, as Dan explored his feelings.

"I feel responsible for keeping things steady until your business is firm on its feet," he began. "I feel responsible to my clients. I don't want to let anyone down."

"If you took that weight of responsibility away, if you didn't have to worry about anyone else, what would you do?" I prodded.

Another period of silence descended.

He took a deep breath. "I'd dive in, whole hog. But, I know I have issues with responsibilities and I realize I wouldn't enjoy the carpentry if I felt driven to make it financially successful right away, and if I left the clinic high and dry. I feel I'd be more comfortable if I could take clients Mondays and Tuesdays, and work with Sabina Wednesday to Saturday. That would give us time to pay off wedding expenses, help Tommy while he's at university, and put a bit aside to create a cushion for when I stop completely."

"Sounds like you have a very good sense of what's best for you right now. Perhaps we should pay attention to how part-time feels first. I don't want you to feel trapped," I expressed in concern.

"Agreed," Dan nodded. "This week I'll be in touch with the clinic coordinator and see about reducing my hours. I think I might also get in touch with a financial advisor to help me map out where I'm going with all of this."

"This week I'll be into the homestretch for our grand opening. Yikes! The times they sure are changing!" I heaved myself out of the swing. "Now, it's time to change position. I need to get horizontal."

"I think I can keep you company." Dan fell into step with me as we made our way to bed.

CHAPTER TWENTY-SEVEN

I took Monday and Tuesday as recovery days. With the holiday and our busy weekend, the team had decided not to take bookings until Wednesday. I slept in. I leisurely caught up on laundry. I sat out in the shade and read a novel for pleasure! I avoided anything strenuous to the mind, body, or spirit. As a result, I felt refreshed when I arrived at Essie's Place for our staff meeting.

"You look good," Tadame commented as she slid into a seat next to me.

"I feel good," I replied. "It was wonderful to have two days in a row where I didn't have to go anywhere or do anything for anyone but myself. You look pretty glowing yourself."

"I'm pregnant!" she blurted out.

"What?" I exclaimed in astonishment.

"I wasn't going to say anything yet. You know I'd decided to stop worrying about it. Then I missed my last period. They've always been erratic, so I didn't think anything of it. All of a sudden, I started feeling woozy in the mornings and the smell of Ronnie cooking eggs just turned my stomach. I was a little suspicious, so I used an old kit I'd pushed to the back of my medicine chest and it came up positive. I bought a new kit and retried this morning. I'm pregnant!" The words tumbled out in a rush.

Cheri scurried in with a basket of scones. She had volunteered to make our snack.

"What'd I miss?" she asked as she plopped the basket on the table and dropped her purse to the floor.

I gestured to Tadame, leaving it to her to share her news. Cheri's squeal alerted the others as they arrived.

Once everyone was filled in, Tadame spoke up. "I know the timing could be better, but Ronnie and I have wanted this for a long time. I want you to know, I won't let you down here. I'll pull my weight."

"And more," Cheri teased.

"Ease up, Tadame." Raman interjected. "You're a partner here with us. We'll work this out as a team. We're delighted for you!"

"Maybe we could become a healing place in a whole new area?" Jace joked.

The others laughed in appreciation.

Leigh, who had been quiet up until this point, offered an opinion. "I believe there is something healing about this place that goes beyond Essie's presence here. It's in the house, the grounds, in us all together."

We all agreed with Leigh's insight. Then, they suggested we put on some coffee and tea to go with our scones and that we delve into the day's agenda. We evaluated the wedding from a work perspective; everything had flowed well. One pottery mug had been knocked off a shelf, leaving a chip on the rim. Raman suggested we buy it and he could follow Sabina's example by planting a small succulent in it, that we could subsequently sell.

Our new cleaning contractors had started the day before. We did a quick tour through and they appeared to have been thorough in their work. Cheri reminded us of new appointments scheduled for the next few days, but our focus was the grand opening on Saturday. Tadame had brought in the newspaper from her apartment and showed us the full-page write-up about us, as well as the ad we had purchased for the Grand Opening. We took time to pour over it and we were pleased with the journalist's presentation of our vision for Essie's Healing Place.

Leigh took us through their preparations for the big day. They had planned a celebrative cake that would be decorated with our symbols and around which we'd take photos. It would be ceremoniously cut and shared and accompanied by a sun tea. Small samplers of Leigh's mousse and other bites of special treats would be offered in tiny paper cups. Sampler mugs would also be used for soup, chili, quinoa salad, and Waldorf salad. Leigh had created a printed menu that included photos and descriptions of foods the café would be offering on a regular basis. They had included a few notes about the healing properties of each as well.

Leigh had also put together mini-bags containing a teaspoon of a dried healing herb mix for cooking. Recipe suggestions were twist-tied to each one. I was thoroughly impressed. Raman held up fifteen millilitre recyclable plastic containers with lids, in which he would be able to offer a sample of his creams to interested persons. Tadame had sample oils that people could sniff.

Cheri showed us flyers she'd prepared which described our fall programs. They could be handed out along with our services flyer and our business cards. In the same manner as our open house days, we would offer regular tours of the grounds and mini-sessions at certain times throughout the day. Melissa would be our official photographer and local media had been invited to the 3:00 p.m. cake cutting. We reviewed everyone's responsibilities for the day. It appeared everything was well in hand and we felt confident from the success of running our open house experiences.

The phone started ringing, so we finished up our meeting. Raman went out to inspect the grounds. Leigh borrowed my car for a grocery run, while Jace followed me into a healing room for another session together. I was getting a massage and we'd continue tapping together for him. Tadame had a reflexology client and Cheri had piles of receipts from the wedding to enter into our spreadsheets.

My massage was excellent; Jace found hidden tension I needed to release. We worked with my stomach again and it felt less embarrassing this time round. After I dressed, we tapped to unearth words that had been spoken to Jace as a child, which continued to influence him. Jace's comfort with hearing Essie had increased significantly, so I was sure one day he'd reach a point of communicating with those beings he'd heard as a child.

I decided to walk the labyrinth before my afternoon appointments showed up. It was cool but comfortable in the shade of the woods. A few leaves were beginning to show signs of yellow and fall flowers sprinkled the forest floor. I slowly wove my way through the labyrinth, allowing my emotions to seep out. As I neared the centre, a gust of wind nudged a blue feather into my face. I caught it in wonder. I knew finding a feather was thought to be an indicator of a message from the angels. Blue feathers symbolized a message of calm and peace. I allowed contentment to flow into me. As I walked my way out, I spoke words of gratitude for all the newness in my life.

Raman was waiting for me, sitting on a bench located a short distance from the labyrinth's entrance. I went to sit beside him.

"How are you doing?" he inquired. "I could feel your sadness when you walked by me into the forest."

I hadn't even noticed him working in the flower beds.

"I'm okay, thanks." I showed him the blue feather. "I needed time to release emotions I'd been storing for a while. The labyrinth is helpful that way. Then, this feather showed up and I let the angels' calm be part of me."

"You're a pretty special lady for the angels to be communicating with you." Raman teased.

"Thank you," I gave honor to his words by not dismissing them. "I feel each one of us who found our way here has something unique to offer. I'm very grateful for the friendships we've formed together." I changed the subject. "Why don't you show me your plans for a greenhouse, so we can see if there's any way we can budget that in this month."

Raman willingly obliged and eagerly began to share his ideas for building a cold frame by using untreated, locally milled wood because he didn't want treated lumber that could leach chemicals into the soil. He'd been watching for old windows at charity stores and had picked up a dozen for under fifty dollars, once he made sure they didn't have any lead-based paint on them. He and Leigh had been chatting and they thought they could build the cold frame off the back side of Leigh's place; that way it would be out of sight of the main grounds. It sounded reasonable to me, so I encouraged him to put it into a proposal with a cost estimate for our next staff meeting.

The next few days slipped by with appointments and final preparations. On Thursday, we had light rain. Thankfully, Saturday dawned bright and clear again. We all arrived early. I stashed a bottle of champagne in the back of the fridge and a bubbly non-alcoholic spritzer for celebrating once it was all over.

Our families were the first to arrive. Sabina and Jack had made it back from their getaway and they stopped in to offer their congratulations and to thank the team for making their special day so awesome. Sabina nabbed one of Leigh's herb mixes and Jack asked Raman's advice about athlete's foot. Ginny and a few of her friends breezed in to sample a few of Leigh's treats and to congratulate us. Some of her friends that had been part of the photo shoot pointed out their pictures on our flyers. Raman's running friends came through and some took advantage of mini massage sessions.

The pace was steady as we welcomed people we knew and others who had heard about us for the first time. Church folks, students, yoga studio members, and even the agent who sold me the house strolled the grounds. The newspaper article and our earlier media forays had obviously reached a wide audience. People of all ages came to check us out. Essie was well-behaved and watched from a distance, according to Cheri.

At 3:00 p.m., the cake was rolled out and photos taken. The mayor of Bright Haven was present and offered congratulations and words of encouragement to our new business. Local politicians expressed their support and best wishes. The chair of the Women in

Business Council stepped forward and spoke eloquently. We felt extremely well feted! The cake was cut and shared around, and more of Leigh's goodies were brought out on trays. The socializing was going along well when I heard a loud voice from the front door.

"Where is he? Where is my Raman?"

"This should be interesting!" Essie expressed excitedly.

I quickly turned to Raman, who shook his head as he made his way to the front door. Cheri was already there, greeting a well-endowed, sari-clad woman, who was standing with a handsome man who bore a striking resemblance to Raman. I nodded my head in welcome.

"Hello, folks. My name is Alisha. Welcome to Essie's Healing Place."

"So, you're her." The woman looked me up and down. "All my son can talk about is Alisha this, Alisha that. He raves on about this Healing Place. Where is he?"

Raman stepped forward and with a firm voice said, "Maji."

She stepped forward and embraced him.

"We have come from India. It is time for you to marry. You have put this off long enough."

Raman removed her arms from around him yet gently clasped her hands. "Maji, I was very clear with you on the phone. I will make my own choice for my wife, when I am ready." He paused and looked directly in her eyes. "I am glad you are here to share in our grand opening because my work and my team are important to me. Come, would you like a cup of tea and some of that cake over there."

His mother proudly stepped toward the café and conversation began to spark again. The gentleman extended his hand to me. "Greetings Alisha, I am Aazvaar, Raman's baba."

I shook his warm hand and took note of his kind eyes.

"Don't worry," he assured me. "All will be well." He moved to join his wife and son in the café. Cheri's eyes were dancing as she looked at me.

A frantic knock sounded at the door behind her. She twirled and pulled it open. This time, a frantic Mildred Smith rushed in, clutching a miniature poodle to her chest. Blood and dirt stained the poodle's carefully trimmed fur.

"Alisha, you have to help. I stepped out of my car to pick up my dry cleaning and Mitzi scooted out behind me. She didn't see the car backing up and she got caught in the wheels. Our vet's away on holiday. I knew your place was close by, so I brought her to you. Can you heal her?" she pleaded anxiously.

"The poor thing! Push those doubts away, Alisha. You can do this," Essie urged.

"Cheri, call the nearest vet clinic. Mildred, bring Mitzi into the back room and place her on the table. I don't know what we can do, but while we wait for the vet we'll do all we can. Tadame, do you have any soothing oils to keep a dog calm? Leigh, bring Toby in. Maybe he can communicate with Mitzi for us and keep her steady. I'm going to assess her energy field now."

As Mildred placed Mitzi on the table and stepped back, I began a sweep with my hands. Having been thrown around by the car, her whole energy field was askew. I sensed some internal bleeding and noted the awkward angle of one of her legs. This was beyond what I usually did, but in an emergency you offer what you can and trust the angels to give their help.

I motioned to Tadame and asked her if she knew reflex points for animals. She knew a few calming points, so she held those as I targeted the internal bleeding. I focused an intense laser beam of energy through my fingers. After five minutes, I rechecked the field and my senses communicated the bleeding seemed to have stopped. I shifted to the broken bone and gently moved it into alignment. I wove around the limb as if I was knitting it back together. After five minutes, I switched to smoothing and balancing Mitzi's scrambled field.

Toby was positioned by Mitzi's head and held a paw gently on Mitzi. Cheri called out that a vet was on his way and should arrive in a few minutes. Before that happened, Mitzi opened her eyes and licked Toby's paw. Mildred exclaimed and stepped forward to touch her beloved pet.

When the vet arrived, he offered a thorough exam and indicated Mitzi was stable enough to transfer to the clinic. He commended whatever we had done because she seemed in a much better state than one would expect for a collision like the one she'd encountered. Mildred thanked us profusely. A few hours later, we heard from Mildred that the scans showed a large internal vessel seemed to have cauterized itself and the leg was not broken, but simply showed a hairline fracture. In the meantime, the others had held down the fort. Raman had taken his parents on a tour of the gardens, along with some new guests who had arrived. Leigh had returned to the café to assure everyone that things were under control. However, the media were still present, so we were receiving a new kind of advertising which I wasn't sure we were prepared to handle.

Finally, five o'clock arrived. Family, friends, media, special guests, and the public were gone. Only the team remained. I pulled out the champagne and spritzer. We set out glasses and popped the corks.

Just as I began to pour, Jace exclaimed, "Stop!"

I looked at him. He was pale and strained-looking. "The voices say stop! The wine is contaminated."

I stopped. "Jace, are you okay?" I asked.

"I'm trying to sort them all out. It's a bit of a strain. Your guardian angel told me about the contamination. Stanley wants me to speak to Essie. There are others, but I told them to be quiet for now. It's too much information for me to handle," Jace shared.

Cheri interjected. "I've just searched for your champagne on the Internet. There was trouble with the corks. A recall was sent out months ago. Jace's right."

"I'm really sorry everyone. I took it from our basement wine cellar; I'm not sure how long it was there." I felt terrible. "Thank you Jace, for opening up to the voices and protecting us."

"You're welcome, but your guardian angel was pretty insistent about getting through!" Jace stated grudgingly. "Once I opened up to that one, all the other voices began to pile through."

"Did you say Stanley—my Stanley?" Essie questioned tentatively.

"Yes, your Stanley. He wants to know why you haven't joined him? Although time is different in his dimension, he misses you," Jace relayed.

"Tell him I love him too. But, I felt my work here wasn't done, so I chose to stay. Why didn't he come and join me?" she enquired.

"Good question!" Cheri encouraged Essie. Then she asked, "Can you come back to this dimension once you've left it?"

"Of course! But many choose not to, because the next dimension is such a place of joy and love without the pain and sorrow that touches this place. Communication between us is cut off, so they're not affected by our experiences here. However, at any time, they can choose to return and be a helping spirit to this world," Essie explained.

"That's so cool," Leigh weighed in. "You decided to stay and help us."

"Yes, but it has also given me a chance to learn so much more than in my lifetime. Jace dear, tell Stanley he's welcome anytime."

Jace cleared his throat and meekly replied, "He

said, he'd think about it."

"The old coot!" We could tell by the tone of Essie's voice that she was miffed. Leigh and Cheri told us she'd stomped off to another room.

"Jace, any more advice from our spiritual advisors?" Cheri asked.

Jace shook his head. "All seems quiet on that front now. It may take me a while to get used to this form of communication."

"I think you handled it incredibly well," Tadame assured him.

"Remember, you're in charge. You can listen or not, as you choose. It's like answering the phone. You hear it sound, but you can ignore it or pick up. It's up to you," I encouraged.

"I like that metaphor," Jace contemplated. "I'll keep reminding myself of that when I start to feel overwhelmed."

"Back to the champagne," Raman drew our attention again. "It just so happens, I put a new, premium bottle of champagne on ice in a cooler in the back of my truck. I thought we might want to celebrate, so I came prepared too!"

Raman went to retrieve it while Tadame poured herself and Cheri some spritzer. Once we all had a glass, I stood up to make a toast.

"We've been on this journey together for a while now, but today marks the official birth of a dream I've held since I was a teenager. I feel so blessed to have each of you in my life, including you, Essie," I called out. "Thank you for the way each of you has stretched and shaped this dream, adding to it in ways I couldn't even have imagined when I first bought Essie's place. Thank you for who you are and who you help me to be."

Tears started welling up, so I raised my glass. "To Essie's Healing Place!"

Cheri gushed, "I love being part of this team and all we're learning together. To us!"

We cheered and Leigh lifted their glass. "Thank you for taking a chance on me, for giving me a home, and being family to me."

"To new beginnings, new friends, and a new little one on the way," Jace raised his glass to Tadame and we all joined in, sharing our joy with her.

"To all that we are yet to become!" Tadame exclaimed.

Raman took my hand and placed his over mine in the centre of the table. "Remember what you came back and shared from that mystic in Hope Falls. It's true. Alisha, you are the heart of this dream, making space for us all and nurturing us along as we've built this together."

With his other hand he took Leigh's hand and placed it on top of ours.

"Leigh, you may be young, but you offer wisdom and goodness in all you do."

Tadame's hand was next on the pile.

"Tadame, you have a gift for keeping us feeling connected."

Cheri reached out to join us as Raman continued. "Cheri, you bring a brightness and light, even when you're teaching us how to use a computer. Jace, you came later, but you exude a trustworthiness that adds to the quality of our whole, and you're making new connections for us in unexpected ways. I don't know where this is all going, but I'm honoured to be part of this exceptional team and I'm ready for whatever comes next!"

We allowed the warmth of Raman's words and our hands to bind us together in a very special way. We finished our drinks and exchanged hugs. I offered to do the final clean-up and soon I was on my own. I washed up the final few dishes and tidied the café. The cleaning crew would be in the next day, so I didn't need to do anything more.

Before I left, I walked from room to room, noticing the transformation that had taken place in each since I first found Essie's place.

"Just look at what we've accomplished, Essie," I whispered as I stood in the Great Room.

I noticed the air rippling in front of me and beginning to take shape. As I shakily drew in my breath and relaxed my vision, my eyes beheld the one who had drawn me to this special place.

"Essie!" I gasped. "I can see you."

"Och, and you're just getting started, dearie," she responded.

"So much is happening; I can hardly wait to see how it all turns out!" I declared.

"Me too!" she affirmed.

ABOUT THE AUTHOR

Rev. Dr. Karen MacLeod-Wilkie was ordained within the United Church of Canada in 1989. She has served in four pastoral charges and is entering her thirteenth year with her present congregation at PEI, Canada. Karen completed her Doctor of Ministry in 2013 at Wesley Theological Seminary in Washington D.C.; her thesis was entitled "A Narrative Approach for Healing Stories of Crisis". Karen has been a practitioner of the Healing Pathway since 2000 and became an instructor in 2014. Karen is a lifelong learner and has attended courses in the US and Canada on topics such as leading in times of change, adaptive leadership, healing pathway, and spiritual direction.

Karen is an inspirational and interactive speaker on a variety of topics. She can be found on YouTube sharing stories about Celtic culture, healing as a ministry, and the Church on Prince Edward Island; she has led many workshops on stress, healing, and humour with health professionals and women's groups, in schools and in churches.

Karen's writing skills have been honed over the years thanks to her work writing Sunday School curricula and developing resources for the United Church. She also has a passion for creative writing—she has written and directed seventeen dinner theatre plays. Contact Infromation: Karen MacLeod-Wilkie, kmacleodwilkie@gmail.com

69214509R10215

Made in the USA
Middletown, DE
25 September 2019